BY DONALD TAGGART

History of the 3rd Infantry Division in World War II

NOVELS:

Reunion of the 108th
Make No Law

MAKE NO LAW

make no law

BY DONALD TAGGART

DOUBLEDAY & COMPANY, INC., GARDEN CITY, N. Y.

1969

All of the characters in this book are fictitious, and any resemblance to actual persons, living or dead, is purely coincidental.

Library of Congress Catalog Card Number 69–20099
Copyright © 1969 by Donald G. Taggart
All Rights Reserved
Printed in the United States of America
First Edition

For

GILBERT L. TAGGART (1890–1948)

and INEZ ISMERT TAGGART (1894–1937)

and for

HELEN B. TAGGART

ACKNOWLEDGMENTS

For help of various kinds the author expresses his grateful appreciation to John N. Bailey, Lois Butler, Canoy Crawford, Curt Gentry, Leo Guild, Franz T. Hansell, Ewing Hass, Louise Reif, Gilford G. Rowland, Walter W. Taylor, and Ramona Veglia. The author assumes all responsibility for viewpoints in this work of fiction, especially in law. If there are any inept interpretations of legal points, they are the author's, not those of Mr. Rowland or Mr. Taylor, both practicing attorneys.

Congress shall make no law . . . abridging the freedom of speech, or of the press . . .

—Excerpt, *First Amendment to the Constitution of the United States*

We believe it to be a principle of our Nation that pre-marital or extra-marital sexual activity is dangerous and unhealthy.

—From *Report of the Subcommittee on Pornographic Literature of the* [California] *Assembly Interim Committee on Judiciary—1959*

PART ONE

Behind a drawn curtain not all movement on the brightly lighted set readily explained itself to the visiting outsider. Five times the number of persons who would appear on-camera bustled about or paused for brief, cryptic conversations that produced quick agreement. To John Hagen it seemed, however, that the general keynote was good humor. These people appeared to know exactly what they were doing and enjoy doing it. He watched two young men push a camera dolly toward the table at which he and the Reverend Bradshaw Coe sat. The seated cameraman cranked a lever to spin his lens turret and said something into the tiny microphone attached to his headset; listened, nodded. Nearby, a man in sports shirt and slacks stood high on a ladder, also dolly-mounted, to make a lighting adjustment. "How's that?" he called out. Someone replied, "That's more like it."

John Hagen stirred in his padded chair and exchanged wary glances with the Reverend Bradshaw Coe. They sat about six feet apart on the outer arc of a crescent-shaped table, facing the curtain some twenty-five feet downstage.

"Here you go, sir," said a man's voice. Arms looped around John's neck from behind; hands clipped on a lavaliere microphone. "Would you like to button your coat over the mike?" the man said. His hands tucked the cord out of sight under the collar and lapels. The Reverend Mr. Coe was being similarly fitted. Other arrangements awaited their absent host. He would sit between Hagen and Coe behind a foot-high lectern with a torpedo-shaped microphone above its sloped shelf with reading lamp.

A pretty, young girl in a black minidress smiled at John Hagen and the Reverend Mr. Coe as she set down a silver tray bearing a glass pitcher of ice water and three tumblers. "Can you use this?" she said, filling the tumblers.

"Yes indeed, and thank you," said Coe. John nodded. She smiled again and took away the tray and pitcher.

Barring the cameras and snaky black cable, the stage was starkly free of clutter. Behind the table was a huge green panel on which was centered a large red shield bearing the symbol EPC, for Edge-water Petroleum Company. To either side, tormentors blocked the wings from audience view. In front of the table a monitor television set faced the participants below camera range so that they might watch themselves if they were so inclined. The onstage cameras were positioned to move in if directed or be swung around toward the audience. Another camera, Hagen and Coe had been informed, was scaffold-mounted in the center of the auditorium.

John Hagen was nervously aware of part of the activity. He was conscious of the pressure of time. One of several deep-voiced young men said to no one in particular, "Ten minutes to warm-up." To John, his own presence was increasingly unreal. He thought that the unwilling star performer in the short, monstrous playlet of an execution must feel the same way. A thousand pairs of hands propelled you firmly yet impersonally toward one point in time when, under glaring illumination, unseen eyes would judge you remorselessly. How you performed, how you died. Finally, time alone assumed the total responsibility. Nothing human, barring a stay, could intercede. The hands, having done their job on the assembly line, were nervously at rest. The clock became the master, pitiless and inflexible. "Look what time it is," said the owners of the hands. "We're not responsible and there is nothing we can do now, because look what time it is." John felt he must be the only one of two dozen persons within view who found it hard to grasp the imminence of a program that would spring to life on a quarter of a million California television screens. What in God's name was he doing here? He felt somehow trapped, seduced, betrayed.

He glanced uneasily at the Reverend Bradshaw Coe and wondered whether that worthy was quite as calm as he appeared. Possibly he was. Coe was clothed in the chain mail of rectitude. His shield against error was simple belief; his steed, right; his sword, truth. Yet he was neither a simple man, or disingenuous.

As though sensing John's speculation, Coe turned his head and said, "Makes you feel like a bug on a pin, eh, Mr. Hagen?"

"All very new to me," said John Hagen politely. After all the bitterness of the last few months he could barely bring himself to be civil.

Coe's answering smile was not quite friendly. It seemed a bit remote, as if he were communing with some private advisory council. Coe was quite short, which new acquaintances were surprised to discover when he stood, for he had a mastiff head. Somewhere in his forties, he was quite prematurely, handsomely gray. His eyebrows were black. His forehead bulged impressively below the deep hairline to meet a large nose. His blue, hypnotic eyes fixed on their object, animate or inanimate, with unwavering certitude. Some injudiciously thought him an ass; many others, a man of undefined destiny. John Hagen shared neither view. He regarded him as a damned dangerous crank with a regrettably large following.

The director came over. His smile must have been a standard instrument, yet it embraced both John Hagen and the Reverend Mr. Coe with seemingly genuine, concerned warmth. "Butterflies?" he said.

John nodded, and Coe said, "Just a trifle, yes."

"If you lacked a little *taut* in this business you couldn't be for real," said the director. He was a slim man in a finely tailored dark suit and faintly blue shirt, with a light-gray silk tie. "I'll tell you something in strictest confidence: Rodge Garry is the keyedest-up guy on the premises." His sly wink was a bid to keep this weighty news inviolate. "At the same time, he'll carry the show. You two have nothing to worry about." Nodding in agreement with his own words, he continued: "You've both seen the show? Right? Then you know that Rodge can sometimes get a trifle abrasive. No question. But now I'll let you in on a little secret. Rodge off-camera is one of the sweetest guys you'll ever meet in this world. That's just between us." He brought his hands together in a light clap. "I guess that's my locker-room speech, gentlemen. I know we're going to have a really stimulating and thought-provoking discussion here tonight. And now you'll excuse me." He crossed the stage to disappear in the wings. He reappeared a moment later in the control booth in back of a man whose head appeared over the top of a large console. The director brushed on a headset and adjusted it. It was his voice that now said, "Three minutes to warm-up, five minutes to opening."

Adjoining the control booth was its twin, the sponsor's booth. John Hagen saw four faces. One was that of his wife, sitting beside her mother. Kris was staring at him intently. As she caught his glance she raised a gloved hand and twinkled her fingers at him. The sick anger again knotted his stomach. She may have bitten her lip but he could not be sure.

John caught himself almost automatically reaching for a cigarette before he realized he had kicked the habit recently. Curious. It must be the clench of nerves. He took up the tumbler of water instead. The ice pinged lightly against the glass. He sipped the cold liquid slowly, expelling a smooth pebble of ice back into the tumbler. He heard Coe experimentally clearing his throat, the first brief grunt followed by two three-note scrapes like the double-clutching of a truck: *ngnh-uh-ngnh . . . ngnh-uh-ngnh!* Getting to you too, eh, Reverend? he thought.

By ones and twos the supernumeraries began to leave the set. The man who had been identified to John Hagen and the Reverend Mr. Coe as the producer linked a friendly hand in the elbow-crook of the two unexplained prosperous-looking men on either side of him and escorted them into the wings. A slim young woman with a pencil stabbed in her hair and a manila folder in her hands conferred with a short, nattily dressed man of about thirty, who was nodding—*yes . . . yes . . . yes . . . yes*—as she spoke earnestly. The man who had okayed the lighting adjustment twisted his neck in one rapid, all-inclusive confirmation, then he, too, entered the wings.

"Thirty seconds to warm-up," said the director. The short man patted the script girl lightly on the cheeks with both hands, and something he said made her laugh. She, too, stepped to the wings, but remained within the sight of John and Coe. The short man shrugged at his coat, grasping the lapels in last-minute adjustment, then walked downstage to stand directly behind the curtain. He stood with his feet slightly apart, his arms at his sides. To all intents he was wholly composed, but John saw him open and close his hands rapidly two or three times. At the last moment he hunched his shoulders high, dropping them as the director's voice said, "Curtain!" The heavy velvet parted to a crescendo of applause. The short man stepped forward immediately to a microphone. Out in the center of the audience the tiny red light of the camera on its scaffold winked on. At the same time the monitor set facing John and Coe fluttered awake. It showed the short man in close-up, embracing his audience, then shushing it with upheld hands. John gazed out at some three hundred people. Rodge Garry's program always attracted turnaway crowds, possibly of the sort that once attended the Circus Maximus and now went to stock-car races.

"Good evening, friends," said the announcer. No trace of his precurtain jitters was evident. "Welcome to 'Sky's the Limit,' the Rodge Garry show. Did you wear your handclapping shoes tonight?" The crowd, well spiked with old familiars, instantly broke into applause. "That's wonderful," said the announcer, beaming, shushing them again. "As always, Rodge and his sponsors, those fine folks the Edgewater Petroleum Company, and the Sierra Television Network are tremendously pleased to see all you wonderful people in the studio tonight. Now, we'll be on the air in less than one minute. Do you see that great big screen up in front of you?" On the stage monitor John could see the center camera swing to a large studio monitor, which, of course, now showed itself. "Well, you people are going to be on that screen in just a few seconds. When Rodge Garry walks out on stage, I'd like to hear you make like thunder with your hands. Can you do that for me?" Wonderfully obedient, the studio captives filled the hall with applause. The announcer beamed at them and stilled them once more. "You are simply beautiful people," he said. "I love you with all my heart." He picked up the microphone and carried it to one side of the stage as a light ripple of laughter stirred and died away. He turned his head to look at the control booth. The director had one hand up, fingers spread. The monitor screen in front of John and his adversary flashed a panel of numbers. A recorded orchestral flourish suddenly cut the silence, simultaneous with the appearance of a title on the screen. The man in the control booth shot out an imperious forefinger. The announcer cried out, "And now . . . the Edgewater Petroleum Company brings you . . . live and direct from Hollywood . . . 'Sky's the Limit'—the Rodge Garry show!" The screen during this speech had first flashed the EPC shield, cutting to SKY'S THE LIMIT, cutting to THE RODGE GARRY SHOW.

To John Hagen all was still unreal, but the sands had run. The program was on the air. He drew a deep breath and hoped that he wouldn't make a complete fool of himself. More to the point, he added to himself grimly, pray that this Garry individual won't lead you down the garden path to anger.

The monitor screen was swiftly rearranging itself in colored, interlocking squares as THE RODGE GARRY SHOW remained, superimposed. The squares alternately framed almost subliminally glimpsed actors, sports figures, politicians, crowd and accident and riot scenes, bikinied girls, the UN General Assembly, a hospital surgery, soldiers in combat, a "flowering rose" of military jets. Each square was wiped by its successor in clockwise sequence. John Hagen took another quick sip of his water as the camera cut to the announcer, who shouted, "Now, introducing one of the most controversial moderators in the country . . . Rodge Garry! And here he is!" His words were taken up in a huge wash of applause. A camera at stage left cut in. It framed a tall, shambling man on his short walk from the wings at stage right to take his place between John Hagen and the Reverend Mr. Coe. He waved carelessly toward the audience. Now an onstage camera panned the busily clapping spectators. Then houselights suddenly dimmed and stage lights were cut off and replaced by a pattern of foot- and spotlights that framed only the three men at the table. The rest of the arena was dark. Garry snapped on his reading lamp.

"Hello again and welcome to 'Sky's the Limit,'" he said. "Glad you folks throughout California came by for another session of talk on controversial, newsworthy subjects." His voice crawled with a flat, understated nastiness.

"The Edgewater Petroleum Company and I have an agreement," he said with a mirthless grin. "I don't make gasoline and they don't tell me what I can talk about on this program. That makes for better gasoline and a livelier show. In case any of you viewers are tuning in for the first time, 'Sky's the Limit' is the program that pulls no punches. If we want to talk about the President of the United States . . . Russia . . . vivisection . . . abortion . . . sex—you name it, we'll talk about it. Tonight is no exception. We've brought together two individuals who say they're willing to defend their respective positions on—pornography. On that provocative note, friends, we'll pause for this message from the Edgewater Petroleum Company." His face on the monitor screen was replaced by an offshore drilling platform in heavy seas. A voice intoned: "The world of oil is a world of adventure. . . ."

"Well, Mr. Hagen, Reverend Coe, I'm glad to see you again," said Rodge Garry, leaning toward them. They had both met him that afternoon in the leather-padded seclusion of the producer's office— Garry with a checkered trousers leg looped over the arm of his chair. "We're off-camera for a minute. If you want to pick your nose, now's your time." At the studied vulgarity, John Hagen frowned slightly. Coe looked startled, then shook his head.

"Good," said Garry. "If there's anything we like, it's a clean show." He grinned his mirthless grin again and opened a folder on the lectern. He began nodding to himself at something he saw there. John Hagen concentrated his attention on the monitor screen, which was displaying a skillfully integrated series of desert pipeline, technicians inspecting a booster station, a huge refinery, close-ups of mazes of multicolored piping . . .

"Twenty seconds," said a voice from somewhere behind the table. John clasped his hands tightly to control a tremor. Garry riffled his papers, studying intently. The Reverend Mr. Coe shifted in his chair. And from the speaker: "Yes, the wide world of oil is a world of adventure. The Edgewater Petroleum Company brings that world to your doorstep. So drive into your friendly neighborhood Edgewater station . . . fill up with high-powered Edgewater gasoline, with the added Element K-Z for extra mileage . . . and drive off into *your* wide world of adventure!" The network announcer's voice accompanied the title flash, THE RODGE GARRY SHOW: "Now, once again, 'Sky's the Limit,' the Rodge Garry show!"

"Introductions are in order," said Garry. He looked up into the live camera. "Now, as just about every adult Californian knows, one of the most talked-about issues on tomorrow's general election ballot is Proposition Number Five. Most of you know it even better as PURIFY, the anti-smut measure. PURIFY is up before the electorate tomorrow because *you,* the people, put it there. It started here in Southern California and became a statewide measure because of a strong campaign. *You,* the people, signed this initiative petition because the politicians up in Sacramento wouldn't act. *You,* the people, said we want some laws with teeth to keep filth out of the hands of our children. Well, the state legislature wasn't listening. So the citizens, reacting in anger, said, 'All right, we'll get up something that the people, *we* the people, can vote on.' And that something, ladies and gentlemen, is PURIFY. If voted into law it will amend the state constitution to put strong controls on smut—*pornography,* if you please. With that, let me introduce two key figures in this campaign. Good evening, Mr. John Hagen, publisher of the Wellbrook *Sentinel.*"

"Good evening," said John, a slight huskiness in his voice.

"And the Reverend Bradshaw Coe—and good evening to you, Reverend Coe."

"How do you do, sir," said Coe.

"Very well indeed, thank you. Now, check me on my facts—although I'm pretty sure I've got everything straight." He shot a glance at John Hagen, as if inviting challenge. John, suspecting the camera might be on him, tried to smile confidently. He felt that the effort did not come off, that he looked nervous and foolish. Rodge Garry looked back at his papers. "About ten months ago you, Mr. Hagen, stirred up quite a fuss in your home community of Wellbrook. Wellbrook is an incorporated city of some one hundred and twenty-five thousand people about thirty-five miles from downtown Los Angeles. You, Mr. Hagen, publish a daily newspaper there with a circulation of about forty thousand copies."

"Forty-one thousand, six hundred and twenty-eight as of yesterday," said John.

"I accept the correction," said Garry with mock politeness. "You'll agree, I trust, that about ten months ago you *did* publish a three-part series on certain establishments in Wellbrook?"

"Bordering Wellbrook," John corrected.

"I'll accept that too. But not too far outside the city limits."

"Correct."

"And the articles in your paper, Mr. Hagen, your newspaper, the *Sentinel,* dealt with pornography. Would you agree to that?"

"Well, borderline pornography, anyway. Trash. Smut."

"Pornography," said Rodge Garry firmly. "You ran this three-part exposé of wide-open filth for sale in two places. Is that right?"

"It's accurate enough."

"Whereupon you, Reverend Coe, pastor of a Wellbrook church, began a movement which soon spread throughout Southern California and the entire state. Am I not correct?"

"Actually, it was a little more complicated than that," said the Reverend Mr. Coe.

Garry waved his hand impatiently. "All right, all right, but at any rate the movement got started. You named it PURIFY. Would you mind telling us what PURIFY stands for?"

"Public United to Restore Innocence to Fair Youth," said Coe calmly. "It is now Proposition Number Five on tomorrow's ballot. We expect and pray to put it over. We—"

"Fine," said Garry. "But I'm not quite done with Mr. Hagen yet. Mr. Hagen, will you answer an honest question?"

"I'll answer your questions honestly, yes," said John automatically editing.

"Yes, honest answers—that's what we're after on 'Sky's the Limit.' My question is this, Mr. Hagen: Did you as a citizen run this series on pornography because you were genuinely concerned—"

"Yes, I—"

"I'm not through, Mr. Hagen. Or—did you as a newspaper publisher print this series simply to grab a little circulation—say, another one thousand, six hundred and twenty-eight copies?"

John hesitated. "Actually—" he began.

"Do you find the question hard to answer, Mr. Hagen? Is it possible you were thinking more about circulation than about your civic duty as a publisher?"

"As an individual I was very concerned. As a publisher I try to do a job for my community."

"Quit evading me, Mr. Hagen," said Rodge Garry, weaving into the famed Garry attack like a copperhead nosing over a log. "If you can't answer that question—honestly, as you promised—I must assume your motives were solely those of the fast buck—a circulation gimmick. Right?"

"Wrong. I visualized the series as a public service."

"With no thought of circulation—is that what you're telling me?"

"I can't separate the two," said John Hagen. "I believe in what I publish. I'm also a businessman, like you're a showman, Mr. Garry. Circulation gives me an audience to tell my story to. You need an audience for your program. Do you believe in what *you* say or are you simply trying to build your audience?"

"Don't be annoyed with me, Mr. Hagen. I'm simply trying to get at the truth here. If you are going to dodge my questions, our television audience may get all sorts of ideas."

"Ask your questions," said John shortly.

"I intend to. We'll assume your complete sincerity in the first instance. And then—to get to the main point—along comes PURIFY . . . a state ballot proposition to clean up the filth. And how did that grab you, Mr. Hagen? Tell us, please."

"I'm against PURIFY, as you very well know."

Rodge Garry brought down his fist on the table like a gavel of judgment.

"Exactly!" he said. "It seems to me that you're in a pretty ambivalent position, sir. You know what ambivalent means, I trust?"

"I think I know the word."

"Well, in heaven's name, explain yourself then!" said Garry, his voice turned raw and combative. "It seems to me that any so-called honest newspaperman—or anyone else who *claims* to be an honest man—can hardly stand on both sides of an issue as important as pornography. Or can he? You, a journalist, who pretends to guard the public interest—tell us, if you can, why you are now saying to the good people of California: 'Ladies and gentlemen, pornography is good for you.' Well, Mr. Hagen?"

John forced a grin. His lips were dry and he licked them. He was instantly aware of his mistake. On television the bad guy, the culprit under interrogation, always prefaced his first lie by moistening parched lips.

"Well, to begin with, you have misstated my position."

"Mr. Hagen," said Rodge Garry wearily. "Do skip the gobbledegook. Now look. You have placed yourself squarely on the record. You have called PURIFY—" A sheet of paper trembled in his hands. "Here it is: 'A measure worse than the evil it was designed to cure. A George Orwellian thought-control bill. A thoroughly bad proposition. We cannot too strongly urge a massive No vote on Proposition Number Five, the so-called PURIFY measure.' Which is it, Mr. John Hagen—yes or no on the control of pornography in California?"

"It is true that the *Sentinel*—"

"Which is you."

"Which is me. The *Sentinel*—like many other newspapers in California, I might add has set forth—*I* have set forth—what I consider good and sufficient reasons to vote No on this measure. Anyone who has bothered to read the *Sentinel* knows what those reasons are."

"Just answer the question—why are you pro-smut?"

"I don't want to spar with you, Mr. Garry," said John Hagen, anger in his voice despite himself. "I don't like smut. I don't advocate it—anything you have said. I do oppose the PURIFY thing, because it's unconstitutional."

"Oh, you think it's unconstitutional, do you? Where did you take your law degree, sir?"

"A responsible newspaperman relies on expert sources, not his own general knowledge, Mr. Garry. I have excellent legal opinion that PURIFY is unconstitutional. Moreover, it would place in the hands of every nut in the state the power to destroy publishing. Maybe it's well intentioned—offered in good faith. So was the Spanish Inquisition. Every tyrant in history—"

"*Ty*-rant, Mr. Hagen?" said Garry. "Do you suggest that the backers of PURIFY—which is favored in the polls, by the way—are you suggesting these three quarters of a million people who signed this initiative petition are *nuts,* Mr. Hagen?"

"I didn't say that. Probably half of them didn't know what they were signing. I *do* say—"

"Nearly a million people heard what you just said," said Rodge Garry severely. "I think we've had enough of you for the moment. Reverend Coe, Mr. Hagen believes PURIFY would put control of obscenity in the hands of the nuts. Are you a nut, Reverend Coe?"

The Reverend Bradshaw Coe smiled. "My friend is slightly intemperate in his choice of words, but I forgive him. I am sure he hardly believes what he says. No, I do not think of myself as a nut. The truth is, however, that the PURIFY measure will stand every constitutional test. What it boils down to, Mr. Garry, is that while there may be laws on the books, who is enforcing them? The people? Ah, there's the rub. Under present law, the people are helpless. We have district attorneys responsible to the people only at election time. The people themselves have no way of making these elected officials do their duty. PURIFY changes that. It empowers the average member of the community to *tell* the district attorney: 'This bookseller is selling material that is a loathsome stench in my nostrils, that is corrupting my children. I demand that you take action. If you don't, I'll have you removed from office.' It's as simple as that. Does that make me a nut? If so, I'll bear the name proudly."

"I guess I'm kind of stupid myself," said Garry. "Seems to me that a law that says you can't put books and magazines about sex perversion and sexual intimacies and bestiality and every other kind of junk right out on the newsstands . . . it seems to me that would be a good law. It seems pretty simple to me too, Mr. Hagen."

"I'm afraid it's too simple," said John Hagen slowly. "And don't continue to misrepresent me. I'm saying there are ways to do this without violating the First Amendment to the Constitution."

"I wonder why every time the good citizens try to defend themselves these days somebody's always hollering about the Constitution?"

"Because it's the only basic protection we've got," said John Hagen.

"No . . . now listen to me, Mr. Hagen. Let's cut out all the fancy words—and I believe in the Constitution just as much as you and the rest of the bleeding hearts—"

"Your words, not mine—"

"—the bleeding hearts, the liberals do. Fact, I think I'm a liberal myself. To me a liberal is someone who believes in freedom under the law. Would you accept that definition?"

"I don't know what a liberal is, Mr. Garry."

"Well, you *do* believe in freedom under the law?"

"Certainly."

"You *do* agree we need laws—along with freedom?"

"Of course we need laws."

"Including laws against dirty books, Mr. Hagen?"

"We've *got* laws against dirty books, Mr. Garry."

"Are they being enforced?"

"I think that the—"

"Are they being enforced?"

"If you'll allow me to—"

"Are they being enforced?!"

"I think so."

"Do you? What about it, Reverend Coe?"

Coe shook his head vigorously. "Mr. Hagen knows that simply is not true. I have seen myself, material that would turn the stomach of a hog openly peddled across the counters right in Wellbrook—or just outside. It is material that corrupts; it definitely has no redeeming social importance—yes, I know that phrase too, Mr. Hagen—material that leads to social corruption, sex crimes, and the destruction of our Christian society. We have set ourselves to stamp it out, and stamp it out we will. That is PURIFY in a nutshell."

"What do you say to that, Mr. Publisher?" said Rodge Garry.

"I'll grant that for sheer volume of worthless trash on the stands— the type of thing Reverend Coe is talking about—yes, we're being inundated. In fact, I've made a first-hand investigation myself since my paper's series ran about ten months ago. But let's be very careful in what we're talking about—right now that's PURIFY. Under PURIFY, which is Proposition Number Five on the ballot, the so-called *average* citizen . . . average, the wording of the measure . . . determines for himself that a given piece of writing is obscene. Now, that could be anything, from the crudest account of a sexual adventure to *Madame Bovary* or the Song of Songs in the Old Testament.

And under the statute as it is written, this individual can say, 'This offends me. Put the bookseller in jail. If you don't, I'll commence legal action to have you thrown out of office.' "

"What is so wrong with that, Mr. Hagen?" snapped Rodge Garry.

"Well, if you want a return to the Dark Ages—"

"May I, Mr. Garry?" said the Reverend Mr. Coe with a forgiving smile.

"Please do," said Garry.

"None of these points is new to the backers of PURIFY," said Coe. "Our opponents have made much of the great works of literature as falling under the ban of prohibition—even the Holy Bible itself, as Mr. Hagen has just done. But this is a quite specious argument. The fact is, as Mr. Hagen knows, that the average, respectable, God-fearing adult citizen is perfectly capable of recognizing pornography when he sees it. Mr. Hagen is, I'm sure, and so are his readers. No one is going to confuse the classics with the kind of thing we're talking about. We've all got to use a little common sense about this."

"Well, as I said, I guess I'm kind of dumb," said Garry. "I don't have any trouble at all recognizing a dirty book when I see it. I'm not so sure I'd be as charitable about Mr. Hagen as you are, Reverend."

"Define me a dirty book, Mr. Garry," said John Hagen. He was aware that he was allowing both men to fight him on their own sophistic terms, that Garry was deliberately baiting him to anger, yet he seemed unable to turn the attack to more favorable terrain.

Garry grinned. "Right here in front of a million viewers, Mr. Hagen? Reverend Coe, can you answer that question without getting us thrown off the air?"

"Indeed I can," said the Reverend Mr. Coe confidently. "A dirty book—but let's be specific and call it pornography—is writing that, judged as a whole according to contemporary community standards, is designed primarily to appeal to prurient emotions. And I will submit again that the average sensible adult man or woman is perfectly capable of putting any piece of writing to that test."

"You're forgetting something called redeeming social importance," said John Hagen.

"Not at all," returned Coe. "If I place a slice of rotten cheese between slices of fresh bread, does it make the cheese any the less rotten?"

"You're saying, then, that the use of one taboo word—taboo according to general social usage, the kind of word we wouldn't use in church, say—one such word would make a work of art obscene, Reverend?" said John Hagen.

"I would say, rather, that there is no reason for using such a word in a work of art," said Coe.

"Let's come off it," said Rodge Garry in a disgusted tone. "We're not talking about works of art and everybody here knows it. Let's quit the nit-picking. Nothing I've heard so far has convinced me there's anything wrong with PURIFY—and I think I've got a pretty open mind on most things. The question, it seems to me, has to do with keeping sexy trash out of the hands of kids. Isn't that the main reason for PURIFY, Reverend Coe?"

"The main purpose, yes. However—"

"Yes, go on, sir."

"I trust Mr. Hagen won't jump all over me when I say this: the way to keep filthy literature from children is to choke it off entirely."

"Keep it from adults too, that's what you're saying, isn't it, Reverend Coe?" said John Hagen.

Coe spread his hands with a shrugging gesture. "If it's smutty trash, why not, Mr. Hagen?"

"Supposing that I, a free-born adult, were the type who likes to read this kind of material?"

"Decent citizens don't want to."

"Who decides who's a decent citizen and who is not?"

"We're not trying to define people, we're defining smutty literature," said Coe with a trace of asperity. "I would ask you pointblank, Mr. Hagen—just why are you so perturbed about a movement to clean up filth?"

"Why are you so anxious about sex, Reverend Coe?"

"I see that we have now descended to the level of personal attack," said the Reverend Mr. Coe dignifiedly.

"Yes. For that I apologize," said John Hagen. "But I must insist—"

"Right about now we'll call a brief time out, but don't anyone go away," said Rodge Garry. "We'll be right back for the second

round after this message from the Edgewater Petroleum Company."
His face on the monitor screen gave way to a smiling blonde at the
wheel of a convertible driving into an Edgewater service station.
John Hagen drew a deep breath in an attempt to control his anger.
He had been warned that Garry's success rested heavily on planting
a series of banderillas in the tender flesh of his victims' sensibilities
until they were stung to vulnerability. He had known, and despite
knowing, had accepted Garry's invitation because he would not for-
feit the arena to Coe. What was unexpected was Garry's unequal
treatment. Indeed, he seemed to have aligned himself with Coe and
against John Hagen.

"You fellows are putting up a good scrap," Garry said. His tone
was entirely friendly.

"I seem to be outnumbered," said John. He instantly regretted
having said it. Garry raised a mocking eyebrow.

"Kitchen too hot for you, Mr. Hagen?"

"Ten seconds," said a voice.

Garry was digging into his stack of documentation again.

". . . And now, once again, 'Sky's the Limit,' the Rodge Garry
show," said the announcer. Garry was looking up into the camera.

"A moment ago our two guests, the Reverend Bradshaw Coe, to
my immediate left, and his opponent, Mr. John Hagen, had begun
a most interesting exchange relating to who reads pornographic
books," said Rodge Garry. "We'll get back to that before the show
is over and before we invite questions from our studio audience.
First, however, I'd like to develop another angle here with some
questions for Mr. Hagen, who is the publisher of the Wellbrook
Sentinel. As you know, we're discussing the issue of PURIFY,
which is Proposition Number Five on the November ballot. Mr.
Hagen is against PURIFY; the Reverend Coe is for it—one of its
leaders, in fact. Mr. Hagen, how do your fellow publishers stand on
PURIFY?"

"Most of them share my position," said John Hagen. "Not all, but
most."

"I see. What are their reasons?"

"I can't speak for them."

"What do you *think* their reasons are, then?"

"Probably the same as mine. They see this ballot proposition as a dangerous threat to the freedom of the press."

"That's a very interesting statement, sir. Tell me this: do you, as a publisher, regard yourself primarily as a guardian of free speech or as a businessman—or are the two inseparable?"

"They're not inseparable, they're two different things entirely. A publisher makes his living from his publishing, true. But he can't stay in business unless he produces a good product."

"From conviction—or what he believes the public will swallow?"

John moved his hand impatiently. "There may be publishers cynical enough to think in terms of selling a bill of goods," he said. "I happen to believe in what I do. If I didn't, I'd be in some other line of business. I don't buy your word 'swallow.' I would use 'accept.' If my community—or that portion of it that subscribes to my newspaper—accepts my product, I figure I'm going a good job."

"All right, but that isn't quite enough of an answer. Now, I, as you may or may not know, have a pretty low opinion of the newspaper business in general. For one thing, whenever somebody—for good reasons, perhaps—won't instantly let a reporter poke his nose in—won't answer the most impertinent of questions—the newspapers start screaming about their God-given right to print the news. But what they're really saying—are they not, Mr. Hagen?—is that if they can't get the news and therefore can't print it, they'll go out of business. So it's all pretty self-serving, isn't it?"

"To some degree. But on the other hand, what you're talking about is the right of the people to know in such areas as government. Whether we're serving ourselves while serving the people, it seems to me, is beside the point."

"To you, maybe. I'll take it a step further. The publishers' general opposition to PURIFY on the grounds of danger to a free press really means that they might themselves have to be more careful of what they print, doesn't it?"

"Perhaps. But the same constitutional amendment that protects my right to publish—all except obscenity or libel—protects you too, Mr. Garry. You defend your right to put on this program. Is that self-serving?"

"Aha!" said Garry. "But I make no high-flown pretensions of

being the guardian of the public interest. I think we perform a worth-while task in exposing a lot of phonies here, and I think that's a good thing. But the main difference between you and me, Mr. Hagen, is that no one has to appear on this program. I invite them. If they accept, I expect straight answers to direct questions. Your paper, on the other hand, frequently prints news about people who would just as soon you left them alone."

"I'm sure of it," said John Hagen dryly.

"All right, let's move on to something else. We've got a general election coming up in about twelve hours. In addition to PURIFY, we're voting tomorrow on a choice for governor, lieutenant governor, attorney general, all state assemblymen, and half the state senators. Let's talk about just one race here—attorney general—because the two opponents are so sharply divided on this PURIFY issue. It's of special interest to the electorate because the attorney general is the state's chief law-enforcement officer. It's of special interest to me because the Democratic candidate, Victor Massoni, was a University of Southern California classmate of yours—right?"

"That's right," said John Hagen.

"He has said, and I quote, 'In my opinion Proposition Number Five will not stand the tests of constitutionality. But if it passes, I will have to uphold it as long as it is the law.' And so forth. So his views seem to coincide with yours. Let me ask you this: Is Assemblyman Massoni, your good friend, classmate, and Democratic candidate for attorney general, your source for saying Proposition Five—PURIFY—is unconstitutional?"

"Many lawyers hold that view," said John.

"That's not what I asked you. I asked if your *bosom* buddy, Victor Massoni, is *your* source?"

John Hagen stiffened suddenly. Was the adjective randomly chosen or accidentally—and why Garry's emphasis of it?

"Your *bosom* buddy Massoni—is he your source, Mr. Hagen?"

John Hagen found his voice. "Yes, but—"

"Well, that's all I asked," said Rodge Garry, his voice now a purr. "Is there something you wanted to add?"

"Only that his opinion has been backed by many others since he gave it to me originally," said John Hagen. He felt perspiration begin to crawl at his armpits. The smell of danger lay in the air. Rodge Garry was eyeing him keenly. He cocked his head.

"The *Sentinel* endorsed Assemblyman Massoni over his opponent, State Senator David O. Hausner, I believe, Mr. Hagen?"

"Yes," said John Hagen shortly.

"Your support is quite wholehearted, I'm sure."

"Of course."

"You and Assemblyman Massoni haven't had any recent falling-out of any kind have you?" said Garry.

"No. Why should we?"

"No quarrel over any recent—developments?" pursued Garry.

Not exactly over what I think *you're* thinking, thought John. Yes, there could be a certain loss of warmth, but you're a hundred and eighty degrees off course. The prime reason is sitting right up there in the sponsor's booth with her mother.

But he must head off Rodge Garry's train of questioning—snap it off decisively.

"Why don't you just say what you mean?" he said.

Garry's head snapped up at the boldness of the challenge.

Yes, I was right, thought John. He knows—he's smelled it out. He's trying to get it across some way without mentioning it directly. We're walking on ground that's treacherous for both of us, and we both know it.

"If there is anything you know about the candidate Victor Massoni that the voters should know, we'd like to hear it," said Rodge Garry.

"Such as what?"

"Anything that bears on his qualifications to be California's chief law-enforcement officer," snapped Garry.

"If you know of anything, I'd like to know what it is," said John Hagen. Now the fine wire of tension stretching between them almost twanged audibly. Garry glanced significantly out at the studio audience and then back at John Hagen.

"Well, let's just get along with our program and see if anything further develops," he said. "Or comes up, as it were." The smirk in his voice said plainly to John, I'm going to nail you yet, my friend. You and Victor Massoni.

In his ten years of publishing, John Hagen's most valuable acquisition had been Quincy Broyles. He still so regarded him, this overweight, deceivingly cherubic forty-year veteran of service on the Denver *Post,* St. Louis *Post-Dispatch,* and San Francisco *Chronicle,* among a half-dozen other newspapers. He had wandered by for a job shortly after John had taken the epochal step of converting the healthy half-century-old Wellbrook *Weekly Sentinel* into a frail but promising six-days-a-week daily. "Why do you want to work for me?" John had said. "The L.A. *Times* or *Examiner* can pay you a living wage." And Broyles had rejoined, "Oh, I think it would be kind of interesting to see how long it takes you to go broke." John Hagen had hired him, needing a city editor, at a salary of a hundred and twenty-five dollars a week. Broyles, under his present title of managing editor, drew down two hundred and fifty and John still considered him underpaid. He had slipped him a sizable Christmas bonus each year for the past three years—years in which the *Sentinel* finally began to fulfill its financial promise.

Broyles in his glass-enclosed office had looked up as John Hagen entered the *Sentinel* city room at eight o'clock of a Monday morning in January ten months ago. Most of the day-side editorial staffers except Maggie Mellody and her girl assistant in Women's came to work at 7 A.M. and knocked off at 3:30 P.M. One man came in at 6 A.M. according to a rotating shift to sort out the accumulation from the AP and UPI tickers, especially from New York and Washington, where it was already 9 A.M. The night side consisted of three regular men—night city editor, whose main job was rewrite, the police-sheriff beat man, and a photographer. In addition, Sports often covered evening events with a man who filed overnight. The day staff rotated assignments on such night meetings as city council, or on important special events. The presses rolled at one o'clock.

Broyles was at his desk unfailingly by seven every weekday morning, a habit he could not break, even when John had named a

city editor and promoted Broyles to managing editor three years before. "My wife and I can't stand each other," was his only explanation when John had asked him why he didn't now catch an extra
hour's sleep.

John said hello to one reporter who didn't look up from his typewriter and another who did, the city editor, whose desk was toward
the back of the room, and the youthful sports editor. Someone
opened the heavy fire door to the composing room and John heard
the tinkle of Linotype matrixes for a moment before the door was
closed. The AP and UPI tickers chattered steadily in their housing
in a corner near the city desk.

"Morning, Quin," said John to Broyles.

"John," said Quincy Broyles. He had a quarter-page-size sheet in
front of him with some tentative page-one stories dummied in.

"What's it look like?"

"Unless there's an earthquake or a big plane crash, we're leading
with a two-car fatal early this morning, one of them Hartmann's
seventeen-year-old daughter. Two others killed."

"No! What a lousy shame."

"Did you know the girl?"

"I met her only once, briefly." The Hartmann Department Store
was his biggest advertiser. Emil Hartmann was a brother Elk.

"A pretty fair story out of Sacramento on an alleged conflict of
interest on the governor's newest appointment to the highway commission. Alleged and denied. Big weekly casualty list out of
Vietnam."

"That goddamn war," said John.

"Yeah. And your friend Massoni is expected to announce for
attorney general. That come as any surprise to you?"

"No. He's talked to me about it, although I haven't seen him for
two or three weeks—a little before Christmas. What's the indicator?"

"He as much as said so in a speech Saturday night in Sacramento.
No assembly votes up there for him. He's quoted to the effect that
there's a need to update, modernize, the A.G.'s office, and he'll have
something important more to say on that Monday, which is today."

"I wouldn't wait on the wire; I'd have somebody get him on the phone. Oh, you did already?" For Quincy Broyles was grinning at him without reply. "Anything else?"

"Not for today, but I want to show you something." Quincy Broyles swiveled back in his chair to move his big belly away from his middle desk drawer. "I didn't want the office to get the idea I'm turning lily-waver or voyeur in my old age," he said. "Take a look at this stuff."

John Hagen glanced at the stack of assorted publications his managing editor had planked on his desk, then looked quizzically at Broyles. "Go on, take a look," Broyles invited. John picked up a paperback with the title *The Private Files of a Psychiatrist* in reverse letters against a solid green background.

"By Doctor Z," he read. "Foreword by L. L. Wentworth, Ph.D."

The cover indicated quality printing, but the pages on inspection revealed a crude, cheap job of presswork. They looked like a short-run order printed directly from type rather than plates. John read at random:

> . . . My beautiful young patient exclaimed: "I had never stroked such a magnificent penis, nor experienced such a thrill of delight as when he began inserting that wonderfully large throbbing organ. . . ."

"Good God, Quin, where did you turn this up?" said John Hagen.
"Read on, squire."

John flipped over a few pages. A troubled young man was relating in minutest detail an act of fellatio with his male "friend." A few pages along, the patient of Dr. Z was a thirty-year-old woman who was understandably perturbed by her affair with a pedigreed collie.

"There's more," said Quincy Broyles.

"Thanks, I get the idea," said John. "What's *your* idea?"

Broyles leaned back in his swivel chair and took a pipe from his vest pocket. He fired it with a kitchen match and tossed the burnt match in the general direction of his wastebasket.

"John," he said, puffing, "sometimes I don't know whether I have lived too long or not long enough. I've seen that kind of stuff before and so have you, I would imagine. From *Tillie and Mac* and French postcards through *A Night in a Moorish Harem*. The difference now is in how it's peddled. I seem to remember a sleazy old boy more years ago than I'm going to admit who ran a kind of junk shop in Denver. He wouldn't sell to kids—we didn't have money anyway. The older ones, the few who did buy, showed it around and some of it got passed along. But I guess the world has changed." He took his pipe from his mouth and waggled it. "That book and the rest of that stuff and a lot more is for sale about three miles from here. Two stores, in fact. Do you know a place called Art's Arcade? Just over in county territory."

John shook his head. "No."

"Another, in the same block as Art's Arcade, is Hank's, a cigar store. It carries about the same brand of material. What else is available, I wouldn't know. And they sell to kids. I see a series."

"So do I," said John Hagen. "Who brought this in? You?"

Quincy Broyles chuckled around his pipe. "No, I'm afraid I'm getting gutless in my declining years. It was young Salzman. He's hot to go. *If.*"

"If what?"

Broyles waggled the pipe again. "He's already out of pocket between ten and fifteen bucks on that stack. He figures to do it up right might cost him at least another twenty or thirty. Also, he'll need some pix. He thinks either this bird Art or the fellow who runs Hank's wouldn't take kindly to a photog."

"I'll okay anything up to seventy five." John Hagen thought a moment. "Hasn't Mike got one of those little—what do you call them—Minoxes?"

"It's possible. I mean, yes, he has. It would be a question of how much available light there is inside those places."

"If anybody can get the shot, Mike can. Also, Mike can handle himself in case he gets caught at it."

"*That* is well known," said Quincy Broyles, smiling. The *Sentinel's* chief photographer, Mike Brescia, had gone directly from high contender for the 1964 Olympic Games boxing team into newspaper photography. His ring experience had proved equally as valuable to him on several occasions as his knowledge of light apertures and shutter speeds.

John Hagen was tapping his teeth with his finger. He dropped his hand and said, "Of course there's another angle here."

"Payoff, of course," said Quincy Broyles.

"Right. That should get Salzman his third installment. Even a denial—which is very predictably what he'll get—is a story in itself. The kid angle. How can this kind of thing go on right under the sheriff's nose?"

"Yes, and civic reaction—ring in the churches, the schools, whoever else is good for an indignant graph or two."

"No shortage in that department," said John Hagen. He smiled. "Sometimes I think some of the people around this place earn their pay."

"Well, a man's got to go someplace in the morning," said Quincy Broyles.

"By the way, let me know when the Hartmann services are going to be held, would you, Quin?" And John Hagen left the office of Quincy Broyles, walking past the adjoining office of his business manager, who wasn't scheduled to come in until nine o'clock, and into his own paneled office. He promptly filed the subject of Art's Arcade and Hank's in an unused corner of his mind. He thought about it only twice during the next week. Then Salzman and Brescia turned in the results of their work and it was very exciting stuff.

— 3 —

The offices were all but deserted. The night city editor was on the telephone. In the composing room several night-shift linotypers were working on classifieds, display-advertising "crap," and whatever overnight straight matter was at hand—editorial page, letters, Pearson, Buckley, Buchwald, and Reston, financial, time-copy wire features, fillers, and the Salzman series. Maggie Mellody ripped off a final line or two of typing, off in her corner cubicle, and zipped the sheet from the machine. John walked over. Maggie was editing her own copy with a fat black pencil. When she looked up, there was a slight frown line between her arching eyebrows, an absent, momentary carry-over from her story, the short transitional period most writers need to readjust from what they have been working on into the here and now.

"Dames," she said. "Messers and mezdams. John, why don't you give me a job on cityside? I get so sick of these damn mezdams and their mad whirls."

"Mad whirl is your idea, not mine. You write your own heads."

"Don't blame me if it comes out 'dizzy spin' one of these days. How's the family?"

"In good shape. I was about to ask you about yours."

Maggie Mellody shook her head. She was a pretty, dark-haired woman in her mid-thirties who was supporting two small daughters from a marriage she had given up on three years before. John had no idea as to whether her former husband was helping support them. He knew little about Maggie Mellody except that she was a fine, competent Women's World editor and an extremely attractive woman with the figure of a twenty-year-old. So far as he knew, she dated no one of the several ostensibly eligible members of the staff.

"It's either one or the other, it seems all the time," said Maggie. Today it's Trudy. Strep throat. Tomorrow or next week it'll be Gen with measles or an earache."

"Cheer up. In no time at all they'll be teenagers and your worries will be over."

"You could have gone all week without saying that."

"Good night, Maggie."

"Good night, John."

He tucked himself into his old Transportation Special, which was parked in its reserved space at the rear of the *Sentinel* building. John Hagen was long-legged, rather wiry, and had worn spectacles since he was eight years old. At thirty-nine he was losing some of his black hair at the part, but not yet enough to concern him seriously. He knew he was not a conventionally handsome man, yet women had been attracted to his strong, well-defined features from the time he had emerged from the down of adolescence at about seventeen. "But if you would only smile more," a bouncy little senior classmate had once wailed at him during a slow number they were dancing at the high-school Spring Prom. "You've got nice teeth, you know." He had grimaced, displaying them all, and she said, "I didn't mean show your tonsils." He did recognize in himself the tendency to grip details, yet he brought the same approach to more important things, too. He wanted typographical accuracy in his newspaper no less than factual content; to him, both were essential. He knew that he was regarded as something of a sobersides, which he regretted. He felt he had a good sense of humor—although who didn't think that of himself? He tried to be a fair employer, and it still bothered him that of seven men dismissed for cause or incompetency in his ten years, two may not have quite deserved it. Of late he had begun more and more to wonder how he seemed to his wife. Kris was revealing an antsiness that she couldn't seem to explain. Was it him, the children, a combination of both—what?

He listened to the car engine a moment before setting the gearstick in reverse. The car was a battered Chevrolet "coop" that had been old when he picked it up two years before. He knew the staff made jokes about his Transportation Special, but hell, it ran well. After all, Kris had her Imperial.

He drove to the alley past a rather unsightly mess of wadded newsprint, making a mental note to have the mechanical superintendent order another dump hopper if necessary. At the alley's intersection with the broad, busy Centinela Avenue he waited for a gap in traffic, crossed, and made his way to the north in the winter darkness.

For several long blocks he was in "old city," the part that had sprung up from 1895 on, and had remained relatively unchanged for the next half-century, growing with measured pace. What had begun as a crossroads hamlet, and by 1945 become a rather smug, self-contained incorporated city of twenty thousand, heard the thunder of immigration with the end of World War II. Major industry was beginning to reach out for land sites, seeking outlying communities of Los Angeles offering water, schools, churches, room for housing, rail service, and friendly local government eager to help out with easement and property-tax problems. Within three years the City of Wellbrook, through annexation and immigration, boasted a population of forty thousand, a Douglas airframe factory, a General Motors assembly plant, and a twenty-store shopping center. That was only the beginning. The citrus groves gave way to the bulldozer, new tracts and even fancier "developments" crisscrossed the rolling hills. Population over the next nineteen years tripled. Now the city joined others like it to east, south, and west, almost indistinguishable to the eye as separate cities, like two score or more other incorporated areas of Southern California. Only to the north, where John Hagen now drove, was "county."

Recalcitrant business and residential property owners had long resisted annexation to Wellbrook. For some five miles, Centinela Avenue meandered through spot-zoned clusters of businesses: super service stations, neon-lighted motels, bars, restaurants, liquor stores, groceries, one-story office buildings, card rooms, cheap furniture marts, garages, beauty shops, self-service laundries, palmists, and massage parlors. Here, no fewer than six apartment complexes of two and three stories huddled together as if for warmth. There, a wooden fence surrounded a vast assemblage of junked automobiles adjoining a garishly painted fence that closed in a drag-strip race track.

He knew the area in a general way and yet he didn't know it at all, John mused as he drove. The youngest reporter on the staff—that would be Salzman—was far more familiar with these precincts. He covered police and sheriff and sometimes municipal court. A lively, curious youngster, he had enterprised those bookstores. John wondered what else might go on out here, aside from a high incidence of peace disturbance calls, drive-in brawls, and drunk-driving arrests by the Highway Patrol. Some of the merchants out here advertised in the *Sentinel,* of course . . . especially two of the schlock furniture marts. But many also took heavy space in the *Sentinel's* principal advertising competitor, the weekly throwaway Wellbrook *Progress & Green Sheet*.

A short ten years ago, when he had acquired the Wellbrook *Weekly Sentinel* to make a daily of it, John himself had been an outsider, an Elsewherean. He had worked twelve, sixteen hours a day at the newspaper to make himself known personally to the city's establishment. He felt he now was at least professionally accepted. He had been able to ease up in the last three or four years. He had caught the surge of a spring tide and moved with it. A sizable percentage of his readers disagreed with his politics but it did not seem to harm the *Sentinel* to any great degree. True, he often heard a ground swell of rumbling that there ought to be a good *conservative* newspaper to give him some competition. The post-World War II prosperity that had transited two brief recessions only to regain its continued high level had made a lot of Republicans out of erstwhile Dust Bowl Democrats of thirty years ago. Now their children, with half-grown children of their own, were also conservatively inclined. The ultra-right United Republicans of California, Young Republicans, and John Birch Society all had quite a few adherents in Wellbrook and environs. An even yet larger group was the comfortably settled, don't-make-waves moderates. While many of these had voted for Ronald Reagan in 1966, enough had also gone for the outspokenly liberal Victor Massoni to send him to the state assembly three times in a row.

John slowed as he came nearly abreast of what he had driven out of his way to see: a small cluster of shops and stores flanked by a service station at either end of the block. The street widened here to permit diagonal parking. Next to the nearest service-station lot an overhanging sign bore the red neon letters ART'S ARCADE. John had already seen it on one of Mike Brescia's black-and-white glossy prints. All diagonal-parking spaces in front of the wide entrance were occupied. He caught a glimpse of several dozen young men standing in front of, or moving about, the long rows of display racks. The two nearest the door looked to be no more than sixteen years old, at most. A long block past was the corner store, Hank's, whose sign was in faded gilt letters flat against a red background on the building itself. The lower half of the plate glass window leading to the corner door was painted black. John could see only the top of a man's head above it. He risked a quick turn of his head as he passed the door. Hank's, too, seemed to be thronged.

Tomorrow's *Sentinel* should be of considerable interest to the proprietors of both establishments.

He made a U-turn a block or so beyond and headed back toward Wellbrook and home.

A new, expensive sedan with a green *A* license plate stood in his curving driveway next to the Imperial. He parked behind the Imperial.

"Hello, stranger," he said to Assemblyman Victor Massoni from the entranceway, by the foot of the stairs. Vic smiled at him from the leather recliner chair, a highball glass at his elbow, and now got up.

"Is that you, John?" Kris called from the kitchen.

"As you can see, I made myself at home," said Vic. Much experience at political greeting had taught him not to apply a crushing grip with his huge, powerful hand. John noted again the profuse wiry black hairs extending to the second knuckle. Vic slapped him lightly on the arm with his left hand, still smiling. "How's everything, Johnny?"

"We're still in business," said John, looking now to the kitchen entrance past the dining room, to Kris, in a black dress. "Hi, honey."

She came into the living room, the short apron slightly breaking the smooth line of her hips, but graceful as a deer, accepting his embrace briefly, turning her head so that he would not smear her lipstick. Tonight she had elected to go with a figure-hugging party dress. "Why so late?" she said.

"Am I late? It's only seven-thirty or so. How's your drink, Vic?"

"I'm okay," said Vic Massoni, but John had already taken the wide-lipped glass from the end table.

"Drink it fast," said Kris. "I'm serving in fifteen minutes."

"Where are the kids?" said John, from the sidebar.

"Pam's in her room. Gordo's over at Jimmy's. He's going to stay all night. I told you this morning but I guess you weren't listening."

"I guess I wasn't. Vic, that's scotch and water, isn't it?"

"Right. Scotch."

"Excuse me," said Kris. She returned to the kitchen.

John settled himself on the sofa after handing Vic his glass and said, "Death to the opposition."

"Cheers," said Vic Massoni. He sipped. "What a week! I don't know how I'm going to make this race and pay attention to business. The majority leader called me up this afternoon to bawl me out for missing roll call this morning. Screw him."

"Anything important?"

"No. He didn't need me and I told him so. They'll futz around for two months before getting down to anything important."

"What *does* bring you here right now, Vic?"

"Dough," said Assemblyman Victor Massoni. "I've got to line up about fifty thousand more just for the primary. If I get over that and I think I will—Katy bar the door. I'll need at least a million. Well, that part doesn't concern me so much right now. There's that group of Democratic fat cats up in San Francisco that'll go with the party nominee after the primary. They're good for fifty or a hundred thousand with their organization alone. And I'll get my share through the central committee—again, *if*."

"How do you stand with the oil crowd?"

"I don't have too many friends there with my severance tax bill," said Vic, rolling his glass between his hands. "By the way," he added too casually, "you're going to endorse me in May—right?"

"Is that what you came over to find out?" said John.

"I'm here because you invited me to dinner, Daddy."

"Is Ernie Gruener going against you in the primary?"

"I think so. He was pretty coy with me when I ran across him a few days ago in Sacramento, but I hear he's just about made up his mind. What difference does that make?"

"I think Ernie Gruener is a good man."

Vic Massoni cocked a quizzical eyebrow. There was no mistaking his racial antecedents in the martial nose, full black hair graying at the temples, the full-lipped mouth in a lower face saved from feminine softness by an almost square chin. His smooth complexion was faintly olive-tipped, becomingly so. As far as John knew, Vic had not found a companion he was serious about in the seven years since pretty, bright little Marie with the enormous eyes had died in fruitless labor, the six-month infant already delivered dead. John was pretty sure he had companions, probably many of them serious about him beyond a night's diversion. He knew from their under-graduate days together that Vic was no monk. Yet even Marie had needed two years past his law school, when Vic was twenty-eight, to pin him down. Now, at thirty-seven, two years younger than John, he seemed set in the role of unattached bachelor.

"Endorsing us both will do *me* a hell of a lot of good," said Vic.

"I can't do *anything* with over half my readers . . . registered G.O.P. They couldn't vote for you in the primary if they wanted to." John smiled. "To some of them I'm that damned Bolshevik who ought to go back where he came from. They've felt deserted ever since Otis Chandler turned the L.A. *Times* into a halfway moderate newspaper."

"Ernie Gruener is a good man, John, one of the best, but I happen to be better."

"Oh, don't get so hot, Vic; you're getting the endorsement. This campaign must be making you nervous."

Vic grinned. "You and that damned deadpan sense of humor."

"Does that mean dinner is ready?" John said to Kris, who had reappeared in the doorway.

"Almost. Could you call Pam?" said Kris, smoothing her dress along her hips.

"Pardon me a minute, would you, Vic?"

He climbed the stairs and knocked. The heavy beat of a rock record pounded through the closed door. Over it he heard her shouted, curiously formal "Enter!" He turned the knob. She was lying with her head away from him. One foot was perched on the knee of her cocked leg. She was wearing orange capris and a psychedelic-patterned pink, orange, and red blouse, and was barefooted. "Hi, Daddy," she said over the noise of the record player.

"How did you know it was me, or rather, I?" he said.

"Don't turn it down!" she protested. "That's the new sound."

"It does seem different. What is it?"

"The Beatles have gone on to positively cataclysmic heights of song-writing and to you it just sounds different," she said.

"I'll admit they sound a lot better," he said, having turned down the volume anyway. "They couldn't have sounded any worse."

"Oh, boy!" she said. She sat up and adjusted herself into the full lotus position. "Am I wanted?"

"You are. And I think maybe a dress."

"There's not a single thing wrong with this outfit that I can see," she said, hands on thighs.

"I'll see you downstairs in a dress, honey. *You* in a dress," he added, for she had begun to giggle.

Pam twisted her wrist extravagantly for the benefit of an invisible witness. "My daddy, he's the editor," she told this unseen visitor.

John smiled and went back downstairs.

He saw impending conflict when his daughter joined them a few minutes later wearing a skirt so short he wondered how she might sit with any decorum. Kris's lips tightened.

"Is that the way your friends are wearing their skirts, Pam?" she said.

"Uh-huh; hello, Mr. Massoni," said Pamela.

"My, you're getting to be quite the young lady, Pammy," said Vic.

"Go change into something longer," said Kris shortly. "Vic, why don't you sit there?"

"But, Mother!" said Pamela.

"We're not going to have any argument," said Kris, a steely glint in her eye. Her daughter glared at her coldly, decided she was outgunned, and returned a few minutes later in a rather shapeless tweed skirt that she must have rummaged from her mother's wardrobe. It came to mid-calf.

Dinner proceeded pleasantly, Vic entertaining them with some backstairs anecdotes about his fellow legislators, as well as the early rigors of a political campaign. The three adults had known each other since college days, fifteen years before; indeed, Vic had stood as best man for John. Following dinner, which featured an excellent roast, they relaxed in the living room over brandies after Pam had gone up to her room to "study." At ten-thirty Vic arose and declared he must leave.

"But you practically just got here," Kris protested. "And how often do we get to see you?"

"Don't worry, I'll be back often enough," he said, smiling. "When I start hitting that old campaign trail I'll need some decent food once in a while. Tonight I've really got to get some sleep. I've got to pry money out of people first thing in the morning."

"Well, good luck, old friend," said John. "Give my regards to the governor."

"I trust your sincerity," said Vic.

Kris was moving around the kitchen, running water over dishes, straightening up, a half-hour later. John came out. "Coming up to bed?" he said.

"In a few minutes."

"Why don't you leave the dishes for Mrs. Glade?"

"I will, but I don't want to hand her a shambles. Really, that girl!"

"What's wrong now?"

"Wearing that—that cheerleader's skirt. Maybe it's time I sat her down to explain that at a certain time men quit looking at females as children. Men of all ages."

"Oh hell, Krissy, I wouldn't make that much out of it. I don't think she was trying to make a display of herself. It was a little short, I admit."

"A little! Suitable for a seven-year-old maybe. I'm not going to have my daughter acting like a chippie."

"Kris, for God's sake, Pam's a good girl. If you make a big thing out of it, you'll only create resentment. Especially if you use a word like that."

"Let me handle the mother-daughter relationship, will you please?"

"Sure, glad to. Only, take it a little easy, huh?"

"Why don't you go to bed? I'll be up in a minute."

He was in their large bed absorbed in a copy of the current *New Republic* when she came in. He watched unashamedly as she removed, first, the party dress, her back to him, then the lace half slip. She unsnapped her garter belt and sat at the vanity table in bra and panties to slide off her stockings.

"Anything interesting at the office?" she said, swinging to face the vanity mirror, glancing at his reflection.

"We're breaking the first installment of a series on some bookstores tomorrow," he said. "It could be very interesting."

"What's that?" she said. She tweezed a vagrant hair from an eyebrow.

"Oh, a couple of stores out in the county are selling raunchy magazines and books. One of the youngsters dug it out."

"What kind of magazines?"

"Sex stuff. Not hard-core, but close to the line. Paperbacks, nudist magazines, flagellation, homosexual. Some of it's aimed at some pretty sad people."

"When you say nudist do you mean like *Playboy?*"

"*Playboy* is a church magazine compared to this type of thing. These are young men and women—models, I think. Showing off what they've got. It's probably within the law—it must be. But it's so damned raw I don't think it should be peddled to kids. Though, Lord knows, they'll see it one way or another, sooner or later."

"Poses?" she said, turning around.

"Not if you mean in coitus. Poses, yes—draped around trees and splashing in streams and sprawled around swimming pools."

"Everything?"

"Everything."

"I think that's disgusting!" She rose from the vanity stool and walked to her closet. Her shapely buttocks moved enticingly in the sheer panties. She shed the brassiere and panties and shrugged on a filmy blue nightgown.

"I guess you know we can't, tonight," she said.

"Oh," he said, disappointed. "Oh well."

"Who buys this type of thing?" she said, getting into bed.

"Men. And some women, I guess. And boys."

"I don't understand it. Why should a woman want to see a man's sex organ? They aren't—you know—are they?"

"No, they draw the line at erections," he said solemnly.

She looked at him quickly to see whether he was teasing. "Are you going to read?"

"No," he said. He laid the magazine on the nightstand and switched off the light. After a few minutes, when he thought she had fallen into her usual quick sleep, he felt her stir.

"John?"

"Mm-hmm?"

"Were you asleep?"

"Not quite."

"Could I ask you something?"

"What do you mean, could you ask me something?"

"This—material. These nudist magazines. When you looked at them. When *you* looked at them. What did you think?"

"Think? That they were a pretty far cry from *Sunshine and Health,* I guess."

"I don't mean that. I mean did they *do* anything for you? Do anything for *you?*"

"Stimulate me sexually?"

"Well—yes."

He chuckled. "The girls are quite shapely."

"It did do something to you, then."

"Not to the extent you mean. Not like being with you, for instance."

He felt and heard her shift position. "This is something I don't understand about men. What is there about *seeing* a woman without clothes on in a picture? Women aren't that way—at least I don't think they are. I'm not. I mean, to see a man in the altogether . . ."

"Well, honey, I guess I can't explain men to you any more than you can explain women for me."

"I think I'm pretty typical."

"Oh, I think you are, but there must be exceptions."

"I just don't understand."

"Nothing we say about it is going to change it, so why don't we just go to sleep?"

"Unh!" she said, and flipped over violently in bed.

— *4* —

The fresh proofs were on his desk. He hung his topcoat on the tree, looking at them. They were on long, narrow sheets of newsprint, jogged together, awaiting his final look. The type itself was undoubtedly already in the page-one chase, presently to be surrounded by the morning's crop of news from the beats and the tickers, to be locked in at twelve-thirty. He seated himself and fingered the top edges of the proofs to count the galleys—one, two, three. Two installments, running about a galley and a half each. About thirty inches per installment, plus a half-dozen photos with each, leading from page one. The third installment Salzman would gather and write this afternoon and the next day. People needed time to read, digest, and let their opinions coalesce.

He had seen the whole story in copy but he wanted to see it again in type. He bent over the galleys, pencil in hand. The headless story began:

smut peddlers ... df .. gal 1 .. etaoins

By Peter Salzman

Sex—raw, explicit, frank beyond belief—is for sale to all comers in two stores in county territory just outside Wellbrook.

It is in books, to be sure—books, magazines and tabloid "newspapers." It is also to be viewed in motion pictures on old-fashioned nickelodeon machines.

The material is readily accessible to children as well as adults. Or so it seemed to this observer during a half-dozen lengthy visits to the two establishments: Art's Arcade and Hank's, both on Centinela Avenue.

Several fly-specked signs posted in both stores caution ADULTS ONLY. Yet I saw boys who looked all of 15 years old fingering, scanning and buying with no questions asked.

Toward the end of a week-long period in which this reporter and Sentinel photographer Mike Brescia both established ourselves as "good customers" we began getting veiled hints that "even better stuff" might be available than that openly displayed on the racks.

Neither of us followed up. But if the material hinted at is any "better" than the goods we both saw and bought, it must be very rank indeed.

Let's see how close it is possible to come in a family newspaper to describing some of the merchandise on sale at Art's Arcade and Hank's. . . .

His telephone intercom buzzed. He picked up the receiver.

"Will you talk to Mr. Wells, Mr. Hagen?" said the receptionist.

"Yes, thank you." He punched the lighted button. "Hello, Harry. How are you?"

"Fine, John. I finished reading it last night. Very interesting indeed."

"Glad to get your reader's opinion. What about the lawyer's slant?"

"Well . . ." The attorney hesitated a moment as if clearing his throat. "I don't think there's anything actionable in there. In a couple or three places there might be a slight modifier—an 'alleged' or an 'apparently'—but to tell you the truth, neither word really removes the sting of libel if there *is* libel. It looks to me as if your man delivered a pretty straightforward account of what he saw and did. There's a bit too much judgmental writing—editorializing, so to speak —but hell, John, this is such a gray area of the law, no one seems to know just where the boundary lines are any more. If there are any. I've looked up *Mishkin, Roth, Ginzburg* and a couple of other landmark decisions—*A Book, Etcetera*—that's the *Fanny Hill* appeal— the book, rather than publisher or author, on trial, strangely—and this business seems to turn back on itself. Ginzburg was nailed for so-called 'pandering,' his advertising rather than content. And that was close—a five-to-four decision. All I can say, if it's of any help, is that what seems pornographic or obscene in any one state at any one given time is possibly just above the line in another."

"You talk like a lawyer," said John Hagen.

"Unfortunate, isn't it? Where you're on pretty solid ground, it seems to me, is the selling to minors. The law is apt to take a different view there. Just be sure your man Salzman is willing to take an oath, if it ever comes to that, that he saw obvious minors purchasing. And that's in both places, not just one or the other."

"Oh, he did indeed."

"Fine. Got time for lunch any time this week?"

"Suppose I check back later. Thanks for calling, Harry."

"Good-by, John."

Quincy Broyles was standing at the door.

"Come in," said John. "It still looks good, Quin. That was Harry Wells. He told me what I pretty much knew already. What've we got?" They were joined by the city editor, Gil Dennis, and for the next half-hour talked over the day's paper. "We'd better step up the press run a thousand or so," Broyles suggested. John agreed. The advertising manager, Will Naismith, wanted to talk about next week's

January Days special; he had six pages' equivalent more advertising lined up than had been expected. "That means about ten to twelve more galleys of runaround copy," said Gil Dennis. "Cripes!" All editorial staff, Quincy Broyles excluded, were required to turn to, in addition to their regular work, grinding out fill for these advertising special sections. Writing on household hints, gardening tips, new trends in design, and similar topics to fill the yawning columns around the ads was considered by one and all to be a pain in the ass.

Before the morning was out there had been a conference with Will Naismith and the *Sentinel's* business manager, Dwight Henry, about several seriously delinquent advertising accounts; a further chat with Dwight about how soon they might add another unit to the web press (a year away, they decided); two charity duns on the telephone, both dubious and therefore refused; and some items in the morning mail requiring his attention: a request to address the state college journalism class next month (accepted), a letter from a firm of attorneys politely reminding the *Sentinel* that both "Coke" and "Coca-Cola" were copyright names and must never be spelled "coke" or "Coca Cola" (bucked over to Gil Dennis), a bill for his USC Alumni Association dues (tossed into his personal file), and three job-seeking brochures (referred to Quincy Broyles). With this activity, he managed to finish reading the proofs of Salzman's story, accept a luncheon date for twelve-thirty with the mayor and city manager at the Cabrillo Club, regretfully turn down a former employee fired two years before for drunkenness who phoned from San Diego wanting to come back to work, hear out the circulation director with his weekly complaint about the truancy of carrier boys, and make an appointment with the ITU business agent to talk over contract, due to expire in two months' time.

Despite a pledge to himself given when he left the office, John Hagen was two hours getting back. As he had suspected, Mayor Ronreif was grinding an ax: the reintroduced bond issue for a City Center, defeated at the polls two years before. The *Sentinel* had opposed it then on the grounds of unrealistic, overambitious goals—chief among them, a Little Theater seating one thousand. It was merely coincidental that Mrs. Ronreif was at the heart of the Globe Repertory Players. City Manager Breckenridge was carefully neutral. The mayoralty was largely honorary but the city manager, who was the chief administrator, served at the pleasure of the seven city councilmen, one of them, the mayor. John Hagen spent nearly an entire hour defending himself against the charge of blocking progress. "That's pure malarkey and you know it, Jack," he finally told the mayor testily. "The all-purpose auditorium, the art and garden center, the offices and shops—okay. But a thousand-seat theater for live productions . . . Who do you think is going to play Wellbrook—Hume Cronyn and Jessica Tandy?" They finally parted with the mayor offering a hearty, insincere clap on the back, saying, "You'll change your mind, I know, John."

"Maybe I will," John said. He walked back to the office, to find three men waiting to see him.

The front entrance had been remodeled several years before so that no non-employee could get past the receptionist without the okay of someone on the inside in authority. Visitors who were vague about their business were met in the anteroom by one of the reporters, who came out from the city room. It was a common and useful arrangement with almost all newspapers. There were the usual cranks to be dealt with, but these were not the only time-wasters for a busy staff. The gamut included, but was not limited to, space-seeking ministers, self-named civic indignation committees, authors with copies of books they had paid to have published, religious-tract pushers, minor-party political aspirants, sonneteers, and advocates of a limitless assortment of Causes, whose invariable need was free publicity in order to raise money. Some of these and other visitors were, of course, on quite legitimate and often newsworthy errands.

Of the three seated men who turned at John's entrance, two wore uniforms.

"Mr. Hagen, these are Deputies, uh—" said the receptionist-switchboard girl.

"Deputy Roberts and my partner Deputy Hosea," said the big man on the left. His face was meaty and bland; his eyes, a washed-out blue. His companion was short and stocky. There was something amused about his expression, as if he were thinking, "Is that the best story you can think up, Clyde?" Both wore suntan shirts, green tunic and trousers, and the large acorn-shaped yellow patch of the Sheriff's

Department on the arm of each sleeve where it joined the shoulder.

"Yes, sir," said John.

"Have you got a minute or two?" said the big man, Roberts.

"Well—" said John.

"This other gentleman was here first, Mr. Hagen," said the switchboard girl. John looked over at the other man, who had not risen but did now.

"Merz," he said. "Merz and Merz Attorneys." He was a small, fierce pigeon.

"Police business," said Deputy Roberts, his bland face turned toward the small man.

"My business is quite important too, Deputy," said Merz sharply.

"Would you mind waiting, Deputy Roberts?" said John.

The officer looked once at his companion, grunted, and they both sat down.

"Mr. Merz, would you like to come in?" said John.

The small man stooped and picked up his leather attaché case. Mary clicked the latch by touching a button and John opened the door, waving Merz ahead of him. Once they were in his office he closed the door. Merz took a chair as John nodded. He snapped the catch of the attaché case.

"I, as I said, am Merz, Kurt Merz of Merz and Merz Attorneys. I have come to see you in the matter of this"—he was holding up a copy of the *Sentinel*—"this article you published today by one Peter Salzman."

"Yes?"

"This is a matter for discretion and quick action. Therefore I came to see you instead of calling you on the telephone." He shook out the paper. His movements were precise to the point of fussiness. "Quite by accident I picked up this copy at the moment it was delivered to the newsstand. This headline, with its label 'The Smut Peddlers,' and 'Stores Sell Sexy Trash to County's Youngsters' . . ."

John leaned forward, brushing a fanned-out array of pink call-back slips with his hand. "Mr. Merz, would you mind telling me whom you represent and just what's on your mind?"

"I happen to represent Mr. Arthur Genesee, Mr. Hagen." His angry pigeon's close-set eyes fixed on John Hagen. "In case the name means nothing to you, he is the owner of the business establishment named Art's Arcade. I read him this article by Mr. Salzman over the telephone. I will not hesitate to say to you, Mr. Hagen, that Mr. Arthur Genesee is very, very disturbed about this gratuitous and unwarranted attack on his place of business. I may go so far as to say he instructed me to commence an action for defamation against you and against the *Sentinel*."

John Hagen slowly opened the desk drawer and took out a package of cigarettes. He was trying to ration himself, with the hope of quitting altogether. He lighted up and puffed in the direction of his visitor.

"Is Mr. Genesee in this afternoon, Mr. Merz?"

"Is he—I suppose he is. Now, I am instructed to say—"

"Can he be reached on the telephone?"

"Mr. Hagen, would you mind if I finished with a matter that is of the utmost importance to you? I would advise you to hear me out."

"Go on, Mr. Merz."

"I am instructed to make a proposition that may offer you a way out of your somewhat difficult and presently hazardous position, Mr. Hagen."

"My—"

"The *Sentinel*, of which you are the proprietor and publisher, has printed a damaging and scurrilous article, libelous on its face, imputing to my client, Mr. Arthur Genesee, actions which, if true, would be criminal; that is, contributing to the delinquency of minors. My client is now inclined to leniency—my doing. He will not prefer a charge of criminal libel, that is, providing you, the publisher, at once cease and desist publication of further malicious and unfounded such articles. As to a civil action, we will weigh the effect of a prominent retraction."

"I'd like to get that in writing," said John.

"The first part of my offer is contingent on your immediate cancellation of tomorrow's article. I'll follow with a letter. As to the retraction—"

"I'm afraid you don't understand, Mr. Merz." He pressed the button over the CITY ED. label on the squawk box.

"Yes, John?"

"Gil, is Pete Salzman available?"

"Yeah, he's on the phone—wait a minute, he's just hanging up."

"Send him in here, would you?"

"Sure thing."

The door opened a moment later, as Merz's face assumed a dubious frown.

"You want me, Mr. Hagen?"

"Close the door, Pete. Pete Salzman, this is Mr. Merz, of Merz and Merz Attorneys. Did you bring some copy paper? No, never mind; here." John pushed a lined yellow pad and a pencil toward him. "Here's a quotation for your third installment. Mr. Merz, who represents one Arthur Genesee, owner, I am told, of Art's Arcade, has offered us a deal. If we lay off on the rest of the series, Mr. Genesee will promise to go easy on suing us. Have I quoted you accurately, Mr. Merz? No, I see I haven't. You tell Mr. Salzman in your own words. Would you go slowly? Pete here is like most American newspapermen—he doesn't take shorthand. Go ahead, Mr. Merz."

Young Salzman cocked an eyebrow. "A *deal,* Mr. Hagen?"

"Yes, Pete. If I understand correctly, Mr. Genesee is highly embarrassed, not to mention wroth. A horse trade, isn't that about it, Mr. Merz?"

The angry pigeon, looking from John to Salzman and back to John, said, "Deal? What do you mean—deal? I have demanded that you halt further publication—"

"Wait a minute, you're going too fast for him," said John.

"I'm not speaking for quotation, Mr. Hagen! I have come in good faith with an overly generous offer that can only benefit both parties. My client, to save him further deliberate, scandalous harassment in his business and embarrassment to his family, and you, by saving you from criminal and or civil action."

"You aren't buying it, are you, Mr. Hagen?" said Peter Salzman. John grinned. The boy saw not only his well-enterprised story, but also a prospective bonus or raise, going into the hellbox.

"Well," said John, stubbing out his cigarette. "I suppose it never hurts to listen to what a man has to say, Pete. The first rule of our business, you know. For instance, here. Mr. Merz has *informed* us that we are wrong, but that if we make suitable amends we may gain immunity from prosecution or other unpleasant legal action. But if you listened carefully, Pete, you'll know that what Mr. Merz *said* was that Mr. Genesee has been nailed but good with a thoroughly researched, accurate, and well-written story. Do you see the difference?"

"I thought you might be amenable to a good-faith offer," said Merz. He snapped shut the attaché case.

"Always try to listen with the third ear, Pete. Oh, before you go, Mr. Merz . . ."

"Publish another article and you'll take the consequences."

"Well, I can't let down the staff. Pete worked hard on that story. And typesetting is costly. On the whole, I think we'll go ahead."

"Very well." The attorney opened the office door and closed it firmly behind him.

"What do you think, Mr. Hagen?"

"Off the record, a bluff. On the record, a bluff. It's a sad and disillusioning business at times, Pete."

Skinny, lithe, and too young to be so irreverent, Salzman said, "Can I quote you?"

"May you; and no, you may not. My name is Hagen, not Hearst. Thanks for coming in, Pete."

Alone for a moment, John Hagen brushed his hand back over his hair. The slight edge of one manhattan with the mayor and city manager had passed. The headache could not be the result of a single drink, surely. He leafed through the message slips: Victor Massoni, left no message; the district superintendent of schools, please call; his dentist's receptionist, setting an appointment for his six-month checkup a week hence; his personal insurance broker, please call; his mother (no urgency), please call Operator Two-Five in La Jolla . . . Nothing immediately demanding here. He buzzed the reception desk on his telephone intercom.

"Yes, Mr. Hagen?"

"Are the two men from the sheriff's office out there, Mary?"

"Yes, they are, Mr. Hagen."

"Let them in and tell them how to get back here, would you,

please?" As soon as he hung up, John Hagen arose to open the door. Presently Deputy Roberts appeared.

"Come in, Officer. You too, Deputy Hosea."

"Mind if I close the door?" said Hosea, his hand already on the knob.

"Please do. Sit down. How can I help?"

Deputy Roberts folded his tall frame, pushing his pistol holster forward as he sat. Hosea stood for a moment longer, then also took his seat with the same habitual displacement of the pistol. He removed his peak-bill cap. Seeing him, Roberts did the same.

"I guess you know why we're here," said Roberts mildly. His hands rested on his beefy thighs, one hand holding the cap.

"Let me guess," said John. "Your visit has something to do with our series on the bookstores."

Roberts' bland face did not change expression. "Right," he said. "Those two stores are in Beat Four. My beat, eight to four this month, and Hosea's here, four to midnight."

"Then what goes on is your responsibility—correct?"

"Well, it's the lieutenant's overall responsibility, but we're the men on patrol. We're the guys that's out there. Okay, now your paper just ran an article that puts aspersions on the law-enforcement officers of this county. I don't mind saying it's pretty hard to live with this kind of publicity. It's bad enough trying to do our jobs, out there day and night, risking our lives on real crime, then have to read newspaper articles like this. Maybe you don't know it, Mr. Hagen, but law enforcement is twice the job it used to be five years ago, if you know what I mean."

"I'm not sure I do."

"S'preme Court," said Deputy Hosea, his cynical half-grin accompanying his scornful tone. "Not only every damn hoodlum in the country has now got more rights than decent citizens, but we've gotta put up with harassment and abuse from the people we're supposed to protect."

"You see, it's like a matter of officer morale," said Roberts. "But right to the point: this business about those two places, Hank's and Art's Arcade. We didn't know what those places were selling. Right, Matt?"

"Right," said Hosea emphatically.

"This is what we don't understand," said Roberts, now almost plaintively, but with a trace of anger showing through. "If what your paper says *is* true, how come you don't tell us first, give us a chance to investigate? No, you people have to smear it all over your front page. What do you think this does to the law-enforcement image?"

"I'm a little at a loss to know what you expect of me," said John Hagen, leaning forward.

"How much plainer can I say it?" said Roberts.

"You maintain that neither you nor Deputy Hosea knew anything about Hank's or Art's Arcade?"

"Well, sure, of course we know they're there."

"You've never been in this Art's Arcade to check on the pinball machines?"

"Them machines don't pay off," said Hosea.

"How do you know?"

"Well, we've both been in those places," said Hosea. "That don't mean we looked at their books."

"Never the least bit curious about why so many juveniles hang around?" said John. "Never wondered why they cluster around the book and magazine racks? My reporter tells me a lot of the rawest stuff is right up front. Didn't it ever occur to you to pick any of it up and look at it?"

"I'm not interested in that stuff," said Roberts, shifting his feet. "Are you, Matt?"

"Hell no!" said Hosea.

"Since you saw the *Sentinel* an hour or so ago, did you check to see if what we said is true?"

"Well, we're gonna check it out," said the bigger of the two men.

"But you thought your first duty was to complain to me?"

"If you want to put it that way. Don't worry, we'll look into it. But this kind of publicity don't help."

"Just makes the job harder," said his partner bitterly.

"*You* don't know what's on sale, but our reporter digs it out. One casual visit. We publicize it instead of coming to you with the information first. So we're hurting your image and striking at officer morale. Do you think it's our duty as a newspaper to do the sheriff's job for him?"

"It looks like you're going out of your way to make us look bad," said Roberts doggedly. "You think you help law enforcement?"

"Strangely, I think law enforcement is your job, not mine."

"It's every citizen's duty to support and aid law enforcement."

"Granted. But if we find dereliction of duty—what then?"

Roberts set his jaw. "Careful, my friend."

"I'm not your friend, Deputy Roberts. I'll tell you quite honestly I think it's amazing you knew nothing about those bookstores. I've been a newspaperman for more than fifteen years. Every good cop I ever met knew his territory like he knew his wife's face. If there was anything funny going on, he had to know about it. And he did something about it—if he wanted to."

"Meaning what?" said Deputy Roberts dangerously.

"Meaning no more or no less than what I said."

"You wouldn't be hinting at anything, would you, Mr. Hagen?" said Hosea.

"I'm not hinting, I'm saying. You make anything out of it you want to. You get the kids out of those stores. That's all you have to do."

Deputy Roberts got up and so did his companion.

"Well now, I'll tell *you* something, Mr. Newspaper Publisher. I don't take orders from you under any circumstances. You hear me loud and clear?"

"Fine," said John. "You do your job as you see fit and I'll do mine."

Roberts stepped over to the desk and placed his knuckles on it. "I just hope you or none of your reporters ever get in any little trouble out in the county, Mr. Hagen," he said softly.

John opened his large left-hand desk drawer. He placed a small tape recorder on the desk. "We sometimes keep a record of conferences with this machine," he said. "Now, Deputy Roberts of the County Sheriff's Department, would you mind repeating what you just said into this microphone?"

"Thank you for talking with us, Mr. Hagen," said Roberts slowly and distinctly. "I'm glad you agree we're doing our job. Shall we go, Matt?"

"Stop by any time," said John Hagen.

He waited until the second of the two deputies had left before dialing Harry Wells.

"Mr. Hagen," said Harry with mock formality.

"Right. I'm beginning to feel like a clay pigeon, Harry. Do you know one Kurt Merz of Merz and Merz Attorneys?"

"Sure. Why?"

"The paper couldn't have been on the street an hour when he came by to see me. Waiting for me, actually. He's representing the owner of Art's Arcade, a man named Arthur Genesee. We really drew blood, Harry. He's threatening all sorts of action—criminal libel, civil libel, defamation. He's willing to deal. Call off the series and retract."

"Oh, he is, is he? Interesting."

"Is that all you can say?"

"What do you want me to say? I told you this morning I think you're on solid ground."

"Well, I hope so. I told him we're going ahead, and we are. The second visit was by two deputies from the Sheriff's Department. They're madder than hops. They left with a strongly implied threat they might do something to me or one of my staff if they catch us out in county territory."

"That's too much," said Harry Wells sharply. "Do you know Lieutenant DeGros? He has charge in this end of the county."

"No, I've never met him."

"He's not a bad guy. I suggest you call him up and tell him what you just told me. Unless I'm sadly mistaken these two clowns made the call on their own. DeGros is no dummy. I doubt he'd hold still for this."

"Harry, I'm not even going to do that. Personally, I don't think they mean it."

"Well, that's my advice anyway. Now, what about that lunch?"

"You're a single-minded bastard. Thursday?"

"Thursday, right. The usual."

By the time Thursday rolled around John Hagen had begun to get a considerable insight into what he and his reporter had stirred up.

Always the approach was oblique.

There was the district superintendent of schools. He was in John Hagen's office by appointment on Wednesday morning.

Elliott Warren was a brisk, competent man in his forties whom John had tried without success to like. He was a doer, a mover, an effective administrator. He walked in an aura, however, of decisive rectitude. To some it smacked of the school principal secure behind his classroom loudspeaker switch, staff disciplinary policies, and warning memoranda to parents. Still, John respected him for his ability to do his job. He had been especially effective in resisting pressures to shelve a basic state textbook titled *Land of the Free,* a several-year target of the right-wing element objecting to its recognition that the United States on occasion had treated its minority races badly. He was concerned at the present moment about a much-needed school bond issue.

"You see, of course, that if the City Center bond measure gets on the same ballot, they'll both go down to defeat," he said toward the end. "There is no question of it. The thing you have to do, John, is resist the mayor's pressure to get that fool thing up before the voters."

"As it stands I don't like the City Center plan," said John Hagen. "But I don't regard it as a fool plan. If some features—"

"Of course it is," said Superintendent Warren. "We need many things far more than we need a City Center."

"It has much to recommend it, which has nothing to do with the urgent need for the new high school. Editorially, of course, I'll do what I can. I think you overestimate my—"

"You're a voice in the community. It's your duty to make yourself heard. By the way, speaking of that, allow me to congratulate you on the exposé of the smut sellers in last night's paper. I read it with keen interest. Any reaction?"

John grimaced. "I'd hope to tell you. There's some talk of a public indignation meeting tomorrow night."

Elliott Warren's smile was condescending. "I've already given my permission to use the high-school auditorium."

"Oh, then it *has* materialized? One of my people is following that."

"Well, you should. I'll support you in anything you do about this racket. Once in a while a teacher confiscates some of this material, I'm told. Have you seen any—well, you must have."

"The reporter-photographer team gathered quite a stack."

"Of course. Just what is it like?"

"You read the first installment. I'd say there is no question of its design—an appeal to prurient interest is the expression."

"The—what, female body?"

"Quite a bit of the female body. Nothing lacking in detail."

"In the course of teaching school for ten years or so before I went into administration, I caught boys—even girls—passing some of this stuff around a few times. I can imagine what it's like."

"Well, these aren't French postcards."

"Oh? But fairly graphic, I'd gather."

"Pretty explicit."

"Indeed? You've—kept it, of course."

"Oh yes. In case we have to defend ourselves in court. We doubt it will come to that."

Superintendent Warren chuckled. "Locked very securely in your desk, eh, John? Good thinking."

"It's tucked away but not in my desk."

"Then you don't have it readily accessible—just out of curiosity, you understand?"

"Would you like to see it?"

"Heavens no. Well, I guess I'd better be going. Give us all your help in keeping that City Center plan off the ballot, John."

There were the several handball players at the Elks Club. John, who had played a fair game of tennis in college days, had accepted a bid to join the Elks several years before, both because of business connections and for the use of its excellent gymnasium. He tried to put in an hour there once a week, swimming or engaging in a pickup game of handball. He was dressing after his shower, several locker spaces away from the powerful, hairy owner of Buck Benson Buick, who was slapping at the roll of excess flesh over the band of his white jockey shorts.

"That was some article in the paper last night, John," he said.

"Like it?" said John.

"I don't know if you could say I liked it," said Buck Benson, pulling on his shirt. "There ought to be some way of running those bastards out of the county. I've got a couple of teenagers myself—boys. If I ever catch them with any of that kind of stuff, I'll kick their tails off."

"Hurry up, you guys," said a man who had appeared at the head of the aisle of lockers. "They only serve to one-fifteen. Did I hear someone talking about that newspaper story? What's this you're threatening to do to your kids, Buck?"

"If you heard that, you got an answer to your question, Larry." Lawrence Maddox, the C.P.A. of the group, was joined by Foster Blake, who owned Wellbrook's best-equipped camera store.

"What're you clowns talking about now—tail?" Blake said.

"You think it's funny, Blake—a store where kids can buy dirty, perverted magazines?" said Buck Benson. He pulled on his pants.

"Oh, that. No, of course I don't, but there must be laws."

"That kind of junk can, you know, really twist a kid inside out," said Lawrence Maddox. "He's not old enough to separate reality from fantasy."

"You're right, Larry," said Buck Benson.

"It can make a degenerate out of a youngster," said Foster Blake.

"Well, that stuff for the fruits, anyway," said Maddox.

"All of it," declared Buck Benson, sitting down to put on his shoes.

"Maybe not every kid," said Blake. He chuckled. "Perhaps you guys won't agree, but I think I turned out normal enough."

"Well, most of us do," said Buck Benson. "Actually, it's my wife —she'd just raise holy hell if she ever caught the boys looking at that stuff."

"I guess it all depends how healthy-minded a kid is," said Maddox. "Did any of you guys ever see a Tillie and Mac book?" He grinned. "Remember the equipment?"

"Like a horse," said Buck Benson, laughing.

"Popeye and Olive Oyl?" said Foster Blake, slapping his leg.

"Kayo and Little Orphan Annie?" said Lawrence Maddox.

"Like wow," said Buck Benson.

"I'll never forget my first stag movie," said Maddox reminiscently. "I was all of sixteen, I guess. It was part of the high-school block society initiation." He winced in recollection. "I never went through so much paddling in my life. They had us stripped naked and painted like a bunch of Sioux. They turned the lights out and showed us this movie, then right away they turned the lights back on, and all the kids that showed you-know-what-kind of reaction got paddled some more. Man, I couldn't sit down for a week. It was that kind of a movie."

"Listen, we better get to lunch," said Buck Benson, standing up.

"We've just been waiting on you," said John Hagen.

"Hey, old quiet John," said Buck Benson. "Tell us about that stuff your reporter collected. You must have seen a slug of it. What's it like?"

"Well, it's not hard-core pornography," said John. "I think the story pretty well described it."

"Those nudist magazines—do they really show everything?" said Lawrence Maddox.

"Totally."

"Good God!" said Maddox. "All the paraphernalia—guys in the same picture with girls—this is right out on the newsstands?"

"All the paraphernalia," said John, smiling.

"Why don't you bring 'em around sometime and let us have a look at them," said Buck Benson.

"Up until yesterday they were on sale. They may be yet, for all I know," said John Hagen.

"Are you kidding? Waste my money buying that junk?" said Buck. "Suppose I slipped up and brought one of those magazines home, where my kids could see it? Like I said, if I ever catch either of them with any of that stuff, I'll kick their tails off. Who wants to match for the lunch?"

There was the delegation from the Wellbrook Women's League for Good Government, a group Maggie Mellody disliked almost solely on the grounds that the two fat *W*s in WWLGG left room for little else in the line if one was trying to write a one-column head using thirty-point type. They called on John Hagen in mid-afternoon on Wednesday to drum up some support for a city charter reform. They argued—and John Hagen agreed—that the original document, drawn in 1921, had grown to an overburdened thicket of grafted-on amendments of piecemeal nature, self-contradictory and outmoded.

"We want the city council to appoint a qualified commission to draft a new model charter for presentation to the voters by next year," said Mrs. Robert G. (Gwyneth) McMoreland, the WWLGG president.

"How can I help?" said John Hagen.

"By giving ample publicity when we make our presentation to the city council three weeks from now, following up with an editorial urging the Council to act," said Mrs. McMoreland. John made a note.

"Fine," he said. "I'll be glad to do it."

"Your newspaper is widely read, you know," said Mrs. Harold B. (Lavinia) Brakebill of the Lemon Hill Brakebills.

"Thank you," said John Hagen.

"That was a highly interesting article yesterday," said Mrs. L. J. (Vyvan) Ogleby, youngest and most attractive member of the delegation.

"Which one?"

"Oh, the article on those places selling the magazines," said Mrs. Ogleby, coloring a little.

"The second part of it is in today's *Sentinel,*" said John.

"Oh. We don't get it at home until four o'clock."

"It sounds just terrible," said Mrs. McMoreland decisively.

"Harold—my husband—rarely swears but he swore right out loud when he read it," said Mrs. Brakebill. "He said he wondered what the sheriff's office was getting paid for."

"They aren't too happy with the *Sentinel,*" said John Hagen.

"I think if people could actually *see* what it is they're selling, they might know how bad it is," said Mrs. McMoreland. "It so happens that about two years ago I was visiting my sister in Santa Barbara when State Senator David O. Hausner spoke to her Parent-Teacher Association on the need for laws to control obscenity. He told us about his Chamber of Horrors. We were all absolutely petrified."

"You didn't tell us about that, Gwyneth," said Mrs. Brakebill.

"Yes I did, Vinny. You must remember. The pictures?"

"Oh. Yes, I do remember."

"What is the Chamber of Horrors?" said John Hagen.

"Well," said Mrs. McMoreland determinedly, "Senator Hausner, as you may know, has made a personal crusade for a strong state law to bring what he calls the 'merchants of filth' under control. He's running for attorney general on the Republican ticket this year, you know."

"Yes, I know," said John Hagen.

"Well, over the last six years Senator Hausner's investigators have made a very complete collection of all the raw, filthy, pornographic books, magazines, motion pictures, and—well, devices—available to people who want to buy them. Not openly, you understand, but he said they're not too hard to find if you—if a person really goes looking for them. He calls this his Chamber of Horrors."

"And can anyone see this?" said John Hagen.

"I should say not!" said Mrs. McMoreland. "He shows it only to public-minded civic betterment groups—those interested in keeping this sort of thing out of the hands of children."

"I see."

"Now that I recall, Gwyneth, you said that he had a few things with him when he made that talk in Santa Barbara," said Mrs. Brakebill.

"Oh yes. *Oh* yes," said Mrs. McMoreland. "I can't—I wouldn't—well, they were simply indescribable." She described them.

And then there was the Reverend Bradshaw Coe.

The Reverend Mr. Coe, pastor of Wellbrook's Second Baptist Church, was, to John Hagen's knowledge, an agile space-grabber. He was the innovator of the sermon topic "Was Jesus the First Hippie?" It got a short paragraph on the Associated Press. An older hand named Chris Smith did the Saturday church page along with daily rewrite and was also the AP stringer. John never learned whether or how the Reverend Mr. Coe made his case on Jesus.

He had met the Reverend Mr. Coe several times in the past four or five years. For all that, he scarcely knew him. On his visits to the *Sentinel* offices Coe was handled by Chris Smith. This time, however, Coe required an appointment with the publisher himself, late on Wednesday afternoon. John sighed. He had his lead editorial yet to finish and it had to go to the machines tonight. He acquiesced, however. The Second Baptist Church, after all, placed a regular two-column, four-inch weekly insertion and was faster pay than most churches. He would just have to stay and finish his editorial after the visit. He went forward to greet his caller.

The short, handsome man with the imposing head had a presence, without question. "I'm so glad you could see me, Mr. Hagen," he said. His handshake was firm. He did not attempt to hold on as some men of God did. His palm was dry.

"My office is back this way," said John.

"I've been in a number of times, of course. Mr. Smith is a delightful person. I'm no wordsmith, to make a small joke, but *he* is. I bring in my X'ed-over copy and he always manages to make it scan." He looked over toward Chris Smith as they walked. Chris looked up vaguely from his typewriter. "Ah there, Mr. Smith," called the Reverend Mr. Coe.

"Hi," said Smith, looking back at his typewriter.

The Reverend Mr. Coe carefully pulled at the creases of his trousers as he sat. The gray suit was well fitted and looked new. "You have a nice office. Are those memorabilia of your career on the walls?"

"Yes, a few. That's me receiving the California State Fair Gold Award for makeup. More credit due my editors than me on that. Bill Mauldin was kind enough to send me the signed original there on request, although I've never met him. I'm in that group shot with the late President Kennedy, taken at the Press Club in San Francisco when he was still Senator Kennedy. That one up there is with Governor Pat Brown. They don't mean anything but they're nice to have. What can I do for you, Reverend Coe?"

"I've often thought you and I should get to know each other better, Mr. Hagen," said Coe, lacing his fingers in his lap. "I was gratified when I received my call to Wellbrook six years ago to learn that the community had such an up-to-date, well-edited newspaper. As I mentioned—when was it—the Rotary luncheon last fall?"

"Thank you, you're very kind."

"Not that I am always in agreement with your editorial policies."

"Even my wife takes issue with me sometimes," said John Hagen. "My father disagrees almost totally with my politics and he's one of my backers. But what can I do for you?"

"You know, of course, that a meeting has been called for tomorrow night as a result of your stories on the smut sellers."

"Yes. We have a story on it in today's *Sentinel*." Peter Salzman had developed the information since John Hagen's talk that morning with the schools superintendent, and turned in a separate story for a page-one box. "Did you have something to do with that?" The short story had mentioned only "civic, religious and patriotic leaders and groups including Mayor Jack Ronreif, the Wellbrook Brotherhood Group, the Affiliated Parent-Teacher Association and the American Legion."

The Reverend Mr. Coe raised an eyebrow. "I saw the notice. It is true I was not mentioned." He smiled forgivingly. "I seek no special recognition, but actually I am in no small degree responsible for serving as catalyst. Contacting a number of persons, I sensed a tremendous upwelling of dismay, anger, and indignation. 'Someone should do something,' was the prevalent mood. I proposed the meeting to one of my brethren, the head of the Wellbrook Brotherhood Group, who requested the use of Wellbrook Union High School. Mr. Elliott Warren, the district superintendent, was quick to give his permission. You're attending, of course?"

John fiddled with a pencil. He had been thinking of how many times as a publisher he had been confronted with this or that pleader for special causes demanding, "What are you going to do about it?" A newspaper, self-appropriating the task of playing civic conscience, frequently was credited with more influence than it possessed simply by asserting editorially that something should be done or not be done. John Hagen assessed the *Sentinel's* function differently. The paper should make plain where the publisher stood on issues. But its more vital function was to find and print the news. That forceful body "the People" required accurate information first. Leadership was a poor second.

"Yes, we'll have a reporter at your meeting."

"That is taken for granted. My question is about you."

"I don't plan to be there."

"Oh, but you must."

Only the memory of his telling Deputy Roberts, "You get the kids out of those stores," checked his impulse to make a short reply to the Reverend Mr. Coe. For the second time that day John Hagen had been told what he *had* to do.

"Mr. Salzman is assigned to cover. He'll do an excellent job, as you already know."

"We need the publisher of the *Sentinel.*"

"Why?"

Coe smiled and touched the side of his nose with his forefinger. "Accept my word that something very important is going to happen at the meeting tomorrow night. Something in which we want your active participation."

"I won't sign that blank check, Reverend."

"Promise you'll attend and I won't ask any other prior commitment."

John Hagen studied the pencil as if it held answers. How long had he used this model without knowing he wielded an EAGLE "CHEMI* SEALED"? So much for his powers of observation.

"All right," he said finally. "I'll come. I don't know what you have in mind but I'll be there, on one condition."

"Name it."

"I've been roped before, Reverend Coe. People have taken the liberty of using my name without my permission. You do *not* have that permission. Is that clearly understood?"

"Please take my word for it, Mr. Hagen."

"I do."

John Hagen now waited for him to get up and leave, but apparently there was more.

"Mr. Hagen, you will forgive my possible naïveté, but I wonder whether I—we of the committee might not ask the loan of the material your reporter collected."

"We've got it put away. You may look at it here, but I can't let it leave the office."

"Fair enough," said Coe. "Tomorrow morning?"

"How about ten o'clock?"

"Splendid," said the Reverend Mr. Coe. "You understand, of course, that in order to deal with an evil you must know its exact nature."

"Of course."

"In my pastoral rounds I must often look on the seamier side of life."

"I quite understand."

"Frequently I find it necessary to steel myself for tasks I personally find extremely distasteful."

"I sympathize," said John Hagen.

"I'm taking your time," said the Reverend Bradshaw Coe. "We'll see you at ten o'clock in the morning. We're a worldly group. You needn't fear showing us anything you have in your—ah—collection."

— *6* —

A glance at his wife told John Hagen nothing. Ever since he had met her in the fall of 1951, he had marveled at Kris's ability to conceal even the deeper emotions behind a pleasant expression. She then had been a pretty eighteen-year-old girl. She now was a beautiful young-middle-age woman.

John in 1949 had just put his two years of Army service behind him, one year ahead of the Korean conflict, and had enrolled at the University of Southern California. He met Kris, a freshman, two years later. As managing editor of the *Daily Trojan* he had assigned himself the task of interviewing some of the new crop. Finding a registration queue near the Men's Gymnasium, he selected a brunette in a calf-length plaid skirt, vivid green cardigan sweater with the sleeves pushed to the elbows, and saddle oxfords. He judged her (incorrectly) to be no more than sixteen, with a delicately curving full mouth, rather high cheekbones, large, guileless gray eyes, and flowing black hair. She was a slim girl of about five foot three with a fine figure and excellent legs. He pulled her from the line over her protests that she did not want her picture taken.

He smiled tolerantly. "I didn't catch your name."

"Kris. Kristina Dryden. Why do you want my picture?"

"Daily Trojan. Now, smile, Kristina Dryden. Freshmen are supposed to co-operate."

She laughed suddenly. "I'm sort of new, Mr. Hagen, but even in Gridley you couldn't get away with a corny line like that."

"Grid-ley, Miss Dryden?"

"Gridley, Butte County, California. Where do you come from that's so much better?"

He got his photo and thumbnail biography. She was, indeed, from the small northern California town of Gridley, her father dead in the Battle of Midway aboard the USS *Yorktown,* her mother remarried and moved to San Francisco. She chose to remain with her uncle and aunt, who owned extensive peach orchard properties. She had come to USC because her father had been an earlier graduate. She struck John Hagen as sweet, very desirable, and highly naïve. She also turned him down for a date. In the year that followed, something happened to Kris Dryden. It was something more than the intense affair she had with a young, married assistant professor of psychology, of which she later freely told John the essential details. A fellow student told him of some vague "pretty wild" happening to which her name was linked, but knew none of the particulars. John refused to believe it of her—whatever it was supposed to be —never asked her about it and was never told. Quite likely some disappointed Don Juan's revenge, he concluded. Certainly his own experience, when she finally consented to date him in the 1952 fall semester, indicated no easy conquest. Quite the contrary. She disliked sex talk, abhorred dirty jokes, and was quite firm in standing off his advances. She'd "neck" a little, but resisted his attempts to take matters any further. To his elation, she accepted his marriage proposal after they'd gone together six months. When they first went to bed together a short time later, he learned why she had shunned heavy earlier physical involvement with him. Deep kissing and a minimum of caressing unshackled a highly sensuous nature—almost mesmerized her. They were married in the fall of 1953 in Las Vegas. The senior Mr. and Mrs. Hagen were disappointed that there had been no formal ceremony, but came through with a handsome check. It enabled Kris to continue into her junior year, majoring in psychology, while John worked at the near-starvation wages paid a copyboy on the Los Angeles *Times*. She was pregnant in December.

Looking now at this lovely, enigmatic woman by his side at the noisy public meeting, John Hagen wondered for about the thousandth time why she had accepted him to begin with, and what secrets she lived with. Of recent months he had sensed a discontentment in her. Did she belatedly regret that she had never completed her college as they had once planned, even after Gordo was born? Was he neglecting her in some way? She professed herself well satisfied when he tried to talk about it, but he found it hard to believe her words.

The gathering was a curiously mixed bag. John Hagen's trained reporter's eye told him that there were about two hundred and fifty in attendance, considering that the high-school auditorium held about fifteen hundred.

On the stage, occupying a row of metal folding chairs, was the ad hoc action group: the chairman of the Affiliated Parent-Teacher Association, a Mrs. Glass; the local post commanders of the American Legion and the Veterans of Foreign Wars, one wearing a blue overseas cap, the other, the same model in olive drab; the president of the Wellbrook Brotherhood Group, Rabbi Gross; the pastor of St. Theresa's Catholic Church, Father O'Hare; the pastor of the Second Baptist Church, the Reverend Bradshaw Coe; the president of the Wellbrook School District, Robert G. McMoreland, husband of the WWLGG's president, Gwyneth; and the county probation officer, Ned Belknap. A vacant chair in the row belonged to the invited representative of the district attorney's office. A scholarly-looking young deputy in eyeglasses, he was presently standing at the microphone centered downstage from the chairs, trying to field a barrage of angry questions. They were thrown from every part of the crowd. On the floor were many middle-aged couples. Most of them probably were parents of youngsters in their teen years. Many in the audience, however, were women in the fifty-and-up bracket and for the most part unescorted, inclined toward grimness of countenance, who attended fiercely to the words of every speaker. They applauded those they agreed with and launched loud jeers when a speech met with their disapproval. Their male counterparts were fewer in number: here and there a bald or graying man, often with upright, dignified bearing suggestive of the military. They were less loudly vocal than the old women, uttering an occasional "Hear, hear!" or "Bosh!" depending on what the speaker had to say. Between times they muttered a good deal.

"Yes, sir?" said the young deputy district attorney to a husky, jut-jawed man who had stood and was demanding attention.

"I've been sitting here listening for an hour and nobody's answered the question yet!" he shouted. The deputy shifted his feet uncomfortably. "As a taxpayer and a parent I demand to know why the district attorney's office don't get out there to Centinela Avenue and shut those places up!"

The audience voiced its approval.

"As I said before, sir, the district attorney's office *does* have the subject under investigation," said the young deputy.

There was a chorus of jeers. An elderly man at John Hagen's left growled, "Evasion! Sheer inertia."

"How long does it take to investigate?" said the man, the cords in his neck bulging. Cheers.

"The matter was only called to our attention two days ago," said the deputy D.A. Jeers.

"That's a lot of double-talk!" shouted the man, sitting down to handclapping and the congratulations of his immediate neighbors.

"*Mister* District Attorney!" cried a small, hawklike woman in black, rising from her seat. Her voice knifed through the mutter like an overstressed drill.

"Yes, ma'am?"

"Why isn't the sheriff's office represented here tonight? Seems to me if anyone ought to be here, they should."

"Yeah, where are they?" "Where's the sheriff?" "Is he too scared to show up?" cried the voices.

"I believe I explained that our office has no jurisdiction over the sheriff. Now, if our own investigation should reveal—"

"What in the hell's to reveal!" yelled a tall man standing up down front. "We all read in the *Sentinel* what's for sale out there! We know the kids are buyin' it! If you guys have got the power of arrest, what's stopping *you* from moving in?" There were loud cheers.

The young deputy waited patiently for the outcry to subside. "Let me explain the legal process involved here—" he began.

"Quit stalling!" a woman's voice screeched.

"If you'll—if I may be permitted—if I may have your attention a moment," said the young deputy as voices overrode him. "I would like to answer that last question," he said, finally getting through. "This is not quite as simple a matter as it may seem."

"Double-talk!" yelled a voice.

"You see," said the deputy district attorney, "in order to proceed we must first find that the material we have under study right now *is* obscene or pornographic, within the meaning of the law."

"Gobbledegook!" yelled the same heckler.

"I do wish they'd let him talk," said Kris quietly to her husband.

"They don't want explanations," said John Hagen. "Explanations complicate simple issues."

"Is it simple?"

"No. Nothing is."

"You see, under the law, based on a number of recent interpretations by the United States Supreme Court—" said the young man at the microphone. He was submerged in a wash of booing.

"If—if—if, as I say," the speaker broke through, "if—"

"If what!"

"If we decide there is questionable material—but more to the point, if we find that it is being sold to juveniles, then we *can* act independently of the sheriff's office. Do I make myself clear?"

Apparently he made himself all too clear. There was further jeering. A man's voice rose above it to shout, "How long will that take—until next Christmas?"

Rabbi Gross had arisen. He was an elderly man. Ancestral sorrow was engraved in his thin face. He stepped up beside the young deputy district attorney and touched his sleeve. The young man twitched as if stung. The rabbi held up a placating hand and inclined his head.

"I would like to resume," he said. The deputy nodded with obvious relief. He returned to his chair.

"My friends, we have now heard from a number of persons about this problem we face," said the rabbi gently. "You have spoken out of the deep and understandable distress arising from a situation over which we have no direct control. What the county authorities are doing—we know the district attorney's office will pursue its investigation and act with whatever power it has. We do not know about the sheriff's office, nor why they did not respond to our invitation." There were jeers, which the rabbi stilled with upraised hand.

"My friends who are here on the platform with me—the parents, the patriotic organizations, my fellow churchmen, and I—we had some discussion before tonight's meeting. Having heard your very sincere views, I would like to propose for you an immediate course of action. Because it is clear to us that the law must move cautiously, but because it is equally clear that some action should be taken at once, I should like to suggest that for now we try the power of persuasion. By this—"

"Rabbi!" demanded the husky, jut-jawed man, standing again.

"Please, sir, if you would—"

"We don't want persuasion, we want those places closed down!" shouted the man. "I move we form a vigilante committee, go on out there, and pull every book and magazine off of those racks! Let's have us a bonfire—tonight!" He was cheered loudly.

"Please. Please. Please," said the rabbi. "Please let me speak. I sympathize, but to break the law is not the way."

"And what if *they're* breakin' the law!" cried the man.

"Please. A mob we are not. If you will hear me out. I am personally convinced that a delegation of citizens, acting with dignity as befits us, should be formed to call on the proprietors of the two establishments in question. It would be a representative group—housewives and mothers, the churches, the schools, the patriotic societies. I would suggest we form such a group here tonight. It should be maybe ten or a dozen of us. I shall serve on it if you should think so, or not, as you wish. And tomorrow this group will pay a call on the proprietors. My friends, shall we not try?" His upraised hands, the appeal in his low, slightly quavering voice left them waiting. The audience was hushed. A woman stood.

"I am Bettyjane Miner," she said. "I have three children. I would like to try what the rabbi has suggested and I would like to serve on the delegation, or committee, or . . ." Her voice trailed off.

"Let's give it a try," said a man's voice.

"No harm," said someone else.

"We are agreed?" said Rabbi Gross. "May I ask first if seven of the nine here on the platform should serve? That is, excepting Mr. Belknap, the county probation officer, and of course our friend the deputy district attorney. Yes? Mrs. Miner, you would join us? Good. A housewife or two more—a father?"

Two women stood, identified themselves in turn, were accepted. A stocky man also volunteered.

"Shall we all meet here on the platform right after the meeting?" said Rabbi Gross. "At this time, then, I should like to introduce once more my colleague, the Reverend Bradshaw Coe of the Second Baptist Church, who has asked to speak."

The Reverend Mr. Coe walked confidently to the microphone, bowing to the rabbi.

"My good friends and fellow citizens," he said. His resonant voice boomed from the loudspeakers. "We have taken an action here tonight that for the moment seems appropriate. I am sure my good friend Rabbi Gross will agree that it is purely a stopgap measure. But we will try to do our very best with moral suasion. If we fail"—he appealed with his hands—"at least we will have tried. But I have something further to say to you." There was a slight stirring in the audience.

"Before I begin, I should like to invite recognition of someone who is here among us tonight. Just before the meeting I asked if he would join us here on the platform. Being a modest man, he declined. Nonetheless he is deserving of our fullest gratitude. At this time I ask that you give him your warmest applause. Mr. John Hagen, publisher of the Wellbrook *Sentinel!*"

Heads turned as the Reverend Coe thrust his arm in John Hagen's direction. As the clapping began, John nodded uncomfortably. Coe indicated with his hands that he should rise. John stood as the applause mounted.

"And his lovely wife, Mrs. Hagen!" called the Reverend Mr. Coe above the noise. John looked down. He saw her lips quirk with irritation, but she had a gently amused smile by the time he had helped her to her feet. They sat down again as the Reverend Mr. Coe reclaimed his audience.

"Of course, this meeting tonight is the direct result of Mr. Hagen's courageous exposé of the merchants of smut through his newspaper," Coe continued. "We owe him a debt of gratitude for what he has done." He smiled. "He doesn't know it, but he isn't through yet. I made him a promise yesterday that I would not involve him in anything or use his name without his permission, and I do not intend to break my word. I am sure, however, that he will be more than happy to give his co-operation when he learns—here and tonight for the first time—what we will ask of him."

John Hagen heard the words in stony silence. Kris nudged him gently with her elbow but he did not look at her. Coe was putting him on the spot publicly, despite what he had said. John Hagen seethed internally. He folded his arms.

"Let me proceed to the point," said the Reverend Mr. Coe. His voice turned soft for the moment in order that his audience might listen the more intently. "When the *Sentinel* began its exposé two days ago, it could not have been more timely. As all of us here are quite aware, the matter of filth on the newsstands, filth in literature, filth in motion pictures has become one of the burning issues of our time.

"There is scarcely a best seller in print that we dare leave around the house for fear that our children may see the utterly foul and depraved scenes portrayed and language quoted therein.

"There is hardly a motion picture on the screens of our neighborhood theaters that we dare take our children to.

"The covers of our magazines—even in the neighborhood supermarkets—have been taken over by nudity or provocative poses even more suggestive than nudity.

"On the wire racks of drugstores, groceries, and cheap bookstores are paperbacks by the hundreds, containing some of the most salacious, revolting, utterly depraved writings the world has ever known. Among them are Hindu and Chinese manuals of physical sex in the most detailed language, leaving nothing to the imagination; unexpurgated texts on torture by the depraved Marquis de Sade;

books by and for lesbians; books by and for homosexuals; books designed to appeal to the utmost depths of lust to be found in the lowest elements of our society.

"They are openly displayed, openly sold—their message of sin, appeals to unbridled lust, instruction and direction and invitation to enter into compact with the forces of evil, laid out in corrupt array—and before the very eyes of children!" The Reverend Mr. Coe was thundering now, his commanding forefinger stabbing the air, then freezing as he stared out at his audience. Kris nudged her husband again. Without looking at her, he took her arm. He felt a shudder. Her hand closed over his.

The Reverend Mr. Coe began again, dropping his voice once more.

"You may have decided by now that we are helpless to do anything about all this. You have heard the representative of the district attorney—quoting the law correctly, I have no doubt—tell us more by implication than direction that it is impossible for us, citizens and taxpayers of California, to do anything about this flood of licentiousness that I have described to you. I will agree that very little *has* been done. We have seen our state legislature, time and again, refuse to pass laws that the people demand, to stop the printing and circulation of pornography. We have seen law-enforcement agencies neglect their sworn obligation to act, even when there *are* laws to govern their actions. We have seen the courts pussyfooting around this dire problem as if nothing could be done to stop it.

"Well, my good friends, something *can* be done and we here tonight are going to help do it!"

There was a great burst of applause. John Hagen finally looked at his wife. She raised an inquiring eyebrow. He shook his head.

"For several months, in my capacity as private citizen rather than minister of the gospel, I have been discussing and exploring this vital issue with a number of persons in Wellbrook and elsewhere in Southern California. They are concerned, as I have been, with obscenity. We have been proceeding quietly, but tonight, for the first time, I have for you an announcement—the first anywhere—the news about PURIFY. I am free to reveal the news because we just yesterday morning learned of some important financial backing that will enable us to go ahead with PURIFY.

"What is PURIFY? It stands for Public United to Restore Innocence to Fair Youth. And how is it going to operate?"

He held up a finger. "One, tomorrow morning, in Sacramento, our
representative will file papers of incorporation with the secretary of
state.

"Two, there will be a formal public announcement of PURIFY
—although I am sure Mr. Hagen's newspaper will carry the first news
story tomorrow—printing what I believe is called a scoop." Two
fingers in the air.

"Three, we will immediately form local committees in every city
and community of Southern California.

"Four, through these committees we will circulate petitions for
signature throughout the entire southland.

"And five, ladies and gentlemen, when we have gathered enough
signatures—and we need about seven hundred and fifty thousand of
them—we will again go to the secretary of state with an initiative
petition. He will place it on this year's general election ballot.

"Do I make myself clear? We are going to amend the Constitution of the State of California through a vote of the people . . .
*and finally get a law on the books that will stamp out pornography
in California!*"

The Reverend Mr. Coe bowed his head, beaming, as the thunder
of approval burst over him. He bowed again.

"And Mr. Hagen—I thought you looked a little apprehensive
when I said I would ask your co-operation in something you knew
nothing about—I'll invite you now to relax. All that I want is your
strong editorial support of PURIFY. Since your newspaper, the
Sentinel, ran that excellent and timely series, we know you will continue to back us in this great crusade against smut. With your support locally and that of your newspaper brethren statewide, we can
only succeed. We are honored to count you with us."

Now the applause again was for John Hagen. Kris squeezed his
hand.

"Tonight we light a torch! We'll touch off a flame that will become a prairie fire of reform sweeping California!"

Again he was applauded.

"Tonight we will begin gathering the first signatures. When we get the petition forms you will be contacted to sign them. I will ask volunteers to take these signup sheets to tables that are set up in the auditorium foyer. There, all those who wish to join us in PURIFY please sign your names—husbands and wives each separately as individual voters." He paused, looking around. "And now—forward with PURIFY!" He stood long, acknowledging the cheers. He then bowed to Rabbi Gross, who was once more coming forward to the microphone.

"Thank you, Reverend Coe," said Rabbi Gross. "What you have said sounds interesting indeed. And now I would ask the several other committee members of our group to come forward to the platform. Thank you all for being here tonight. The meeting stands adjourned."

—7—

"You're angry, aren't you?" she said. He followed the headlights of the Imperial around the swooping curve of the auditorium parking lot exit.

"Yes, of course I'm angry. This isn't the first time something like this has happened. Ethics of courtesy seem to go out the window when some of these advocates of Causes—cap *C*—go into action. They bay on your trail like a Mississippi bloodhound. You can't refuse; the tone of voice is always the same. I don't care whether it's the American Red Cross, Little League, litter on the sidewalks, Big Brothers, or PURIFY. 'Oh, we know the *Sentinel* will support us,' they say. 'Let's go on to other business.' Well, the girl might love to go to the dance but she wants to be asked." He slipped the car into northbound traffic.

"That man frightens me." He shot her a quick glance. She was hugging herself although it was an unseasonably mild January night.

"Coe? He's harmless, I'm sure."

"*Are* you?"

"Of course. Tonight he had a handful of genuinely concerned parents and a whole lot of fringers whipped up to march on Sacramento if he asked. Tomorrow will be a different story. In cold, practical fact, to gather three quarters of a million valid signatures in California costs about a quarter of a million dollars. There's some rule of thumb—two bits a signature, I think it is. Get a million to allow for a generous number of throw-outs. With all due respect for the zealous pastor of the Second Baptist Church, it just won't happen."

"Yes, but he hinted at a big . . . what did he say about important financial backing?"

John Hagen grinned wryly. "Well, he's promoting. Confidence is the name of the game. I remain to be convinced that PURIFY is any more than the Reverend Mr. Bradshaw Coe. Oh, he may have some help outside Wellbrook, but I doubt that it amounts to a hill of beans."

"To coin a phrase," she said.

"Public United to Restore Innocence to Fair Youth. God!"

Gordo was sprawled on the sofa with his feet on the leather hassock watching an Andy Griffith rerun on the color TV. To his teachers, his grandfather, and on his birth certificate he was Allan, after John's father. But because of a fancied resemblance to the dark-haired, bright Pepito of Gus Arriola's comic strip, which the *Sentinel* carried, he had become—by some curious transmutation—Gordo, the comic strip's namesake.

"Hi," he said.

"Hello, sweetheart," said his mother. "Did you get your homework done?"

"Uh-huh."

"Is Pam home yet?" said his father.

"I think so," said Gordo absently, his attention riveted on Andy Griffith, who was talking to his skinny, pugnacious deputy.

"Gordo, is your sister home?" said John Hagen. "Could you spare us your attention for just one moment?"

"Huh? Yeah, she come in about a half-hour ago. She's upstairs."

"I'm glad she come home," said John Hagen. "She's went upstairs, did you say?"

"She's what? Aw," said John Hagen's son.

"Tell it like it is. Sometimes I feel downright disorientated."

"Aw," Gordo said again.

"John," said Kris.

"Just having a little father-and-son—pardon me, dad-and-boy—colloquy, aren't we, Gordo?"

"If you say so," said Gordo. His voice slipped into its new, low register.

"John," said Kris. "And sweetheart, I think you'd better go to bed. It's almost ten o'clock."

"It's over at ten o'clock, Mom."

"Not including the closing commercial, nine fifty-seven," said John Hagen.

"Yeah, man, but they always tag off with another little bit," said Gordo resentfully.

"I bow to that," said John.

"I think I'd like a cup of coffee," said Kris. "Would you, dear?"

"Yes indeed, man," said John.

The boy's eyes flicked to his father an instant and back to the television set. His thin, sharply defined face was dispassionate.

They were seated at the dinette table, John stirring his sugared coffee when the finale music clicked off. Gordo in his tight white permanently creased pants and short-sleeved black jersey wandered in barefooted and made for the refrigerator.

"Milk," he said, lifting out a half-gallon carton. He took an eight-inch glass tumbler from a cupboard and dumped it full. It went down his gullet in three long draughts, his youthful Adam's apple bobbing. He seemed to debate having another; instead, he filled the glass with water in the sink and returned the carton to the refrigerator.

"How did you like today's issue, son?" said John Hagen.

"Fine. Can I say good night now?"

"Can you? You just did."

"Yeah, well . . ."

"See anything in there of interest?" pursued John.

"Oh, it was—you know. Like the usual."

"I'm suddenly curious, Gordo. Do you ever read my newspaper?"

The boy seemed to need a place for his hands, finally shoving them in his tight hip pockets. "Some."

"It's really his bedtime," said Kris, turning her cup in its saucer.

"Well, call it the one-minute closing tag. What do you find of interest in the *Sentinel,* Gordo? The international news? The stories out of Washington? The local scene? Or all of it?"

"It's kind of hard to say." Gordo took one hand from his pocket and scratched his nose. "All of it, I guess. I mean, I guess it's like it's interesting to somebody, Dad."

"How about the series we just finished today?"

"Series?"

"Sleep tight, son," said John Hagen.

"Good night, Mom-Dad," said Gordo.

"Good night, darling," said Kris.

"Night, son," said John.

Kris sipped at her coffee, cradling the cup with both hands. Finally she said, "I wish you wouldn't."

He smiled at her. "I guess I was a little rough with him. Truth to tell, he makes me feel more uncomfortable than I do him. I can't find any point of contact."

"How long since you've really tried? Do you remember when you used to swing him between your legs; how he'd chuckle and scream? When you wrestled on the floor with him? I did most of the fault-finding then. Now it seems you two are always at swords-points and I'm the peacemaker. Funny, when you were pouring the most of yourself into the paper was the time you paid the most attention to him."

"He was the cutest little guy, wasn't he?"

"Honey, the thing he doesn't know how to cope with, can't handle, is your sarcasm."

"Mostly his language, Krissy."

She shook her head. "He's well adjusted to his group. That's *their* language. You could have it lots worse."

"Would it be too much to ask the boy even to read the newspaper?"

"I don't think it's even relevant. How old were you when you took an interest in your father's brokerage business?"

"Touché." John smiled again. "Even today it seems a supremely dull business to me."

"Did you know that your son is terribly proud of you, John?"

He was pleased. "It doesn't come through."

"He's not going to jump in your lap. Already he's a man physically."

"Yes, I've noticed."

"And from now on he'll be competing with you even more strongly. Do you realize that he'll be eighteen in just three and a half years? He's in that terribly difficult position of wanting your love but moving away from you too, which he has to do. He'll be anything but effusive. He won't ask you for affection. Maybe he doesn't read the *Sentinel,* but he's proud his father is not a bookie or a ditchdigger. He's told me so, in the most casual way possible; any other way would be un-cool. If you listen, he's saying a great deal."

"But all the reaching out has to come from me?"

"It's an inarticulate age. Their language isn't ours. With his peers, I imagine Gordo has a great deal to say."

"Kris, do I verbalize things too much?"

"Sometimes. If you don't want any more coffee, I may as well turn off the pot."

He looked at his cup thoughtfully. "I wonder what else I can do, being me? How do I know whether a concept is valid unless I test it with words? To me, an idea has to be put in language. It's like hitting a golf ball or designing an airplane. It's impossible to fool the ball or the plane. It flies or it doesn't."

She touched his hand. "That's your life style and I wouldn't change it. But try to give yourself a chance with your son, John."

"In other words, I should shut my big mouf once in a while."

She looked at him steadily. "Do you know, sometimes I love you very much," she said.

— *8* —

John Hagen stopped by the city editor's desk. "Morning, Gil," he said.

"Sounds like you had a lively time last night, John," said Gil Dennis. "Salzman filed overnight."

"Let me see the carbon," said John. Dennis flipped through a sheaf in a basket. The story was toward the top. John took the five sheets and read quickly until he found what he was looking for. "Here, Gil, these two graphs about me. Kill them."

Dennis separated the page, circled the passage with a single swirl of his pencil, and wrote KILL–GD over the paragraphs. "Copy!" he called out.

A kid with long sideburns got up from a typewriter, where he had been batting away idly, and sauntered over.

"Proof desk," said Dennis. The kid took the page and walked away. "Salzman called in and asked the okay to cover that delegation this morning," Dennis said. "Nine o'clock. It's not his shift but it's his story and he wants to stay on it."

"That's the other thing I wanted to say," said John Hagen. "Let him make his arrangements to get his information by phone. He's not to accompany the committee. Having a *Sentinel* reporter along —especially Salzman—would just put up a red flag."

"Well, we need the lead," said Dennis, squinting up over a cigarette.

"Of course. Although the chances are, there won't be any very conclusive results. Not today—much as I wish them well."

"What's with this preacher Coe anyway, John?" Dennis took the cigarette from his mouth but not in time to flick off a half-inch ash, which dropped in his lap.

"All I know, you know," said John Hagen.

"We need a good righthand story," said Gil Dennis.

"Maybe the Queen and Philip will announce they're divorcing."

"Maybe Ev Dirksen will announce for Gene McCarthy."

At ten-thirty Quincy Broyles stood in John's doorway with a tear-off from the wire in his hand.

"Yes, Quin?"

"Gil Dennis thought you'd like to see this," said Broyles, puffing comfortably at his pipe.

The item was brief:

SACRAMENTO (AP)—A SOUTHERN CALIFORNIA GROUP CALLED "PUBLIC UNITED TO RESTORE INNOCENCE TO FAIR YOUTH" FILED ARTICLES OF INCORPORATION WITH THE SECRETARY OF STATE TODAY.

THE GROUP ALSO TOOK OUT PAPERS FOR AN INITIATIVE PETITION.

AVOWED PURPOSE OF THE NON-PROFIT CORPORATION WHOSE INITIALS SPELL "PURIFY" IS TO GATHER SIGNATURES FOR AN "ANTI-OBSCENITY" MEASURE ON THE NOVEMBER BALLOT.

THE APPLICATION LISTED R. BROOKS NORTON AS PRESIDENT, PERRY M. TUNMAN, VICE-PRESIDENT, AND THE REV. BRADSHAW COE AS SECRETARY-TREASURER.

John Hagen pursed his lips. "Mm," he said. "R. Brooks Norton I know. He's president of Shasta Savings and Loan. Who is Tunman?"

"If you buy a Higashi camera, lens, or binoculars anywhere in thirteen western states you're buying from Tunman," said Quincy Broyles. "He and the Madrone Distributing Company are one and the same. Japanese optics, shavers, power tools, kitchen appliances, and I don't know what all."

"Big?"

"Very big."

"Where do you pick up these impedimenta, Quin?"

"I'll have to think about that," said Quincy Broyles.

John Hagen looked at the dispatch again. "Now, how would a two-bitter like the Reverend Bradshaw Coe tie up with men like that? It doesn't make good sense."

"Maybe your man is not a two-bitter."

"That thought has just occurred to me. How is Gil playing this?"

"He's given it to Chris Smith to rewrite for a sidebar under the page-one head with a one-column mug."

"I hate to give him the play, but in a sense it's our own story."

"That it is," said Broyles. He looked critically at a pipe that had gone out. "Oh, Gil says to tell you that so far this morning Queen and consort are happily wed. He thought you would like to know."

"What else is new?" said John Hagen, returning the tear-off to his managing editor.

John leafed through his morning harvest of junk mail, which he had set aside earlier, and plopped most of it into the wastebasket. Included was a revolutionary new plan of executive life insurance, a tearful dun from a Boys' Ranch somewhere in Oregon, the announcement of a Surefire Way to Increase Your Circulation 10% in 30 Days (give a steak-knife set with each new subscription), the Whittaker-Baxter propaganda clip sheet (which Quincy Broyles had slipped in deadpan, knowing John Hagen's distaste for its pro-utility arguments), and a multicolored flyer and brochure packet with coupon for A Book That Should Be On Every Publisher's Desk. His telephone rang.

"Mr. Hagen, there is a Mr. Davis out here to see you," said Mary, the switchboard receptionist.

"Who is he with?" said John. He floated the brochure for A Book That Should Be On Every Publisher's Desk into the wastebasket.

"He wouldn't say, sir."

"Then tell him I'm busy."

"Yes, sir." She clicked off.

At eleven-thirty he got up and went out into the city room.

"Salzman phone in his story, Gil?"

The city editor pointed to Chris Smith, who was hunched over his typewriter. He was banging away with two fingers of each hand, taking the information from the headset. He growled something into the mouthpiece, listened a moment, and resumed typing. A moment later he ripped the sheet from his machine and said, "Copy!" The ambling kid with the sideburns brought it over to Gil Dennis. John read over Gil's shoulder:

new lead—smut—salzman/smith

Two county territory bookstore proprietors today promised a "civic cleanup" committee headed by Rabbi Norman Gross that no minors will be permitted to buy "questionable" books or magazines.

At the same time they xxxxxx denied they had previously permitted such purchases, despite evidence to the contrary turned up by a Sentinel reporter as related in the Sentinel earlier this week.

The ad hoc committee of 12, formed at a public indignation

meeting last night in the Wellbrook Union High School auditorium, paid calls starting at 9 o'clock this morning on Arthur
Genesee, owner of Art's Arcade, and Henry (Hank) Buttles,
proprietor of a cigar store named Hank's, both in the 21490
block of Centincla Avenue.

The committee's xxxxxxxxx mission was to urge removal of
borderline smut from the racks or, failing that, ask the owners
not to sell such material to persons under the age of 21.

According to the Rev. Bradshaw Coe, pastor of the Second
Baptist Church, a committee member, the group's reception this
morning was "polite but somewhat aloof."

Genesee told the committee, according to the Rev. Mr. Coe,
that he planned legal action against the Sentinel for the newspaper series.

Sheriff's Lt. Lucien DeGros, who heads county law enforcement xxx for the area that includes Art's Arcade and Hank's,
could not be reached for comment.

. . . . pickup earlier   ####

"We've got to go with this, John," Gil Dennis said with a meaningful glance at the clock.

"I've read it," said John Hagen. Dennis quickly slugged *2-B-2*
on the story and handed it to the copy chief, whose semicircular table
adjoined.

"Is he suing us, John?" said Gil Dennis.

"Not so far," said John Hagen. Which seemed true up until that
time but not at ten minutes past twelve noon, when he left by the
front for lunch. A heavyset man in a rumpled brown suit got up as
John closed the inner office door.

"You John Hagen?" the man said.

"I'm Hagen."

"You're served," said the man, shoving a folded sheaf of papers
at him. John automatically took it. The man said, "So long," and
opened the front door, closing it hastily behind him.

"That was Mr. Davis," said Mary from behind her switchboard.

At two o'clock John Hagen was on the telephone to Harry Wells.

"Well, our friend Genesee's done it to me, Harry. Defamation
and malicious libel. Merz and Merz attorney for the plaintiff."

"Uh-oh. Who's named and what's the amount?"

"The Sentinel Publishing Company, Inc., its president and publisher John A. Hagen, Peter Salzman, an employee of the Sentinel Publishing Company, and John Does one through ten, begging leave to amend without prejudice. A cool quarter of a million dollars."

"Send it over," said Harry Wells. "We have ten days to answer. Frankly, I didn't think he'd do it, but nothing is certain in law. We'll file a general denial of allegations, of course."

"What then?"

"See what comes," said Harry Wells cheerfully. "There's an excellent chance it will never go to trial. But I have to have the papers, so shoot 'em over."

"Well, I don't want the damn things," said John Hagen.

The Reverend Bradshaw Coe gained admittance to the inner sanctum at a little after three o'clock.

"An excellent news story, excellent, Mr. Hagen!" he exclaimed. He insisted on shaking hands. "We've done a good day's work, but now the real work begins. What did you think of my little surprise last night? Took you somewhat aback, did it not?"

"I wasn't expecting public attention," said John Hagen.

"It's an unfortunate aspect of doing the public's business. Like you—and like me. Now, let's talk about your editorial support of PURIFY. If we work fast, you shall have the privilege of being the first newspaper in California to line up behind it. Let's see . . . since you have no newspaper on Sunday and today is Friday—"

"Reverend Coe, I haven't—"

"—and unless there is time to write your first editorial for tomorrow's paper—"

"—said I would yet offer the *Sentinel's*—"

"—Monday it will have to be, I suppose. Can you be ready with your editorial for Monday?"

"Reverend, if you please."

"Sir?"

"At this point I know just two things about PURIFY. One is that you have announced it. Two is that you and your associates have filed articles of incorporation."

"Why—yes." The Reverend Mr. Coe smiled tolerantly. "Of course. I am so caught up with enthusiasm I had forgotten that all I've given you so far is lip service. But see here." He drew from his breast pocket a single sheet of paper and extended it. "Here is the general wording of the petition. It still needs work to get it into perfect legal form, but this basically is what we plan to incorporate into the measure. We are in the process of getting literature. We'll have it from the printer next week. Look this over, if you would."

John accepted the sheet and spread it out. He read:

INITIATIVE PETITION

We, duly registered voters in the State of California, legally resident at the addresses shown hereon, do hereby petition for a measure to be placed before the Voters of California at the General Election next succeeding the filing of this petition, the measure to be worded as follows:

The Constitution of the State of California is amended by adding an Article entitled *Control of Literature* and the following language:

Whosoever sells or causes to be sold any printed material that, in the judgment of the average person according to contemporary community standards is lewd, lascivious, indecent, obscene, or pornographic and is designed to appeal to the prurient emotions, is guilty of a misdemeanor; and on conviction thereof, shall be sentenced to a mandatory term of confinement in the County Jail for no less than 30 days or more than 90 days *and* shall be fined the mandatory sum of no less than $500 or more than $1,000. Whosoever commits a second or subsequent offense under this provision who has previously been convicted of a misdemeanor under this provision is guilty of a felony; and on conviction thereof, shall be sentenced to a mandatory term of confinement in the State Prison of no less than one year or more than five years *and* shall be fined the mandatory sum of no less than $5,000 or more than $10,000.

Removal for Failure to Act: Any District Attorney who, on complaint by a citizen under this provision, fails to prosecute the person or persons complained against, shall be removed from office by due legal process on the complaint of the citizen who has failed to obtain the redress sought under this provision.

As he looked up, John Hagen was aware that the Reverend Bradshaw Coe was eyeing him intently. Coe immediately dissembled with a smile.

"It's quite hard-hitting, isn't it?"

"Yes it is," said John. "This is what you're presenting to the citizens, is it?"

"Yes. As a matter of fact last night we gathered one hundred and twenty signatures of people who want to sign the official petition when it comes out. Committees are forming throughout Southern California. We expect to have the requisite signatures in two months' time. We are quite serious, you see."

"So it would seem." John reread the language. "Don't you think the penalties are a little extreme?"

The Reverend Bradshaw Coe frowned. "For the panderers of filth to our children, Mr. Hagen? Stern, yes, and rightly so. Extreme, no. It will have the support of every decent citizen of California. We know it will have the wholehearted backing of the newspapers . . . starting of course with the *Sentinel*."

John tapped the paper with his finger. "Can you leave this with me, Reverend Coe?"

The Reverend Bradshaw Coe appeared a trifle taken aback. "Why —yes, of course. I have any number of copies. But may I be so bold as to inquire . . . well, frankly, Mr. Hagen, I sense a certain reservation on your part. But surely I'm mistaken?"

John inclined his head. "I haven't said no, Reverend. I ask only that you let me study this a day or two. You're asking a snap judgment on something quite far-reaching. I'll need to look this over carefully."

"Well—" said Coe. He smiled again. "I *am* a bit disappointed, but then I shouldn't let my enthusiasm carry me away. That is, I wanted the *Sentinel* to be the first with its commendatory editorial early next week. However, you're right, of course. Shall I come back Monday?"

"How about Tuesday? Tuesday morning at ten o'clock?"

"I'll be here promptly. And of course I urge your most prayerful consideration, Mr. Hagen. I feel sure that you will help carry our banner in this crusade." His eyes narrowed slightly. "I might add only that we have the most powerful support in this movement. Men of good will, decency, and—ah, strength." He rose briskly. "Well, so much for that. Let me repeat how grateful the entire community is to you, Mr. Hagen. I'll tell you frankly that we had those two men terrorized this morning. Oh, they covered up nicely, but underneath they're pretty shaky."

"My lawyer will be glad to hear that," said John Hagen. Once more he found himself taken by the hand.

Matters were relatively quiet for the rest of the day. The *Sentinel* published its smallest edition on Saturday, with much of its material prepared earlier, such as the church page. At the very outset John Hagen had determined that a small daily could not compete for Sunday attention with a giant like the Los Angeles *Times*. Hence, with no Sunday paper, late Friday afternoons were usually pretty slack. Quincy Broyles stuck his head in at five o'clock to bid him a pleasant weekend. They chatted a moment about the legal action, then John resumed his work on the second of two Monday editorials. His mother called at five-thirty to remind him that he, Kris, and the children were expected for dinner Sunday.

"Oh, we'll be there, Mom," he said with a guilty start. He had noted it on his calendar pad but had forgotten to tell Kris. She was slightly annoyed when he telephoned her immediately after his mother's call.

"Why doesn't she call me on these things?" said Kris.

"An old habit, I guess. Remind me to ask her to do that the next time."

"I really don't care if this is the arrangement you prefer."

"Oh, cut it out, will you, hon?"

He had just typed the ### on his editorial when he became aware that Maggie Mellody was in his doorway.

"Oh, hi, Maggie," he said, startled.

"John, I wonder if I could ask you for a ride."

"Sure. What happened to your car?"

She placed her elbow against the door casing, her wrist curved against the angle of her jaw. "That damned mechanic promised me he'd have my bug out by four o'clock, then phoned at four-fifty to say I needed a new remulgus or something. He can't get it now until Monday morning."

"So you'll need a ride Monday, too." He slipped the cover over his battle-scarred Underwood. "Listen, why don't you take my Chev and keep it over the weekend?"

"Oh, no; that leaves you without wheels."

"We've got the family car."

"I think I'll cry."

"Not on my carpet. Are we ready?"

They left by the back door, which adjoined the composing room door.

"I hope you can drive this monster," he said.

"The staff thinks you should donate this car to Bill Harrah for his museum."

"I should fire the lot if that's the best they can come up with."

They got caught up in the Friday evening juvenile mating dance of "cutting the gut" on Centinela Avenue. Cars formed a steady procession.

"I guess Trudy and Gen will be a part of this scene in just a few years, I regret to say," said Maggie.

"Would you go back yourself and do it all over again if you could?" He glanced at her. She wrinkled her nose.

"Not for anything. I'd opt for a permanent twenty-five. That's still young enough to, but old enough to decide." She was silent a moment. "Or so I tell myself. You can fall at any age. My second was at twenty-eight, and now I've got two little girls. I love them both dearly, but sometimes I wish . . . Oh, don't mind me, I guess I'm just tired tonight."

He braked for about the twentieth time. "I don't really know anything about you, Maggie."

"Where shall I start?"

"That's not an invitation. Yes, I guess it is, but only in a general way."

Maggie Mellody put her hand on the top of the seat cushion, near but not touching John Hagen's shoulder. "I took journalism at Missouri, as you know. I was married in college. It was annulled by his parents because he was underage. I was broken-hearted. Now I think it was a good thing. One of us was bound to outgrow the other."

"You think you would have outgrown him," he stated flatly.

"You're very perceptive. I *know* I would have, but I was a very bitter eighteen at the time. Well, that lasted me until I was twenty-eight. Not that I've ever been a man-hater." She looked at him just as he looked at her. "He was a husky, beautiful, sexy—telephone installer. Oh, I tumbled but hard. Do I have to suggest what the trouble was?"

"Maybe I might guess."

"Right for the money. A husky, beautiful, sexy telephone installer. Those *broads!*"

John Hagen steered around the last of the cars, a Mustang with two young girls, and accelerated to thirty-five.

"You asked me one time if I liked the job," said Maggie. *"Whether* I liked the job? Well, I like newspaper work better than anything else I can mention, so I guess the answer is yes. The *Sentinel* is a good sheet to work for. So are you good to work for."

"But you also think you could fall again."

He sensed her eyes on him. She said, "He'd have to be someone pretty special."

"I'd take that for granted," he said.

– *9* –

The mid-morning air was crisp, the sky overcast. As they neared La Jolla, John thought about the father and mother they were on their way to see. His father was now in his seventieth year and generally as healthy as his mother at sixty-five. It was his father and his father's friends who had made it possible for John Hagen to become a publisher ten years before.

John had not always been able to talk to his father, but when he had gone to him with his idea he was listened to carefully. This was business.

"Seventy-five thousand for plant and equipment," said his father. "Seems like a lot for a broken-down weekly. How much of it's usable for a daily newspaper?"

"The building, two Linotypes, the Ludlow, the Elrod, the chases and furniture, the proof press, the stones and tables, the casting furnace, plus a complete job shop. We'd need a web press, a couple more Linotypes, stereotyping equipment, more of everything else, including back and front office space. There's a twenty-year-old Hoe for sale right now up in Seattle. We could squeeze into production for two hundred thousand dollars."

"What makes you think you know enough to publish a newspaper?"

"I don't," said John Hagen honestly. "But I know news, and I know what advertising is, and I know what the potential is out there in Wellbrook. I'll hire the advertising and business brains, and, frankly, work my ass off."

"You will indeed. Democrat slanted, of course."

"Politically independent."

"Yes, I know you political independents. You analyze fearlessly and independently and somehow it always comes up Democrat. Let me think about it."

That had been ten years ago. After five years John had exercised an option permitted him under contract to purchase forty shares from his four partners at the original value of forty thousand dollars. He used the shares as collateral for the money he borrowed from the bank to make the purchase. At this point the newspaper had begun to turn the corner, and the bank was pleased to make the loan. The shares made him a 20 per cent owner. Within another five years the business and property had boomed to a healthy appraised value of about six hundred thousand dollars as the community burgeoned. One fifth of that belonged to John and Kris. Eventually another 20 per cent would pass to them by inheritance.

He knew that he had been incredibly lucky. He also knew how much of himself he had put into the *Sentinel*. It was no more than other men had poured into other enterprises: only a sizable chunk of their lives.

Barely five years ago both children would have come tumbling out of the car and raced up the broad macadam driveway to greet their grandparents. Now John and Kris actually led, with a slightly sulky Gordo and an aloof Pam trailing by a few steps. They had been fighting.

"Hello, hello!" his mother said. John kissed her and she embraced Kris. "Kris, dear. How nice you look. And Pamela, darling . . .

kiss Grandma, sweetheart. Gordo, honey, you're *such* a handsome young man . . . are you too big to hug your grandmother? I didn't think so. Come in, come in!"

John Hagen watched his father come forward as his mother herded them in, a hand on the shoulder of each child. Was he walking more slowly than he had at their visit three months ago? His normally rather grave, even stern face seemed a little thinner, but his color was good and he was smiling.

"Well, Kristina my dear"—pecking her cheek—"and John"—shaking his hand with a still strong grip.

"Dad."

"Hello, Father," said Kris.

"And the young man here . . . how are you, Allan?"

"Fine," said Gordo.

"And my little sweetheart, Pamela. Kiss for the old man?"

"Hi, Grandpops."

"Let me take your coats," said his mother. "I've got a nice big roast. You still like pork, don't you, John?"

"I haven't changed."

"No, you always did like pork. Why don't you all go into the living room?"

"What about a drink?" said Allan Hagen. He was comfortably clad in old, but quality, gray tweed trousers, moccasins, and a gray wool shirt. "John? Kristina?"

"Nothing for me, thanks," said Kris. "Oh, maybe a little Coke."

"Bourbon and branch?" said John.

"Never took to scotch, did you, John? I guess Pamela and Allan will have some Coke, eh? Of course. I won't join you if you don't mind. I take my two ounces along toward bedtime."

"Are you still playing a little golf, Dad?"

"Yes, that stupid game," said Allan Hagen at the sideboard. "Twenty years ago I came within five strokes of shooting the age I am now. Now I'm lucky if I break ninety. You getting any exercise these days?"

"I try to work out at the Elks once a week."

"The Elks. How come they never put you up for the—what's the name of the country club?"

"Lemon Hill. They did, three years ago. We wanted to wait until we had more time and money. We may join this year."

"But you still haven't taken up golf?"

"Nor likely to, but they have a good swimming pool and fine clay courts."

"Tennis. I guess it's a good game but I never played it. Coke for you, Kristina . . . Pamela . . . and Allan. And your highball, John. Let's relax. Son, how's it going?"

"Well, you get your copy of the paper."

"Yes. And I suppose you're going for Massoni for attorney general. Despite the fact that as far as I can see, he's not remotely qualified."

"And Hausner is?"

"Yes, if you come right down to it. Besides, he'll have opposition within the party before the primary. I can think of two or three men including Hausner better qualified than some red-eyed young leftist barely out of law school."

"Oh goodness, are they at it already?" said John's mother to Kris as she came back from putting away the coats.

"Vic Massoni had a good solid six years' law practice before he went into the assembly," said John. "Two in the public defender's office. And he's been five more years *making* the laws. Voted outstanding freshman assemblyman by the press corps in his first year. Was offered and turned down a municipal judgeship two years ago."

"The governor probably wanted to get him out of his hair."

John grinned. "Besides, Ernie Gruener is also running on the Democratic ticket in the primary."

"It beats the hell out of me how you can go on year in and year out deciding every Democrat is the best man for every office."

"Not true. I've gone twice for Tom Kuchel for the U. S. Senate."

"That's the worst thing you could have said. If Kuchel's a true Republican, I'm Franklin Delano Roosevelt."

"Best man your party has had for fifteen years."

"Oh Lord!" said Allan Hagen ducking his head in disgust.

"How are the children doing in school?" said John's mother. Scarcely a thread of gray as yet touched her naturally brownish-auburn hair, and her gray-green eyes were as keen as they had been when John was a boy. "Let's see, Gordo, you'll be entering high school this fall, won't you?"

"Yeah, I'll start as a soph'more."

"And Pamela, honey, how is the seventh grade treating you?"

"Okay, Gramma." Pam and her mother had waged war that morning. Pam had elected to put on bell-bottom pants and a crazy blouse. She was now wearing a becoming yellow dress. She was beginning to develop a figure, although yet a very slender girl.

John's mother still preferred to do her own cooking, even though the Allan Hagens could more than afford a cook. She did have a housekeeper in, five days a week, although John suspected she worked right along with her.

Since his retirement at sixty-five, giving up his salary but not his interest in Hagen & Dunwoody, Allan Hagen had begun to share some of his wife's devotion to plants and flowers. He was also an ardent member of and heavy contributor to the United Republicans of California, although limiting his participation to attendance at UROC conventions. John Hagen had long ago learned how fruitless it was to argue politics with his father. They spoke two different languages. Nonetheless, argue they did. Still, they had become the best of friends since John had struck out for himself in business. John knew also that his father was quite proud of his success. He expressed his pleasure in such statements as, "Well, I see we had another good year. You're keeping the shareholders happy."

Sitting nearest his father, John now found himself in one conversation while Kris and his mother were in another.

"What's doing on that threatened legal action?" said Allan Hagen.

"It's happened," said John. "We ran a little squib on it in yesterday's paper but you won't get that in the mail until tomorrow."

"You mean you've been served?"

"The corporation's been served, I've been served, the reporter who wrote the story has been served, and any one of ten John Does will be served if they're identified."

"How much?"

"Two hundred and fifty thousand dollars."

"Any chance of losing?"

"Harry Wells tells me anything can happen in a courtroom, but we're in the strongest possible position. He thinks the man has very little chance of winning anything, even a token dollar. The facts are correct, so it goes to the question of malice. The old saying is, 'The greater the truth, the greater the libel.' That means simply that the truth is not a complete defense if it can be proved the publication was actuated by malice. A newspaper is an instrument of community betterment, or should be. We'll go in—if we do go in—with the posture of having exposed a condition that was harmful to the community."

"You think it might not go to trial?"

"Harry thinks it might not."

"What's your insurance?"

"Anything over thirty thousand dollars."

"Is Wells a good lawyer?"

"Obviously *I* think so or we wouldn't retain him. Yes, Harry has a fine reputation."

Allan Hagen tugged at his earlobe. "One other thing I'm curious about—this man Coe. Who is he?"

"Well, what I know, you know. I don't know whether he's sincere or a publicity hound. Or both. They're often found in combination. Even Jesus wasn't averse to a little puffery, while no one questions his motives."

"Well, I'm not equipped to argue about that and neither are you. But this Coe, is he going anywhere with his campaign?"

"I didn't think so at first, but now I know he's got strong money behind him."

"Are you planning to take a position?"

"I haven't yet decided. I'm having lunch tomorrow with Vic Massoni. I want to get his opinion. Personally—I've read the document— I think the proposed constitutional amendment has penalties out of all proportion to the problem, but then I'm no lawyer. If that's the final conclusion, it's hands off. I mean that I won't support it but I won't oppose it either."

"It sounds to me like a good proposition. I'll think so even more if Assemblyman Victor Massoni is against it. The goddamned pornographers are flooding the land with trash—as you just said in the *Sentinel*."

"Yes, but do you burn the haystack to get rid of the fleas?"

"If they're hopping into the house I would."

"Well, the issue is moot at this point."

"What if he puts this thing over? What if they should get it on the ballot?"

"I'd rather deal with that question if and when it becomes fact."

"I see that you've made up your mind."

John laughed. "Dad, some day you and I may agree that black is the color of night."

"I wouldn't bet on it."

"I think we're just about ready to sit down," said John's mother. "Does anyone want to wash their hands?"

The John Hagen family left for home just at dark. "Don't stay away so long," said Allan Hagen at the car door.

"We want you to dinner at our place next time," said Kris.

"We'll see. I'm getting too old to enjoy driving much any more."

"Good-by, my dears," said John's mother. "Please be careful. And do come again soon."

Settled into the soft, humming monotony of the drive homeward, John Hagen presently said, "What's the word from Mother on Dad?"

"Good."

"I thought he looked a little thin."

"You're right. The doctor told him to lose ten pounds and he has."

"I didn't think I was wrong. Oh, I'll give the old man high marks. He's always had a simple code and he follows it. If it's right, that's it—full steam ahead."

"Well?"

"Well, what?"

"Aren't you the same way?"

"Do you think I am, Kris?"

"Yes. I just said so."

"That's strange. I'd have said I was a marvelously complex creature with all sorts of hidden swirls and facets invisible to the naked eye. Inscrutable to a fault."

"You're full of whimsy, for sure."

"But not complicated."

"That isn't fair. I think I was paying you a compliment."

"Oh well, in which case."

"Dad?" said Gordo.

"Yes, son?"

"You and Grandpops don't agree on much, do you?"

"I think he's wonderful," said Pam.

"Who said he wasn't?" said Gordo. "I mean, like who asked?"

"Grouchy old bear."

"To answer you in a word, Gordo, no," said John Hagen. "But it's mostly a difference of personal philosophy. Your grandfather is a gentleman of the old school. He clawed his way up from a bank messenger's job and he did it all by himself. No help from *his* father or anyone else."

"Isn't he pretty rich?"

"Extremely well off."

"Does that mean he's rich?"

"I'm sure he's worth well over a million dollars. Maybe two."

"That's a lot of loot."

"It's a good deal of money. Having made it all himself, he's impatient with people who haven't made it the way he has."

"Does that mean he's selfish?"

"No, I wouldn't call him selfish. I think he lacks understanding, that's all. And don't forget he's old, and older people rarely change their ideas. That may be true of your father, as far as that goes. Would you say so, Kris?"

"Why are we only going fifty-five miles an hour?" said Kris.

— *10* —

He met Vic at twelve-thirty at Emiliano's, a first-rate restaurant owned and firmly run by an aging ex-bootlegger. He bowed them to a table and left them with menus when they both declined a cocktail.

"Well, pal," said Massoni, laying one muscular hand over the other. "What's current in the newspaper biz?"

"We're on the street every day but Sunday. What's new in the political biz?"

"How much time have you got? Actually, you know more than I do. Since I saw you last week I've been in Sacramento just two days. I got my ducks pretty well lined up financially, so now I've got to get back up there and buckle down. The Speaker hopes to line it up with the senate president pro tem to call a recess around May fifteenth so all we lawgivers can get out and hustle the hustings."

"Two and a half weeks before the primary? Oh, come off it."

Vic Massoni winked theatrically. "I'm accepting a lot of speaking engagements between now and then. And finding it convenient to call on a lot of editors. And making a lot of get-togethers here and there, like testimonial dinners for my fellow seekers after money—the mother's milk of politics, to quote Jess Unruh. So how's Kris and the family?"

"Fine. I guess we should order now. See anything that appeals to you?"

"Everything," said Vic Massoni. He patted his belly, which actually looked to be quite flat and trim. "But suppose I settle for the diet lunch. You can afford that, can't you, Johnny?"

They ordered.

"Got all the money you need, huh, Vic?" said John.

"There's no such thing," said Massoni. He sipped at his water. "But I've got enough to let a few people know I'm in the race. I'm lining up some editorial endorsements, too."

"Bully for you."

Although two years John Hagen's junior, Vic Massoni had been a fellow member of the USC class of '53. A high-school "football knee" had barred him from military service but not the college varsity. He completed his pre-law, then sailed through law school to pass his bar first time out, while John was serving his newspaper apprenticeship on the *Times*.

"I've got something I want your opinion on," said John Hagen when the waitress had removed their plates and brought coffee.

"For free, no doubt."

"No doubt." He extended the copy of the Reverend Bradshaw Coe's provisions for an initiative petition. "Mind scanning this?"

"What's this? 'An Article entitled *Control of Literature* . . . Whosoever sells or causes to be sold . . .' Mm-hmm . . ." He bent his head over the document with suddenly intensified interest, now tracing with his forefinger, frowning. "And . . . what's this? 'Removal for Failure to Act . . .' *Shall* be? 'Shall be removed from office'?" He looked up quizzically. "Is this somebody's idea of a joke, Johnny?"

"It's that bad, is it?"

"The goddamned thing's preposterous!"

"I rather thought—"

"Let me reread it."

John Hagen smoked what he swore to himself was positively the last cigarette he would smoke that day as Vic Massoni leaned back in his chair and examined the document once more. He began shaking his head as he lowered it finally.

"Who dreamed this up, anyway?"

"It seems to be the idea of a committee of which the Reverend Bradshaw Coe is a prominent member. You know Coe, of the Second Baptist Church?"

Vic Massoni groaned. "Oh yes, I know him. In my first year he wanted me to put in a bill outlawing prostitution. I told him there were adequate statutes to let local jurisdictions take care of the problem—if there was any problem. Every time there's some half-baked bill on books or magazines he bombards me with letters. I thought of devising a form letter of appreciation just for him. He's real hipped on the topic. This one really takes the fur-lined pisspot."

"In detail—what's wrong with it?"

"I'll name you a number of things right off the top of my head. It fails to meet the constitutional tests for defining pornography. It virtually hands over police powers to even the dullest illiterate. It removes from the district attorney any exercise of discretion in the matter of prosecution. It denies every judge the right to grant probation. Want more?"

"Yes."

"As it's written, almost anything you can name comes under the ban of the statute. Hell, a rape story in the *Sentinel* could be offensive to someone under this language. Anything. It's just absolutely —outrageous is the word."

"What would be the effect of such a law?"

"To choke the courts and D.A. offices, for one thing, until the state supreme court got around to throwing it out." Vic Massoni looked startled. "By God, there's something else! The state constitution being governing, this could supersede every other law on the books dealing with obscenity, lewdness, and what-all in literature. Now, think about that a moment, Johnny. What happens when this is declared unconstitutional? That means there isn't a single statute left until the legislature can pass some hurry-up new laws. In the meantime—chaos. That's the way it looks to me anyway; my horseback opinion."

"Anything else?"

"Well, yes; the penalties are utterly medieval. Hell, even the minimum penalty for armed robbery is only five years."

"All right. That's all I need to know."

"You don't mean to tell me you've been asked to support this?"

"That's the general idea."

"I don't suppose I have to ask, but—"

"No, you don't. I'd pretty much made up my mind already. But thanks for the reinforcement. Oh, but if it gets anywhere and you get elected, Mr. Attorney General—"

"Lord!" said Vic Massoni. He wiped imaginary sweat from his forehead with the back of his hand.

"Well, you must admit it poses interesting possibilities. Mind you, I don't think for a minute they're going to muster three quarters of a million valid signatures. But what if they do? Won't you have to take a position?"

Vic Massoni shifted his chair and crossed his legs. "You are talking about political dynamite, Johnny. You see, I'm aware there's a problem. Maybe you saw the attorney general's report not too many months ago."

"No, I don't think I did."

"I may be able to find a copy and send it to you. I won't try to gist it for you, but this twilight-zone junk is a multimillion-dollar business here in California alone. You might want to look into it just for your own information one of these days. The angle of attack, it seems to me, is pandering to juveniles. Personally I don't care if adults stuff themselves on porny until it runs in their shoes. But kids are a different proposition. A child is a peculiar creature in law—almost a non-person. Only in very recent times, for instance, has a court held that a child has the right to counsel in a lesser criminal proceeding—and that is still very widely violated in the juvenile courts. He can't vote but he can be sent to fight. He has no right to live with a parent of his choice in a broken-home situation; his wishes are a factor to be considered, but it's strictly up to the court. He may legally drive a car at sixteen and lawfully shoot a weapon and be capable of knocking up a girl but he cannot get married without a parent's or guardian's consent. No judge in the land will deny his parents' right to teach him that God is purple and lives in a 7-Up bottle, though the kid may have worked through the Easter bunny myth at the age of three. He can own real property but can't dispose of it without someone else's permission, he can't drink anything alcoholic, or stay out after an arbitrary curfew any hick police chief chooses to lay down. He can't change his name until he's twenty-one if his divorced father objects. You can't kill him but you can beat him, so long as you don't maim or unduly mark him. He must go to the school you send him to and obey the worst jackass of a teacher set over him while he's there. Everything I've named comes under the head of protecting the child. He's a non-being who in all respects becomes a person under the law only when he reaches the age of twenty-one. After that he can do almost anything he can get away with as long as he's quiet."

"You're hinting that a child is different," said John Hagen.

Vic Massoni grinned. "Mildly alluded to. In the matter under discussion, the law recognizes the duty and responsibility of the parent to provide moral guidance along with food, clothing, and shelter. Thus—to bring my little lecture to a point—you, the parent, have the right and duty to control what your child reads. That can be very narrowly limiting while he is under your rooftree. In short, reading material that may be legally permissible for you, as an adult, to buy—

or to be sold, in present context—may be deemed unfit, hence illegal, for him to buy or to be sold. And that is where I think the law can be made to stick."

John Hagen discovered he had lighted another cigarette quite from force of habit. He *must* knock this off any day now.

"So is there enough law?"

"It might be spelled out a little more clearly—with respect to juveniles, I must emphasize again. As to adults—well, photos of coitus, that sort of thing—there is plenty of law now under general obscenity statutes. And a constitutional provision such as this thing here—it's exactly the wrong way to accomplish any control. It's anxious, hysterical, and, I'm sure, unconstitutional as all hell. It's vague, meaningless, and almost impossible to enforce." He leaned back in his chair. "Have I answered any questions?"

"Yes. Wouldn't you have to take a position?"

Vic Massoni grimaced. "I don't want to be tagged as the man who favors smut. And I can't see explaining in twenty-five words or less what I've just taken ten minutes to highlight for you. Let's just hope that the specific issue doesn't get posed as a ballot choice, and, two, that I'm artful enough to be for good law enforcement and against sin in general so as not to get my back against the wall."

"You'd advise me to oppose it, but *you* won't?"

"I'm a professional politician, Johnny."

"That doesn't satisfy me, Vic. You're running for the state's top law-enforcement job. Suppose you and PURIFY both get voted in?"

"Johnny, the best way to kill a bad law is to enforce it to the letter. I'd have no other choice—except to resign."

John Hagen folded his napkin. "Well, I hope if it gets on the ballot you'll tell the voters what you've just told me."

"I think you're taking it too seriously. You and I know what the problems are, and they're not smut. Racial disturbances, narcotics, crime syndicate money in business—these are some of the real problems. Smut is mostly a gut issue. No one's ever proved a link between pornography and sexual misbehavior, but try to tell that to anxious parents who also happen to vote. What I'm saying is, don't ask me to stake my campaign on it, because I won't." They both rose from the table. John hit him on the arm playfully with his fist.

"I think I know you too well, Vic. If you know it's wrong, you won't be able to keep quiet."

"I just hope the baby is stillborn," said Vic Massoni.

— *11* —

Promptly at ten o'clock Tuesday morning the Reverend Bradshaw Coe bustled in confidently. After the almost mandatory handshake he seated himself, at John's invitation.

"I have never seen anything fire the spirit of so many people so quickly," he said briskly. "Can you imagine, Mr. Hagen, committees are forming in every suburb of Los Angeles, in the cities of Pomona, Santa Ana, San Bernardino, the beach cities, Redlands, San Diego and environs—in short, everywhere. But that isn't my biggest news. I have asked, and been readily granted, a nine-month leave of absence from my pastoral duties in order to devote my full time and efforts to directing PURIFY. Oh, we have a monumental task ahead. Gathering signatures will be the work of the committee volunteers but that is the easiest part of our mission. Between now and November we intend to mount a massive educational campaign. It will sweep PURIFY to an overwhelming victory at the polls. My associates—my fellow officers—Mr. Perry M. Tunman, who is head of the Madrone Distributing Company, as you know, and Mr. R. Brooks Norton of Shasta Savings and Loan are agreed that early newspaper support is necessary and desirable. It is purely coincidental, but Shasta Savings and Loan is a regular *Sentinel* advertiser, is it not?"

"Yes, we enjoy their business," said John Hagen.

"As a matter of fact, I believe, the Madrone Distributing Company also controls a lot of what I think is called co-operative advertising for Higashi optical products and other goods."

"I have no idea. What has that got to do with PURIFY?"

"Oh, nothing whatsoever," the Reverend Mr. Coe said hastily. He dissembled with a gesture. "I just mentioned it in passing. But now, because I am sure you have many things to do and so have I . . .

did you have the chance to examine our petition carefully? I trust you did."

"I did."

"Excellent. How soon may we expect our maiden editorial, if I may so term it?" He leaned forward in his chair.

John Hagen had the document centered on his desk. He touched it lightly with his finger. "I am afraid I'm going to have to disappoint you, Reverend Coe. I do not believe I can endorse PURIFY."

The Reverend Bradshaw Coe stiffened. "I—I don't understand, Mr. Hagen."

"Simply what I said. I cannot place the *Sentinel's* support behind your proposal."

"I see. I see. Then you are going to oppose PURIFY?"

"No. If there is any legitimate news about PURIFY, we'll run it, as we try to run all important news. Editorially, for now, I intend to remain silent."

"I'm sure I am entitled to ask why."

"Of course you are. I have checked with competent legal sources. I am advised that the provisions here are unconstitutional."

The Reverend Mr. Coe frowned. "The measure is being drawn by an attorney for Mr. Norton, sir. He is a highly paid corporate lawyer. Do you imagine that he would be party to anything that is in conflict with the Constitution?"

John Hagen smiled. "Well, I suppose it's possible to find lawyers on both sides of anything you'd care to name. However, I also respect my source. That being the case, I'm afraid our support is out of the question."

The Reverend Bradshaw Coe shook his head. "You are making a grave mistake, Mr. Hagen. This issue—this measure—is properly drawn, it's legal, and most of all, it is morally right. I find it hard to believe that any family newspaper could even consider withholding its backing from something as good and needed as PURIFY. The *Sentinel*, most of all. How many days has it been since you were blasting smut to the high heavens?"

"The *Sentinel* opened up on a local problem specifically involving sales to minors, Reverend. I think we did some good; I don't know. We intend to check back on it within two or three weeks."

"But you are talking about one small area and not the basic issue!" cried the Reverend Mr. Coe. "We are striking at the very roots of the problem. And you won't join us?"

"The *Sentinel* is just one small daily newspaper."

"That is entirely beside the point. In fact, the major daily newspapers throughout California have been curiously silent on this vast problem for many years. PURIFY springs from the grass roots. The smaller newspapers are the closest to the people and can influence the mass of voters in a way the big newspapers no longer can."

John smiled. "I'm not too sure of that, Reverend. Sometimes I think the *Sentinel* can't even influence my own wife. I wish you luck, but you'll have to run your campaign without my support."

The Reverend Mr. Coe leaned forward urgently. "Before I take your answer as final, Mr. Hagen, there is something I want you to see. I believe you still do not realize the enormity of the problem. Now, there is in our state legislature a man who has devoted most of his political career to fighting pornography. You know State Senator David O. Hausner, do you not?"

"Yes, of course. He's running on the Republican ticket for attorney general."

"Exactly. One of his major planks is going to be a cleanup of literature and films. Mr. Hagen, have you ever heard of Senator Hausner's Chamber of Horrors?"

John Hagen frowned in recollection. "Oh, yes, one of the clubwomen mentioned it to me recently."

"I think you should see the Chamber of Horrors before you definitely decide against endorsing PURIFY."

"From what I've heard of it, I doubt it'll change my view."

"Mr. Hagen, I think there is a good chance it may."

John shrugged. "Well, I like to think I keep an open mind." He smiled. "Don't we all? I'll look at it if you like. How and when?"

The Reverend beamed. "Splendid!" he said, getting to his feet. "I'll be in touch with you shortly. And don't underestimate us, Mr. Hagen. We have a powerful movement generating. I think you'll end up on the side of good."

A three-alarm fire nearly on deadline promptly drove the Reverend Mr. Coe and his mission from John's mind. He scarcely gave him another thought for a week. Then a telephone call from Coe reminded him. The Chamber of Horrors *and* Senator Hausner would visit the *Sentinel* at 2 P.M. the following day.

PART TWO

Everyone in the California state capitol knew State Senator David O. Hausner. Not just his colleagues, the secretaries, the clerks in the Bill Room, the assemblymen, the clerk of the senate, the sergeant-at-arms and his deputies, the governor of the moment—but literally everyone under the dome knew Senator Hausner. He was hard not to know. For one thing, he had been a "Solon," as the Sacramento *Bee* termed it, for eleven years, and an assemblyman for five two-year terms before that, for a total of twenty-one years. For another, he was a man who displaced a lot of air: six feet, five inches by two hundred and fifty pounds or thereabouts. He dressed as if he bought his suits off the pipe at Robert Hall and was too impatient to have them altered except at the waist and cuffline. In an era of attention by politicians to television "image," he wore his graying hair no longer than an inch, with a high washbowl trim all round. He specified creased sleeves on his suits and was never seen without a huge silver tie bar bearing the insignia of the American Legion, of which he was a Past National Commander. His fifty-plus-year-old countenance was that of a YMCA counselor or Boy Scout leader, curiously cherubic for all its strength of jaw and direct, piercing gaze, as though nature had decided to allow him maturity of years without the penalty of lines. His manner was consistently hearty, manly, open. "Want a bill? Dave Hausner will introduce it for you," was a byword among a number of the several hundred lobbyists who plied their trade at Posey's, the Firehouse, Frank

Fat's, and wherever else good food and drink was served. Most of all, the Honorable David O. Hausner was known, however, for The Bill. Hausner's Bill. Dave's Bill. He had introduced it twelve times. Eleven times he had seen it die in committee or go to a more lingering death at the hands of "interim study."

When general legislative sessions had been limited to odd years, State Senator David O. Hausner had dropped The Bill in the hopper every other year, starting in 1947. Since the jobs of senator and assemblyman had become full-time, every-year occupations, Hausner now trudged to the front of the senate chamber every January third to eighth—depending on the fall of the calendar—and dropped his latest version of The Bill on the desk. The Honorable David O. Hausner was, it seemed, deeply concerned with the public's morals. He had spent a good part of his life trying to legislate his fellowman's behavior without troubling to ask his choice in the matter. Yet he was a very well-meaning soul and liked by his colleagues, even though he amused them ("There goes Dave with The Bill—now I know we're in session again"), and he was an announced candidate for the Republican nomination for attorney general this year.

"Mr. Hagen, you have some visitors," said Mary on the telephone intercom. "They say they're expected."

"You wouldn't mind telling me who they are, Mary?" The *Sentinel's* office receptionist-switchboard operator at times displayed a slight touch of density. John didn't know whether it went with the phase of the moon or lack of sleep.

"Oh, it's Reverend Coe and Senator Hausner, sir. And some young man. They're all together."

"Mr. Hagen, how are you this afternoon?" said the Reverend as John came out to the *Sentinel's* reception area.

"I'm fine," John said. "Senator, how are you?"

Hausner shoved out his big paw. "Mr. Hagen, it is a pleasure to see you again!" he roared. "I know I'll never get your backing, but I respect a worthy foeman, yes indeed. And this young man is Bobby Ladd; Bobby, meet Mr. Hagen."

"How do you do, Mr. Ladd."

"Hello, Mr. Hagen," said the young man with almost military crispness. His grip was firm.

"Bobby's doubling as driver and committee representative," said Senator Hausner, beaming on him. "One of these days this young man is going to get his bachelor's degree and come to work for me up in Sacramento. Meantime he picks up a salary taking the Chamber of Horrors around to the various communities as a committee educational program. Yes indeed."

"Fine. Let's go back to my office," said John.

Seated, the Reverend said, "Senator, would you like to speak your piece?"

"Glad to!" the Honorable David O. Hausner said, smiling broadly. "Mr. Hagen, spite of you being on the other side of the political fence, I know you are a good, upright, honorable citizen."

"Thank you."

The senator waved his hand. "Not at all. And were you aware that you are not unknown outside this community?"

"I didn't know my fame had spread," said John.

Senator Hausner guffawed. "You're a modest man, Mr. Hagen. May I call you John?"

"It wouldn't be the worst thing I've ever been called."

Hausner bellowed his laughter again. "As a long-time politician I share that privilege," he said. "But to get down to business: I'm here to talk about PURIFY."

"So I understand," said John politely.

"You, as a publisher, must be aware that for almost my entire legislative career I have been trying to place a strong section in the penal code dealing with licentious books, magazines, and motion pictures," said the senator. "My colleagues, love them all, in their wisdom, as the expression has it, have seen fit to deny me the satisfaction of getting the measure passed."

"I know you haven't had much luck," said John Hagen.

"Luck has played no part in it, if you'll forgive me, John." He tapped out an enumeration on his huge fingers: "The lobbies for the motion picture industry, the book publishing industry, the magazine publishing industry—there's your answer. Next to oil, agri-business, and alcoholic beverages, Hollywood and the publishers are among the strongest and best-heeled lobbies in the statehouse. I've been around them for better than twenty years and should know. Now, my good friend the Reverend here and some equally good friends over in Los Angeles have PURIFY going for them. Need I say that its passage would fulfill my life's ambition?"

"I know about your long fight," said John.

"For which I respect you. My arguments, if you can call them that, are of a graphic nature. As you must know, I have sat on or chaired, on a more or less continuing basis, a committee—called by various names in several successor versions. It is a joint senate-assembly committee to investigate sex in literature and films. During these many years, our staff people have assembled one of the most unbelievable collections of material in the world. It pales description, John; it must be seen to be appreciated, to use that word in its true sense. I call it my Chamber of Horrors.

"I have revealed it here and there to groups of concerned citizens —parents and taxpayers. It illustrates more tellingly than ten million words what my career-long fight has been all about. You say you have an open mind, John. Prove it. Look at this parade of filth. Do that and then tell us you won't support PURIFY."

"All right, let's have a look at it," said John. "Are you back in the parking lot?"

"Yes, sir," said Bobby Ladd.

"We can go back through the city room."

The large van had been repainted white from its original army olive drab except for the rear bumper, which was diagonally striped with bands of orange and black. The vehicle sat in the middle of the lot. Bobby Ladd strode to the cab, opening the door to reach up and press a button. Hydraulic machinery whined. A metal staircase folded against the rear doors arced over slowly to touch the ground. The young man slammed the door and walked back, pulling a key chain from his pocket.

"There are only two keys to the Chamber of Horrors, and I have the other," explained Senator Hausner as Bobby Ladd climbed the steps and unlocked the door. "You'll notice there's no identification. We don't want to tempt the wrong element to break in. This is a highly valuable collection."

Bobby Ladd threw open the double doors. John saw a black

wooden panel about two feet from the rear of the bed, which effectively blocked any view of the interior. The young man snapped a light switch.

"After you, Mr. Hagen," said Senator Hausner. "You, as a newspaperman, may consider yourself unshockable, but I think I can guarantee you this is going to shake you up a little."

John Hagen climbed the stairs with something of the sensation of entering a boardwalk fun house. Bobby Ladd had stepped around a set of black baffles. John followed. On the inside, his first impression was that of a heavily stocked curio shop.

Steel shelving rose to the ceiling in the center, dividing the interior into two corridors. Each side also carried shelving, making four rows in all. A small sign affixed to the center uprights proclaimed:

CALIFORNIA'S SHAME!!!

"The Chamber of Horrors"

This Sickening Display Is
An Example of What
Your Child Might See

The lighting was subdued. It came from both a rank of overhead bulbs aligned with the corridors and individual lamps at the top of each shelf with long, narrow metal shades deflecting the light downward. There was the soft, steady note of an air conditioner. Altogether, the effect was sepulchral, with the dark background of the paneling behind the shelving, the monotonously circulated air, and what apparently was a sound-deadening material serving to heighten small sounds: footsteps, the faint clank of coins and keys, breathing. Bobby Ladd hovered at the far end of the left corridor, his usual guide's role pre-empted for this occasion by his employer, Senator Hausner, who now stood at John Hagen's shoulder and was trailed by the Reverend Bradshaw Coe.

"We begin here, John," said Senator Hausner. Gone was the booming voice, replaced by a quieter, almost anticipatory tone, like that of a tour guide at the threshold of the Louvre. "The exhibit is arranged by categories, or groupings, so that the full range may be given maximum individual attention. Now, I have been looking at this sort of thing for years, yet let me tell you, it is no less revolting to me now than when it first came before my eyes. First, on your left, the two racks of comic books, so-called. Would you care to examine one or two?"

John Hagen obediently selected a crudely printed, garishly colored booklet with an amateurishly drawn Daisy Mae. A ridiculously muscled Li'l Abner stood in the background. In case anyone should miss the point, the less-than-gifted artist had surrounded Abner's exaggerated male bulge with radial lines. And on the very first page the action began: an aggressive Daisy Mae coaxing a timid Li'l Abner into a haystack. She had divested herself of clothing by the third page, the balloon reading, "Aw, come on, Li'l Abner, it ain't gonna hurt you none." On the fourth page he had dropped his trousers to reveal a phallus of frightening proportions. Except for the dramatis personae, the plot played out as predictably as the type of thing John Hagen had first viewed behind the junior high school bleachers about twenty-seven years before. He returned *Daisy Mae and Li'l Abner* to the rack.

"Now, wouldn't that make you vomit, John?" said Senator David O. Hausner.

"Mm," said John.

Well, here were old friends, *Tillie and Mac* . . . and two other old acquaintances, *Popeye and Olive Oyl,* neither male figure a whit depleted for all his many years on earth . . . and a whole range of others, some new, some venerable standbys: *Kayo and Little Orphan Annie* . . . *Batman Meets Batgirl* . . . the Phantom reaching across time to mate with Little Redwing . . . *Tarzan and Jane* (were or were they not married?) . . . *Terry and the Dragon Lady.* . . .

"Disgusting!" exclaimed the Reverend Mr. Coe, who had edged up close enough to peer over John Hagen's arm.

"All right," said John, who had actually looked into two of the books cursorily and only glanced at the range of other titles.

"Now, here," said Senator Hausner, with difficulty moving past John in the narrow space between shelves and indicating the display on the right-hand side of the aisle, "these are the pornographic paperbacks. Here, I'll show you one at random." He selected a volume, *Diary of a Nymphomaniac,* which looked well thumbed. The senator fanned it open, leafing rapidly, saying even before he found it: "Now, on page twenty-three . . . let's see . . . twenty . . . twenty-one . . . twenty-two . . . here we are—twenty-three. Would you care to read that, John?" One large finger trembled slightly as he touched the paragraph, handing the book to John Hagen. John read:

> My very crotch tingled with mad anticipation to be possessed, crammed full by the beautiful, engorged thing I held in my hands. It throbbed under my touch; it was so soft of texture, yet so hard. . . .

"Very reminiscent of *Ulysses,*" said John Hagen.

"I beg your pardon," said Senator Hausner.

"Mollie's soliloquy. You've read it, of course."

"Is that in Homer?" said Senator Hausner. "Are you sure?"

"I had reference to Joyce. This is much more poorly written, of course."

"Terrible, terrible!" said the Reverend Mr. Coe, craning his neck.

The paperback shelf, as expertly sampled by Senator Hausner, contained some fifty or more titles, such as *Go Down In Joy* . . . *A Bellboy Tells All* (subtitled "Fun and Games in a Resort Hotel") . . . *My Five Hundred Men* by A Famous Actress (Anonymous) . . . *The 10-Inch Stud* . . . *Any Color Will Do* . . . *Deflowered!* . . . and *I Want It—Now* ("The True Story of a Girl With An IN-SATIABLE APPETITE").

"Tck!—Tck!—Tck!—Tck!" from the Reverend Mr. Coe.

"We move along to this choice collection," said Senator Hausner. "These are the homosexual publications."

"Male or female?" said John Hagen.

"Male, of course," said Senator Hausner with the chiding air of the teacher for a backward pupil. "The lesbian publications are next."

It was indeed a notable collection, lovingly gathered, professionally displayed. In the next twenty minutes, guided slowly along right- and left-hand shelves and around the opening at the front to come back the other side, John Hagen saw more publications, photographs, drawings, and devices than he might ever in his life have dreamed existed. There were both black-and-white and color photos of persons in various aspects of sexual congress . . . men and women, men and men, women and women, and assorted varieties, without regard to race, color, or, presumably, creed. One section was devoted to the instruments of torture ("discipline") and restraint ("bondage"): whips, leather straps, paddles, and switches, and ropes, harness, handcuffs, leg irons, and chains. Elsewhere were rubber and leather and plastic phalluses, ranging to heroic dimensions, penile "splints," artificial vaginas, and electric vibrators shaped like the male organ. Books illustrated as many as a hundred positions of coitus, many a challenge to all but a rigorously trained athlete. Various publications were aimed at some of the many fetishists: buttocks, thighs, feet, breasts, and black-stocking, lingerie, shoes, leather. . . .

They were at the end of the second row. Bobby Ladd pressed a button on a large cabinet on legs that was braced to the rear panel. A garishly lighted picture jumped up on the self-contained motion-picture screen.

"Now, this, John, is only one of a hundred films in our collection," said Senator David O. Hausner. "I've seen them all. Ah yes, 'Three-Ring Circus'—very typical of its type."

The epic unfolded swiftly. Scene: the living room of an apartment, sparsely furnished. Enter tired-looking blonde in negligee, holding highball glass. She looks quickly toward door. Subtitle: THE PARTY GUESTS ARRIVE. Girl walks swiftly to door, opens it to crowd of merrymakers: three men, two women, men all somewhat on the emaciated side, only one woman at all pretty. Subtitle: THE PARTY GETS GOING. Men undressing women, women undressing men. Close-ups of buttocks, breasts, sexual organs. Now one couple engaged on couch, two others on floor. Much writhing, milling about, inexplicable camera work making it difficult to tell which particular duo involved at given moment, including numerous angles and explicit close-ups. Successive subtitles: ONE AND ONE . . . BOY/BOY . . . GIRL/GIRL . . . 'HEADING' HIM OFF AT THE PASS . . . RIDING THE STALLION . . . AROUND THE WORLD . . . TWO ON ONE . . . THREE-WAY SANDWICH . . . TRY THIS ON YOUR PIANO. . . .

The Reverend Mr. Coe's breath was hoarse in John Hagen's ear.

He punctuated the sequences with "How awful." . . . "Wicked, wicked!" . . . "Unbelievable." John glanced at him. His gaze was rigidly fixed on the screen. He looked at Senator David O. Hausner, who licked his lips and said, "We have many like this in our collection."

The picture ended quite abruptly in a tangle of bodies that would have put Laocoön and company to shame.

"Well!" said the Reverend Bradshaw Coe, blinking his eyes rapidly, a dazed expression on his face.

"Well, John?" said Senator Hausner. He licked his lips again. "What do you think now?"

"I think you've got yourself quite a gallery," said John Hagen.

"Bobby, you can lock up and take off for the weekend," said Senator Hausner. "You're due in San Bernardino on Monday. May we go back to your office, John?"

John Hagen sat thoughtfully at his desk. The sheer intensity of the barrage to which he had just been exposed left him with the sensation of having stepped from a cascade of raw sewage. The labyrinthine passages of human sexual stimuli and response were indeed awesome. John had read or heard that the incidence of mental illness among psychiatrists and psychoanalysts was quite high. Could repeated cries of "Help me to understand myself—help me!" in time erode one's own protective barriers? Did the stoutest explorer venture furthest into the chambered depths only at the peril of his own sanity?

"You're disturbed, aren't you, John?" said Senator Hausner. He leaned forward, pointing an accusatory finger. "Have you begun now to understand what we're up against? Do you know now why I call that my Chamber of Horrors?"

"Mr. Hagen, I get the feeling that maybe PURIFY does not seem to you so extreme after all at this point in time," said the Reverend Bradshaw Coe, smiling gently.

John turned his gaze on him. "I think I understand several things," he said slowly. He looked back at Senator Hausner. "And yes, I am disturbed, Senator. It's quite a parade of muck when you put it all together. But now let me ask you some questions. First: all this material you've got in that van—is all of it readily and openly for sale?"

"Our investigators bought it all, John. Does that answer your question?"

"Not quite. I mean, could a child walk into a store and purchase any of those items?"

"No, but he could by mail," said Senator Hausner. "You see, a great amount of what you saw is advertised in cheap magazines. Children, as you know, all have money these days. What is simpler than clipping a coupon with a check mark where it says, 'I am over twenty-one,' and mailing it in?"

"The lists are sold, Mr. Hagen," said the Reverend Mr. Coe, his fingers laced. "Your child might innocently answer an ad for stamps and shortly find himself the target of smut advertisements. Successive contacts can lead from invitations to purchase the lesser items to the very worst that you have seen."

"I'll buy that," said John Hagen. "But I also know there is federal legislation pending to choke that off. Soon a person will only have to write a letter demanding his name be taken off a mailing list and the mailer must take it off, under penalty of federal law."

"We haven't got that law yet, John," said Hausner. "And even when we do, I personally have my doubts as to how strongly it can be enforced. These fly-by-nights are as thick as fleas in a haystack. Give us PURIFY and at least we've got a big stick to beat 'em with when we catch them."

"There's another thing," John pursued. "Your collection seems to make no distinction between the truly hard-core pornography and the twilight-zone stuff. Now, it seems to me that when it comes to those photographs, the stag films, the items in that category, we have law enough already to take care of it."

"Not strong enough," said Hausner firmly.

"Not nearly strong enough," said the Reverend Bradshaw Coe. He frowned. "Mr. Hagen, as far as I am concerned, every single thing you saw in there today is hard-core pornography. The books, the devices, everything, is corrupting of innocent children. *I* can make no fine distinctions. God knows the effect even one of those filthy paperbacks will have on a young boy or girl. One thing leads

to another, until finally a once fine, bright, promising youth is perverted, degraded, a burned-out shell. You smile, Mr. Hagen; it is no
joke! Our mental institutions are filled with sex maniacs! Why do you
think they are there? It is precisely because they filled their minds
as children with the type of filth and slime that you have seen this
very afternoon. And there is only one way to deal with the problem:
smack the manufacturers and the publishers and the sellers with an
iron fist! PURIFY will do that."

"But if you make no distinctions, Reverend, don't you strike at
worthwhile books along with the trash?" said John, fingering his ear.
"And along the way, deny any of it—the good and the bad—to
adults?"

The Reverend Bradshaw Coe squared his shoulders. "Primarily
we need to protect the children," he said. "That doesn't say that
possibly some adults don't need the same kind of protection. A rapist
is a rapist, Mr. Hagen."

John Hagen brought his hand down softly on his desk. "At that
point we part company, Reverend. I'll disregard the rapist figure; I
do not believe that words or pictures can make anyone do anything
he isn't inclined to do anyway. But what really disturbs me is your
posture of deciding what *I* can or cannot read."

"Now, let's look at this thing calmly," said Senator Hausner
tolerantly. "John, you're an educated man, a community leader, and
a family man. We don't need this law for you. It's the others—the
lonely, the maladjusted, the sick perverts. And the children most of
all."

"Senator," said John Hagen, "you have made a career out of
chasing the smut peddlers."

"Yes, I am proud to say."

"Isn't it quite a large business, Senator?"

"Large!" said Senator Hausner incredulously. "It's a thirty-
million-dollar business here in California alone!"

"Where do those thirty millions of dollars come from?" said John
softly.

"I don't see your point," said Hausner.

"Doesn't it come from the buyers of this material?"

"Absolutely. Of course."

"Thirty million dollars is a lot of money," said John Hagen. "It would seem to me there must be an awful lot of perverts, if I follow your argument."

"You're just playing with words, Mr. Hagen," said the Reverend Mr. Coe. His equanimity was gone.

"I am indeed. I make my living with words. Tell me, Reverend, and you, Senator: you have both seen quantities of pornography. Has it harmed either of you?"

"No," said Coe.

"Of course not," said Senator Hausner, now himself a bit testy. "I regard myself as a well-balanced man. Likewise, I so regard Reverend Coe. And you."

"Isn't that much like the attitude of people who drive cars? Have you ever met anyone who didn't think he was a good driver, but that there are certainly an awful lot of bad drivers on the road?"

"Yes, and crazy people think they're sane. That doesn't make them any the less crazy," said Senator Hausner.

"But where is your dividing line, Senator?" said John Hagen. "Suppose for the sake of argument a well-balanced man—whatever that may be—derives enjoyment and stimulation from a spicy picture?"

"I think we're getting nowhere," said the Reverend Mr. Coe impatiently. "The well-adjusted simply don't."

"How did that stag film affect you, Reverend Coe?"

"Sir?"

"I said, how did that stag film affect you?"

"Utterly disgusting!" said Coe vehemently. "It made me want to turn my eyes away."

"But you didn't, did you?"

"Of course not," said the Reverend Mr. Coe. "How can you fight the enemy if you don't know his face?"

"Had you seen the film before?"

"Once only."

"Why was it necessary to see it again?"

"Now-now," said Senator Hausner. "We're getting lost in semantics here. John, a man-to-man appeal. We want your support for PURIFY. Yours and your fellow publishers'."

"Senator, the measure still bothers me," said John. "I wish I could give it my backing. I don't like this wave of trash any more than you do. But I still think we're hung up on a constitutional issue. I think we can do better. You'll have to forgive me, but I just can't go along."

"Shall we go, Senator Hausner?" said Coe, rising.

"Give it some prayerful thought, John," said Hausner, also getting to his feet.

"I will tell you one thing, Mr. Hagen," said the Reverend Mr. Coe, his blue, hypnotic gaze fixed on John's face. "The community will not be sympathetic to your position."

"Threats, Reverend?"

"I imply no threat of any kind. I speak only the truth," said Coe. "I say that you must either be for us or you are against us. Measure the consequences if you fail to act in the best interests of the community."

"In your opinion, Reverend?"

"In the opinion of right-thinking persons, Mr. Hagen."

"Such as yourself?"

"I count myself as only one among many."

"Reverend Coe, will you excuse me now?"

"Now, I uh—" said Senator Hausner.

"Thanks for coming in, Senator," said John Hagen.

The Reverend Mr. Coe stared in defiance a moment longer, snorted, and turned on his heel.

"Good afternoon, John," said Senator David O. Hausner. And then he too was gone.

"Well, squire," said Quincy Broyles a moment later. "Wasn't that the Honorable smiter of smut with your friend Coe?"

"Senator Hausner, no less. I'm still under siege over PURIFY."

"They're a persistent tribe," said Broyles. He pushed his big belly away from the desk and leaned back in his swivel chair, fishing a wooden match from his pocket. "About thirty years ago in St. Louis with the *Post-Dispatch* I covered a hot-eyed Gantry who'd elected to take on the burleyque. I was a smart-assed young squirt but I had to play it straight. You can't mock evangelists in that part of the

country, then or now. Well, every night he'd sound the last hallelujah
at about ten o'clock, then I'd hop in his Cadillac with him—we got to
be pretty good friends—and we'd drive to one of the theaters, a
different one every night. He'd watch the performance nearly all the
way through. I'd watch him mostly. He took it all in. Toward the
end he'd stand up and start denouncing at the top of his lungs.
They'd throw him out, of course. Next night he'd be thundering
hellfire and damnation on them *dins* of iniquity. On one ride he
confided his main mission in life was to keep little girls with them
real cute little legs under them short little skirts from growing up, as
he put it, to become like unto hoors and Jezebels. He just couldn't
say enough about the awful temptations that awaited them cute little
girls with them cute little legs, so sorta sturdy and pink."

– *13* –

The first clue that anything out of the ordinary was afoot cropped
up in the weekly Wellbrook *Progress & Green Sheet*. John Hagen
picked the copy out of a rosebush and took it to his office one
morning.

For several years the *Progress* had stuck like a fleck of gravel
between the *Sentinel's* toes. It was too small to give unbearable
pain, but privately was too irritating to ignore. Editorially it was a
joke. "News" copy for page one was anything from a local wedding
(generally called "nuptials") to a service station Grand Opening.
Visually the *Progress & Green Sheet* was a tossed salad of incom-
patible type headlines, often pasted just slightly askew over vari-
typed columns of body copy. The whole was run off on an old web
press in a barnlike structure near Centinela Avenue a couple of
miles over in county territory by a former journeyman pressman
named Richard Berry, who was also the publisher. He had a staff of
fifteen, including three advertising salesmen. Early every Wednesday
morning copies were thrown on the driveways, rooftops, and shrub-
bery of fifty thousand houses within and outside the Wellbrook city

limits. There, a third to a half of the total stayed until retrieved and dropped, still banded, into garbage cans. Still, enough copies were opened and scanned for grocery and other special sales to give the *Progress & Green Sheet* leverage in draining off some accounts that otherwise might have gone to the *Sentinel*. Even major stores like Hartmann's might splash four pages in the *Sentinel* but also throw a half-page bone to the *Progress*. Officially the *Sentinel* did not recognize the weekly throwaway's existence, although a lot of its copy was a rewrite of *Sentinel* stories. Once as a joke Maggie Mellody had run a wholly fictitious wedding story, which was picked up *in toto*.

John had been at the office nearly an hour when he received his first call about the *Progress & Green Sheet*. His copy lay banded on his desk. The caller was Harry Wells, the *Sentinel's* attorney.

"My wife told me to tell you to take a look at this morning's *Progress,* John. Got it?"

"Yes, right here."

"What does it say?"

"Hang on." John Hagen punched the Hold button and rolled the rubber band from the folded mass. He spread the paper before him. A glaring red bannerline spread the width of the page:

'SENTINEL' SPURNS SMUT MOVEMENT

Below the sheet's gaudy logotype was a three-column headline:

**Local Newspaper Declines Support For
'PURIFY' Anti-Pornography Initiative**

The story led off two columns wide:

> The daily Wellbrook *Sentinel's* publisher, John A. Hagen, has told the local backers of "Public United to Restore Innocence to Fair Youth"—PURIFY—that his newspaper will not support the worthwhile movement.
>
> A source informed the Progress & Green Sheet that Hagen has flatly refused to endorse the PURIFY initiative petition, which seeks to gain a place on the November ballot for an anti-pornography constitutional amendment.
>
> The petition reads as follows:

John Hagen's eye jumped to the rest of the story following the petition:

> The Progress & Green Sheet's informant said: "We find it strange indeed that Wellbrook's only daily newspaper, which just a short time ago virtuously beat its breast about allegedly smutty materials on sale locally, will not back a major campaign to do something constructive about this issue.
>
> "We are sure Mr. Hagen has his own reasons for declining his newspaper's support, but it is his newspaper and he can do as he chooses."
>
> The Wellbrook Progress & Green Sheet wholeheartedly approves of PURIFY and urges all its readers to sign the PURIFY initiative petition when it is presented to them.

"Harry?"

"Yes, John. Thought maybe you'd hung up."

"No, I'm still here. Well, this is what my competition has to say. A mixture of bad reporting and opinionating . . ." He read the complete text to Harry Wells.

"That's all of it?" said Harry.

"In its entirety. Topped by a red four-alarm banner."

"Mm-hmm. Your friend Coe?"

"Who else? What do you think?"

Harry Wells coughed. "Well, it sounds like there's nothing libelous as far as I can tell. Whoever wrote it carefully laid it out to suggest something that isn't true, but avoided actually accusing you of favoring pornography. Now, as I see it, there are two ways to go. The first—"

"Harry."

"The first is—"

"Harry. Listen to me. We're going to say nothing. Ever since this little back-alley sheet started publishing we've declined to recognize it. We're not going to start now."

"That's your business, John. But is this the end of it?"

"I certainly won't dignify this in the *Sentinel*."

"My other idea is a good, stiff letter from me on my office letterhead strongly suggesting that the *Progress* lay off or face legal action."

"No. I won't give them the satisfaction. Coe either, for that matter. He may want a fight but he'll find it hard to battle an opponent who ignores him."

"Well, you're the publisher."

"I'm the publisher."

He had called Quincy Broyles in and was showing the piece to him when his intercom buzzer sounded again and Mary at the switchboard told him his wife was on the telephone.

"Excuse me a moment, Quin. Yes, hello, Kris."

Her voice sounded as if she was fighting for control. "John, did you pick up that terrible *Green Sheet* from the lawn this morning? Did you?"

"From the rosebush, yes. And yes, I've seen the article. How did you—?"

"Mrs. Glade brought her copy. It's her day to clean. How could they . . . ? I've already had telephone calls from three of my friends —Sarah Norden, Fan Drill, Bess Lanterman. John, this is awful!"

"Quin, would you . . . ?" Quincy Broyles nodded in quick understanding and went out. "Kris, let's talk this over—"

"Talk over! I don't want to talk anything over, I want you to say something in the paper. Deny it, tell the readers what a big lie this is. You've got to do something!"

John Hagen gripped the receiver tightly. "Actually, it isn't a lie. Come on, Krissy, let's not get hysterical over what some irresponsible—"

"Hysterical! You're right I'm hysterical! Are you just going to sit down there and do *nothing* about this?"

John Hagen sighed. "Kris, listen to me, please. Are you listening?"

"Yes, I'm listening. I want to know what you're going to do."

"Kris, I am not going to do a thing. For ten years I've published a clean, newsy, responsible newspaper. I've called every shot as I've seen it. My God, Krissy, how many times have I had the Birchers and the mental health and the anti-fluoridation nuts on my back? Don't you remember the *Land of the Free* hassel—people calling in to cancel their subscriptions, threatening boycott, picketing? Don't you remember the anonymous letters, the—"

"John Hagen!" Her voice lanced through. "I'm trying to tell you something very important and you want to make a speech. Don't you know we have to live in this town?"

"Yes, we *do* have to live in this town. You and I have to live in this town and the Wellbrook *Sentinel* has to live here too. Some irresponsible printer with a cheap throwaway rag takes a swipe at me . . . what am I supposed to do? Run howling to the hills? I've already told Harry Wells—"

"Who *cares* what you told Harry Wells or anyone else? Would you like to know what Fan Drill said to *me?*"

"You know what I think of Fan Drill."

"Right now I don't care what your opinion is. That cutesy-wutesy little giggle; then, 'Kris, isn't it simply awful what some people will print these days? Can you go around saying things about people that aren't true without being sued?' How would you like that bitch saying something like that to you?"

"Par for the course."

"Yes, and Sarah saying, 'Well, anybody who knows John Hagen knows exactly what kind of a man he is, and those who don't—well, who cares?' Do you begin to get some inkling of what I'm talking about?"

"Kris. Krissy—please. Nothing would please those people at the *Progress* more than if I rose to the bait. For five years we've never given them the slightest nod of recognition. They're not a newspaper, they're a glorified handbill. Now they've shot their bolt . . . what more can they say?"

"John Hagen stands on principle like a dignified—stuffed shirt!" She was both crying and angry.

"Kris!"

"People will think I'm married to some kind of dirty old man!"

"Oh, good God! Now look, I've got work to do. You take a tranquilizer and settle down. I've got to hang up now, Kris . . . Kris? Kris?" He replaced the receiver slowly. His head had begun to throb. He opened a desk drawer, where he kept the bottle of aspirin. His telephone buzzer sounded. He picked up the receiver hastily. It wasn't like her to change her mind so quickly, but then . . .

"Mr. Hartmann would like to speak to you, Mr. Hagen."

"Oh. Yes, of course." His biggest advertiser. He stabbed the lighted button. "Hello, Emil. How are things with you this morning?"

"Well, of course the daughter last month," said the low, deep voice.

"I was so terribly sorry, Emil."

"I know, and thank you. We try to bear up, but it's hard."

"There's really no consolation, I know."

"Uh—John, what is this dreck I read in the *Progress and Green Sheet?* What is this silliness about innocence and fair youth and what's it got to do with you, hey?"

John Hagen caressed his temple lightly. "I had to turn someone down on a pet project and I guess he got mad, Emil."

"Yeah, yeah, that comes through all right. But explain me just what it's all about."

"Well, I guess it's pretty much there, except it doesn't say why I won't go along with this thing. I think it's a dangerous proposition. You can see that for yourself if you'll read it over carefully."

"I read it. I don't know, John, I don't pay much attention to these things, maybe I should. This is some kind of law to clean up book-stores—what you were writing about a couple weeks ago?"

"Sort of, Emil, but much too drastic."

"I see. Whyn't you sue the bastard, whoever's responsible?"

"Because it's true as far as it goes."

"You going to answer it then?"

"I'm not going to give them the time of day, Emil."

"Oh. Yeah. Well, you got a good newspaper there, John. You know what you're doing. Only thing is—well, hell, never mind."

"No, tell me."

"Well, you know, John. We don't want anyone to get any funny ideas. But like I say, you know what you're doing. How they doing on that school bond proposition?"

"I've talked with Elliott Warren, the superintendent. It looks like it's going to get on the ballot."

"Good. I'm all for it. We need that new school. Let's get together for lunch one of these days."

"Sure thing, Emil. And thanks for calling."

"Well, I got kind of curious, I guess. Be good, John."

All through that day John Hagen heard from an amazing number of friends, business acquaintances, and civic figures about the blast in the *Progress & Green Sheet*. Not one was overtly unfriendly. Many were concerned, indignant. Some, like Mayor Jack Ronreif, were pointedly supportive, in search of future horse trades. Many, like Buck Benson of Buck Benson Buick, were heavily jocular. As the day grew late it was the attempted humor that wore the thinnest. By late afternoon John Hagen was nearly tempted to abandon his position of lofty disregard and compose an editorial reply that would peel three layers of skin from the *Progress*. A personal call by Rabbi Norman Gross shored his weakening resolve. On admittance to John's office he looked about almost shyly, as if doubtful as to why he had come. A slight old man in a dark, neat suit, he shook hands with John Hagen before removing his black hat.

"Rabbi, I'm honored."

A smile lighted the rabbi's careworn face. "I am sorry we have not known each other better, Mr. Hagen. I thought maybe it is time that we do."

"Thank you," said John, smiling in return. "How can I help you?"

Rabbi Gross waggled a finger in negation. "Perhaps I can help you, which you haven't asked me. I am offering support for a position. Like many others I read the attack on you today. The undeserved innuendo I do not like. The night of the meeting, the Reverend Mr. Coe showed me his petition. To me it is sending an army to capture a field mouse. I cannot believe such a problem exists we should treat it as one with serious crimes like second-degree murder, felonious assault, rape. I joined with the committee because we cannot be outside in that which concerns the community. Also, there is perhaps the poor, sad, withdrawn child to whom the wish-fulfilling fantasy is the reality. So. We do what we can to keep the literature of such nature from the hands of our young. But to class the panderer with the murderer is to yield our sense of values. The obscenities that should concern us more are war, class hatred, racial discrimination, brutality for brutality's sake. Some anxious persons will take you to task that you do not choose the easy road to simplistic solutions. I feel that you should remain calm and firm. So maybe I am asking for something after all."

"You're giving, not asking. I appreciate the trouble you took to come over, Rabbi."

Rabbi Gross shook his head. "This is a strange time. We apply our fervors to professional football games, wars, and hatred out of fear for the dissenter—all the wrong things. We cannot absolve our guilt for our sins of omission, so we transfer it elsewhere. We over-react to the emotional. Often this is for good, but it is not cool reason, applying the test of right. Courage is needed to resist that which is wrong."

John Hagen fingered his chin. "You give me too much credit, Rabbi. I haven't dug that deeply into the basic moral issues of the thing I've been attacked for. I'm not mounting a pulpit against PURIFY; I've elected only to adopt a hands-off position. With luck, I won't have to speak up at all."

"We shall see, my friend," said Rabbi Gross.

— *14*

It was only mid-February, but already the slow roll back from the winter solstice showed in lingering daylight when John Hagen left his office. It had been an exceedingly trying day. At times he wondered why he had ever yearned to be a newspaper publisher. This was one such time. He was warmed by the rabbi's totally unexpected visit, but paradoxically made to realize by it that the snide piece in the *Progress & Green Sheet* had stung more than he had admitted even to himself. Most people want to be thought well of, he mused. I am no different. As our friend Sarah said, anyone who knows me knows exactly what kind of man I am. Yet how can that be true when I am not sure myself? Granted even that a good family friend like Sarah can "know" me, how many people in this community can make even that claim? A thousand perhaps? . . . A thousand with whom I have actually more than a nodding acquaintance? My newspaper goes into forty thousand homes, but that does not imply acceptance of John Hagen, only of the *Sentinel*. And in that audience, of course, are a good many who take violent exception to our outlook on the edi-

torial page. They read the *Sentinel* because it is the only daily newspaper Wellbrook has, but they would cheerfully accept a competitor
strong enough to run me out of business. There must be many in
these comfortable houses I am driving by right now who are utterly
delighted at what they read today in the *Progress & Green Sheet.*
That'll show that liberal, high-minded son of a bitch. Who the hell
does he think he is, anyway, refusing to support a good movement
to clean up filth? Maybe what this town needs is another newspaper.

The children knew without being told that there was strain between their mother and father. Kris dished up the evening meal, a delicious beef ragout, in unsmiling silence. Conversation during the
meal was perfunctory. Kris had just cleared the table, with Pam's
help, and was serving a pudding when the telephone rang.

"I'll get it!" cried Pam.

"Maybe it's for me," Gordo protested, but his sister was already
out of her chair and running to the alcove.

"Hello," they heard her say.

"Whoever it is can call back after dinner," Kris called.

"Fat chance of getting her off the blower," said Gordo.

"Where did you pick up that word?" said his mother.

Pam uttered a gasp that was almost a shriek. All heads jerked
around. "I—I . . ." She put the receiver down in its cradle, her eyes
wide with fear.

"Pam, what is it?" said John.

"It's—it's—I can't tell you."

"What do you mean, you can't tell us?" demanded her mother.
"Who was that and what did they want?"

Pam lowered her head and swallowed in agitation. "It—it was
something perfectly awful," she said in a small voice.

"Something . . . ?" her mother began, and then looked at John.
"Was it something nasty, Pammy?" he said.

She nodded. She stood, still stricken, by the telephone.

"Come and sit down, dear," said Kris. "Come eat your dessert."

Pam's hand went to her mouth. "Oh, Mother, I couldn't. I feel as
if I'd been . . . Oh God!" She turned suddenly and ran from the
alcove, out into the hallway, and up the stairs.

"I'll—" said John Hagen.

"No, let me," said Kris swiftly. She arose, placing her napkin on the table in the same graceful movement, and left the room.

"What's wrong with her?" demanded Gordo. His words were unsympathetic but the tone in which they were spoken was not.

"I think your sister has just had to listen to some sick person who likes to make filthy telephone calls, Gordo."

"You mean like he cussed her out?"

"Dirty words, son, worse than cussing out."

"Why'd anybody wanta do a thing like that?"

"I don't know, but there are people who do it. Some obscure sexual drive. I know only a little about it. Gordo, you've read of men exposing themselves in public? Do you know what that means?"

"Well—uh, yeah, I guess I do."

"I think it's kin to the same twisted impulse. Sex has many faces. One of them is self-exposure, another is talking dirty to a woman or a girl. In both cases the offender gets his thrill by knowing he's made his victim think about sex or sexual intercourse. His way of doing it shocks them deeply and that is his satisfaction."

Gordo's expression was guarded. "Sounds pretty freaky to me."

"To me too, but remember, son, a person like that is sick."

Presently Kris came back downstairs, her lips compressed. John said, "Did you find out—?"

"Later," she said curtly.

John Hagen was leafing through the *Saturday Review* after Gordo had gone up to bed, when Kris came out of the kitchen. She took a dress from a rod in the downstairs closet and her sewing box from the shelf. John turned a page, waiting. She threaded a needle and began fixing a hem that had torn loose. He lowered the magazine.

"Well?"

"Well what?" She lifted the hem and examined it with elaborate care.

"Let's not play games, Kris."

"Do you want me to repeat, word for word, exactly what some filthy stranger said to your daughter? Something outside her knowledge but fully understandable to a girl of twelve. She was utterly horrified."

"Well?"

Kris finally looked at him. " 'Would you do it?' he said. 'With the mouth.' "

"Lord!" he said.

"It's nothing to do with you, of course."

"What!"

"I said, don't blame yourself in any way for it. I'm sure that out of about sixty thousand homes some pervert picked the residence of John A. Hagen wholly by accident. Just ran his finger down the listings and stopped at ours."

He heard her in astonishment. "Well, of course. What else did you think? It happens all the time. The answer is very simple. We'll just get an unlisted number tomorrow."

She bit off a thread. "Do you suppose it would have happened if you were a little more interested in answering that awful piece in the *Progress?*"

"Well, we got around to that finally. Do you honestly think there's a connection? And if so, why?"

"Of course there's a connection. It's just too coincidental."

"You know, Kris, I think you actually believe what you're saying. That if I had come forth in today's *Sentinel* with an angry blast, our daughter would not—entirely by accident, remember—have answered an anonymous telephone caller. That's almost paranoid."

"Paranoid? Mentally ill? Am I mentally ill, John?"

"Krissy, please. You know you're not. And you know the incident tonight *was* coincidental. Maybe not quite. John A. Hagen is a publisher—remember? It says so on the *Sentinel* masthead. We could be a target for any reason."

She smiled thinly. "Target. Yes, that's the word. I think until you publicly speak up, we'll all be targets. Come out for this silly proposition of Coe's or come out against it, but don't lie back letting people think the worst."

"Well, I'm not going to answer."

"Is that all you think of your family?"

"I think pretty highly of my family—all of it."

"What is this stupid principle you're hung up on, anyway? What harm would it do you to say something?"

"For the same reason, Kris, that we rarely answer the letters in the

Our Readers Write column. Irresponsible, illogical, misinformed—
we run every kind of letter but libelous or obscene. We don't feel it's
our job to dignify every one with a reply."

"Dignify. You keep using that word."

"Recognize, if you wish. Elevate to a status they don't deserve.
I'm not running for office, I'm trying to run a newspaper."

She dropped her sewing in her lap. "I feel put in the wrong somehow. Maybe it's my tone of voice. So let me ask you again in the
nicest way possible: would you kindly let our friends know that you
are a clean-minded, decent man who happens to believe the way
he does for the following reasons?"

John Hagen sighed. "Krissy, I have to be just a little bit stubborn
on this."

"You won't do it?"

The telephone rang. Kris laced her fingers together in her lap.
"Would you care to answer the telephone, dear?"

"Yes, I'm about to."

"Be dignified."

He was in the alcove by the third ring. He picked up the receiver.
"Hello?"

"Hagen?" said a man's voice.

"I'm Hagen. Who is this?"

"So you like shitty books, you filthy bastard? How would you like
to eat—?"

John Hagen depressed the cutoff button. He replaced the receiver
and looked up a number in the directory and dialed it. Presently a
man answered.

"Joe? John Hagen."

"Yes, John!" said the district superintendent of the telephone company. "What can I do for you at this hour?"

"We're getting some filthy calls. I'd like to order an immediate
disconnect—now, tonight. I'll arrange for a private listing tomorrow."

"Did you try to hold the caller on the line? Or could you next time,
and arrange with a neighbor to call in for a trace? We like to catch
these characters. They give us a lot of trouble."

"We're pretty upset tonight, Joe. If you could just arrange for a
disconnect."

"Will do. I'll have you cut off in ten minutes. Awfully sorry, John."

"Thanks, Joe. Good night."

"Well?" said Kris.

He shrugged. "It may have been the same man. You heard what I said."

"Loud and clear. I'm going to bed."

John Hagen had no way of knowing until next morning that Peter Salzman, his youthful reporter, had tried to call him well after midnight from the sheriff's office substation jail.

— *15* —

It seemed they were all in on him at once: Quincy Broyles, for once looking anything but placid; Gil Dennis, tight-lipped and grim; and Peter Salzman, a purple bruise under his left eye, puffy face, and a swelled lower lip. Pete was slim and curly blond. He had large, thin sensitive hands, a long curving nose, and a wide full mouth. In another fifteen years his Jewishness would become more emphatic, in a nose grown more authoritative, the undercurl of his lower lip more pronounced, the eyes more knowing. As of now, he was a sleepy and dully angry young man, beat up and perturbed.

"Pete, what the hell?" said John Hagen. He had not had time to seat himself. The other three were grouped just inside the doorway.

"Tell him, kid," said Gil Dennis. Gil had joined up after an apprenticeship and journeyman service with the San Jose *Mercury* and a brief stint as assistant city editor with the San Diego *Union*. He was fast and he knew how to deploy a news staff.

"I'm due in municipal court at ten o'clock," said Pete Salzman. His youthful voice trembled, most likely as much in indignation as agitation. "You remember that big deputy sheriff Roberts, Mr. Hagen? He's on night shift now. I was taking a recheck on Art's Arcade, about ten o'clock. They've cooled it since the series. There are still kids in there, but if they're letting them buy, they didn't while I was there. Anyway, Roberts came in. He gave me the old hard eye and then went over to Genesee, the owner, the guy who's suing us.

They were talking as I went out. I guess Roberts saw me get in my car. Anyway, on the way back here with a couple of little stories to write I stopped at a bar. I swear, and I can prove it by the bartender, I had one draft beer. One, period. We talked baseball. I left at about ten-forty. I drove off and got just about a block when I saw the red dome light flashing. I stopped. Roberts came up to the door. He told me to get my ass out of the car. And when I was a little slow"—Pete Salzman's voice quavered—"the big bastard grabbed me by the arm and jerked me out." Salzman touched his lip lightly.

"They booked him for resisting arrest," said Gil Dennis. His voice was icily furious. "They couldn't make a drunk charge stick."

"Get Harry Wells, Quin," said John Hagen. "Call him at his home if you have to. Go on, Pete."

"There was another smaller guy with him, named Hosea," said Salzman. He drew a deep breath, attempting to achieve calmness. "They made me bend over the fender and they gave me a complete frisk. When I said what's the problem, Roberts said, 'Don't get smart with me, you drunked-up little bastard.' 'Drunk!' I said. 'One beer?' 'Catch him, he's running away,' Roberts yelled. All of a sudden I'm on the ground. Honest to God, Mr. Hagen, I was still bent over the car when this other guy slugged me from the side, right here under the eye. Then Roberts grabbed me by the shirt. He lifted me up and really let me have it—open-handed slaps. It hurt like hell—really stunned me, too. Then they threw me in the car and took me in. They wouldn't even let me make a phone call for two or three hours. They wouldn't call a doctor when I demanded a blood test. But they booked me for resisting arrest. Then they went away and left me in that damned holding cell. When I yelled out after an hour—I didn't even have my watch—this desk sergeant told me to shut up, he was trying to find some film for the camera, and until I got mugged and printed, no phone calls, so pipe down. They can sure make you cool your heels once that sliding steel gate locks on you. Well, when your phone was reported out, I called the bail bond office. The man didn't show until about five o'clock. He was sleepy. His answering service had got him out of bed. To top it all off, when I walked out at close to six o'clock I had to call a cab. They'd had my car towed and impounded."

"I've got Wells on the line," said Quincy Broyles. He handed the receiver to John and stuck the pipe back in his mouth.

"Harry, we need some representation," said John Hagen without preliminary. "The big deputy and his sidekick ran in Pete Salzman last night on a drunk driving pretext, beat hell out of him, and booked him for resisting arrest. He's due in court at ten o'clock."

"Salzman? Isn't he the reporter that—?"

"He's the reporter that. It smells to high heaven. I'm going over with him. I'd appreciate it if you could meet us there."

"Make it nine forty-five. Give me a chance to talk to the boy."

"Nine forty-five it is."

"That'll be Department Two, the municipal court."

John Hagen hung up. "We've got about an hour, Pete. Have you had any breakfast?"

"I don't think I could eat anything, Mr. Hagen."

"Well, let's go out and you have a try at it. After court I want you to go home, take a slug of whiskey if you need it, and get some sleep. And don't come around tonight."

"Who'll cover the beat?"

"You think you're the one indispensable man around here?" said Gil Dennis brusquely. Peter Salzman managed a grin.

"Sure. I thought you knew that."

The courtroom in the new wing of the city hall was half filled when John Hagen and Salzman arrived. Here and there an attorney leaned over to beckon a client outside. There were some women, usually with a son or husband. A few were defendants. A heavy proportion of the waiting group were young men, several with long hair and outwardly scornful. There was quite a lot of milling around. Nervous, subdued conversations created a continuous buzz.

"Hello, John," said Harry Wells. "Hi, son. Let's just step outside a minute, shall we?" They followed his large, plump figure, expensively clad in a lightly checked gray suit. Harry Wells led the way to a side wall, away from a dozen or so other persons.

"This is Pete Salzman, Harry. Harry Wells, Pete."

"Hello, Pete," said Harry Wells. He had a big, smooth face with almost oriental eyes and a firm, confident mouth below a carefully trimmed black mustache. He was a suburban city lawyer with nothing of the small town about him. He had the largest law practice in Wellbrook and had argued cases before district courts of appeal, federal courts, and the state supreme court.

"How do you do, Mr. Wells."

"I've looked at the calendar. We've got a good hour before we come up, Pete. Suppose you tell me what happened?"

Less distraught now, Peter Salzman related the story he had told an hour before. Harry Wells pinched his lower lip.

"Yes, I can see they really worked you over," he said when Pete had finished. "Now, let's see, you went directly from the arcade to the bar. How much driving time?"

"About five minutes."

"So you got there at about what?"

"Oh, maybe ten-twenty."

"And left at about ten-forty. One beer, you're sure?"

"I'm sure," said Pete Salzman tightly.

"If he says it was one beer, it was one beer," said John Hagen.

"Yes, of course," said Harry Wells. "Would you excuse me a moment? I want to get a look at the complaint before court convenes. I'll be right back." He walked over and pushed his way through the swinging doors. Pete Salzman shook his head.

"Honest to God, this is fantastic," he said.

"Harry Wells is a good man, Pete. Just don't let anything bother you. Do what he tells you and you'll be all right. Oh, and by the way, his services, the price of your bail bond, the cost of getting your car back, they're all on the *Sentinel*. Maybe you'd better see a doctor too."

"I'll be all right, but what if these characters can make this stick? My word against theirs."

"Let's just let Harry do the worrying for now."

He rejoined them after about five minutes. He looked disgusted.

"It's pretty shaky, but they're going through with it. I had a little talk with the prosecutor—the deputy district attorney. I think he has his doubts, too, but your man Roberts swore to the complaint. You are alleged to have swung on Hosea when ordered into the patrol car. Well, we'll see about this. When we go up, I want you to say only two things. Acknowledge that you are Peter M. Salzman, and when the judge asks you how you plead, say not guilty. I'll take care of the rest. Okay?"

"Sure," said Pete Salzman.

"Let's go get a cup of coffee. We have nothing but time."

When they returned a half hour later, the court was still dealing with a variety of drunk driving, disturbing the peace, and battery cases. It was another droning thirty minutes by the courtroom clock before the young deputy D.A. at the table to the left of the bench looked up and said, "Peter M. Salzman."

"Peter M. Salzman!" cried the bailiff. He was a big, complacent Wellbrook cop. He looked about curiously. As Harry Wells and Pete Salzman came forward past the railed barrier, Harry Wells leading, there was the trace of a friendly smile on the bailiff's face. He and Salzman probably knew each other from Pete's frequent court and police beat coverage.

"Are you Peter M. Salzman?" said the deputy D.A.

"I am."

"You are charged with violation of Section Six-Nine, California Penal Code, resisting an officer of the law in the performance of his duty, a misdemeanor," said the deputy D.A. "Are you represented by counsel?"

"I am his attorney," said Harry Wells. "If it please the court, we wish to waive the reading of the complaint and the court's statement of the defendant's rights. We are ready to plead to the charge."

"Very well," said the judge. "I take it your client is aware of the possible penalties if he pleads guilty or nolo contendere, Mr. Wells?"

"He is, your honor."

"All right, how do you plead, Mr. Salzman? Guilty or not guilty?"

"Not guilty, sir," said Peter Salzman firmly.

"Do you wish trial by court or trial by jury?"

"We request trial by jury, your honor," said Wells.

"Trial by jury." The judge consulted a paper. "Trial is set for two weeks from today at ten o'clock. Is that agreeable with you, Mr. Wells?"

"It is agreeable," said Harry Wells.

"And the district attorney's office?"

"Agreeable," said the deputy D.A., scratching his nose.

"Your honor, I wish further to request that the defendant be allowed to go free on his own recognizance," said Harry Wells. "He is gainfully employed by the Wellbrook *Sentinel* newspaper, has never before been arrested, and is well vouched for by the *Sentinel's* publisher, Mr. John Hagen, who is in this courtroom today."

The judge glanced over at the deputy D.A.

"No objection," the young prosecutor said.

"Defendant is freed on his own recognizance," said the judge. "Your client understands that he is not to leave the county without permission of the court, Mr. Wells?"

"He understands that, your honor."

"Very well," said the judge. "Who's next?"

Wells, Pete Salzman, and John Hagen left the courtroom.

"What now?" said John.

"The first business we have to take care of is of the utmost importance, Pete," said Harry Wells. "You are going to the district attorney's office and swear to a complaint against Roberts and Hosea for assault. As soon as they're picked up, I'll have a court order requiring a complete physical examination of both men. If they're totally unmarked, as I'm sure they are, it might be a little hard for a jury to believe that you tackled these two big, strong men—sober at least, as you were. The second thing I want you to do is make an immediate appointment with a doctor for yourself for the same purpose. John, can you spare a photographer?"

"Not only can I spare a photographer, but he'll also be shooting on assignment for the *Sentinel*," John Hagen said. "In fact, I'll meet you both at the district attorney's office. I've got to make a phone call."

The district attorney himself was in the distant county seat, but Wellbrook had a branch office, housed in rented quarters in the Wellbrook City Hall, consisting of two deputies, a legal stenographer, and a receptionist-typist to handle a volume of local misdemeanor complaints. John Hagen arrived there with Mike Brescia, the burly chief photographer of the *Sentinel,* and a *Sentinel* reporter named Al DeWeese at about the time a deputy D.A. was hearing Pete Salzman's story behind closed doors, with Harry Wells. The receptionist, whose sister worked in the *Sentinel's* accounting department, wanted to know whether Mr. Hagen wished to ask to join Mr. Wells and Mr. Salzman, but John Hagen said no, they'd wait until he came out. They sat. John filled in DeWeese on the story, as much of it as he knew. DeWeese made notes on a wad of copy paper. Mike Brescia waited, seemingly bored and disinvolved, his heavy battery pack, strobe light, and Mamiya C-33 camera lying on the plastic-covered sofa by him. When John Hagen had finished, Brescia, fingers laced together as he sat leaning forward staring at the floor with his elbows on his knees, looked up and growled, "That bastard Roberts. I'll meet him sometime when he's out of uniform."

"I think one *Sentinel* staffer in trouble at a time is enough, Mike," said John Hagen, but he smiled. Brescia continued to look morose.

"One poke, that's all," he said. "Two maybe."

"When Pete comes out I want you to get a two-shot close in of him and the deputy district attorney," said John. "Al, you wrap up your story when you talk to the deputy and Pete and then phone it right in. We're pretty close to deadline."

"Right you are," said Al DeWeese. He was sandy-haired, middle-aged, and quietly competent without much flash to his copy.

"We're going to hit this one hard," said John Hagen.

That afternoon he had a surprise visitor.

— *16* —

He was wearing a neatly pressed, hard-finish suit and lighter gray hat and his name was Lucien DeGros. He was a lieutenant in the Sheriff's Department. By chance, he and John Hagen had never met before. John's first reaction was surprise that he was such a small man. His immediate second impression as DeGros spoke was that here was a truly tough, businesslike man—tough in a way that had nothing to do with biceps. He had an intonation savoring of a New York West Side background, shaded a little by exposure to the blander California climate. He spoke directly to the point, yet John Hagen sensed that he would never let a word slip unintentionally.

"I've just finished booking two of my men on a charge of assault and battery, Hagen," he said. "Your boy Salzman signed a complaint through the district attorney's office."

"Yes, he was advised to, Lieutenant, and I'm glad he did," said John Hagen coldly. He was still furious at what he was sure was a wholly trumped-up act of revenge.

"Yeah," said DeGros ruminatively. He had the most penetrating blue eyes John had ever seen; they seemed to knife like a laser beam into the hidden secrets of the cerebrum. "I want you to know two things, Hagen. One is that I had no knowledge that Art's Arcade was selling dirty books to minors. The other is that when I found out Roberts and Hosea made that call on you it was entirely on their own hook. When I found out I tore a chunk of skin off. Now I've got a real mess on my hands. It's not about to get better when The Man sees a copy of today's *Sentinel*."

"You've seen it yourself, I take it?"

"I've seen it." Mike Brescia's photo of the battered Pete Salzman with the deputy D.A. was splashed four-column on page one. The second paragraph noted that Salzman had counter-complained against the two officers and that a warrant for their arrest had issued at *Sentinel* press time. Brescia, following orders, had been present that afternoon at the bookings. Those photos would run tomorrow with another page-one story.

"I don't know about you, Lieutenant, but those two roughnecks of yours have got a mess on their hands," said John Hagen. "Several weeks ago I sat right here while Roberts warned me that neither I nor any of my reporters had better get into any trouble in their territory. I'll so testify in court. If this wasn't a deliberate act of retaliation, I never saw one. I don't care whether you concede that or not. No one is going to walk on one of my people and get away with it. We're going to print the news come hell or high water—or plugugly deputy sheriffs."

"I'm not here to fight you, Hagen, I'm here to clear up a couple of things," said Lieutenant DeGros gruffly. "I'd rather have the newspapers on my side; I don't like heat. Off the record, I got plenty from the Old Man on those bookstores and I'm going to get more when he hears about this business today. This is a political year and he's up for re-election. What I'm telling you is that Roberts and Hosea can face the music alone. They're going to resign the force."

John Hagen could not quite conceal his astonishment. "That's quite a development," he said. "When did this all come about?"

"About one hour ago. They're resigning on account of poor health. If they don't, I'll have 'em up on a couple of charges including unofficerlike conduct and another one I don't see any point in mentioning."

John raised an eyebrow. "Like accepting a payoff maybe, Lieutenant?"

DeGros' penetrating blue eyes bored into John Hagen's. "You said that, not me, Hagen."

"You understand of course, Lieutenant, that I have no control over what Pete Salzman does from here on," said John Hagen. "In addition to pressing his charges, he also might have a first-rate civil suit against those two men and against the county."

"That's their problem. Those two dumb assholes got themselves into this, they can get themselves out."

"What's your position going to be in court when you're called on to testify about their character?" said John.

DeGros did not so much as blink. "That to the best of my knowledge they were good officers and that I was sorry their health was so poor they had to quit the department. That I had their word for it that Salzman took a poke at one of them. Like I told you, Hagen, I'm not here to fight you. I want to get along with you. I think you're for good law enforcement as much as I am. I just want to get rid of these two guys and let this whole thing blow over. But for the sake of my own job I can't risk admitting I had a couple of stupid hooligans working for me."

"All right, we understand each other," said John.

"Thought I'd better clear some things up," said Lieutenant DeGros.

"By the way, what about the bookstores?" said John.

"I personally told this guy Genesee and Hank Buttles that if they ever sold as much as one dirty magazine to one juvie I'd start a roust like they'd never seen."

"Fair enough."

Lieutenant DeGros got up. "Maybe one of these days I'll be in a position to do you a little favor. I only want one thing myself."

"If you mean play down this story, not a chance, Lieutenant," said John.

"Nobody asked you to," said DeGros a little sourly. "I just want you to know I'm an honest cop and I'm trying to run a good show. Just don't go out of your way to make us look bad."

"Fair enough," said John Hagen, shaking hands with him. DeGros eyed him for a long moment.

"You ought to loosen up a little bit, Hagen," he said. "You don't seem to be a bad guy."

John laughed. "Thanks for dropping in, Lieutenant."

— 17 —

Five miles east of town off the interstate freeway, the campus of the California State College at Wellbrook was first glimpsed on a high promontory south of the highway. Thence it sprawled gracefully over a broad valley to another cluster of buildings on the heights to the east. John Hagen had attended its dedication nine years before, when the Wellbrook *Sentinel* itself was but one year old as a daily.

He veered away from the interstate at a green sign with white letters marking the offramp: *Cal State College.* He had notes for his talk in his pocket, but imagined the lecture would be pretty informal. Cal State Wellbrook, he knew, had a lively journalism department—taught by a former USC classmate—reflected in its daily newspaper, the *Vaquero.* He looked forward to the morning's encounter, but his mind was not entirely undistracted. Deposition taking was to begin next morning in Genesee *v.* Sentinel Publishing Co. et al. Despite Harry Wells's confident attitude, a libel suit was always a matter for concern. As even Harry admitted, anything could happen in a courtroom.

He was also disquieted by a piece of intelligence from Will Naismith, his advertising manager. It might be nothing or it might be a straw in the wind. At any rate, Will had told him that morning that the *Progress & Green Sheet* had picked off a good account, the Emporium Furniture Mart. It was a third-rate store in county territory, true, and its merchandise flashy and cheap, but it had also been spending about two thousand dollars a month with the *Sentinel* for three years.

"Frankly I don't understand it, John," Naismith had told him worriedly. "I know the *Sentinel* pulls for him, but go figure a hardhead who knows everything there is to know about advertising. He just says he's going to try the *Green Sheet* and radio awhile and that's it. I tell him he's making a mistake. He says if he is, that's his funeral."

"Well, you'll work on him, I know that, Will," said John.

"Oh, I'll work on him, but for now we've lost the account."

The disturbing thing was that dropping this major piece of business reversed a practically unbroken upward trend. The *Green Sheet* during its existence had picked up new business before in competition with the *Sentinel*. It had also taken small accounts away, as well as getting its share of some big ones. But this was the first time the *Sentinel* had out and out lost a larger established customer to its throwaway rival. As Will said, perhaps it meant nothing except a schlock merchant who knew it all. And perhaps it was something else again. Well, no sense brooding about it. The *Sentinel* would still come out, every day but Sunday.

The paved road wound around the football field and forked. The left fork led along a curving ascent to the east heights of the main campus. At the top was an asphalt-surfaced area surrounded by posts threaded by a cable. The sign read *Visitors Parking*. From there it was but a short walk along the road to a sidewalk leading to the Quad. The Liberal Arts Building was past an archway. Classes had just ended. Young men and women were strolling between buildings, pausing at the concrete benches around the center fountain, or enjoying the warm sunshine on the lawn.

Smoking a pipe by a pillar at the main entrance to the Liberal Arts Building was John's former University of Southern California classmate Larry Gulick. As John approached, Larry took the pipe from his mouth and stepped forward to greet him. He was a blackmustached, swarthy man of stocky build. At one time he had wanted to be a foreign correspondent for one of the wire services. The academic world had beckoned to him after his eight years' experience with the Associated Press in San Francisco and the Copley Newspapers.

"You're right on the button, John," said Gulick. His grip was powerful. "Had no trouble finding the building, did you?"

"Hello, Larry," said John Hagen, smiling. "You forget that I saw this place for the first time before you did."

"So you did. All ready with an inspirational talk?"

"Will the economics of the newspaper business do?"

"I count on you for something better than that," said Gulick, replacing the pipe. "How've you been?"

"Oh, pretty well. Yourself?"

"First rate. I've just become a father for the fifth time."

"I'll be damned! What's the division?"

"This one's a girl; makes three and two boys. Ages from two weeks to twelve years. How's Kris? Haven't seen her in years."

"She's fine. And my brood of two seem healthy and alert."

Gulick peered at him shrewdly. "You've been having your fun with the *Green Sheet* lately, haven't you? What's going on over there anyway?"

"Suppose I tell you about it over lunch, if I'm invited."

"Yes, a meal goes with. I think we'd better go in now."

"Lead the way."

"I'll warn you," said Larry Gulick, holding the door for John, "I've got a stimulating bunch here. You may get challenged on some of your most cherished concepts. I do, all the time."

"I'll try to be brave. As I remember your invitation, it was twenty to twenty-five minutes of talk and the remaining twenty-five minutes in free-wheeling discussion."

"Make the talk about twenty minutes. Don't worry about the discussion. You'll get questions, I guarantee you. Up these stairs ahead."

The classroom was stepped like a theater, with five rows of wooden armchair seats. About twenty young men and women looked expectantly at John Hagen from their seats. Others were still entering and finding places, in a free exchange of banter and uninhibited laughter.

"The real work is done in the *Vaquero* offices next door," Larry

Gulick told John. He led the way to a table with two chairs in front of the green "blackboard." He moved behind the far chair. "Sit down. I'll make the introduction in a moment."

John Hagen pulled out his chair, seated himself, and looked up at the assembled group. In the very first row a very pretty young girl tugged at a miniskirt to very little avail and made a back-of-the-hand remark to her right-hand neighbor, a sharp-faced young man with a Mephistophelean black beard. The young man laughed and said, "You *gotta* be kiddin'!" Next to them a chunky boy in white stay-pressed pants, bilious-green sport jacket, and red turtleneck sweater stared fixedly at John Hagen from behind gold-rimmed spectacles. A fat, solemn girl in a pink sweater, with thin gold pendant, checked skirt, and brown loafers, toyed with a ball-point pen, looking away as John's gaze rested on her a moment. For the time being the rest were just faces. Larry Gulick said to a tall, husky boy who had just entered, "Would you shut the door please, Mr. Stavros?" The lad gave a mock salute and pulled the door to.

"Good morning, ladies and gentlemen," said Larry Gulick. "With us by invitation this morning is the publisher of the Wellbrook *Sentinel,* an old friend of mine, Mr. John Hagen. Mr. Hagen and I were classmates and fellow journalism students at the University of Southern California back in the Dark Ages—the years nineteen forty-nine to nineteen fifty-three. It was an era during which, as I'm sure you know, Senator McCarthy was not Eugene but Joe, of Wisconsin, and it included the period of hostilities between the United Nations and the People's Republic of North Korea. During this time, as if I had to remind you of our differences in age, most of you here were born. I would like to emphasize one point, if you please: we were *not* the goldfish swallowers." There were a few smiles. "We—Mr. Hagen and I—and our contemporaries indulged in no such foolishness. Our *schtick* was panty raids." He got a groan or two. "Mr. Hagen apprenticed on the Los Angeles *Times* right after the Los Angeles *Daily News,* the late lamented liberal newspaper, was done in by the combined whipsaw of the new *Mirror,* the *Herald and Express,* the *Times,* and the *Examiner.* As you know, only the morning *Times* and the afternoon *Herald-Examiner* now survive. So much for that."

He cleared his throat. "I see no point in lengthy biographies. Mr.

Hagen bought an old weekly ten years ago and converted it into a daily. And that is the *Sentinel*. It enjoys a liberal reputation in Southern California equaled perhaps only by Tom Braden's Oceanside *Blade-Tribune*. I rate it as an excellent, well-balanced medium-size daily. I think Mr. Hagen has done a good job with the *Sentinel*. Now I'll let him speak for himself on the topic of 'The Responsibility of the Publisher.' John, the floor is yours." Larry Gulick extended his hand, palm upward, toward John Hagen and sat down.

"I'm pleased to be here," said John, having gained his feet. "I'm always glad to talk to fellow journalists. And before launching into my quite informal talk, I'd like to correct a misimpression. Your professor I remember quite well as an able newspaperman, both on the *Daily Trojan* and in his career with the AP and Copley. Now, as you know, many a good story can be ruined by too careful checking. As an old spoilsport I must point out that *I* do not have nor have I ever had any souvenir panties in my possession. If Professor Gulick chooses to remember that aspect of our college days, you are free to draw your own conclusions." There were some snickers. Larry Gulick grinned as John looked at him.

"I don't know why you men and women wish to enter journalism," John Hagen continued. "I do not know that you all intend to. I know only why I did. It was simply because it seemed and still seems to me to be, next to skydiving, which I've never tried, one of the most exciting jobs in the world. And, begging the pardon of any skydivers among you, considerably more meaningful. A lot of newspaper work is as dull as any other work. You'll find that out. But a good story is still fun to dig out and satisfying to see in print. Even the most jaded of old newspapermen still feels a high degree of personal accomplishment in doing something ahead of the competition, finding an angle that no one else has thought of, or writing it better than anyone else—or all three."

As he developed his topic, feeling more at ease with his audience by now, John Hagen let his eyes glance around the room, lingering on individual faces. They were giving him careful, unblinking attention in a way that the young now seemed especially to have made their own. They had a marked air of cool thoughtfulness, accepting nothing ready-made, buying nothing without testing it, rejecting the phony instantly, ready to pounce at the slightest hint of meretricious reasoning.

He glanced at his watch. He had been talking for some eighteen minutes.

"If I have a philosophy, it is that a newspaper and its publisher owe the readers honesty, insofar as honesty is possible," said John Hagen. "It is that a newspaper must inform. In informing, a newspaper must try to give as many sides of a question as it is humanly possible to give. To guard against unconscious bias; to credit even your opponents with having reasons for thinking the way they do; to try to understand and to report those reasons, even when you think they are wrong. Justice Holmes expressed it, in another context, as freedom for the thought that we hate. As a publisher I try to keep that in mind. I hope I'll never get to thinking I am so god-like that I'll stop trying to get behind the other man's point of view. Within my limitations, that is the guide I try to follow." He looked at Larry Gulick.

Larry nodded and said without arising, "Thank you, John. Let's open it up now to discussion. Questions?"

"Mr. Hagen," said the bearded young man in the front row. John inclined his head. "How can you stand there and say the newspapers are doing a job when they're all so uptight about my generation they don't even know what's going on on the campuses? Can you answer that one honestly?"

"I'll try," said John Hagen. "I agree with you that there's a lot of hysterical treatment by a large segment of the press about the present ferment on the campuses. I'll agree there hasn't been enough first-hand investigation when there is a protest or a sit-in or a rally or even a riot. A paper *does* go to press every day; news is history written in a hurry. Perhaps there is not always enough analytical follow-up. And sometimes it's a little hard to understand just what you people are angry about. I can only say that I think the *Sentinel* does try."

"Does it?" said a voice from one of the back seats. The tall, husky young man Larry Gulick had addressed as Stavros stood up. "A year ago there was a big protest rally here on campus over napalm in Vietnam and U. S. Navy recruiters. The *Sentinel* sent one photographer and one reporter out to cover the story. I don't know who all the reporter talked to besides the president, the dean of students, the student body president, and a couple of straight-arrow types in business administration. The story came out like we were a bunch of rah-rah kids with spring fever. We had a serious gripe. It was a deadly serious protest, but you sure as hell wouldn't have known it from reading the *Sentinel.*" The young man sat down.

"Would it surprise you to know that I agree?" said John Hagen. Several of the students exchanged cynical smiles. "It was our first local and locally covered protest. We goofed. We'll try to do better in the future."

"Will you?" said the pretty miniskirted girl down front. "Have you got anybody on your staff young enough to see it like it is and tell it like it is?"

"Well, I'm going to say something about the other side too," said John. "I credit you people and your generation of people with the utmost degree of seriousness and sincerity. But you won't agree with me at all when I say I find there is often a greater effort on the part of my age group to understand *you* than you are willing to make to understand *us*."

There was a collective groan. From somewhere a male voice said quite distinctly, "Oh, bullshit!"

"Wait just a minute," said Larry Gulick. He looked up into the classroom. "Everyone's entitled to his point of view, including the author of that earthy expletive just now. Speak as frankly as you wish, but keep the barnyard out of my classroom. I apologize, John."

John Hagen smiled. "Well, I *have* heard the word before. May I amplify my challenge? You'll pardon this touch of old-fogeyism, but I'll say that there is a degree of unanimity among the New Left, which some or many of you subscribe to, that seems to brook no argument. I'll offer the statement that a lot of your group often present simplistic solutions for the world's problems. It may surprise you to know that we know about the problems too. Maybe finding the answers is a little bit tougher."

"I'd like to ask the publisher of the Wellbrook *Sentinel* why the over-thirty set is so scared of us," said an attractive girl in the second row.

"Isn't that a rather arbitrary division?" said John. "Over thirty, under thirty? Or am I just picking a point?"

"I think you are, yes, and you haven't answered my question," said the girl coolly.

"I beg your pardon; I haven't. I can't speak categorically for your elders. I can only answer in a general sort of way. If you mean far-out dress, I admit it has taken a bit of getting used to. If you mean a degree of outspokenness on everything from the military draft to drugs, maybe we needed shaking up. Perhaps we have not been too willing to accept the idea that young people really do have something to tell us. I personally do not feel threatened, but I know that there are those who do. I'll remember to try to keep my own pipelines open."

The tall boy, Stavros, stood again. "We're talking about the press and we're talking about the generation gap," he said, his hands in his hip pockets. "It seems like a good time to bring this up. A few weeks ago your newspaper, the *Sentinel,* got all excited about dirty books being sold in a couple of bookstores. Made a great big thing out of it. I'd like to know just what's the big hangup about sex?" There was a general chorus of agreement.

"Hangup?" said John Hagen puzzledly. "Is that your idea of a hangup?"

"Well, yes," said Stavros. "Who the hell worries about dirty books and magazines except *old* grownups? Uptight grownups."

"Frankly, I don't quite know how to answer that one," said John Hagen. "It seems to me that there is an age for innocence and an age for growing up. When I say innocence, I don't mean what you think I mean. I mean simply the joy of remaining a child for a while. It seems to me that learning the seamier side of sex through the type of thing the *Sentinel* was writing about deprives a young boy or girl of learning the beautiful side of our sexuality."

"You admit, then, that sex is really beautiful and right?" said the fat girl in the pink sweater.

"True loving sex, yes," said John.

"You mean between married adults, don't you?" said the bearded youth in the front row.

"No, I didn't say that," said John. "I speak of the normal hetero-sexual relationship between mature men and women."

"Why do you use the term normal?" demanded Stavros. "Is there anything abnormal about homosexuality?"

"You'll have to go to a psychologist or a psychiatrist for the answer to that one. Yes?"

"I'd like to pursue this particular thing about sex books," said a man in one of the rear seats. "Did you know that about a year or so ago over in Denmark they took off all the limits on what they could print and sell? And did you know that after all the excitement, the sales of pornography dropped off?"

"I've heard that," said John. "I don't know whether we're ready for that degree of license in this country or not. And I'm not sure I am quite ready to accept the fact of my own children reading some of the stuff I've seen that makes sex out to be something leering and ugly."

"How do you know they haven't?" said another voice.

"I don't," said John Hagen.

"How do you even know whether they're interested in that junk?" said the pretty miniskirted girl. "How old are they?"

"Twelve and fourteen, and I don't."

"Mr. Hagen," said the chunky boy with the bilious-green coat and gold-rimmed spectacles, "why is it that rape is such a staple fare of the newspapers? Is it because it sells newspapers?"

"Yes," said John Hagen. "A qualified yes. Everything that goes into a newspaper represents the editor's idea of what will sell his newspaper. There's an old saying in the business that the public casts its votes every day with dimes."

"I thought you said that your philosophy was honesty with your readers," the chunky boy rejoined. "What's honest about the way you guys report a rape story? I mean, some female gets taken by force. Half the time it's some alcoholic broad who went with the guy by choice and he gets mad when he finds out she's been puttin' him on. Well, that's neither here nor there maybe, but there's a sniggering thing about rape stories. Why can't you be honest and tell it like it is or don't tell it at all?"

John smiled. "Language and all?"

"I personally don't think there ought to be any limit at all. Can words kill you?"

"Let me answer that in two parts," said John Hagen. "First, in a rape story—who and what the victim may be. We will report the general facts except the name, including how she came to find herself in her precarious situation. As to totally cataloguing every person we write about—what would you like? Suppose I said Banker Jones, who sits on the city council, is a greedy note-shaver, or Millicent Van Astor of the Junior League once ran off with an itinerant scissors-grinder when she was fifteen years old? This too would be honest. And the publisher would be up to his ears in summonses on his very first day of business."

"I don't think there should be any censorship at all," said a girl in the fourth row.

"Do you work on the *Vaquero?*" inquired John.

"No, the *Word*. That's our magazine. Whenever we get a contribution that really lays it on the line, we have to fight for every sentence. I think if a person has got something true and valid to say, that person ought to be allowed to say it."

"That would tend to eliminate the editor, would it not?"

"It's not his job to make moral judgments," said the girl spiritedly. "Who appointed him God?"

"Let me see if I follow this argument," said John Hagen. "If the editor is not allowed to determine or at least interpret standards of taste, then there should be no standards whatsoever imposed. Is that about what you're saying?"

"There should only be standards of good writing," said the girl firmly.

"With no words of any kind barred?"

"Yes."

"Interesting. Yes?"

"Could I make a comment that's a question?" said the attractive girl in the second row.

"Or even a question that's a comment," said John.

"Well, it seems to me from reading about Pulitzer and Hearst and Captain Patterson and the rest of those old boys—the ones that really bore down on love nests and chorus girls and sugar daddies—those people sort of set up patterns that a lot of your editors don't question to this day. I mean, sex sells. Only, be moral about it at the same time. Give the morons lots of good, juicy sex to drool over, then say, 'Isn't this simply terrible!' I think your rape stories fall in the same category. The word is hypocritical."

"I'll agree," said John. "The *Sentinel* tries to hold down on this type of coverage."

The girl shook her head. "I guess I didn't make my point broad enough. You quoted some old saying about the public casting its votes with dimes. But who are you talking to in your paper, using these tried-and-true, hackneyed formulas that have been passed down for eighty years? The same people who grew up on this same kind of junk and have come to expect it. Not just the *Sentinel,* but all newspapers. When are they going to do a little honest soul-searching?"

"There is much room for improvement," said John. "We'll look to your generation to show us how."

"We get under your skin, Mr. Hagen?" said a man's voice, and there was some laughter.

"Time for about two more questions," said Larry Gulick.

The man up in the rear who had spoken about Denmark said, "Mr. Hagen?"

"Yes?"

"Back on this pornography question. What's bugging all these people that spend their time poring over dirty books and say, man, would you look at this, let's get up a law? It's in the papers all the time. What's with them?"

"I'll have to beg the question," said John. "I don't know."

"Don't you have any idea? Like, they make a holy war out of it."

"My thoughts on this may be no more valid than yours. The speed of what I'll call the frankness explosion has been truly amazing. Now, the development of our attitudes—toward life in general, others, our political convictions—is not an overnight process. We are the sum of our total environment from earliest childhood, even infancy. This includes our beliefs and attitudes toward sex, surely one of the strongest and most influential drives that shapes us. Our total sexuality, I mean, not 'drive' in the sense of the sexual urge. And out of these lifelong influences of environment, each of us tends to think a certain way—this is my point of view, formed over thirty-nine years; that is yours, formed later. Thus what to you may be matter-of-fact, standard openness of language in writing, to me may be alarming. My reflexes are triggered and I respond."

"Yes," said the man, "I can understand that. You react. That's normal; we all do. What I'm talking about goes a hell of a lot further. Some of these people are as scared of sex in books as they are of communism. I mean, paranoid."

John smiled. "I've had some experience of that."

"Don't you think there's a kind of vicarious enjoyment involved here? Like, they're scared and fascinated at the same time?"

John Hagen tugged at his earlobe. "Well, you're leading me out of my field of competence. I've had no extensive training in psychology, merely one college course. I'd say, first, that there is much—call it simply honest concern about the tidal wave of trash being spewed from the presses these days. Whether it harms us to any great degree, I'm not prepared to say. I believe *I* do not take an extreme position on it. As to voyeurism and the vicarious enjoyment of something you publicly deplore—yes, I think that there is some degree of that too."

"You mean, they get their jollies respectably."

"In a manner of speaking. It's quite complicated, I'm sure."

"Any more questions or comments?" said Larry Gulick.

The pretty, miniskirted girl said, "Do you think, Mr. Hagen, that the newspapers, yours included, are doing an honest job of political reporting?"

"All I can say is that I think we try."

"Why don't you just admit you're married to the Establishment, the status quo?"

"Maybe I am—I don't know," said John. "But change does not come by minority revolution. Most change, in fact, evolves. Look how far we have come just in our attitudes toward the black man in the last few years."

"You mean, just because it's not fashionable to call us niggers in public any more?" This from a Negro girl.

"I mean an honest groping for solutions to a centuries-old problem," said John Hagen. "A start has been made. It will be up to people of your generation—and your children—to carry it on."

"Isn't that pretty platitudinous?" said the chunky boy.

"Maybe. Do you disagree with its truth?"

"One more question or comment," said Larry Gulick.

"Yeah," said the boy Stavros, who seemed to like to stand up when speaking. "I'll speak for myself only. I don't think there's been any real dialogue here today. I don't think there can be—I'm talking about newspapers now—until you publishers quit patronizing things you don't understand. And won't make any effort to understand. You reflect middle-class, middle-aged, square attitudes instead of trying to learn. Your readers get a jumbled-up picture of riots, grass smoking, folk rock, light shows, draft-card burning, and sex, and that's us. When it isn't frightening you, it's funny to you. Until you get down to where the happening is, your newspapers will go on serving up the same tired jazz they always have. But I like your guts coming here; maybe you learned more than we did."

"Thank you, Mr. Stavros," said John Hagen. "Maybe we don't use the same brand of semantics. I can only say to all of you, if you'll accept a word of advice, learn the English language. That's your tool if you're going into journalism. Then use those words to strike for what you believe in. I know, certainly, that you have the forthrightness of your convictions. At your age, principles are all that count. Fine; I hope you hold onto that point of view. I hope you can, when you start bumping into some of the harsher realities."

"Thank you, John," said Larry Gulick, standing. "I trust the hazing wasn't too painful. I face it three times a week. That's it for today, ladies and gentlemen."

They found a corner of the pleasantly airy cafeteria away from the faculty section. "One of these days we'll get our own lounge," said Larry Gulick. "Couple of years maybe. It depends on the legislature making the appropriation. It's been a tough period for higher education."

"Well, Larry," said John Hagen, salting his meatloaf, "how does teaching compare with the newspaper business?"

"I love it, frankly," said Gulick. "There *is* no comparison. I have to remember only to keep from getting the sole-authority complex. Here, I'm the only guy with a newspaper background. That makes me the top man in my field."

"I should think, from the last hour, that there's no danger of complacency."

Gulick grinned. "Welcome to the club, pal. Yeah, these kids are really fantastic, John. Throw out everything you think you know about this current crop. They call 'em the Now generation; I'd call 'em the *What for?* generation. They question everything—you got a sample of that. They simply won't accept without proof. Even when you think you're pounding along in perfectly logical order, they challenge. Even if they think you're right, they'll tell you you're wrong. It's in the order of things. It should keep me alive, young, and alert for a long time. Now, what's with this *Progress and Green Sheet* brouhaha? Whose toes did you step on?"

John Hagen briefly related the events of the previous weeks, Larry Gulick munching away and nodding from time to time.

"I think some people aim to use the *Green Sheet* as the voice of opposition to the *Sentinel* on PURIFY," John concluded. "From what I know of the publisher, his convictions are purchasable. We'll rock along; I'm not too worried."

"Uh-huh. Say, how's old Vic doing?"

"Vic Massoni? Too early to tell, really. He and Ernie Gruener are the only good Democratic bets in the primary."

"He went with Kris at one time, didn't he." The emphasis was on "didn't," making it an assertion rather than a question.

"Vic? Vic and Kris? No, never."

"In college? I was sure they went together at one time."

"It's news to me." John's forkful of lettuce stopped halfway between his plate and his mouth. Then slowly he put the lettuce in his mouth, scarcely tasting it.

"College. What a long time ago and no time at all," said Larry Gulick. Man, those years really do fly. Have you ever been to a class reunion, John?"

"I'm sorry; what did you say, Larry?" said John Hagen.

The receptionist in Harry Wells's office said, "He's expecting you, Mr. Hagen. I'll let him know you're here. Would you care to sit down?"

"Yes, thank you." Just yesterday Dwight Henry had completed a full set of documents relating to the corporate structure and finances of the Sentinel Publishing Company. John had these with him in an attaché case along with personal bank statements, tax records, and other financial data. He sat and crossed his legs and waited until the door to Harry Wells's inner office was opened by Harry.

"Good morning, John," said Harry Wells. "Come on in. Brought a lot of paper with you, I trust?" He closed the door as John walked in. "Have a seat. We'll have a reporter and a notary up here. Merz said he'd be along at nine-thirty. Let me explain just what we're doing and why. Now, we're taking depositions today only on your finances. Today and maybe tomorrow. Normally this would be inadmissible as evidence. However, along with general damages, Genesee is asking punitive damages, which does make it admissible. He is entitled to go into your financial picture to a considerable degree."

"I see."

"Today's session is only the first round. It's the plaintiff's show, because he asked for it and I saw no reason to stall. However, let me tell you the rest of it so you'll know what to expect in a few months, when I call Genesee in for interrogatories. The general purpose of deposition taking is to save time in court by establishing the pattern of the case before the trial. We're aiming at two things: impeachment and discovery. The first is laying the groundwork for self-contradiction in court. That is, if a witness says one thing under oath in deposition and another in court, we can use that to impeach his own testimony during cross-examination. Discovery is the right to learn the nature of your opponent's case and who his witnesses are ahead of trial. This enables you to prepare your own case. It saves nasty little surprises in court."

"All right," said John Hagen. "I guess that's clear enough. When do you think this will come up for trial?"

"My guess would be next January at the very earliest. Maybe much longer. The superior court calendar is pretty well jammed up. Meanwhile, we can hope the plaintiff will change his mind. Maybe you'd like to know that I already have an investigator quietly at work on Mr. Arthur Genesee. You know, if you allege that I have damaged your reputation and you sue me, I am entitled to the broadest possible leeway in exploring your whole character and background. The going can get pretty sticky for the plaintiff if it can be shown he hasn't got too much character and reputation to damage."

"It sounds like a pretty nasty business."

"Well, if somebody throws a punch at you, you don't stand there and let it land without trying to block and counterpunch," said Harry Wells.

Presently the receptionist announced the arrival of the notary, the reporter, and Mr. Kurt Merz, all within a few minutes of each other.

"I guess we'd better get the show on the road," said Harry Wells. "Answer all his questions frankly and honestly, John. If he gets off base, I'll step in." He arose and went to the door. John heard his greeting and then, "No, Ethel, we only need you for the swearing. Just the one witness. Shall we go in?"

"Good morning, Mr. Hagen," said Kurt Merz, still the angry pigeon.

"Good morning, Mr. Merz," said John, accepting the attorney's handshake. An efficient-looking girl with glasses had carried in a Stenotype case. She looked around for a place to set it.

"This is Miss Galloway of the Ace Reporting Service and Mrs. Clary, the notary public. Miss Galloway, you may take that chair right there. Mr. Merz, you may sit there if that is satisfactory to you."

"Perfectly satisfactory," said Merz briskly, seating himself and opening an attaché case. There was silence for a few minutes as Miss Galloway set up her machine, tested it, and then said, "Ready."

"Mr. Wells, do we agree that this gentleman here is John A. Hagen, a defendant in Genesee versus Sentinel Publishing Company et al.?" said Merz.

"Yes, I'll stipulate that."

"Would you swear the witness in the proceedings, Mrs. Clary?"

"Would you raise your right hand," said Mrs. Clary, a spare, middle-aged woman with a crisp voice. "Do you, John A. Hagen, swear that in the testimony you are about to give, you will tell the truth, the whole truth, and nothing but the truth, so help you God?"

"I do."

"That's all, and thank you, Ethel," said Harry Wells. "Mr. Merz?" Mrs. Clary went out, closing the door behind her.

"Stop me if there is anything to which you object," said Merz to Harry Wells. "I would like the record to show in Arthur Genesee, plaintiff, versus Sentinel Publishing Company, John A. Hagen, Peter Salzman, et al., defendants, that appearing were Messrs. Merz and Merz, represented by Kurt Merz, Esquire, eighteen-nineteen Olive Street, Wellbrook, California, as counsel for the plaintiff, and Harry Wells, Esquire, three-ten Professional Building, Wellbrook, California, as counsel for the defendant. Off the record, Miss Galloway: Mr. Wells, shall we stipulate to the reporting?"

"By all means," said Wells.

"Let the record show," said Merz, "that it was stipulated between counsel for the responding parties that said deposition . . ."

The formalities droned on.

Merz looked at Harry Wells. "May I proceed to examine, Mr. Wells?"

"Please do," said Harry.

"Mr. Hagen, you are the publisher of the Wellbrook *Sentinel*, a daily newspaper, are you not?" said Merz.

The long day had begun. . . .

With a break only for lunch, the exhaustive examination went on until five o'clock. During this time, with only occasional interpositions from Harry Wells, Merz established the *Sentinel's* and John Hagen's complete financial standings. That John Hagen was a 20 per cent shareholder in a private corporation whose present worth on the market was about six hundred thousand dollars. That the most recent full calendar year's earnings after taxes had been ninety-four thousand, four hundred and fifty-one dollars and eighty cents on gross earnings from newspaper, engraving, and job printing out of six hundred twenty-two thousand, one hundred and eighteen dollars and four cents. That of the net, forty-four thousand-plus had been placed in reserve, and fifty thousand divided five ways to shareholders: ten thousand dollars to each. That total reserves exceeded a hundred thousand dollars, 90 per cent of which was invested in common stocks. That Mr. Hagen drew the salary of fifteen thousand dollars per annum for his dual services as editor and publisher. And much, much more, to the most miniscule detail: personal property, equity in house and how held, automobiles, insurance policies, cash in bank—average amount of savings—investments or other holdings, if any, personal or joint debts, monthly installment payments—how much originally and how much now—amounts of state and federal taxes paid on how much gross income for each of the past five years. No facet was too small for Mr. Merz's searching eye, including even such items as monthly expenditures for food, gasoline, clothing, insurance, medical and dental care, entertainment. In the sum six and a half hours he explored every aspect of the newspaper corporation's past earnings, reserves, assets, liabilities, cash-flow and cash position, and of John Hagen's personal financial standing.

"Now, Mr. Hagen—"

"Pardon me, Mr. Merz—off the record, Miss Galloway—how much more time do you think you will require?" said Harry Wells.

"As a matter of fact, I believe I am almost through. Mr. Hagen —back on the record, Miss Galloway—have you any other personal assets of any kind or any other sources of income?"

"No," said John.

"No other insurance policies, no other—"

"I'll enter an objection," said Harry Wells tiredly. "His answer was entirely responsive."

"The question stands. No other thing or property of any value or any other source of income, no matter how insignificant?"

"No."

"Bearing in mind, of course, Mr. Hagen, that you are as fully under oath as you would be in a court of—"

"You are baiting the witness, Mr. Merz," said Harry Wells testily. "My client is fully aware that he is under oath and he's aware of the penalties for perjury. He has twice replied 'No' to your question. I hereby advise him to refuse to answer the same question a third time."

"No further personal liabilities or debts or other obligations of a financial nature that you are aware of other than those to which you have testified?" pursued Merz, undaunted.

"No; no others that I am aware of."

Merz shuffled some papers and put them back in his attaché case, snapping it. "I am through with the witness, counselor," he said.

"All right," said Harry Wells, "and we're off the record now. I'll be in touch later on as to examination of *your* client."

"And when do you think that will be?" said Merz, peering suspiciously.

"I can't say at this time. What about Peter Salzman? Do you plan interrogatories of him, and if so, when?"

"I'll let you know," said Merz, rising. "I'll also let you know when I'd like to examine Mr. Hagen, Mr. Salzman, and any others on the action itself. I'll expect a signed transcript of this hearing within two weeks. Good evening, Mr. Wells, Mr. Hagen."

"Good-by, Mr. Merz."

They waited until he had left the office and Miss Galloway had also packed her equipment, made her farewells, and left.

"How do you feel?" said Harry, smiling wearily.

"Wrung out. Totally drained. I feel as if I'd been tacked to a board and dissected with a dull knife."

"Come on," said Harry abruptly. "I'll buy you a drink."

— *19* —

A good newsman suffers from a schizophrenic-like malady to which doctors also are prone. Neither wants human suffering, yet it is most productive of both news and the kind of medical practice that leads to the improvement of the healing arts.

For some two weeks following the deposition taking, airplanes quit crashing, no major earthquakes dislocated the earth's crust, and the world capitals took on an unwonted placidity. Even Vietnam provided only the usual enemy body count and the periodic "we are winning" announcement by an American general.

This morning brought no significant change in the news barometer. Publisher, managing editor, and city editor held their usual weekday conference. This took place as a rule in Quincy Broyles' office a few minutes after John Hagen came in, customarily at about 8:30 A.M. The early, tentative page one was the main order of business. A late-breaking top story could and would alter this showcase page. Otherwise the early decision stood.

Gil Dennis, the city editor, did have some news on the domestic front this day, despite the doldrums. The trouble was that it was nothing for the *Sentinel*. His cold green eyes narrowed, he said, "I hear you've converted to communism, John."

"Lenin, Mao, Stalin, or Trotsky?"

"Now, you don't expect these people to make fine distinctions like that, do you?" said Gil.

"Specifically, *what* people?"

"Specifically, I don't know. It came from two sources. Chris Smith's wife's sister and Al DeWeese's female cousin. The Smith relative heard it in the Safeway last night and the DeWeese connection, at a bridge party yesterday afternoon. The two versions jibe closely enough as to make it seem something more than coincidence. It seems that the publisher of the Wellbrook *Sentinel* is a no-good, rotten commie."

John sighed. "Whose finger did I pinch in the door *this* time, Gil?"

"It goes like this. Pornography is eroding and rotting our moral fiber, which takes away our will to resist our enemies. Therefore, it must be a communist plot. Since you won't take a stand on Public United to Restore Innocence to Fair Youth—which neither party could remember, by the way—called it simply PURIFY—then you must be part and parcel of that conspiracy. Dig?"

"Yes, I dig," said John dryly. "*A,* dogs are canines. *B,* wolves, who are dangerous animals, are canines too. Ergo, *C,* dogs are dan-

gerous animals. It's as simple as falling off a syllogism. Pool, which
starts with *P* and that rhymes with *T* and that stands for trouble.
Trouble in River City."

Quincy Broyles had been listening silently, sucking on a dead pipe.
Now he spoke up: "An organized whispering campaign?"

"Three guesses," said John Hagen. "The *Land of the Free* textbook
story all over again. Remember, Quin?"

Quincy Broyles shook his head. "Trying to hang a Dirty Old Man
tag on you could be much worse, John. It's like planting a rumor
that So-and-So has homosexual tendencies. What is So-and-So going
to do about it? Can he buttonhole everyone he knows and say,
'The word is going around that I'm a faggot; I'll have you know
I'm as heterosexual as you are'?"

John Hagen laughed. "That's an idea. I'll run a page-one editorial.
I'll say the rumors about my communist-oriented salacious proclivi-
ties are slightly exaggerated."

"Just thought you'd like to know," said Gil Dennis, sounding a
trifle miffed.

"Gil, I'm glad you told me," said John. "I don't believe in slay-
ing the messenger who carries bad news. Which reminds me, what
has the staff picked up lately on the PURIFY campaign for signatures?"

"I was going to tell you about that too. I had Al DeWeese run a
little spot check yesterday afternoon. Pomona, Oxnard, and Long
Beach have nothing on it—positive *or* negative. But Santa Ana,
Pasadena, San Berdoo, and San Diego all report it seems to be taking
hold, from all they can hear. And of course you already know they've
got card tables set up in front of half a dozen supermarkets here in
Wellbrook. They seem to be filling up a lot of petitions."

"I've seen them," said John. "Maybe I took this bunch too lightly.
Their deadline is July thirty-first to get on the November ballot.
Perhaps they'll make it."

"No statement until then, John?" said Quincy Broyles thoughtfully.

"Quin, how in the world can you take on something that doesn't
officially exist?"

"I guess you can't," admitted Broyles, refiring his pipe.

John Hagen shook his head. "We're in a really hysterical era," he said. "The conservatives proclaim that law and order is the only answer to racial problems. The boys on the far left say the only choice is to plow up the whole system and redeal from chaos. And there is a school preaching that words no longer have meaning, that the soapbox, not the message, *is* the message. I have the feeling that a man of reason like a Lincoln or an Oliver Wendell Holmes would throw up his hands in despair. Or simply throw up."

Quincy Broyles was once more befouling the air with his pipe. He took it from his mouth, smiling gently. "You know from your history, John, that Lincoln was surrounded by just as many jackals and just as much hysterical nonsense as the twentieth century ever produced. And Joseph McCarthy, *that* McCarthy, wasn't even a patch on the Bolshevik demon of the twenties—Attorney General Palmer, Sacco and Vanzetti—which *I* can remember. And don't forget, Justice Holmes was as damned by some in his time as Earl Warren was in *his*. Maybe not so loudly nor by as many, but then mainly because he was so often with the minority."

"If you guys will excuse me, I've got a paper to get out," said Gil Dennis.

"If you hear any more of that gossip, I'd appreciate knowing about it, Gil," said John Hagen.

"All the news, all the time," said Gil, waving his hand.

"Quin," said John, "where is the right spot to stand these days? Is there a right spot? Look at me right now—caught between a libel suit for a story on smut pushers and those who think I'm soft on the racket."

"A rock and a hard place," said Quincy Broyles. He was watching John narrowly.

"When the truth is, I haven't yet *done* anything, aside from authorize the Salzman series and refuse to give in to the Reverend Bradshaw Coe on a bad piece of legislation."

"You're fur 'em or you're agin 'em," said Broyles, rapping out his pipe in the metal floor-stand ashtray. "But where in journalism school did they ever teach you you could stand in the middle? Ain't no such place, squire."

"But God damn it, all I'm trying to do is run a decent newspaper!" said John Hagen. He slammed his hand on the desk in a rare display of anger. "Is ordinary common sense out the window in this decade —or are my own values awry? My God, there are important things going on in the world! And I stand impaled on a cross of pornography nailed to total censorship."

"What you have here is a simple visceral issue, John," said Quincy Broyles patiently. "The fluctuation of currency, the significance of the fighting in Nigeria, de Gaulle—who can understand these things? Sex in books—ah! Instant comprehension. Lends itself to quick opinion. Does she or does she not? . . . that is the vital question of the day. The point of the whole argument, squire, is that very few arguments are worth a damn." He peered quizzically.

John frowned. "I don't follow you."

"Simply that on matters sexual my opinion is worth not a particle more than yours—or a particle less. Look, there hasn't been a time in the history of mankind that people haven't been hung up about the sexual urge. Every given society in every time has tried to set rules. Some of them have been extremely weird, and in some societies —even today—extremely cruel. In our own so-called civilized land we have strong overlays of inherited puritanism, an official morality handed us by the church, and a hodgepodge of laws across the fifty states that belong to Hawthorne's age. People look over each other's shoulder, wonder what the other guy knows that they don't, worry about what's 'normal.' The whole thing is highly charged with emotionalism. Yet few of us are able to admit that what we call our ideas are only our personal prejudices. I don't know of any other area, including religion, where so much guff is peddled as gospel with as little foundation."

"How does all that help me?" said John.

"It doesn't. I'm just ruminating. You've taken what I think is a sound position, but again, that's just my own prejudice talking."

"Big help," said John. "Do you think even her hairdresser knows for sure, Quin?"

"If she does, she's not telling it around, squire."

20

"It's up to you, Pete," said Harry Wells. Peter Salzman sat with John Hagen in Harry's tastefully paneled office. Since Salzman's arraignment he had obtained two continuances. Because the two cases were inextricably tied together, the lawyer for the two ex-deputies, Roberts and Hosea, had done likewise.

Harry steepled his hands, his elbows resting on his desk. "The case was paper thin to begin with," he said, speaking as much to John as to Pete Salzman. "I told you that the deputy district attorney, young Greives, had his doubts at your arraignment. But with two officers of the law making the accusation, he had little choice but to follow through. Now, what's happened is that he's been talking with Hilby, our other deputy D.A., the one that issued the complaint against Roberts and Hosea on your charge. Hilby is scheduled to prosecute on that, since Greives couldn't very well prosecute you, then turn around and prosecute *them* on a counter-complaint arising from the same incident. Clear, so far?"

"I follow you," said Pete Salzman quietly.

"Now, enter the attorney for Roberts and Hosea. They are no longer officers of the law, which makes a big difference. So we now have the offer of a deal. Greives is receptive because he's dubious about his chances, and district attorneys don't like to enter cases they don't think they can win. Hilby is not, because he thinks that not only are you going to be acquitted, but that he can nail Roberts and Hosea. But both Greives and Hilby agreed to leave it up to you. Roberts and Hosea will withdraw their charge if you'll agree to drop yours."

"Could I ask you something, Mr. Wells?" said Salzman.

"Of course."

"Why did those two guys file the charge in the first place?"

Wells shrugged. "Having worked you over, which is really all they wanted, they had to book you to give it the semblance of authority.

I think they regretted it the next day, especially when you filed your own complaint."

"What do you think, Mr. Hagen?" said Pete Salzman. He chewed his lip.

John shook his head. "I risk nothing, Pete. You do."

"Yes. Of course there is a chance you might be convicted, Pete," said Harry Wells. "Juries can be funny animals. If it happened, we'd appeal, of course."

"But ultimately, whatever penalty might be handed out, it doesn't involve me or you, Harry," said John. "If there were a jail sentence to be served, Pete is the one who'd have to serve it."

"I know that," said Pete Salzman firmly. "And I've been around that county jail farm. No thanks. I'm still asking you, Mr. Hagen— what would you do?"

"I won't make the choice for you, Pete."

"I didn't ask you to. I asked what *you* would do."

"You get no help from me, Pete, sorry."

"Mr. Wells, what if I was acquitted and they were convicted? Wouldn't I also have the grounds for a civil suit?"

"Of course you would, Pete. However, let me point out that those two men probably have no money. You might win a moral victory but no cash."

"Well," said Salzman, "I'll admit I wanted to punish them, but at least they were fired—maybe that's enough. I don't want to stand trial myself; I'd just like to forget the whole thing."

"I think that's the best choice," said Harry Wells. "I think one phone call to the district attorney's office will do it. I'll get you the word this afternoon."

"By the way, you haven't heard what those two fellows are doing now, have you, Pete?" said John.

"I haven't heard a rumble," said Pete Salzman. He rose to his feet as John did.

"Maybe they'll get out of town now," said John.

PART THREE

21

A red-eyed but triumphant Vic Massoni announced to an equally sleepy John and Kris Hagen at 2 A.M., June fifth, in his Los Angeles campaign headquarters: "I'm in!" They had driven over at his invitation the evening before, to celebrate or commiserate, as the case might be.

The champagne corks started popping at nine o'clock as the early first count from the primary came in from San Francisco, where votes were cast by machine. It favored Massoni over his Democratic opponent, Ernie Gruener, by a substantial thirty-five-thousand-vote margin. "Just between us it doesn't mean a goddamn thing," Vic said quietly to John and Kris as a whoop went up from the large roomful of celebrants. "I figured to be strong there. Ernie voted against a Bay Area Rapid Transit bill and the *Chronicle* and *Examiner* both took out after him. Let's wait and see how Southern California goes —especially main L.A. and San Diego." But by two o'clock the tide seemed to be running heavily for Massoni from nearly everywhere except the cow counties.

"You figure you're in, with only a small part of Los Angeles counted?" said John as a group of tipsy well-wishers wended in and out to slap their candidate on the back.

"Yeah—thanks, Henry, you too, Evan—yeah, those precincts out around Hollywood are the tip-off. The polls showed I was going to lose there and I'm winning. I expect Ernie to concede by ten o'clock in the morning."

The secretary of state's semi-official (but highly accurate) count three days later showed, in the race for attorney general on the Democratic side, Massoni, 1,945,620, to Gruener, 1,404,803. It also showed David O. Hausner narrowly defeating his opposition on the other ticket to become the G.O.P. candidate and Vic Massoni's opponent in the November general election.

A week later the secretary of state announced that the movement called Public United to Restore Innocence to Fair Youth (PURIFY) had filed petitions bearing the signatures of more than one million persons, verified by their respective county clerks to be currently registered voters. He would assign it a number on the general election ballot sometime after July thirty-first, according to the United Press International wire story that John Hagen saw (and published). Number One was already assigned to the Cal-Vet farm and home loan bond issue, the story continued. From a separate source UPI had learned the PURIFY backers were hoping for Number Two.

Late in June there was the surprise announcement from the Weekly *Progress & Green Sheet* that the sheet was to start publishing three times a week, starting in August. "A newly organized, fair-minded, unbiased Conservative newspaper, reflecting the prevailing philosophy of the community," said the announcement blazoned in twelve-point type over the two right-hand columns of page one. John Hagen read the news with outward calm but intense inner irritation. He called in his top staffers as soon as the *Sentinel* had gone to bed.

"I think we're slipping up somewhere here," he told them with icy calm. "You can't have a build-up like this without the word getting around. Dwight, don't you talk to the paper salesmen? And what about new equipment? They can't run three a week with that junk they've got. Will, don't the advertisers talk to your salesmen? A sheet can't step up that much without sounding out the prospects."

"Honest to God, there hasn't been a single rumble, John," Will Naismith protested earnestly.

"You're sure? Well, of course you are, you'd have told me otherwise." John looked around, frowning in concentration.

"Backing," said Quincy Broyles. "Where's the backing coming from?"

"Just what I was thinking," said John Hagen as Dwight Henry, the business manager, nodded. "They'll need a bundle. All right, here's an instruction to everyone: Find out."

As it turned out, John Hagen first learned the information himself. His informant was the president of the Wellbrook First Savings & Trust Company, a stubborn holdout from affiliation with one or another of California's large banking chains. "It's Los Angeles money, John," he told the *Sentinel* publisher over lunch. "Some of it's from the president of Shasta Savings and Loan, a man named Norton."

"Would any of it also come from the Madrone Distributing Company—or do you know?" said John.

"As a matter of fact, yes. How did *you* know?" said his surprised luncheon companion.

"Sheer guess. You're sure of your information?"

"I am." Calmly.

"Where did you get it?"

"I have my sources. It doesn't look as if the Dodgers have much chance at the pennant this year, does it?"

To Quincy Broyles later that afternoon John Hagen said, "I think our PURIFY friends see a chance to do two things—plug their project and try to run me out of business."

"We'll give 'em a race for their money, won't we, John?"

"Oh, that we will, Quin," he said. "That we certainly will."

Midweek seemed the best time to get his workout at the Elks Club. He couldn't always spare the hour and a half it took out of his day, but the afternoon calendar today was fairly light. By arrangement he met his usual group: Buck Benson of Buck Benson Buick, Lawrence Maddox, the certified public accountant, and Foster Blake of the camera store. They had a fast set of four-man handball, John Hagen teaming with the heavyset but quick-moving Benson against the other two. They beat them two games out of three. They all had a quick shower, brief dip in the pool, and another shower before dressing for lunch. Foster Blake detained John Hagen for a moment at the dining room entrance. He seemed a trifle uneasy.

"Not the place to bring this up, John, but the salesman from Madrone Distributing Company was in this morning," he said. "I

carry a heavy line of Higashi opticals and electronics, you know.
Sole franchised dealer, in fact. Cameras, lenses, binoculars, micro-
scopes, tape recorders." He rubbed a palm over his lapels as if to
wipe away perspiration. "Now, I want you to understand this is
none of my doing. I don't even know what the hell it's all about."

"What what's all about, Foster?"

"Well," said Foster Blake nervously, "there seems to be some
doubt about continuing to get the Higashi co-operative schedule of
advertising for the *Sentinel*. I just wanted you to know what he
said."

"For the *Sentinel?* Do you mean, just the *Sentinel?* Or is there a
general cutback?"

"No, the *Sentinel*. He said the word is, it depends which way you
go on something. A word to the wise."

John Hagen ran it over in his mind. "Madrone Distributing Company? Madrone Distributing—oh, yes, it rings a bell. Its president is
a man named Tunman. Perry M. He is an officer in a group that
calls itself Public United to Restore Innocence to Fair Youth."

Foster Blake raised an eyebrow. "Oh, is *that* what the guy was
talking about?"

"Apparently so," said John Hagen. "Well, well."

"You know that Madrone picks up fifty per cent of the tab for
my advertising, don't you, John? I mean, this kind of a thing could
cut the hell out of my twice-weekly insertion."

"A very subtle gesture indeed. Well, Foster, you're caught in the
middle and I'm sorry, but I'm sorrier for Mr. Tunman. Please convey this message to his salesman: the *Sentinel,* effective immediately,
will accept no more Higashi advertising. I'll send you a letter on it
this afternoon, in fact. Now perhaps we'd better join Buck and Larry
in the dining room."

Foster Blake caught his arm. He was a tall, powerful man who
had been a regional tennis champion in his younger days. There was
a note of strain in his voice. "Hey, wait a minute, pal. You can't
do that to me. Now that I know what they want—what's so wrong?
Maybe you better go along if you know what's good for you."

"Take your hand off my arm, Foster," said John Hagen. "That's
better. Please understand me, there is nothing personal in this. But

I've just been threatened in a very distasteful way with a form of economic boycott. It is better termed blackmail. If I knuckle under to that kind of pressure, I'll have to shave in the morning without a mirror. I might expect this of the principal in your distributing house, but not of you. I'm sorry, Foster. I'm canceling out Higashi immediately."

"Well, listen to me good, big shot! You just canceled out Blake Camera too. Maybe you don't know it, Johnny boy, but there's been an awful lot of talk about the *Sentinel* in the last few months. Yeah, and about you, too. I'm not the only one either. Buck Benson in there's another. First, you won't help clean up filth, then you got your staff being arrested right and left; well, Johnny boy, you might just find a lot of people pulling out their ads. Flat on your ass, big boy. Flat on your ass."

"Are you going in to lunch, Foster?"

"You fuckin' well know I am."

"Then would you please offer my regrets to Buck and Larry? I have an urgent appointment back at the office."

"Maybe you won't even have an office one of these days."

"Enjoy your lunch," said John Hagen.

He returned to the *Sentinel* parking lot, entering the city room through the rear door next to the composing room. In the pressroom, he knew, make-ready was in progress, awaiting only the plates for page one and the jump page. Several staffers looked up. City editor Gil Dennis was one. John Hagen signaled for him to come into his office. Quincy Broyles, at his desk calmly chewing a sandwich and drinking milk from a thermos cup, winked placidly, swallowed, and said, "What's the matter, squire?"

"Could you join me in my office when you've finished your lunch, Quin?"

His rotund managing editor gulped the last of his milk and brushed crumbs from his lap. "Just finished."

John nodded shortly and walked along toward his office, glancing into advertising director Will Naismith's cubicle. He was out, probably at lunch with an advertiser. Dwight Henry, the business manager, was busy at an open ledger in his own office.

"Staff session, Dwight. Can you tear yourself away for ten minutes or so?" said John Hagen.

Dwight, a dry-as-dust middle-aged bachelor whose camellias were a passion nearly equal to that for a clean set of books, adjusted his glasses. "Certainly, John, certainly," he said. There was no curiosity in his voice or expression. To Dwight Henry, what was, was.

Gil Dennis and Quincy Broyles both entered his office ahead of him. Dwight Henry followed shortly. John Hagen buzzed Mary on the telephone intercom. "Please leave word for Mr. Naismith to join us at a staff meeting in my office when he returns, would you, Mary?"

"Yes, Mr. Hagen."

"Make yourselves comfortable, fellows," said John. Quincy and Gil Dennis chose spots at either end of the brown leather sofa. Dwight Henry perched on a chair facing John's desk. John picked up a long-bladed copy shears, a desk top decoration, souvenir of his days on the *Daily Trojan*. He tested the points idly with a forefinger. He looked around at his top staff. A better crew no publisher could ask for—these men, together with the absent Will Naismith. Men who knew their jobs, who were dependable, who liked the sheet they worked for. Quincy Broyles had been with him from the beginning and Dwight Henry almost as long; Gil, half that time, but he had nailed down his job solidly in his first week; and Will Naismith was in his sixth year, three as advertising manager. An excellent staff, one to be proud of.

"I've just come from a most curious encounter," said John Hagen. "If I seem put out, it's because I am. Maybe I had best review our position so—oh, hello, Will. You're back early."

Will Naismith was a grinning, sandy-haired man whose choice of suits today was a gray tweed. He waved his hand at the assembly in general. "The ad director of that new supermarket they're building ten miles out on Central Boulevard," he said. "The competition's after him too. Right now he's very noncommittal and busy, so we cut it short. What's the mafia session for?"

"Have a seat," John Hagen said unnecessarily. Naismith had already selected a chair next to Dwight Henry and flopped down on it. "I had just told the others I've just had a weird and highly annoying experience. Now, all of you here have been through some campaigns with me. We had the battle of the schoolbooks and the fluoridation hassel. You'll remember we got quite a lot of heat in each case—some canceled subscriptions, a lot of abusive mail, and some direct confrontation both here in the office and personally, outside. We may be in for another tussle. A different sort. It may amount to nothing, but I feel it is necessary for me to warn you that it could be more."

"What's up?" said Will Naismith, eager as always to move the conversation along. It was part of what made him a good salesman; he could interrupt without giving offense.

John Hagen looked down at the copy shears. "As you know," he continued, as if no one had spoken, "we've been the object of attack in a minor way. I refer to the *Progress and Green Sheet* and Reverend Coe's PURIFY. So far, the so-called attack has resulted in nothing more than my getting a lot of good-natured ribbing plus some nasty letters and phone calls. Most of the ribbing good-natured, that is, and none of it bad. 'Has resulted' should read 'had resulted.' Not a half-hour ago I experienced something truly vicious. One of my handball partners and sometimes opponent, Mr. Foster Blake of Blake Cameras, delivered a none too veiled threat to cancel his advertising. In justice, I should say it wasn't his idea. It was that of his Higashi supplier, the Madrone Distributing Company. The principal, Quin"—he nodded at Quincy Broyles, who nodded in return—"is of course Perry M., as in Mike, Tunman, prominently identified with the PURIFY movement. Go for PURIFY or we pull our co-op schedule was the blunt warning. Brace yourself, Will. I've told Mr. Blake to pass the word back that as of this moment, Higashi advertising is out of the *Sentinel*. Will you this afternoon write and send a letter to Blake so informing him, and why?"

Will Naismith shrugged and nodded. "If you say so, John."

"Actually," John added dryly, "it's merely a formality. Mr. Foster Blake turned extremely ugly and informed me that I had just canceled the entire Blake schedule."

Dwight Henry clucked. "That's a good account, John."

"In terms of how much?"

"Something like two hundred and fifty dollars a week."

"Average?"

"Well, yes. He goes much heavier at Christmas, of course."

"I suppose we'll just have to get along without it," said John Hagen. "That's not the whole story, of course. If it were, I wouldn't have bothered calling you in. As I say, I may be taking an alarmist position, but what I know, you all should know. Mr. Foster Blake then most charmingly informed me that there, in his words, has been a lot of talk about the *Sentinel* and a lot of talk about me in the last few months. By Buck Benson, for one, he said. That I might just find a lot of others pulling out their ads. Any questions so far?"

Quincy Broyles rapped his pipe sharply against the floor-stand metal ashtray. "That kind of chicken maneuver, eh, John? I've seen it before personally. It can hurt sometimes, but usually it never amounts to a fart in a windstorm."

"I'm not pressing the panic button on the basis of one angry advertiser," said John Hagen.

"Of course, if there was an organized conspiracy, that would be something else," Quincy Broyles said, testing the draw on his pipe, removing it to load it from a leather pouch. "The most recent case I know of was when the gamblers ganged up on Hank Greenspun over in Las Vegas a few years ago. He took it to court and got a ruling that if they advertised in the *Review-Journal* they must also advertise in the *Sun*. That's something to keep in mind."

"I remember the case," said John Hagen. "I'm not sure that applies here—nor, as I've said, that it is even going to happen. But I want you all to look out for any indicator that this might be anything more than one petulant individual."

"Wouldn't Will be likelier than anyone else to pick up on that?" said Gil Dennis, scratching his chin. Gil's cold green eyes, set deep in a rather narrow face, flicked over at Will Naismith.

"Most directly, yes," said John. "But cityside might also overhear rumblings, if any. I want to know immediately if they do. It could have a very direct bearing on my own actions."

"How do you mean that, John?" said Quincy Broyles. He emitted a weak puff of smoke.

"Well, as you know, I've elected so far to lie doggo on PURIFY. It's my feeling that even adverse publicity is what these people want to help their movement along. If it starts gaining in the polls and begins to look possible—well, we'll see. How do the rest of you feel about it? Quin?"

Broyles fumbled for a wooden match. Flicking it on his thumbnail, he fired his furnace again. "Known you for ten years, John. I don't" —*puff, puff*—"really think you need my opinion, because I suspect you know exactly what you'll do in the contingency you speak of. But"—*puff, puff*—"since you ask, I'll say it. I'd tell them to bugger off. I never liked pressure from a reader, an advertiser, or my own wife, and I'm too old to change now. I think the strategy is sound. Ignore them as long as you can. Comes a time you can't, tear off a strip of their hide and lash them with it."

The quiet hum of a small electric clock on John Hagen's desk intruded during a moment of silence. Then all felt a slight tremor and heard a muted thunder as the web press cranked up.

"Dwight?" said John.

Dwight Henry cleared his throat twice. "I don't know what to say, John. I'm better at running your business office than—well, I'm not a newspaperman, never pretended to be. The operation's in fine shape financially. You know that. I guess if we dropped a lot of accounts it could hurt us, but right now we're well above the line. I'm sorry I can't have an opinion on this other thing."

"Will?" said John Hagen.

Naismith spread his hands. "You know the competitive picture, John. Radio, plus the neighboring dailies when an account is out in fringe territory and can go either way. And of course the *Green Sheet*. I don't know how much that jerk outfit is going to hurt us, but I can guess. My experience is that most advertisers never get the results from a shopper that they can from a regular, well-established daily. Times that I know of it's been tried, the big accounts, like your department stores, nearly always find out they're hurting. Sooner or later they switch back."

"We've taken up enough time now," said John. "We'll just keep our eyes and ears open."

He had accepted the Friday invitation weeks before, thinking, naturally, that Kris would be attending with him. But late this afternoon he had just scratched a line through the notation *Art/Gdn Recptn* when Mrs. Harold B. (Lavinia) Brakebill, of the Lemon Hill Brakebills, called. Besides her efforts on behalf of the Wellbrook Women's League for Good Government, Lavinia Brakebill was allied with Mayor Jack Ronreif's wife in two cultural activities: the Globe Repertory Players and the Wellbrook Art and Garden Society (WAGS). Kris was slightly under the weather, and John Hagen first had feebly tried to plead that as an excuse. Mrs. Brakebill was not to be put off. "You must come, Mr. Hagen, with or without your wife," she said crisply. "This is the official preview of our semi-annual art show and we expect you." Because Harold B. Brakebill was a member of the family that held controlling interest in the Lemon Hill Shopping Center and owned outright the larger of two Ford dealerships, a hardware, and a quality furniture store, it had seemed politic to capitulate gracefully.

The Art and Garden Center, a sprawling one-story building of wood, glass, and fieldstone a half mile from the "old city," was heavily crowded this evening. The society arranged three major affairs annually: an art exhibition early in the year and again in summertime, and a flower showing in April. Other, smaller events were sandwiched in between. Tonight, Wellbrook's moneyed and social and civic figures had come to sip champagne, stroll the many passages created by fixed and movable panels, and view the paintings and statuary created by an ever-growing colony of regional artists. The week-long showing would be open to lesser citizens starting the following evening.

John Hagen, freshly shaved and wearing a dark suit, moved slowly through the throng. He was greeted everywhere—by Lavinia Brakebill and her husband, a compact, harmlessly glowering man in his forties; by the schools superintendent, Elliott Warren; by

Mayor and Mrs. Jack Ronreif; by dozens of others. Many asked whether his wife was with him. From time to time there was the lightning flicker of a strobe light as one of Mike Brescia's two photographers took group shots under Maggie Mellody's direction. The champagne moved briskly at two separate cloth-draped tables. A brassy combo in a corner added to the din of the conversation.

Momentarily by himself, John Hagen stood in front of a huge splash of blacks and whites labeled "OPUS II," bearing the price tag of $250. He mused that none of the artists underestimated his or her worth.

"Would you buy it?" said Maggie Mellody softly.

"Oh, hello, Maggie. It does have a certain appeal, doesn't it?"

"I wouldn't either," she said.

"Where's Ben?" he said, referring to the *Sentinel* photographer.

"I turned him loose to shoot a few *objets d'art* without people. We got about all the group poses we needed. Where is Mrs. Hagen?"

"She doesn't feel very well this evening. How do you like this one?"

"You wouldn't think me a lady if I said."

"It does have a certain—mm, ah "

"Titled 'Regeneration.' "

"I'm afraid we both do see the same thing. Are you enjoying yourself?"

Maggie rolled her eyes comically. She was stunning in a short-skirted green dress and matching bracelet with dangly earrings that set off her high-piled dark hair.

"It's the usual traffic," she said. She patted her handbag. "I've notes on messers and mezdams that look like the same messers and mezdams from the last ten occasions . . . or affairs, as we social writers term it."

"Hey, Mag—'scuse me, Mr. Hagen," said a short, blond young man who was strapped up with camera gear.

"Hello, Benny," said John Hagen.

"Need some help, Ben?" said Maggie.

"No, but I wonder, you said you wanted this stuff first thing in the morning. I need about two hours to soup it up and print it. It's nine o'clock. . . ."

"In other words, you want to take off?"

"Yeah," said the young man. "You ready?"

"I wasn't quite, but if you have to leave," said Maggie. To John she said, "Ben's got the wheels."

"Is there a problem?" said John Hagen. "Is it a question of a ride?"

"Oh, heavens, I wouldn't impose."

"Not at all."

"That's awfully kind," said Maggie. "Go ahead, Ben. I want an eight-ten of the best shot of each group and whatever good shots you got separately."

"On your desk tonight. Good night, Mr. Hagen, Maggie."

"Good night, Benny," said John.

"Oh there you are!" exclaimed Mrs. Jack Ronreif. "Mr. Hagen, I do so want to talk to you for just a moment about the City Center. Could I drag him away for a while, Mrs. Mellody?"

"In about half an hour?" said John.

"Fine," said Maggie Mellody.

Mrs. Ronreif, a pleasantly slender woman in her thirties, took John Hagen's arm and steered him to a group that included her husband, Lavinia Brakebill and her husband, and a youthful man with intense eyes and a sparse black beard. They had chosen a spot too near the brassy combo, a distinct handicap to conversation.

"I found him," said Mrs. Ronreif. "Mr. Hagen, I'd like you to meet Dr.—" It sounded like "Frannis" but John Hagen couldn't be sure. He leaned in.

"The doctor is professor of dramaturgy at the state college," Mrs. Ronreif said to John. "We're talking about the need for the City Center."

"—But of course you people need a cultural center," said the professor after draining his champagne glass. "Oh yes, thank you, I will"—as Harold B. Brakebill took the glass from him and went in search of a refill. "I can't see that it should even be necess'ry to argue the point."

"But Mr. Hagen here doesn't think so," said Mayor Jack Ronreif jovially. "Do you, John?"

"You're not exactly stating my—"

"Oh, re-a-lly?" said the professor. "For what reason do you oppose a City Center, Mr. Hagen, or is it on the same old tired grounds of cost?"

"Cost against need," said John Hagen. "It seems to me that possibly on a scaled-down—"

"But, my dear man, you've a highly prosperous community here, one that's lit'rally crying out for a center of the arts. The money can be *found,* don't you see?"

"We need a new high school, which I regard as the first—"

"I don't see why we can't have—" said Mrs. Ronreif.

"It seems to me—" said Lavinia Brakebill.

"I see no issue of a choice between guns and butter, as it were," said the professor, raising his voice. "Naturally you need a new school, and you shall vote it, and you shall maintain your streets and support your fire department and all that, but along with these facts of daily government, you clearly have in this community the wealth to build, as well, a core of creativity; it is not enough to say, 'That would be nice if we could afford it,' because you *can* afford . . ."

John Hagen closed the door of the Imperial behind Maggie Mellody and came around to get in behind the wheel.

"Always at work, aren't you, John?" said Maggie, smiling.

"It goes with the territory." He started the engine. It purred softly. "Let's see, you live north, don't you, Maggie?"

"Mm-hm." She tucked one leg under her and placed her arm on the back of the seat. "This is nice of you."

"How is the bug running?"

"Very well, thank you. It's a good little car."

They cruised north, Maggie humming a little tune to herself, past the Freeway West upramp and under the freeway itself past the city limits, entering a brief stretch of industrial park area, beyond which lay a residential tract. Presently there were spot-zoned clusters of business establishments.

"May I be terribly bold?" said Maggie Mellody.

"That wholly depends on the area of boldness."

"How would you like to buy me a nightcap?"

"Don't you have a sitter situation?"

"No. That is, yes, but she keeps them all night when I'm out on evening assignment. She lives quite close; it's a very nice arrangement."

"I'd be pleased to buy you a nightcap. Any suggestions?"

"Oh, there are any number of places along here. In fact, just ahead there on the right—see it?"

"I do." He slowed and pulled to curbside by a one-story white building marked by a red neon sign of a martini glass and olive in outline. The roof was limned by two parallel tubes of neon.

"Gaudy but clean," Maggie Mellody decided.

Inside, a girl in a quite abbreviated black skirt and black net stockings looked over at them, as did the bartender. Two couples occupied a booth on the right toward the rear, where the jukebox was throbbing with the emphatic beat of a rock number. Another couple had their heads together at the bar. John Hagen looked at Maggie, inclining his head toward a near booth against the mirrored wall.

"Fine," she said. He moved the table so that she could slide in more easily. He followed. The girl in the abbreviated skirt and black net stockings came over and took their orders.

"That champagne," said Maggie. "I can't handle it." She moved to cross her legs. There was a whoop of laughter from the foursome at the rear. "Ten to one, a dirty joke," said Maggie.

"I won't take the odds."

The girl brought their drinks and made change on the webbed lining of the tray, leaving the tray. Maggie lifted her glass.

"Well . . ."

"Our very good health," said John.

Maggie lighted a cigarette and exhaled, making a small *O* of her full lips, resting her chin on the hand that held the cigarette.

"Mama's ill tonight, huh?"

"Just a little touch of something or other."

"She seems like such a nice person."

"Thank you. Do you have any folks, Maggie?"

"Only a father, and he lives in the Middle West. Iowa. I haven't seen him in five or six years. He didn't approve of my marriage in college. He was right, of course. He met my second husband only once. He didn't approve of him, either. We've hardly anything in common—if we ever had. He's a retired salesman, lives with a brother and his wife on their farm. I grew up in the Middle West, but it's not my dish. I think I'd prefer the East. So saying, I find myself a Californian." She made a little *moue,* lifting her drink once more.

"You were divorced three years ago?"

"Yes. A little more than."

"I don't want to get terribly personal—"

"Oh, go ahead."

"I just wonder that a pretty woman like you wouldn't have found someone by this time. Or that someone wouldn't have found you, to say it better."

She looked at him carefully. "I wasn't planning to tell you for a long time, but I have to," she said. "I've found a somebody."

"No!" said John. "Do I know the lucky guy?"

"As a matter of fact, you do," she said. "It's Vic Massoni."

"V—well, I'll be a striped ape! Vic! Where in the world did you ever meet him?"

"It was about a month ago. There was a Wullug—Wellbrook Women's League for Good Government meeting I covered. He was there and someone introduced us. We've—seen each other a few times since. Not enough with this political race, darn it."

"Maggie, I'm delighted! Why did you keep it such a secret?"

"Because I didn't dare think he could be for real. I learned he was."

"Real as real." He clapped his hand lightly to his forehead. "Sometimes I wonder what I use for brains. I could have introduced you two a long time ago."

"Do you think I'm doing the right thing, John?"

"I'd bet on it."

She smiled. "I'm scared, John. Gosh, the third time—it's just gotta work."

"I know it will. I guess that means I'm going to lose a good society editor. When's it going to be?"

"Right after the election, win, lose, or draw. Yes, I'll be leaving the paper."

"Let's have another drink on this development."

The waitress again took their order.

"You know," said Maggie, "I'll be glad to get out of the rat race
—the personal rat race, I mean. I'd almost given up hope, to tell
you the truth. That's why I can't believe my good luck even yet.
Oh, don't misunderstand me, there were plenty of men quite willing
to provide the therapy they were sure I needed. All in the spirit of
willing self-sacrifice, of course. I've even had a few proposals along
with the propositions. But you'd be surprised how few truly eligible
unmarried men there are." She grimaced. "Or how many married
men looking for a fast romp, for that matter." She looked at him
earnestly. "I really hated the rat race, but I'll be perfectly frank,
I'd have gone stark staring mad without adult companionship once
in a while. And that's the rat race. Yet I didn't want to be promiscu-
ous either and I don't think I was. I—"

"Stop," said John Hagen. He held up his hand.

"Don't be silly, you haven't been cross-examining. In fact, that's
one of the things I respect about you. I think your wife must be a
very lucky woman. Does she know it?"

"Thank you, Maggie," he said, without answering her.

"I'm way out of bounds, I know that. Maybe it's the alcohol. Do
you know, I thought of making a pass at you one time?"

"No, and I'm glad you didn't. I don't know what I'd have done."

"Tell me something, John?"

"If I can."

"Have you ever been unfaithful to your wife?"

He took a drag on his cigarette before answering. "No," he said.

"Never came close?"

He shrugged. "It depends on what you mean by close."

"Close."

He considered it. "Yes, I did. There was a time or two. Once at
a CNPA convention I got a wide-open invitation—she couldn't have
made her meaning clearer. There was an interval between the time
she offered and the—appointment. I chickened out. Since I had
planned to go, I suppose you could say I was unfaithful."

Maggie Mellody smiled. "Did you ever tell her—your wife?"

He returned her smile. "No, I may make my share of mistakes, but I'm not essentially stupid."

She regarded him through half-closed eyes. "What about—? No, I shouldn't ask."

"Has Kris ever been unfaithful to me? No, I don't think so."

"Would you want to know about it if she had?"

He hesitated. "No."

"Do you think you would leave her if she had and you found out about it?"

"I can't even think about it. Would I leave her? How can I say? I think that if she ever wanted *me* to leave, I would."

"Why don't you just tell me to shut my big drunken mouth?"

"You're neither drunk nor do you have a big mouth. You have a woman's natural curiosity."

"Tell me about Vic, John."

"Well, that's a pretty big order. We were classmates—you know that. He lost his wife—you probably know that too." She nodded. "He's my best friend and I think he's going a long way in politics. He has a driving ambition. I don't think he'll even be satisfied with attorney general, if he makes it. Governor, maybe; U. S. Senator, possibly. Maybe even higher. You're in for a rocket ride, Maggie."

She hugged herself. "I can hardly wait."

He glanced at his watch. "I think I'd better be getting you home and myself home. Okay?"

"Ready any time you are, Mr. De Mille."

John Hagen usually was a careful driver, as he was careful in everything he did. What happened, then, was simply the result of split-second indecision at the amber light at the intersection of Centinela with Rosebury, followed by the wrong choice. Rather than screech to a panic stop, he elected to step down on the accelerator. The light turned red before he was halfway across. A pickup truck whose driver was timing the changing of the lights on Rosebury roared down on him, horn blaring furiously. In a desperate instant of shrilling tires and the horrendous clash of metal John Hagen felt his car slewing, righting, stopping, and he heard the tinkle of glass.

"I guess I did it that time," said John, feeling pretty stupid. "Are you all right?"

"Scared, otherwise okay. You?"

"I'm fine, but, my Lord, Kris's car! Well, let's see just how bad it is." Already cars were stopping as he got out. A young man was running up from the far side of the broad intersection.

"You run the goddamn light, you son of a bitch!" he yelled hysterically. He couldn't have been much more than twenty—dark, lean, and muscular. He fetched up breathlessly in front of John, tensed as if ready for combat. "You ruint my goddamn pickup, you bastard! Lemme see your goddamn driver's license!"

"Calm down, son, everything's insured." The youth, he decided, was more frightened than angry, and also in a hurry to establish blame. "You may have been coming a little fast."

"Goddammit, you run the light! What am I s'posed to do, fly over you? Now lemme see your driver's license!"

"Will one of you people call the highway patrol?" said John Hagen to the dozen or so deadpan spectators who had gathered. No one moved. John heard a man's voice say with satisfaction: "Man, an Imperial, reckon that's five hundred bucks' repair work right there, easy."

"Yeah, 'n' how about the front end of that pickup?"

"Maggie, would you call the highway patrol?" said John. She had got out of the car and come round to stand by him. "You *are* all right, aren't you?" he said. He was still considerably shaken himself.

"Just scared, but it's all over. Thank God no one's injured."

"My goddamn neck hurts somepm awful," said the young man angrily.

"I'll call," said Maggie. She was anticipated. A motorcycle idled down. A husky officer in the tan uniform of the California Highway Patrol put down his kickstand and dismounted, drawing off his gloves, looking around as he did so. His radio honked something loud and incomprehensible. He lifted the microphone and said something into it. "Ten-four!" blared the voice of the dispatcher. The officer walked over.

"Hey, listen, Officer, this guy—" said the young man.

"Wait a minute. Is anybody hurt?" said the patrolman.

"Yeah, my neck hurts," said the young man. The officer stared at him. The young man glared back defiantly.

"Are you one of the drivers?" said the officer.

"That's my pickup over there."

"How bad does your neck hurt? Can you move your head?"

"Well, it hurts when I do," said the young man, who wore blue Levi's and a gray jersey and sported long sideburns.

"Do you need an ambulance?" said the patrolman.

"Naw, I guess not."

"Are you the driver of this vehicle, sir?" the patrolman said to John Hagen.

"Yes, I am."

"Let's have a look at it." The officer moved past John around to the right rear, John following. The fender was thoroughly crumpled and the bumper and rear deck considerably mangled. "Look, will you drive forward out of the intersection?" said the patrolman. "The tire's going to rub but it's only about twenty feet. I think the tow truck can pull that fender out with the winch. You do that while I get a look at the other car. All right, everybody, clear the intersection! Come on, now, get out of the street! You wait for me by your car if you would, sir."

"He run the goddamn red light!" the young man complained to the officer, tagging along as the patrolman strode off to the far side of the intersection. "Just shot right out in front . . ."

"It happened so fast," Maggie Mellody said. They were sitting in the car. The officer had moved his motorcycle out of the street and set out flares. Meanwhile a highway patrol sedan with two more men had arrived. One of the two helped the motorcycle officer take skid measurements while the other held a flare and directed traffic around them. About twenty persons strolled from the Imperial to the pickup and back on changes of the light, admiring the damage.

"I'm afraid it was my fault," said John Hagen. "He did come sliding through pretty fast, but he had the light with him."

"Now then," said the motorcycle patrolman a few minutes later, "let me see your driver's license please, sir." He studied it a moment and looked up. "Aren't you the publisher, sir?"

"Right," said John.

"I'm sorry, sir, but I'm going to have to cite you. The evidence is that you ran the light."

"Well, we had the yellow light part of the way through, and the other man was really barreling," said John.

"I'm going to cite him too, if it will make you feel any better," said the officer calmly. "You were both at fault to some extent. I'd say you and Mrs. Hagen were pretty lucky you didn't get hurt pretty bad."

"I am not Mrs. Hagen," said Maggie Mellody.

— *23* —

Normally John did not go to his office on Saturday. Today was an exception. A number of minor tasks that he had shoveled to one side awaited his attention. Kris had accepted his story of how the Imperial had been damaged, including the part about giving Maggie a ride home. He did not mention the drinks. On Monday, he said, he'd turn it over to the insurance people and get it fixed. He returned home late in the afternoon. Kris was on him almost as soon as he had closed his own front door.

"I thought we had an unlisted number," she said sharply.

"We do."

"Well, it isn't private any more. I've had two of those calls in the last half-hour."

"Dirty?"

"Worse. Threatening."

"Well, we'll get it changed again."

"How did they get the number?"

"Haven't you given it out to people you know? Perhaps you have it listed in one or another of your membership rosters."

"I hadn't thought of that. The bulletin of the Women's League carried my name and address and telephone number this month."

"So there you are."

Her hand went to her mouth in sudden dismay. "But do you realize what that could mean? That someone *I* might know has—connections."

"Yes." He looked at her steadily.

"But that's frightening. I might expect this from strangers. Not from people we know."

"The question is, what's it all about?"

Her expression was exasperated. "Because of this silly PURIFY thing and your refusal to speak up on it. Now even friends of ours may be turned against us over this nasty business."

"Some friends."

The telephone rang. Kris started perceptibly. "Not another?" she said tensely.

John lifted the receiver and said hello.

"Do you know where your kids are right now, Hagen?" said a man's voice hoarsely.

"Identify yourself," said John sharply.

"I don't need to, you commie bastard. But if you think anything of those kids, you'll sell that cheap, filthy newspaper as fast as you can and get the hell out of Wellbrook."

"Your call is being recorded and monitored," said John. "Hello?"

He returned to the living room to find Kris looking at the *Sentinel,* somehow too intently. Without looking up, she said, "It doesn't seem to me as if any family should have to put up with this."

"What do you suggest we do, Krissy?"

"I feel a wind, a current. Those nasty rumors about you. These telephone calls. The feeling that even our friends may be deserting us. I feel all of a sudden that something is going to happen to everything we have—wash it all away. John, I'm just plain scared!"

"Hon, there's nothing to be afraid of. Any coward can make a telephone call. Suppose I do strike out with a strong editorial. I think it would only intensify things."

"You'd at least clarify your position, John Hagen."

"And then what?"

"Oh, I don't know. I guess I really don't know anything any more."

At table Sunday night, Gordo unexpectedly blurted out: "Dad, what's this business about you and some kind of political thing?"

"That is a good, broad question," said John, buttering his baked potato. "Could you narrow it down a little?"

"Well, like a couple of the guys were sayin', you know, you were supposed to do something you wouldn't do, or like that. Something to do with—uh—books. You know."

Pam peered at her brother from behind her harlequin glasses. She wore them to correct a mild hypermetropia—a word she had discovered meant far-sightedness and delighted in using. "I know what he means," she said. "PURIFY, isn't it, Daddy?"

"What's with this 'he means' bit?" demanded Gordo. "I'm right here across the table, kid."

"I will have no squabbling," said Kris. "Yes, that is what Gordo refers to. It is something certain people are talking about. About the *Sentinel,* your father's newspaper, and a political campaign called PURIFY. Your father has been asked to endorse it. He will not, nor will he speak out against it. He will not tell the people why. That is about right, isn't it, dear?"

"Just a little slanted, but essentially correct, yes, hon. The *Sentinel* believes the measure is bad and will not support it."

"Saying a newspaper believes or does not believe is a formal, in fact rather strained, way of saying its publisher believes or does not believe," said Kris.

"Gosh, are you guys fighting?" said Gordo.

"What business is that of yours?" said Pam.

"What business is it of yours what business it is of mine?"

"I do believe that if you two children cannot utter one single word without this eternal bickering back and forth I shall go mad," said Kris. "Pamela, do you know that almost every time your brother says something you tease him?"

"I'm sorry, Mother. But he's got no business to ask—"

"Your father and I *do* disagree on this point, in answer to Gordo's question. I don't think you would call it fighting."

"What did the couple of guys say about me?" said John Hagen.

"Well, like, it was their folks said, you know, that there must be something wrong with the *Sentinel,* it wouldn't sort of do what it was s'posed to. I didn't make this up, Dad. One of the guys said his old man said there must be something wrong with a newspaper that didn't want to clean up—p'nography?"

Kris clapped down her fork on her plate. "Said what!"

"Well, you know. I mean, that's all this guy said."

"And what is this guy's name, Gordo?" said Kris.

"Uh, Benny. Benny Giordano."

"Is that Doctor Giordano's son by any chance?" said Kris.

"Yeah, his old man's a doctor. Yeah, that's the guy."

"My, we're getting quite a reputation. Wouldn't you say so, dear?"

"Well, Krissy, people are entitled to their opinions," said John Hagen. "I'm sorry if the good respectable doctor thinks I'm in league with the devil. On the other hand, you will recall that Doctor Giordano believes the United States should have used the hydrogen bomb in Vietnam, and is one of the few medical men I know of who stoutly opposes fluoridation of our drinking water. Which remains unfluoridated, by the way, thanks to him and others."

"I wonder that you couldn't, for heaven's sake, speak up once— just once—to explain yourself?" said Kris grimly. "Once, for my sake, for the children's sake?"

"Aw, Benny Giordano don't bother me none," said Gordo.

"If I have to defend myself against the Giordanos of this community, maybe I'd better get into some other line of work," said John Hagen.

"There are some innocent bystanders, too."

"Are we truly hurting, Kris? Is my business off any? Is this nonsense costing any of us our health or appetite?"

"Well, it's causing me embarrassment—and as you have just heard, embarrassment to your children."

"What can we do, Krissy?"

"I don't know. I'm getting to be a bundle of nerves. Children, you are excused."

The Monday morning *Progress & Green Sheet* carried a delightful page-one story. Running under a three-column headline:

Sentinel Publisher Is Unhurt
But Cited in Auto Accident

it concluded:

> Woodcock, who was also cited, claimed neck injuries. Neither Hagen nor his passenger, a Mrs. Maggie Mellody, was hurt in the 10:30 P.M. crash.

"Well, I see we're getting ample publicity," was Kris's caustic reaction that night. The next evening she was forbiddingly silent. The children were quick to notice, John saw, but were too tactful to comment. Presently Pam and Gordo left the table. Kris began removing the dirty dishes.

"Let me help," John suggested. She shrugged. In deep thought, he stacked some plates and carried them to the kitchen. They crossed paths on his return trip. When he came back into the kitchen with the rest of the load, she was spraying warm water over the dishes preparatory to putting them in the dishwasher. He sat down at the kitchenette table, which was near the sink. She glanced at him meaningfully.

"Where are the kids?" she said.

"Gone upstairs, I believe."

"That's good."

"All right, what's on your mind, Krissy?"

"What makes you think anything's on my mind?"

"Let's quit playing games."

Without a word she reached into her apron pocket and pulled out a folded paper. She tossed it on the table. He frowned and opened it.

Dear Mrs. Haggen [he read]

Why don't you ask your husband what he and that Melody female was doin in the bar together about a half an hour before that accident last Fri. nite?

A. Nony Mouse

John looked up. "Well?"

"She's very pretty, isn't she, John?"

"Maggie is a very pretty woman, Kris. And this is pretty rotten."

"Yes, I think so too."

"Hon, don't read something into this that isn't there."

"Oh, what makes you think I'm doing that?"

"Yes, I bought her a drink on the way home."

"Yes, I know you did."

"Well, where's the harm in that?"

"None whatsoever. Just one tiny, tiny thing, John. You forgot to tell me about it."

"I can't see that it makes any difference."

"Then why didn't you tell me?"

"I didn't tell you something else, either. For your information, Maggie told me that she's going with Vic Massoni and that they're going to get married."

The news cracked her facade. She turned toward him, eyebrow raised. "Vic and this—woman—are going to get married?"

"That's right, Vic Massoni and Maggie Mellody, it seems, met each other about a month ago and have been going together."

Her air of studied indifference returned. "I wish them every happiness," she said. "And you too, dear. I'm going away for a while."

"You're what!"

"I'm going to visit my mother in San Francisco."

"You're—for how long?"

"Oh, a week maybe."

"I see. Are you taking the children?"

"No, Gordo's got his summer job at the pharmacy, and Pam is planning some kind of outing with one of her friends."

"What about the cooking?"

"Mrs. Glade will come in full time. She's a very good cook. Oh, and too old to bother you."

"Kris, there is absolutely nothing going on between me and Maggie Mellody!"

"I'm glad to hear you say so."

"Well, it's true, goddamn it!"

"Did I say I doubted your word?"

"Well, it's pretty obvious you do."

He stared at her. She was making much more of her small task than it justified.

"When are you going?" he said.

"Tomorrow. I've already talked to Mother."

"Hell, you don't even like her."

"I haven't seen her in so long. She *is* getting old."

"I wish you wouldn't go," he said.

"You haven't considered my feelings on this bad publicity we've been getting, thanks to you. I see no reason to consider yours now. You know I've been upset. Now I learn you've been buying drinks for one of your female employees and hiding it from me."

"Oh, Lord, you'd think I'd been sleeping with her." She turned to him again, eyebrow lifted. He shrugged helplessly. "All right, think what you like. I've told you the truth but you want to believe something else."

"I didn't say anything. Should you have a guilty conscience?"

"What are you going to do in San Francisco anyway? Ride the cable cars? Visit Fleishshacker Zoo? Feed the pigeons in Union Square?"

"Oh, I'm sure I'll find something to do," she said.

Wellbrook was served four times daily by a twin-engine helicopter to and from the Los Angeles International Airport. There Kris would board a PSA jet and be at San Francisco International within the hour.

"Send me a funny card from Fisherman's Wharf," said John. "A view of Alcatraz: 'Wish you were here.'"

"Try to behave," said Kris. She kissed the air by his cheek and walked away, hips swinging, as the young man who doubled as office manager and dispatcher opened the wire mesh gate. A youth was loading luggage for a half-dozen passengers. The agent brought up the rear and handed a manifest to someone inside the chopper. He released the latch that held the door open. A hand caught it as it swung in. A few seconds later a starting engine whined, an engine coughed, a puff of dirty smoke was whipped away in the north wind, and the long, floppy blade began to turn. Its counterrotating mate moved, picked up speed. Suddenly the young man made an upward movement of his hand. The downward draft whipped his pants legs. He ducked away, holding his hand to his cap. Within seconds the ungainly craft was up and gone, taking its clatter with it. John walked slowly back to his car, feeling suddenly lost.

On the way to the office his anger began to rise. By the time he walked through the rear door from the parking lot he was seething with icy rage. They (whoever "they" might be) were going to run him out of the community with rumors and anonymous letters, were they? Quincy Broyles waved at him as John passed his office. He nodded to him. He strode into his own office, shut the door, and instructed the switchboard operator to intercept all calls. He jerked the cover from the typewriter, fed a book of copy paper into it, and stared at the machine for a full five minutes. Then his fingers began to dance over the old Underwood.

−24−

Late in the morning Vic Massoni called from Sacramento. After the preliminary chitchat, he said, "Main reason for the call, Johnny, is my oil severance bill. It went to interim study just before adjournment, you know. They're starting hearings on it next week and I want a little grass-roots support for it."

"You know where the measure's going, don't you, Vic?" He waved at Maggie Mellody as she passed his door and got a warm smile in response.

"Sure. It's got all the chance of a clam in a kitchen. But I'm going to bang the drums as loud as I can. One of these days the California taxpayer is going to realize what a free ride these fat cats are getting."

"Besides which, they won't contribute to your campaign."

"Besides which, they won't contribute to my campaign."

"I can put my heart into that one, Vic—and have before. Are you sending a release, or what?"

"A short covering release and a position statement to all the papers today."

"Fine. By the way, you old SOB, congratulations."

"On what?"

"Maggie told me."

"She did, did she? Well, doggone her!"

"You're getting a great gal there, Vic."

"I know it, pal, I know it. So how are Kris and the kids?"

"Fine. Kris should have landed in San Francisco about two hours ago. We'll be making do with a housekeeper for a few days."

"That's right, Kris's mother lives up there—down there—whichever it is."

"Yes, that's where she is."

"Nothing wrong with the old lady, is there, Johnny?"

"Don't try to entrap me with questions like that, counselor. If you refer to the good woman's health, I believe it is all that might be desired."

"I know you love her dearly, old buddy. You give me a good editorial now, hear me?"

"Just rush me the material."

"Will do. By the way, I may be in the city in the next few days. I'll give Kris a call if you'll trust me with the number."

"I haven't got it here, but it's under Wellesley, on Green Street. Wellesley like the school."

"I went to Bennington myself. Be good, careful, and like that, Johnny boy."

"I'll try. Say, Vic, I'm breaking an editorial on PURIFY tomorrow. I've just written it."

"Well." Vic's voice was noncommittal.

"That's all you've got to say?"

"I thought you'd come to it eventually. Is it pretty strong?"

"As strong as I know how to make it."

"I hope it does a little good in the community. The statewide polls say this thing is gaining a lot of steam."

"Uh-huh," said John Hagen, fiddling with a pencil. "When are you going to get on record publicly about it?"

"As soon as Hausner challenges me on it. Then I'll say in a nutshell just about what I told you several months ago. That I think it's unconstitutional, but that I'll uphold it if I'm elected and it becomes law."

"He seems to be making a major campaign issue out of it."

Massoni chuckled. "That's old Dave. You know that annual bill he introduces? Around the capitol they call it Hausner's Pubic Hair Bill."

John laughed. "Great! Take care of yourself, Vic."

"Likewise, Johnny."

He waited until eight o'clock that night before calling, hoping Kris might call him. Her mother answered.

"Oh hello, Mother," he said. It was a term that even after more than fifteen years still stuck in his throat. Yet Kris had asked it at the beginning, and John Hagen was ever an obliging man when so small a point was involved.

"Why, hello, John," she said. There was, as always, the suggestion of archness to her voice. "I suppose you'd like to talk to your wife. She's right here; we've been having a regular mama and daughter talk."

"I'll bet you have. How have you been?"

"Oh, a little better, thank you. The stiffness has nearly gone. I'm still having the tummy trouble. The doctor has put me on a very bland diet. He's also told me to watch my weight. My ankles, you know—I've always had quite slender ankles—and he doesn't want them bearing too much weight. I got over my cold. But I'm not complaining."

Poor Kris, thought John. A week of this?

"I'm glad the main ailment is better," he said, without asking what it was. "So you're enjoying a nice visit, you two?"

"Yes, I'm glad she came, John. Perhaps I don't see her often enough, if you know what I mean."

"No, I don't know what you mean, except that perhaps you don't see her often enough."

"Just a mother talking, John; you know how they're always children to us, no matter how grown up, and if they're having little problems, we like to know about them. I just know that everything will work itself out in the end. These little difficulties can all be ironed out. I know you're trying as hard as you can. It isn't always easy being a woman, John. It takes a lot of help from a strong husband at times like these—but of course I don't have to tell *you* that. Do I?"

"I don't think so," said John Hagen. "Would you mind if I spoke to Kris now?"

"Yes, and be patient with her, will you, John?"

"Yes."

"Here's Kris."

"Hello, dear," she said.

"Krissy? I'd ask did you have a good flight and is the weather nice, but I guess now I don't feel up to it. Just what in the hell is your mother talking about? What have you been telling her, anyway?"

"Oh, John, you know Mother."

"I sure do. You haven't answered my question. She talks as if this cabin fever of yours is terminal."

"Oh, did you get that impression?"

His knuckles tightened on the receiver. "Yes, frankly. I thought you never told your mother anything important about us."

"I don't really."

"Can she hear you?"

"Oh, yes, it's lovely."

"All right. Then let me ask you questions you can answer yes or no. I take it that since you got there you've spent all your time with your mother?"

"Oh yes."

"And she's pumping you?"

"Uh—yes and no."

"Meaning she's trying to?"

"That's pretty much it."

"Kris. Krissy, this is important. Have you given her the impression that there is something seriously wrong with our marriage?"

"John, dear, it's a matter of proximity."

"Yes, of course," he said. She had just given him their old code for *I can't talk; there's someone here.*

"I'll try again. Would you prefer I not call you the rest of your visit? Give you the chance to be completely *away?*"

She hesitated. Then she said in a small voice: "I'll leave that up to you."

"All right," he said, trying to keep the disturbance from his voice. "We'll try that. You are sticking it out for the week?"

"I think so. Yes."

"Then I hope you get the chance to do something besides hold mama-daughter talks. Which reminds me, I was talking to Vic Massoni today. He said he might be in the city in the next few days; said if he was, he'd give you a call."

"Yes, he did already."

"Oh? You didn't tell me."

"You didn't give me the chance to."

"Sorry; you're right. Well, I suppose I don't have to tell you we all miss you. The kids said to say hello. I hope a few days of that San Francisco air will do you all sorts of good."

"What does that mean?"

"I mean simply, have yourself a good time."

"Thank you, dear. Is Mrs. Glade working out all right?"

"Yes, splendidly. She cooked us a nice rib roast tonight. Pammy and Gordo are behaving themselves, I'm busy, everything's fine, so don't worry. I guess I'd better sign off now. Say good night to your mother."

"All right, hon."

"I love you."

"I'm glad."

It was a thoroughly unsatisfying talk. He hung up too soon to remember to tell her that he was finally running the PURIFY editorial next day.

—25—

The Wellbrook *Sentinel* became the first Southern California newspaper to issue a strongly condemnatory editorial on Public United to Restore Innocence to Fair Youth. A number of other publishers were not long in following suit, but John Hagen was the first. He played it on page one, under a thirty-six-point head with a twenty-four-point kicker:

EDITORIAL

The Sentinel Opposes PURIFY

As a rule the Sentinel eschews gossip and unfounded rumor, believing a newspaper's job is to print only fact.

For several months, pressure has been brought on the Sentinel publisher to lend this newspaper's editorial support to an initiative proposal called Public United to Restore Innocence to Fair Youth. It is best known by its acronym, PURIFY.

The measure, which has qualified for the November general election ballot statewide, would, if passed, place a strongly worded, extremely punitive section in the state constitution to deal with the sellers of smutty literature.

The Sentinel has declined so far to speak out on PURIFY. At the outset there was doubt as to whether its backers could gather the requisite 750,000-plus signatures to place it on the ballot.

That doubt was removed in June.

We now speak our piece. The Sentinel is firmly and unalterably opposed to PURIFY.

Our hand has been forced because of the latest rumor making the rounds. It even tops the story of some months ago that the Sentinel's publisher must be a communist because he would not come out for PURIFY.

That was ignored as too ridiculous to deserve comment.

Now, however, it is being whispered that John A. Hagen himself must be a pornographer, a secret publisher of smutty books. Else, why would he not back PURIFY?

We would like to ignore this, too, but we choose to take note of it publicly, because it is an even more insidious type of story.

In short, the time has come to nail the lies. And in doing so, we feel it is necessary to point out briefly (to enlarge on at a later date) why the Sentinel is against the measure known as PURIFY:

· It is unconstitutional as drawn. Competent legal opinion informs the Sentinel that the state supreme court (or even lesser courts) would so hold.

· Its penalties are equivalent to those handed out for such crimes as second-degree murder and armed robbery.

· It deprives district attorneys of any discretion whatsoever in prosecution.

· It removes from the courts any power to give or withhold probation—to suspend sentence.

· It pre-empts any and all law now on the books dealing with written obscenity or pornography.

These five reasons alone are sufficient to say PURIFY would be extremely bad law. There are others, but for now these are enough.

The Sentinel realizes that there is a problem of trashy or obscene literature. Our readers will recall the Sentinel's own series earlier this year, publication of which embroiled the Sentinel in litigation that is yet to be heard in court.

But if law is needed in this field, it should not be a Draconian statute like PURIFY. Medicine that threatens the patient's life while killing his germs is much too drastic treatment.

So, beginning now, the Sentinel urges and will continue to urge a No vote on PURIFY in the coming November election.

And neither the Sentinel nor John A. Hagen will swerve from this position—regardless of threats, ugly rumors or anything else anonymous cranks may choose to employ against us.

Would the real sneak who started these outright falsehoods care to stand up?

He had shown the piece to Quincy Broyles pre-publication. That rotund gentleman, leg cocked comfortably over his other knee, had read it in silence, puffing steadily on his pipe. Finished, he jogged the sheets together and handed them back. "Good-*o*," he said.

"Suits you, does it, Quin?"

"Suits me right down to the ground. I've been uneasy about you, squire. This business is doing something to you. I'm glad you're bringing it out in the open this way."

"Of course there are always those who think that where there's smoke there's fire."

"I covered a lot of arson cases," said Broyles. "The one who reports the fire is quite often the one who set it."

Between the hour of publication and six o'clock John Hagen heard from a number of persons, personally and by telephone. Several of the staff let him know quietly they liked his editorial. Superintendent of Schools Elliott Warren called to congratulate him, effusively; so did Rabbi Norman Gross, quietly. And there were others, not all of them in favor of his stand. One unidentified woman, almost incoherent with rage, assaulted his ear for approximately five minutes, seemingly without drawing breath, and ended by slamming down the telephone. "Fornicator" was her final word for the publisher. Several others, who did give their names, disagreed in milder voice. All first made it a point to emphasize that Mr. Hagen was a man of honor and certainly no one could blame him for getting angry at ugly rumors, and they would too, and most people might react the same way, but . . .

But. One pleasant-voiced woman who identified herself as Ida Mears, mother of three, struck the note for the more reasonable group. "I read your editorial and I signed the PURIFY initiative, Mr. Hagen," she said. "I recognize that what you said about this measure being quite drastic may very well be true. But may I tell you, as a mother, why I am quite concerned that something be done? Please understand, I am anything but a prude."

"Please do," said John.

"About one year ago my middle child—my son Raymond, he's twelve, very bright, very energetic—Raymond mailed off an innocent-looking coupon for a set of barbells. He's just at an age when boys do that, want to start building their muscles. Well, I don't know what some of those people do, trade off their mailing lists or sell them or what, but in the last twelve months, Mr. Hagen, my son has been the recipient of some of the most disgusting mail I have ever seen in my life. When I discovered what it was I began intercepting everything, and when I had a big stack of it I mailed it off to the post office department. Well, they assured me of their complete co-operation in a letter, they would warn the senders and so on, but still the mail keeps coming. I mean, from everywhere: North Hollywood, California; Brooklyn; New York; Chicago; Washington, D.C.; Newark, New Jersey; Miami . . . just everywhere . . . but just an awful lot of it from Southern California addresses. I know there is a law now that you can write the sender and make him take you off the mailing list, but there just seems to be no end of new addresses. It's like turning on a faucet you can't turn off."

"I appreciate your concern, Mrs. Mears," said John. "Believe me when I say I deplore this widespread racket as much as you do. But striking at one evil with another, in my opinion, is not the way. Do you see my position?"

"Mr. Hagen, I believe in freedom of speech as much as you do," said Mrs. Mears. "But I think there is a limit."

"So do I," he said.

I believe in freedom of speech. It was a recurring theme. Yet always there was the point at which each caller said, *"but."* And it was when each specified at what point he or she believed firmly a line should be drawn that John Hagen acquired further insight into just how much or little the Bill of Rights meant to different people. There was an almost uniform certainty as to where the "but" began. "I believe in freedom of the press, but they ought to arrest the people that put out that *Playboy*." "I'm all for the right to print anything you want, but I think some of these here pocketbooks are just too plain damn much." "There ought to be some way to stop those cheap tabloids—the ones that print all those stories about rape and incest and wife-swapping; how can they say the Constitution was meant to protect that kind of garbage?"

Can it be, thought John Hagen wearily, that my editorial missed so badly? Have I so misgauged my audience that a majority disagrees with me? I have taken unpopular positions before. Yet always a strong undercurrent reassured me that much of the community disowned the extremists. Did I stir something here too emotional for common-sense logic? I believe I am in the right—but what is right?

The mail next day was heavy. Along with the usual run of advertising insertion orders, solicitations, checks, subscription orders and cancellations, and invoices—none of which he saw—were the first of the two unsigned letters in response to his editorial. One, crudely block-lettered in pencil, said:

YOUR AS BAD AS ALL THOSE POYNOGRAPHERS
HAGEN WHY DONT YOU STOP AND TAKE A GOOD
LOOK AT YOURSELF OR WOULD IT MAKE YOU PUKE!!!

The other, typed in red, was a bit neater:

Dear Sir,

Who made you an authority on this viscious dirty racket PURIFY will clean up? Read what the Citizens for Decent Literature have to say that Venerial Disease is DESTROYING a whole generation of Youth which is a direct result of these filthy books and magazines on the newstands every time you turn around.

You should be ashamed if you call yourself a publisher! If you do not stop and take heed. We are serious.

ONE WHO KNOWS

John Hagen got up and went into his managing editor's office.

"Quin, I think sometimes when we try to teach the staff that it's Smithsonian *Institution,* not Institute, and not to use *infer* when they mean *imply,* we should furnish examples."

"What's on your mind, squire?"

"You might want to post these two models of style, punctuation, and grammar."

Quincy Broyles scanned both notes quickly. "Well, at least one of them is signed," he said.

John dropped into a chair. He stared absently at the partly tilted venetian blinds. They revealed the alternating shadows but not the form of passing traffic on Centinela Avenue. "You know, Quin, I have a funny sense of having been tugged into my present spot. Instead of acting, I reacted. I find I'm not in a very aware position. I pride myself on trying to be an objective observer. Yet I jumped into a public statement on selfish grounds—because I was personally attacked. I believe my instincts are sound, but what do I know about the other side of the coin?"

"You're working your way through an argument," said Quincy Broyles, puffing.

"I am. Vic Massoni tells me PURIFY is bad law. I agree with him. Still, I ought to know much more about the whole field that brought it about. For one very good reason." He stood and walked over to the window. "Because I think that from here on out it's going to be sock-it-to-me time. And I'm It. These nuts here"— he waved at the letters on Quincy Broyles' desk—"don't bother me. But when responsible people start asking me, 'Do you know the whole extent of the problem?' I'd better have the answers."

"What have you got in mind?"

"Some firsthand investigation. Take two or three days and see what I can turn up. It can't be any research in depth, obviously; just plow a little deeper than I have. I think I must, if I want to hold a dependable position."

"Sounds logical to me, squire." Quincy Broyles refired his burner. "Of course you're talking about a lot of study in a very limited time."

"Well, call it a short cram course," said John. He riffled the venetian blinds with his finger. "I ought to get some kind of toehold anyway. I'll trust you to keep the *Sentinel* chugging away for a few days."

"Oh, we'll get a paper out," said Broyles.

John Hagen made several telephone calls and was on the freeway to Los Angeles in the old Chevy before noon.

— 26 —

He had talked to attorneys, law-enforcement agents, a pamphleteer, editors, psychologists, a post office inspector, and even a somewhat amused publisher of erotica. By the end of the third day John Hagen felt nearly inundated. One could search for a point of view and feel that he had found it. He would then encounter equally positive conflicting testimony, uttered in the same deep chest tones. Only one conclusion was irrefutable: that the question of what might or might not be obscene in print, pictorial rendition, or motion pictures was almost totally hemmed in by more opinion, sophistry, bias, shallow conclusion, and emotion—and supported less by provable fact—than any other field of study he had ever encountered.

Here was the graying attorney at his massive polished desk, a Goya original on one wall, a signed Picasso on another. He spoke gently, from time to time lovingly fingering a black onyx miniature bust of Nefertiti on his desk:

"I don't know what you mean by hard-core pornography, Mr. Hagen. Have you studied any of the recent appellate decisions in this field? The Fresno conviction, *Sex Life of a Cop*—were you aware that it had been reversed on appeal? The Luros case in Sioux City—reversed? All constitutionally protected materials. I can't argue alleged effects of this type of material on the reader, although there are only too many in my profession who are willing to do so. How can they know? I am only concerned that the publishers I represent stay within the law. Neither Aday nor Luros were my clients, by the way."

"All right," said John. "What about under-the-counter merchandise—the very basic photos, films, and drawings depicting the act of sexual intercourse and the various perversions? Would you call this constitutionally protected?"

The attorney smiled. "Are you aware that two justices of the United States Supreme Court have consistently maintained that a state is totally without power to control or punish the distribution of *any* writings or pictures upon the grounds of their obscenity?"

"But a minority view, is it not?"

"That doesn't say it is wrong. The great danger in censorship, Mr. Hagen, as I'm sure you know if I understand your position correctly with respect to PURIFY, is that there is no stopping point once it starts. Are you aware of the difference between *malum prohibitum* and *malum in se?*"

"I don't believe I am."

"*Malum in se,*" said the attorney, turning the Nefertiti bust so that it faced him, "is that which is and always has been recognized in all societies as wrong in itself. Murder is the classic example. *Malum prohibitum,* on the other hand, is that which is wrong because the law says it is wrong. A prime example is income tax evasion. In the United States it is a criminal offense. In most European countries it is only a civil matter. If you're caught, you pay up but you don't go to jail. As far as I am concerned, the production and sale of so-called smutty literature is strictly *malum prohibitum*. Like many sex offenses—acts between consenting adults—you have a crime without a victim."

"How do we know?" said John Hagen. "Take a book glorifying deviant sex—homosexuality. Can we say it might imply a certain degree of acceptance, and therefore influence some susceptible young boy?"

"I wouldn't make any such assumption," said the attorney.

"Do you grant the possibility?"

"Is homosexuality acquired or hereditary, Mr. Hagen?"

"I don't know."

"Nor do I. But I strongly feel that if a boy, a man, is susceptible to deviant behavior, he'll find what he's looking for sooner or later, and it won't be in the pages of a book."

"But couldn't that book or those pictures in a magazine help promote those subconscious impulses?"

"What about the sight of nude buttocks or male sex organs in a shower room, Mr. Hagen? Which do you honestly think would be the more stimulating: the actual flesh or the pale reproduction of it?"

Here, in the rigidly furnished quarters of a U. S. Post Office inspector, spoke a man who compared his task to that of sweeping back the incoming tide with a kitchen mop:

"California owns the dubious distinction of supplying between nineteen million and thirty million dollars' worth of sex-oriented material to the country each year. It depends on whether you take the state attorney general's guess or that of the *Wall Street Journal*." The government man, a mild-mannered individual who might as easily have been a hardware salesman or county clerk, removed his half-rimmed spectacles and caressed the bridge of his nose. "We deal with complaints by the thousands about the mailings and we get them from all over—the Middle West, the South, the East Coast, and the western states, of course."

"What is the nature of the complaints?" said John.

"Parents, mostly," said the federal man, replacing his glasses. "They want to know why the United States Post Office handles the mailings of advertisements for sex books, magazines, films, and devices. Their kids get on some kind of mailing list. Well, there's a big business in list brokering around the country. There are as many as a hundred brokers. The big mail-order operators also compile their own lists through cheap come-on advertisements in the girlie and nudist magazines. Either way, there's quite an interlocking system, with hundreds of *dba*'s—"

"*Dba?*"

"Doing Business As—*dba*. Any one of the bigger operators can have dozens of names and scores of mail drops. Suppose you, for example, answer an advertisement for a magic sex elixir. That gets your name on a list as someone who may be interested in sex literature and sex devices. Suppose your initial return comes from Fly By Night Scientific Research, P. O. Box Oh-oh-oh, Los Angeles. That's only the beginning. Soon you'll be getting mail from San Diego, Grand Central Station post office in New York, Pennsylvania, Guadalajara, Brooklyn, Maryland, New Jersey, you name it.

" 'All right,' you say, 'I have no reason to complain.' In a sense you asked for it. But supposing it's your boy. He sends off for a stamp kit. Juveniles are prime candidates for lists. The next thing you know, your boy is getting the same treatment. Someone sold his name and address to a list broker. He in turn rents this name and thousands of others to one mail-order sex-device or sex-book dealer after another. Each one makes thousands of mailings at a crack. All they need is about a two per cent response on any mailing to make a thousand per cent or more return on the mailing cost. The profits can be fabulous. Well, it's true that you, as a parent, can insist that your son's name be taken off the Fly By Night Scientific Research mailing list. But that's only one of prospective hundreds. Well, we know pretty well which major operator is responsible for which *dba*'s. Under new law we can help in getting your son's name off all of a particular firm's lists. But that is only one firm and one individual. Multiply in the millions and you'll get an idea of the extent of our job." He looked gloomily out the window.

"The post office regards itself as a censor then?" said John Hagen.

"Not at all," said the inspector sharply. "But as an agency of the U. S. Government we are certainly obliged to help people protect the privacy of their homes against material they do not want."

"But hasn't the post office in the past planted advertising as a means of trapping the mailers of pornographic materials?"

The federal man gave John Hagen a long look. "I have no official knowledge of any such activity," he said.

The offices of the Blue Pacific Publishing Company were in a new, five-story building in Van Nuys, in the San Fernando Valley. His appointment with the editor had taken six telephone calls to arrange. The first was to a former *Times* colleague who now worked on the *Herald-Examiner*. He in turn had telephoned a friend in North Hollywood who made a living of sorts supplying manuscripts to Blue Pacific for paperback publication under a half-dozen "bookline" names. The friend, a former screen writer with a serious drinking problem (John was told), had then talked to the Blue Pacific editor, then called the *Herald-Examiner* newsman, who in turn called John to give him the editor's telephone number. The sixth and last call was by John Hagen to the editor.

The initial response was cautious. "Is this for publication?" the man said.

"Not directly, no," said John. He explained his role and the purpose of his investigation.

"Oh hell, come on over," said the man. "We've got nothing to hide."

John stepped from the self-service elevator at the fourth floor into a gardenlike reception area. A stunning blonde smiled at him from behind a Danish-style desk that adjoined a switchboard. "May I help you?" she said pleasantly. John gave his name and she said, "Oh yes, he's expecting you, Mr. Hagen." A moment later another equally shapely young woman in a provocatively cut miniskirt appeared in the reception area from one of two corridors that led to the rear.

"Mr. Hagen?"

"Yes."

"Would you come this way, please?"

She led him past a series of open cubicles. Except for one rather severe-looking older woman with glasses, the emphasis in female help, judging from the three girls they passed in the corridor, seemed to be on youth and beauty. John Hagen heard voices and typewriters, saw a bearded man look up from his keyboard, scowling at something, and in still another office he exchanged glances with a middle-aged man in shirt sleeves who was talking rapidly into a telephone.

"How can I help you, Mr. Hagen?" said the editor. John had been told he was but one of several senior editors of Blue Pacific Publishing Company. He was a man in his middle forties, with a thin, intelligent face, black-framed spectacles, and reddish mustache, who lighted one cigarette after another.

John briefly sketched the story of the *Sentinel's* January series on Art's Arcade and Hank's and his own position with respect to PURIFY.

The editor laughed. "You think they'll ever get that passed?" he said.

"I don't know. There seems to be a lot of sentiment for it."

"Nevah hoppen," said the editor firmly. "People will talk one way and vote another. But go on—you've got some questions?"

"Yes. What does Blue Pacific Publishing Company publish?"

"Well, we've got six paperback booklines: Baroque, Nighttime, Bard, Jupiter, Cosmos, and Revelation. Eight magazines: *Celebrity Secrets,*—that's like *Confidential*—then there's *Uncensored, Peephole, Sly, Body,* and *Romp,* which are girlie magazines, and two nudist pubs —*Island Nudist* and *Bare Journal.* Some other stuff."

"What?"

"Some other stuff. Excuse me." The editor picked up his ringing telephone, to which was attached a recording device. "Yeah?" He listened for a few minutes, punctuating the lengthy narrative from time to time with a "Yeah" or "Uh-huh" or "Sure." Finally he said impatiently, "Well, about six things, if you wanta know. In the first place, I need forty thousand words minimum as I told you in the first letter. In the second place, you take about twenty pages to get her in the sack—who do you think you are—James Gould Cozzens? Third, way too much dialogue, not enough action. Four, not graphic enough, I mean nitty-gritty, no holds barred. Five, I want more deviation—you've gotta keep piling it up, not just the same old thing over and over. Okay, six, give me some colored skin for variety—black, yellow, brown. And get a black stud in there with a white girl, that turns 'em on like nothing else. Now, when do I see your rewrite?" He paused, studying John Hagen's face. "All right, two weeks. Yeah, you've got a basically good story there, now let's get some meat on those bones. Okay, good-by." He dropped the receiver on the hook. To John he said, "Not a bad writer but he tends to get too high-toned for our kind of reader. What else do you want to know?" He lighted a cigarette from the butt of the last, then crushed out the stub in a half-filled ashtray.

"How do you distribute your publications?"

"Rail, truck, any common carrier, direct to distributors. We don't fool around with the mails. In the first place, we ship bulk. And in the second, Uncle Sammy is always sticking his nose in and it's just too damned much trouble to have to explain everything. We operate clean, always have. We've got diplomas from the U. S. Supreme Court to prove it. Listen, Mr. Hagen, sex sells. If it didn't, we wouldn't be in business. You think I've got any illusions about the quality of the stuff we put out? It's trash, sure, but how is it any different basically from the so-called classics like *Lady Chatterley* and *Ulysses?* Do you think *Chatterley* sold up in the millions because D. H. Lawrence is a beautiful writer? Go on, tell me another. You ask your average reader what the heroine's first name is and catch the blank stare. They don't care if it's Connie or Esmeralda, most of 'em just flipped over until they found the places where Mellors put the fat part in. You ask me if we're creating taste or meeting it and I'll give you a real quick answer. Somebody out there is buying this stuff —does that give you any ideas?"

"What your man probably neglected to tell you is the original beginnings of Blue Pacific," said a young deputy attorney general to John Hagen. He swiveled around in his chair and opened a drawer in a green filing cabinet. He removed a manila folder after a brief search and turned about again. "The principal in Blue Pacific Publishing Company is a man named Smith. Plain, ordinary Smith, although he has called himself Courtney and has also been known as Ravell, Johnson, and Bradley. He served two years in Joliet for assault with intent to kill back in the nineteen thirties, a short jail term on Riker's Island in nineteen thirty-nine for pandering—pimping— and did a one-year bit in Washington, D.C., in nineteen forty-five for writing bad checks. He came to Los Angeles in nineteen forty- seven and presently came on the mail-order market with a so-called electric massager. It was nothing more or less than a hard-rubber device in the shape and size of an erect penis, incorporating a Japanese-made electric vibrator. It cost him from approximately two dollars and fifty cents to three-fifty to have made and he sold it in three models, the cheapest of which was eighteen ninety-five and the most expensive, twenty-four ninety-five. Using a rented mailing list, he cleared about a hundred thousand dollars in one year. He branched out then into so-called splints, phallic extenders, dildos, and artificial vaginas. Because of the quasi-medical nature of this material it was impossible for local authorities in several states to make any sort of conviction stick. In the meantime he moved out into publishing. Today he is one of the largest sex-oriented paperback and girlie magazine publishers in the United States. And the strange thing is, he still keeps on with the mechanical devices as a sideline. It's too profitable for him to drop, in spite of the millions he's made in the publishing business. These people are actuated by greed to an extreme degree, Mr. Hagen. They'll do almost anything for a dollar."

"Do you regard this man Smith as one of the worst operators?" said John. It was getting on toward five o'clock. He was tired from a long day.

"No. He's bad enough, but I think the publishers of the sado-masochistic stuff are even worse," said the deputy attorney general, returning the folder to the filing cabinet. "Have you seen any of that type of thing?"

"Yes, I saw Senator Hausner's rather complete collection."

"Senator Hausner. Oh, yes," said the young attorney noncommittally.

"He may be your boss one of these days," said John, smiling.

"I know. Do you know his opponent at all?"

"USC classmate of mine, as a matter of fact. My newspaper is supporting his campaign."

"How do you figure Assemblyman Massoni's chances?"

"It's hard to say. We've moved into a sort of conservative climate the last few years in California. Maybe the pendulum will swing the other way this year. I don't want to run past your quitting time, but I do have a couple more questions."

"Fire away."

"Where, if anywhere, is there a dividing line between the books and magazines that are sold openly and hard-core pornography?"

The young deputy attorney general smiled ruefully. "Well, the most recent experience has been that almost nothing in type can be successfully prosecuted up through all levels of appeal. There is, however, an exception. We now have a ruling from the Supreme Court that it is illegal to sell this borderline printed material to children. That goes against the bookseller, mainly. There's something else working in many small communities that has nothing to do with the courts. You're a small-town news dealer, let's say, and you put some of Blue Pacific's paperback line on your racks. There's a complaint. The cop on the beat pays you a call. 'Take it out or I'll arrest you,' he says. You don't argue, you take it out. In small towns the law can exert a lot of personal pressure on a bookseller that isn't possible in a city like Los Angeles, San Francisco, or New York. There isn't enough of a business loss with one small-town store for the publisher to take a conviction through all the appeals."

"What about photos?"

"I don't know where the line is," the attorney admitted. "Oh, photos of the sex act are no problem. The dealer pleads guilty, takes a slap on the wrist—a fine or a short jail sentence—and that's it. The same for out-and-out stag films. The defense attorney knows he can't win and doesn't even try in most cases. He just pleads his man guilty and tries for a suspended sentence on probation. If you'll excuse the expression, we call those 'fuck' books and films. A lot of them come in from Mexico and Europe. They're nowhere the problem this twilight-zone stuff is that we've been talking about—like the Blue Pacific line. The hard stuff is too dangerous for your average bookseller to handle." He looked at his watch.

"Just one more question," said John Hagen. "What do you, the police, and the district attorneys think about PURIFY?"

"This is entirely off the record, I hope, Mr. Hagen."

"Completely."

"Considering that Senator Hausner, as you say, may be my next boss. We don't like it. The D.A.s and police alike think some stronger obscenity statutes are needed. Some very careful work over several years has gone into drawing up the kind of language we think will stand the constitutional tests. Now, I give Senator Hausner and the PURIFY people all credit for sincerity, but a lot of good work is going to go down the drain with this measure. It's my considered opinion that even if it passes, it won't hold up."

At the suggestion of the deputy attorney general, John Hagen strolled Los Angeles's Main Street between Second and Fourth, where the stores specializing in borderline smut clustered. It took two hours to make the tour, entering each establishment. By the third, the pattern was established; by the sixth, deadly in its sameness. Here were the virtually unfurnished and usually high-ceilinged large rooms, walls and center portion lined with decked troughs of magazines, paperback books, record albums. Each display was ar-

ranged by category. The male homosexual material, such as the magazines of nude "models," the muscle books, and the organized-society
publications by and for the gay set were all to be found in one section. The material devoted to whipping, or the various other forms
of torture, combined with a wide selection of printed matter dealing
with restraints, called "bondage," occupied still another area. In one
limited section might huddle the marriage and sex manuals (some by
recognized and respected authorities) together with pseudoscientific
esoterica under imprimaturs like Inter-Family Research Foundation, dealing with variant aspects of physical love-making, alternately
lip-smacking and tut-tutting. Here and there books or magazines
whose covers hinted at the very nadir of depravity were sealed in
polyethylene bags with price tags as high as $9.95. Nudist magazines
took up much shelf space. On the covers the genital areas were
blacked out but no such proscription was applied to the inside pages.
John Hagen wondered why the publishers bothered, unless it was to
forestall complaints by the parents of juveniles. Each establishment
was ruled by a man sitting quietly at a cash register located near the
door, nearly always behind a gate or a counter. He made no effort to
catch his patrons' eyes, nor did customers (who looked quite "average"), look at each other's faces while browsing. The almost endless
repetition—the same magazines, books, outsize tabloid freak papers—
led to an inescapable impression that the oft-invoked "average" man
might sooner expire of boredom than from overwhelming shock.

"So you took a tour for yourself?" said the psychologist. He was a
comfortably plump man in his fifties whose listed credentials in the
Yellow Pages included Family, Teen-Age, and School Counseling.
He leaned back in his leather chair. The crinkle at the corners of his
eyes hinted at amusement. "And have you come to any conclusions
yet, Mr. Hagen?"

"One for sure. There is certainly a flood of this junk."

"Indeed there is. But as to its effects—what is your opinion about
that?"

"This is the one thing I find hardest to pin down," said John.
"There's a great deal of excitement about obscenity in print. I myself
authorized a newspaper series about it on the local scene. But at this

point I'm not sure I know much more about the subject than I did at the beginning—except, of course, that I've since been exposed to a lot of actual materials I'd never known existed."

"You came to me, then, for an authoritative opinion?"

"Yes."

"I can't give it to you."

John raised an eyebrow. "No opinion at all?"

The psychologist shook his head. "I do not say I have no opinion, I say I have no authoritative opinion. I can tell you only what I personally believe as do a goodly number of my colleagues. Which is that the few pathological people who are trying to control everything we see and read are a far greater danger than that posed by pornography."

"It is your view, then, that erotica cannot trigger bizarre behavior?"

"Of course it can. So can a panty-hose advertisement in your newspaper or the sight of a woman's legs in street dress. Generally speaking, however, sex offenders are among the stupider element of our society and they're action-oriented. I doubt, for example, that many potential offenders would or could take the time to read a sex paperback."

"By and large you do not think pornography is harmful then?"

"I do not. The great majority of people would eventually turn from it after a certain period of exposure, largely out of ennui. It tends to a considerable sameness. Perhaps you've found that out?"

"I have indeed."

"Generally, to those who need it, pornography serves as a harmless outlet rather than a dangerous stimulant. A man who masturbates in his bathroom to the photo of a man and woman coupling is hardly apt to be a rapist. The rapist often erects his own images. Frequently rape is an act of impulse, occurring on a moment's notice when object and opportunity come together—in police slang, the "hot rapist." And the taking by force or the threat of force often is the necessary element of the whole act. The offender may even be impotent in more conventional circumstances."

John Hagen fingered his chin. "You see some of the smut fighters as pathological, Doctor?"

"The worst ones, yes. They may have deep fears or anxieties about their own sexuality and be attempting to deny them. The rationale they offer is that they fear the effects of sex-oriented material on others, especially children. There are others who privately enjoy pornography. They find joining movements against it an excellent, socially acceptable means of access to it. Most others fall into neither camp, feeling that pornography must be evil because that is the prevailing social view." The psychologist shrugged. "I do not advocate it myself. It is degrading of sex and of the human spirit. Yet I feel that its alleged power to destroy is as mythical as the potency of the evil eye. I personally deplore the daily diet of sadism to be found on television shows more than I do overt pornography."

The publication office of *Smut-Alert* proved to be the Liberty Bell Bookstore, on a side street between Hollywood and Sunset boulevards. A bell rang as John Hagen entered. The forward part of the small store was much given to displays of works by such authors as Ralph de Toledano, Ayn Rand, William F. Buckley, and Robert Welch. A man who came up from a room in the rear identified himself as the proprietor as well as editor and publisher of *Smut-Alert*. The hum of a lithograph press came through the open doorway in back.

"Yes, I've been putting out *Smut-Alert* for eight years," the man said. His eyebrows contracted with suspicion. "Official organ of the Southern California People's Cleanup Committee. A going group before anyone ever heard of the Citizens for Decent Literature or PURIFY. Don't get me wrong—fine organizations, splendid efforts, but we have done the real pioneer work in this field of investigation. Supported by donations from public-spirited groups and individuals throughout the West. Perhaps you heard of our campaign against the *Dictionary of American Slang*." His voice quavered with indignation. "Filthy words throughout. We republished pages—especially a certain part of the *F* section alone, if you know what I mean. Made a wide distribution—to our entire mailing list. And can you imagine: the publisher threatened us with suit over the copyright, made us cease distribution."

"What are your guidelines?" said John Hagen.

"Best authorities," said the man promptly. "Here, read this."

He held out a sheet of paper. "See this excerpt? Taken from a Chicago Police Department training bulletin." John read:

> Sexual arousal from obscene literature has been responsible for criminal behavior from vicious assaults to homicide. In the case of sex murders, the killer is usually an avid reader of lewd books and magazines. Sex criminals read this sexually stimulating material and are clearly influenced by it.

"Do you feel you are making progress?"

"Great strides; of course we are making progress. Thanks to us, large numbers of people have joined in to help get PURIFY on the ballot. Not our program, but we support it wholeheartedly."

"What evidence do you people have of a causal relationship between sex literature and sex crime?"

"Would you take the word of J. Edgar Hoover?" said the publisher of *Smut-Alert*. He drew himself up with the air of a man who has said all there is to be said on a subject.

And finally Smith himself, principal in Blue Pacific Publishing Company. Through his counsel, the attorney John had first seen, Smith consented to see the *Sentinel* publisher, but only on two conditions: it must be in the lawyer's office and nothing was for publication.

"I told everything to the attorney general's office anyway," said Smith. He was a dark-visaged, craggy-featured man in his fifties with perpetually moving eyes. His suit was obviously expensive. A huge diamond ring glittered on the pudgy little finger of his left hand. "I only said I'll talk to you because I heard about you. You're the guy who took on the preacher wit' this political deal. Right?"

"How did you know about that?" said John Hagen.

"Word gets around," said Smith. He grinned contemptuously. "You take yourself real serious, I bet. Fixin' to get yourself crucified, Hagen. You ain't on my side, that's for sure."

"No, I'm not."

The attorney, who was toying with the black onyx bust of Nefertiti, looked at his client warningly but said nothing.

"All you guys give me a pain in the tokus," said Smith. "There ain't a dime's worth of difference between you and the preacher. I know what you done over there in Wellbrook. Got yourself a first-rate lawsuit out of it, didn't you? Serves you right. The trouble is, Hagen, you're buckin' human nature, like tryin' to stop people from screwin'. How many laws they got against that? Hey, Max, how many laws they got against screwin'?"

"A considerable number of statutes in the several states deal with extramarital cohabitation," said the attorney.

"Yeah, considerable. They pass all kinds of laws. You think that stops a guy from gettin' a little when he wants it? All right, they try to stop me from printin' what the public wants to read. You see any difference? They don't care what the U. S. Constitution says, hey, Max? Well, listen, Hagen, I didn't invent sex and I ain't forcin' no one to buy what I print. So I made a pretty good buck in the last twenty years, how do you account for that? And I had to stand up for my rights every foot of the way."

"Just how much money *have* you made, Mr. Smith?" said John Hagen.

The Blue Pacific Publishing Company proprietor grinned. "Why don't you ask the man with the whiskers? I notice he ain't too particular about where my money come from, even if his boys in the post office kept tryin' to put me out of business. I paid enough taxes last year alone to build ten post offices."

"Would you say you'd made a million in twenty years? Two million? Ten?"

"I made a dollar," said Smith, twisting the huge diamond on his pudgy finger. "You're a publisher, Hagen. How much money have you made?"

"What do you think will happen to your business if PURIFY becomes law?" said John. Is it a man like this that I am risking my career for? he thought. "Where in journalism school did they ever teach you you could stand in the middle?" Quincy Broyles had asked rhetorically. "Ain't no such place, squire."

"I believe that is a quite hypothetical question," interjected the attorney.

"I hope they put it over," said Smith.

"You can't be serious," said John Hagen.

"No? You read that law?"

"Yes, of course."

Smith snorted. "Wait'll they start goin' after those high-priced guys in the East," he said. "Yeah, you know, the big boys with the respectable names. They put out a lot of shit in a fancy binding and say it's literature. Me, I live across the tracks; me, they take off on because I don't make no bones about what my stuff is. Yeah, let 'em get that law on the books. They'll be so busy goin' after some of them big dirty-word books my enterprises're just gonna be one of the crowd." He grinned at the lawyer. "Tell 'im, Max."

"The Constitution should be an umbrella over all, not just a favored few," said the attorney.

"You favor PURIFY then, Mr. Smith?" said John.

"Didn't I just tell you? And when the courts wipe it out, it clears the whole bit off the lawbooks. I mean, *no* law."

"Is this your interpretation?" said John to the attorney.

"Anything I might say would be purely speculative," said the attorney.

"Okay, play it cool, Max," said Smith.

"There is a lot of money behind PURIFY," said John. "If you favor it, as you say, might I assume you are secretly contributing to it?"

"You're dreaming," said the Blue Pacific publisher contemptuously. "Let those damn fools spend their own money. They're helpin' me and they don't know it."

— 27 —

The telephone buzzed a half-dozen times before the receiver was lifted.

"Yes?" said his mother-in-law. She always answered with quite perceptible suspicion, reflected in that imperious *"Yes?"* John had often been tempted to ask her, "Why can't you say 'hello' like everyone else?"

"This is John, Mother. How are you?"

"Oh, hello, John. Oh, I don't complain. I hate to say it but I think I'm about to catch another cold, when I just got over one. I still have the little stiffness; I've been using a cane, you know. That's why I took so long to answer the telephone. And I'm trying to be good about the bland diet but I do have this positive mania for sweets."

"That's ni—yes, it must be an awful temptation. Is Kris—"

"—Not candies so much, but Blum's does make such wonderful cakes—"

"Yes. Do you suppose I might talk to—"

"—So delicious, but absolutely loaded with calories."

"Mother," said John quickly, "is Kris there—could I talk to Kris?"

"Why—why no," she said. "As a matter of fact, this friend of yours, Assemblyman Massoni, invited her to dinner. They left—oh, thirty minutes ago."

"Well, good," said John Hagen. He covered his disappointment. "I told her she ought to get out somewhere while she was in the city."

"Oh?" said Mrs. Wellesley. She could pack more innuendo in one syllable, John thought, than most persons could in a one-hour oration. "Then you—well, I wasn't quite sure you would approve."

John frowned. "Approve? I don't understand."

"Oh dear, I hope I didn't say something I shouldn't have. I know how much you trust your wife, John."

"Mother—" he began, breaking off to keep from saying something he knew he'd be sorry for. "Vic Massoni is a very old friend to both of us. He said he might call. I assumed it might include some sort of invitation. Krissy went up to San Francisco because she wanted to see you and because she was feeling a little moody. I'm glad she has gone out with Vic Massoni."

"Yes, of course," she said. Her tone said, "I don't believe you for a minute."

"Actually, all I'd called about was to see if she's coming home tomorrow."

"Well, she hasn't said anything. I guess you *are* missing her?"

"We all are. Would you leave her a note to call me if she doesn't get home too late?"

"How late would too late be, John?"

"Any time before midnight. Would you do that?"

"Why, of course, John. You know I retire early these days, never later than nine-thirty, that's another thing my doctor is very strict about. Not that he has to be, really; somehow when you get to my age you're ready for early beddy-bye. I suppose it's just another one of those penalties of age, along with the aches and pains and tummy troubles and diets and all that sort of thing. But I don't complain."

"Good night, Mother."

"Good night, John."

The bell of his bedside extension telephone jerked him from sleep. At first he fumbled with the muzzy notion that it was his alarm clock, remembering within drowsy seconds that it hadn't a bell but a flat, continuous drone. His hand found the phone and carried it to his ear as he sat up. He snapped on the light, trying to focus his vision.

"Hello?"

"Checking up on me?" said Kris.

"Wha—huh?—is that you, Kris?"

"Who else would it be? What is so urgent that I have to call you at two-thirty in the morning? Is someone ill?"

"Two-th—wait a minute!" His vision was now unscrambled. According to the small electric alarm clock it was actually nearer three o'clock. What did anyone do until three o'clock, when all the bars, by California law, closed at two? "Did you just get in?" he said.

"No, I did not just get in, but I did just find Mother's note on my pillow. You didn't answer my question: is anyone sick?"

"No, but—"

"Then what is it? Did Mother tell you I'd gone out with Vic Massoni? Is that what's bothering you?"

"Will you listen to me, for God's sake, Kris? I did *not* ask you to call at this ungodly hour. I *did* ask your mother to leave a note saying call at any time up to midnight. And no, no one is sick. I only wanted to find out if you're coming home tomorrow and when, so I can meet you."

"Oh," she said. "Oh. She forgot to say anything about time."

"I hope you had a good time," he said, thinking, *I'll just bet she "forgot."*

"Yes, we had a wonderful evening," she said. "Dinner at Doro's, then we went to see The Committee in North Beach, and after that, a late snack, and home. Vic was wonderfully attentive, and I'm afraid we talked a great deal about you."

"Did you, now?"

"Well, yes. Is that so strange? You're mainly what we have in common."

He lighted a cigarette, reminding himself that he was going to quit the habit any day now. "I wasn't questioning that," he said.

"In any case, yes, I'm coming home tomorrow. I'll be on the two-thirty helicopter."

"Well, fine, honey. The children asked, and I wanted to know too, so I guess that's about it."

"All right. Shall we say good night?"

"Yes. I love you, and good night."

"Good night, dear."

He waited to hear the receiver click before hanging up. Vaguely disturbed, he lay for what must have been a half or three quarters of an hour before he could coax sleep once more.

He had never seen her prettier nor looking happier. The 'copter blades had scarcely stopped turning when the young dispatcher was at the door. Kris was the first to step down. She waved as she saw him. She had on a white dress that he didn't remember, green shoes with matching bag, white gloves and hat.

"Hello, darling!" she said as he came to meet her. Her embrace and kiss were fervent. "Miss me?"

"Just a little."

"Uh-huh. Me too. I'm glad I went but I'm gladder to be back."

"You look wonderful, sweetheart."

"Thanks. It was a good flight. Isn't this beautiful weather?"

"How was the visit?"

"Oh, just heavenly. It turned out to be a simply wonderful visit after all. I've so much to tell you. Mother and I got along surprisingly well after all. Either she's mellowing or I am. And Vic and I went out, as you know."

He was guiding the Chevy into traffic. "Had a really good time, eh?"

"Oh, yes! I *do* think Mother's taking on a little bit about her age; after all, sixty-six isn't young but it isn't really ancient, either. But she's doing pretty well. We had a lot of good, honest talk, and one evening she had some friends in for bridge. A man about her age and his wife. I thought it would be just ghastly and it turned out to be more fun! She has a marvelous cook. And one day—Friday, I think it was, we took a long drive up into Marin County: Muir Woods and then over to Bolinas and Point Reyes, and for a wonder it was a clear day—just beautiful—even if it was a little windy. And I went shopping. And on Sunday I took her to twelve o'clock brunch in the Starlight Room of the Sir Francis Drake. San Francisco just seemed to turn on its best weather for me the whole visit. This morning she and I had just a little time to wait at the airport; the chauffeur had instructions to come back and pick her up in an hour, and we were very daring—we had two cocktails in the airport lounge. I told her we'd really like her to come visit."

"You did, eh?"

"Mm-hmm. You could stand her for a few days."

"Oh, I can get along with the old girl. The main thing is if you're happy."

She squeezed his arm. "I can't tell you; I feel like a different person from a week ago."

He smiled at her and returned his attention to the road. "That's the best news I've had all year."

"She said she'd come a little later in the year—around late October maybe."

"Well, that's fine."

"I'm awfully glad to be home, though."

He had permitted himself the luxury of leaving the office early to meet her. He returned for an hour or two to do some inescapable chores after dropping her off at home, but left again at about five o'clock for an early dinner. The children were delighted to see her, of course. Mrs. Glade started the dinner but left when Kris said she'd serve it, wanted to serve it. It was a good evening. Pam and Gordo were on their best behavior, Kris sparkling, John quietly happy.

Later in the evening they talked.

"Krissy," John began hesitantly. He searched for a way to begin. She gently stroked the short hairs on the back of his neck. "One week ago you went up to San Francisco—cold, distant, and suspecting me. Even last night you still sounded out of sorts. Today . . . tonight—what happened to you in San Francisco? You came back so different."

She looked at him searchingly, as if for oblique meanings. She continued stroking the back of his neck.

"I—I guess I was pretty upset," she said finally, in a low voice. "All that strain, plus that awful letter. It's just that—well, I guess I had a good long week to think about things. My husband, my family, my home—especially my husband. Why I married him in the first place. My dirty little suspicions." She looked at him anxiously. "You didn't have anything to do with that woman, did you, John?"

"Limited to drinks and conversation."

"I guess I knew it all along. I wasn't thinking too clearly."

"You are now?"

"I think I am now. But—darling, is all that nastiness still going on?"

"I'm afraid so, Krissy. I finally ran a blistering editorial."

"You did? Did you save me a copy?"

"Yes. It's on the secretary. It stirred up the animals even more."

She was silent for a long moment. "Hon, I wonder, is it worth it?"

"I'm not too sure myself. We could probably get a good price for our shares. But I wouldn't even think of it right now, Krissy—not until I've seen this thing through to the election. If they run me out —well, it's a point of pride now. I may be kidding myself, but I think I'm fighting a fight for a lot of people. I'm not even thinking of the specific issue, only whether a band of fanatics can have their way through intimidation."

"Well," she sighed, "I just hope we live through it."

In the late hours they made love, talked softly and contentedly about small matters, then made love again and fell asleep in each other's arms.

The bomb went off at exactly 3:53 A.M. on a Thursday morning just three weeks later. The precise time was established by the night booking sergeant at the Wellbrook police station, who heard the blast and automatically looked at the wall clock. There were no witnesses to the planting of the explosive.

The night crew of compositors had gone off shift at two o'clock, leaving only Al DeWeese pulling the night city editor assignment to face the drear morning hours. He was heavily jolted by the explosion but unhurt.

John Hagen was aroused from a light, troubled sleep by an insistent pounding. He was vaguely aware that his telephone had rung several times—one short ring each time. Even though he had installed an automatic answering device, with a recording mechanism that invited the caller to leave a name and number, there had still been some nasty, threatening calls. Kris stirred uneasily and muttered something unintelligible. John felt his way to the wall closet, identified his bathrobe by feel, and slipped it on over his pajamas. Kris murmured again. John opened the bedroom door quietly and went downstairs.

The heavy pounding had begun again a second or two before he opened the front door against the night chain. "Who is it?" he said.

"Patrolman Bennett, Wellbrook police, Mr. Hagen." A face appeared at the narrow opening. "We tried to call you and all we got was a recording. Your place has been bombed."

John shook his head in an attempt to clear the fog. "My place?" he said. He closed the door to slip the chain and then reopened it wide. A young, beefy patrolman holding a long flashlight stood on the welcome mat. In the driveway sat a black and white sedan, its engine purring softly.

"Somebody set off a bomb at your newspaper, sir. We thought maybe you oughta come down."

"Was anyone hurt?" said John Hagen. The initial shock of incredulity passed swiftly. "Were any of my people hurt?"

"No, sir; your man DeWeese is kind of shook up but he's not hurt."

"I'll be down right away."

"If you want, sir, we'll wait and you can ride down with us."

"Thank you, Officer. I'll be with you in five minutes."

Fumbling in darkness for a pair of trousers, John heard the rustle of bedclothes. "What is it?" said Kris.

"Trouble at the plant. Somebody set off a bomb."

"A bomb!" There was violent stirring, and Kris snapped on the lamp. "Somebody bombed the *Sentinel?* But who—"

"I'm going down with the police now. Go back to sleep."

Kris's eyes were round with fright. "They're trying to kill us and you say go back to sleep!" She swung her legs decisively out of bed. "John, what are they doing to us?"

"Hon, I don't know, I don't know." He adjusted his trousers and pulled a heavy sweater over his pajama top, then stepped into a pair of loafers. "I'll let you know when I get back." He shot a quick glance at her face. Her hand was at her mouth, her eyes wide with shock. He sought for a word of comfort and could not find it. "It'll be all right, Krissy," he said inanely and swiftly left the room.

The patrol car, with another policeman at the wheel beside Patrolman Bennett, backed quickly from the driveway as John Hagen slammed the rear door. The vehicle was equipped with a wire mesh screen between front and rear seats with no window cranks or interior door handles. John felt like a burglary suspect on his way to a booking.

"Can you tell me anything about it?" he said to the silhouetted figures up front. Patrolman Bennett turned half about in his seat.

"All *I* know is, it went off sometime a little before four o'clock," he said. "About thirty minutes ago. It was against the back of the building in your parking lot. It blew a hole in the wall big enough to step through. The chief's there now."

"I see," said John, but he didn't see at all. He was just beginning to take in the full outrage of the act. Faceless telephone calls and letters were one thing, explosives, quite another. It occurred to him with suddenness that at least one of his vicious slanderers was possibly demented enough to attack him or his family personally— physically. The *Sentinel* and its publisher were no strangers to blind, cowardly letters in the mail. But this was now a totally new ballgame. The quiet, sprawling city of Wellbrook seemed in the faint first light of false dawn to take on a new shape, a new dimension. Behind the sleeping town were the silently crawling tentacles of the jungle. He silently groaned in contemplation of what this latest incident might do to Kris.

The squad car drove around back into the *Sentinel* parking lot. At least fifty persons were milling about. Several black-garbed, helmeted firemen shuffled their feet by a pumper truck. Three more police cruisers stood at hastily chosen spots, their revolving domes flicking red beams over the crowd like channel lighthouses. A dozen figures were clustered by the composing room rear wall. The interior light shone through a hole. The scene was additionally illuminated by police car spotlights. Patrolman Bennett opened the back door for John Hagen.

"Bill," John said to the police chief, and, "Hello, Chief," to Wellbrook's fire chief. They both turned. Somebody said, "It's Mr. Hagen." Mike Brescia, John noted, stood by grumpily with his camera, looking recently awakened. Gil Dennis, the city editor, was there, too, probably summoned by Al DeWeese.

The hole in the concrete slab wall was, indeed, big enough for a man to step through. In fact, a fireman was at the moment doing just that. Mike's strobe light winked. There was a faintly acrid odor.

The police chief, a tall man in mufti, said, "This is a real bad business, John. Same time, the clumsy bastards apparently just dropped a bundle of dynamite sticks and flagged ass."

"It was dynamite all right," said the fire chief.

"One of the boys found this on the parking lot," said the police chief. He held a sheet of notepaper, a handkerchief between his fingers and the paper. "No, don't touch it. Sacramento may be able to pick up a latent print." In the uneven light John saw the red-crayon scrawl:

JUST A FRIENDLY WARNING HAGGIN— GET LOST!!!!

"Two hours earlier they'd have got one of the linotypers," said Gil Dennis grimly. "A piece of concrete as big as your head smashed the keyboard."

"No witnesses at all?" said John. He couldn't take his eyes from the hole in the wall. His sense of personal assault was overwhelming.

"Not so far," said the police chief. "The only clue we have is from the attendant at the all-night Enco station. He said a blue sedan, he thinks it was a Pontiac, about a 'sixty-four, came barreling along the street just a minute or two before the blast. That's five blocks from here. Pretty skinny clue. Now what would anyone want to do a thing like this for, John?"

"I guess someone doesn't like me," said John Hagen with a dry amusement he did not feel. "Where is Al DeWeese?"

"I told him to go home," said Gil Dennis.

"I got all I could from him for the time being," said the police chief. "I'll talk to him again later today. He's in a little shock, although he turned down my offer to have one of the boys drive him. All he knows is he thinks he could have heard a car but he's not sure. He said the blast damn near knocked him out of his chair."

"The dirty sons of bitches," John said bitterly.

"You make a connection, John?"

"There's no doubt in my mind at all. For some time now I've been getting threats over the phone and in the mail."

"How come you never reported them to the police?"

"Because it's happened before in past years. They all turned out to be as hollow as a rain barrel."

"Is there anyone you suspect?"

"Can we talk it over in private?"

"Sure thing."

A thought jolted him. "Chief, my family. I want protection for them."

The police chief smiled. "Well, it happens I already told Bennett and his partner to kind of cruise your neighborhood the rest of the night after they brought you here. We'll work something out for the next few weeks. Let's go inside. At least you don't need your door key."

"Not at the moment," said John. He ducked and stepped gingerly over a ragged cornice. Inside, he shook his head in disbelief. Normally only a night light would be burning in the vacated composing room, but someone had turned on the full bank of ceiling fluorescents. A police photographer was shooting the interior scene, the scattered shards of concrete, the hole, the Linotype with the smashed keyboard.

"A rotten business," said the police chief.

John's stomach was knotted with a growing anger. Never a man of violence, he had had his last fistfight in his sophomore year of high school. But he felt at the moment that he would like to have his hands around the windpipe of the man who had bundled the dynamite and lighted the fuse. Had the murderous fool even known or cared whether the back shop was empty when he planted his charge?

"My office," he said. Gil Dennis had followed him into the building. Now, needing no instructions, he headed for his desk to summon help to get out an early extra edition. Already a telephone was ringing in the city room, one of four left plugged in when Mary closed the switchboard at night.

"Well, John, suppose you tell me anything you know," said the chief.

"You're aware that I've been the object of some nasty talk."

"Yeah. I've heard it."

"And you know how it started?"

"Right." The chief looked a little uncomfortable. "You made yourself kind of controversial over that PURIFY thing. Is that what these phone calls and letters you've been getting are all about?"

"Yes."

The chief rubbed his chin. "You suspect anyone?"

"Directly, no. The Reverend Bradshaw Coe is a top figure in PURIFY, but, my God, he's the last person in the world I'd accuse of having a hand in this. And Berry over at the *Green Sheet* has stirred up a lot of dust, but hell, that's just business competition.

I'm as much responsible myself as anybody. I declared myself on this issue—"

"I saw the editorial."

"You know this community, chief. We've got a wide band of right-wingers. They range from moderate or even heavily conservative Republicans, some of them my friends, all the way through the Birchers to the Minutemen. I would like to think this is not an organized conspiracy. I'm not even sure the whispering campaign is. I think some ding-a-ling decided to strike a blow for God and country by blasting a hole in my building. On his own. A nasty, mischievous crackpot."

"I'd be sort of inclined to think that way myself," said the chief. "I've got some friends in the Birchers, John. Well, think of them what you want, they're not activists—not this way. I mean, even I agree with some of their ideas. I don't know about any Minutemen in Wellbrook. I think those guys are more hot air than anything else."

"All right. But someone *did* set off a bomb."

"Yeah, we've got that. You save any of those letters?"

"I've got several here. I threw a lot of them out."

"Let's have 'em. And I want you to turn over all the rest you get. They may not be of any use but we can check them against the files. We'll make a full investigation of course, John—places that sell dynamite and so on. Maybe we'll get a tip, never can tell. What are you going to do meanwhile? Take a little vacation maybe? Get your wife and family out of town?"

"I'll have to talk to my wife," said John Hagen. "Personally—just read the *Sentinel* today, Bill. Do you need me any more right now?"

"I can't think of anything more for the moment."

"Would one of your boys be good enough to run me home?"

"Least we can do," said the chief.

A light was on in his house as the police cruiser pulled up into the driveway. The sky in the east was lightening.

"Thanks, fellows," said John. He got out and walked up to his door. He rapped on it and Kris opened it against the night chain and then let him in.

"Kris—"

"Come on, I've made some coffee." She was in her peach-colored peignoir and slippers. He closed the door and relatched it and followed her into the kitchen. Her own half-filled cup on the dinette table and half-dozen cigarette butts in an ashtray told their own story. She poured his coffee and sat down. "I've been going crazy, thinking. What is it, John?"

He told her what little he knew. "I won't even swear it's PURIFY, Kris," he concluded. "Maybe someone has just decided it's time to run me out of town."

"But it's all so savage," she said. "Like it's another country. People don't go planting bombs in a civilized community."

"People don't go shooting Presidents and civil rights leaders and presidential candidates either. But they have."

"What do we do now?" She held her coffee cup between her hands, looking at him over it.

"How would you like to take the children and go away for a while?"

"Without you?"

"I'm not leaving now."

"Why can't you?"

He drew a deep breath and exhaled slowly. "I just can't, Krissy."

"Would it hurt you to go away for two or three weeks or until school starts? Give the police a chance to find out who did this? Do you think they couldn't run that goddamned newspaper for just one day without you? Do you?"

He bowed his head over his laced fingers. Finally—hearing her quickened breath—he said slowly: "I am not leaving Wellbrook at this time. I can't and I won't. I think very much of my family, Kris, and that's why I think I'd like you to take Gordo and Pammy and go somewhere. When this all blows over, I'll take a vacation. I've got to get dressed now and go down to the office."

The city room was a controlled powerhouse of energy, like a boiler under a tight valve. It was only six o'clock but nearly the whole day staff was on the job, rushing to get a paper on the street by eleven o'clock, three hours ahead of normal publication. The telephones were ringing with calls from Los Angeles, San Francisco, even New York. Chris Smith had telephoned a quick first take to the Associated Press in L.A. The *Herald-Examiner,* UPI, *Examiner* in San Francisco, and *Time* and *Newsweek* now were all demanding further details along with AP. Quincy Broyles and Gil Dennis had roughed out page one with a single eight-column Armageddon screamer in wood type:

SENTINEL BOMBED!

with a six-column photo on the left and the two-column main story leading under a second head from top right. John Hagen knew better than to bother his city editor for longer than it took him to nod approval. "Leave me room to start a boxed editorial on the lower left-hand side, Gil," he said. He walked into his office and closed the door. He instructed Mary by telephone intercom, "No calls from anyone, and that means anyone, Mary." He fed a book of copy paper into his old Underwood and paused to marshal his thoughts. He then began typing, and typed almost without stopping for twenty minutes. He ripped his second book from the machine, slipped it under the first, and looked quickly over his handiwork:

EDITORIAL

Cowardly Blow in the Dark

Early this morning a person or persons unknown made a coward's reply to the Sentinel's editorial policies. He or they lit the fuse on a bundle of dynamite and scurried off into the night.

The blast blew a man-size hole in the back wall of our composing room. By sheer luck our printers had all gone home, or at least one man would have been killed. As it was, only the wall and one expensive typesetting machine were damaged, and I thank God that was all.

The Sentinel points the finger at no one, suggests no name and offers no sure motive for this murderous act. Without proof, I can—at this early hour—say only that the police are investigating.

It may be stated accurately, however, that whoever chose this violent course almost certainly did so as a means of warning me to sell out and leave this community.

The scrawled note in the parking lot made that plain. Illiterately punctuated, it said: JUST A FRIENDLY WARNING 'HAGGIN'—GET LOST!!!!

I, the Sentinel publisher, have for a number of weeks been the target of scurrilous, anonymous letters and telephone calls, at the office and at my home. Many of these sneaky messages identify the Sentinel's editorial stand against Public United to Restore Innocence to Fair Youth—Prop. 5 on the November ballot—as the motive for the invective.

Whether this morning's outrage was prompted by the Sentinel's denunciation of PURIFY I cannot say. I know none of the movement's public leaders is in any way responsible for this criminal act.

Regardless of my political differences with the principals behind Prop. 5 and theirs with me, I am positive they have no more knowledge at this point of the bombing than have I.

I DO believe it reasonable to suspect that some one of the anonymous letter-writers or telephone callers who resent the Sentinel's position on PURIFY is one of the bombers—if there be more than one.

I hereby serve notice that I have not the slightest intention of budging from Wellbrook or of selling the Sentinel. Nor do I intend to withdraw the Sentinel's editorial opposition to Prop. 5. It is a thoroughly bad measure and I hope it takes a decisive and deserved beating at the polls come election day in November.

To my enemies of the night who hide behind unsigned letters, the anonymity of the telephone and dynamite:

DO YOU HAVE ANY FURTHER QUESTIONS?

John A. Hagen

Long before the *Sentinel* extra could hit the street, the news was on radio and television. The calls began flooding in. John Hagen, having lifted the injunction against incoming calls, began accepting them from those he knew. He was deeply depressed over the act of violence and over Kris. Yet his spirits could not help lifting somewhat by the outpouring of indignation, shock, anger, and sympathy that came across the wire. I *do* have friends, he thought, decent people who bitterly resent a senseless act of terrorism against a neighbor and who protest violence in their community. Harry Wells and Elliott Warren in quick succession, and then Rabbi Gross and

Fred, his insurance agent, and others. Some he knew only casually, like Pete at the service station where he had his car lubed, the new manager at the Elks Club, his barber, and Emiliano, the restaurateur.

There were other interruptions, including the area correspondent for the Los Angeles *Times,* who had arrived early with a cameraman and wanted a statement, and calls from several radio stations, each requiring recorded interviews by telephone, each on a crash basis. An insurance man came over to view the damage, bringing *his* photographer, and the police chief paid a call to ask some more questions. No, they had no solid leads as yet; no real leads at all, in fact. Then his father telephoned in some agitation from La Jolla and John spent some time convincing him that he was in no personal danger, which he himself wished he could believe.

The extra hit the streets at just five minutes after eleven o'clock. The staff already had been working at fever pitch for thirty minutes pounding out copy for the regular edition. Vic Massoni was on the wire at eleven-thirty from San Diego.

"What the hell's going on, Johnny?" he said. "I just heard the report. Is everyone crazy?"

"Well, some crackpot stuck dynamite at the back door this morning, Vic. All kinds of fun."

"Sweet Jesus Christ. The AP said nobody was hurt."

"Luckily."

"How's Kris taking it?" he said. Instantly John wondered why that had occurred to him so quickly.

"She's pretty nervous and unhappy."

"I should think so. God, what a rotten business!"

"To change the subject. How's the campaign going?"

"Well, you've seen the polls."

"Yeah, Hausner's got a little edge on you."

"That's why I'm giving it everything I've got."

"Attaboy. I'm still waiting for that statement on Proposition Five —PURIFY, remember?"

"Later, Johnny boy."

"I'll rely on it. See you, Vic."

The denouement came several weeks later, at a time when John had begun to worry about a very serious drop in advertising. It was so irrelevant, so ridiculous, that John began to wonder whether the whole world was upside down.

—29—

There were three of them. Not one looked to be over eighteen. The chief of police had them in his office, together with a couple of other officers and a gaunt, morose man the chief introduced as Sam Golden of the public defender's office.

"Here's your bombers," said the chief. "For your benefit I'll repeat what the boys have told me while they're in your presence—right, Mr. Golden?"

"I don't want any more questioning right now," said Golden dispiritedly.

"Correction," said the chief. "The burden of the confession was freely volunteered and you were here, Mr. Golden. Boys, did I warn you of your rights against self-incrimination?"

The three, who were seated together on a bench, looked at each other. The middle one, a thin, dark youngster wearing desert boots, faded Levi's, and a knit jersey, said, "Yeah."

"Did I tell you anything you said could be used against you?" said the chief.

"Yeah," said the boy again.

"Did you not volunteer freely and of your own accord, in the presence of one another, that you set off an explosive charge at the *Sentinel* building several weeks ago?"

The boy nodded.

"Why?" pursued the chief.

"Aw," said the boy on the left, a well-dressed, husky lad wearing glasses. "You had us. What the hell?"

"I don't want you to plow any new ground here, Chief," said Golden. "The parents are on the way over and they'll probably want their own lawyer."

"Everything I'm asking is already being typed up," said the chief. John Hagen got the impression he was showing off a little. "Now, boys, did you tell me why you set off that dynamite?"

Again the three boys looked at each other. Finally, the thin boy said, "We was high."

"What do you mean, high?" asked the chief.

"Stoned, man. Flaked out on caps. We had this here dynamite, see, and it seemed like a good idea to, like, make a noise. You know?"

"Where did you get the dynamite?"

"Aw, some construction shack out in the hills."

"Did you take it with any purpose in mind?"

The chunky boy said, "Man, it was there, we just took it. They shouldn't leave that stuff layin' around."

"So you were high and decided to make a noise," said the chief. "Why the *Sentinel* building?"

The thin boy said, "On accounta what they're sayin'."

"On account of what who's saying?" said the chief sharply.

"Oh, people. About this here *Sentinel*."

"You'll have to do better than that, son."

"Well, Benny here," said the lad, nodding at the chunky boy, "he heard his old man tell my old man the guy that puts out that filthy rag, he calls it, oughta be tarred and feathered. Said the *Sentinel* was, like, a disgrace to a decent community."

"Did your father say why, Benny?" said the chief, addressing the boy with glasses.

"Aw, I don't know, it was somepm like a political thing, you know?" said Benny. "He said those guys'd be lucky if somebody didn't set fire to their building one of these nights. Bill's old man said, yeah, we oughta run 'em outa town."

"But you don't know why?" persisted the chief.

The boy shrugged.

"So you boys got high on pills, cruised over to the *Sentinel,* lit the fuse, and took off, isn't that about it? You decided to pull a silly stunt that could have killed a man, just on account of some vague rumor you overheard—right?"

The thin boy said, "Man, high is high. You know?"

The chief of police looked at John Hagen, who was frowning. "That's the main part of it," he said to John.

"May I talk to the boys?" said John.

"Go ahead."

"Boys, do you know me?" said John. All three shook their heads.

"Do you know my name?"

"Haggin?" ventured the thin boy.

"It's Hagen. I own the building and the newspaper. Did any of you ever hear of something called PURIFY?"

Again the three looked at each other. "Called what?" said the third boy, the medium-sized youth on the right who had not spoken before.

"PURIFY, this political movement I think the two fathers were talking about."

"Was that what it was?" said the chunky boy, Benny.

"That's what I'm asking you," said John grimly.

"Like, who knows?" said Benny, shrugging.

"Don't you feel any remorse?" said John tightly.

"Huh?"

"Are you sorry you did what you did?"

"Yeah, I guess so," said Benny.

"Yeah, we're sorry," said the thin boy.

John shrugged helplessly. "Thanks for quick work, Chief," he said. "It's all so senseless."

"Yeah," said the chief disgustedly. "You punks, somebody oughta knock your brains out!"

John Hagen turned away wearily.

— *30* —

He drove west on a mission of desperation. The broad roadway of El Camino Drive wound gracefully past one of the newer, more graceful subdivisions, Sierra Verde, rolling gently over broad swales on which the oaks had been mercifully spared. It curved to the northeast and dipped into the small business district of Lucerne—two dozen stores, several service stations, two bars, and a bus station. Past Lucerne he pulled the Chevy down carefully at a stoplight controlling cross traffic on the El Camino–Park Estates Boulevard intersection. He turned north on Park Estates Boulevard. The midmorning traffic thickened as he cruised at a comfortable thirty-five miles an hour. Although it was a week past Labor Day the air was uncomfortably warm; it had been an extremely dry summer. Park Estates flowed in a long, looping S-curve, through a cut in Lemon Hill, the citrus trees long since replaced by streets and multi-level houses. Beyond lay the vast sprawl of the Wellbrook Shopping Center. The largest of some one hundred businesses in a series of interconnecting quadrangles surrounded by acres of striped asphalt was Hartmann's Department Store. Three stories high, it dominated the central quadrangle.

He parked aslant fully seventy-five yards from the arcade leading to the garden court interior of the central quadrangle. The low-ceilinged arcade was lined with shops: a jeweler, shoe repair, boutique, bookstore, beauty parlor. The main entrance was on the other side of the building, the direction from which most traffic entered, but there were doors into Hartmann's from the garden court as well. He chose the nearest and found himself in the luggage and leather department. He rose on an escalator to the second floor and proceeded through linens and draperies, furniture, and lighting fixtures to the corner suite that housed the business and administrative offices. A pleasant, gray-haired woman said, "Good morning, Mr. Hagen. Did you wish to see Mr. Hartmann?"

"I would like to, thank you," said John.

"Let me see if he's free," she said. She pressed the button on an intercom, then lifted the receiver from the top. She gave the message and listened a moment. "Yes, sir," she said. "He asked if you'd wait, he has one of the executives with him."

"Thank you." He sat on a plastic and chrome sofa and reopened the letter. It was brief, formal, and devastating. He reread it carefully, but it told him nothing new. He refolded it and tucked it back in his inside coat pocket.

For quite a long time he sat. For a while he leafed through a copy of *Women's Wear Daily* from the end table. Eventually it palled; he had too much on his mind. He glanced at his watch. He had been waiting twenty minutes.

The secretary, who had turned to her electric typewriter and was whisking through a letter, stopped and picked up the intercom receiver. "Yes, sir," she said, and hung up. "You know the way back, of course, Mr. Hagen?"

"Oh yes, thank you."

Emil Hartmann was behind his large, new, no-nonsense desk. Seated next to him was an elegantly turned-out young man in a black suit, who looked at John unsmilingly. Emil, a brother Elk, was portly in gray double-breasted, almost totally bald, and had an impressive, fleshy nose. He wore rimless eyeglasses with gold temples. Now he rose, saying, "Hello, John," shaking hands, adding, "I guess you know my advertising manager, Jim Stern."

"Yes; hello, Mr. Stern." John was not at all well acquainted with him. This was Will Naismith and crew's normal territory, but the present situation was anything but normal.

"How are you, Mr. Hagen?" said Stern, also shaking hands.

Emil Hartmann reseated himself. "I guess I don't have to ask why you came, John. I could have told you to save the trip. We made a business decision. So what more could I tell you?"

"Emil, it doesn't add up," said John quietly. "You've been advertising with the *Sentinel* since I first went in business—since you had the store down on Centinela Avenue. You've grown on *Sentinel* advertising. *This*." He took in the office and by implication the huge store. "We've been pulling business for you for ten years. And now, with a history like that, suddenly you tell us you are cutting us out completely on contract renewal next month. Emil, it simply doesn't make good sense. You need the *Sentinel* as much as the *Sentinel* needs you."

"If I may comment," said Mr. Stern. "We talked this over very thoroughly. Now, we've found that we can buy nearly twice the space in the *Green Sheet* for what we pay for the *Sentinel* and get at least ten thousand more circulation."

"Yes, and how much of that is paid circulation?"

"Well, I don't think that is too important," said Stern. "The shopper has become a very big thing in a lot of communities. And now that this one has gone three a week, which is the frequency we buy the *Sentinel*—"

"I'll invite you to make a test," said John Hagen. "Hire a man, three men, ten men for one day. I'll pay for it. Send them out at eight o'clock of a Monday, Wednesday, or Friday morning. Have them count every house they can in one eight-hour day and have them count every *Green Sheet* that's still lying on the lawn. We estimate that between fifty and seventy-five per cent of their copies don't even get picked up except to throw away as garbage. People *pay* for the *Sentinel*. Not one gets tossed unread."

"Well, John, we tried advertising some specials in the *Green Sheet* we didn't advertise in the *Sentinel* and they pulled real good," said Emil Hartmann. "So we began to ask ourselves, do we need the *Sentinel* all that bad, especially when the other paper's got saturation coverage? We decided the answer was no."

"Is that the whole basis for the decision?" said John.

"Purely business, like I said," said Emil Hartmann.

John Hagen looked from one man to the other. Stern was finding something interesting about the fingernails of his left hand. Hartmann was beginning to rock back and forth as if impatient for his visitor to be gone.

"I see. Emil, mind if I have a word with you in private?"

"John, I'm not going to change my mind. The decision's made."

"Surely after a ten-year association you can spare me a minute."

Stern looked coldly at John Hagen and then at the owner. An expression of annoyance crossed Hartmann's face. Then he grunted and inclined his head toward Stern. His fingers laced, he made a small gesture with his thumb. Stern rose immediately and left through an interior doorway, closing the door behind him.

"Emil, there is some other reason," said John Hagen. "A business like yours was not built on snap decisions. You've always been a strong-minded, independent merchant and a good citizen of the community. I remember your work in the first school bond election."

"John, listen—"

"—Your leadership in the beautification program, the zoning fight, the way you spoke up when the pressure was on Elliott Warren about the sex-education program in the schools—"

"—All some time ago."

"Not that long ago."

"I got a big investment here."

"Of course you have."

"Time it takes. Time and energy and worry. You know what I'm getting at? A store's got to keep right on top—the competition is terrific. Everything we sell, somebody else sells. We've got to sell at the right price, give good service, and keep our good will. You understand me, John?"

"Of course I understand."

"A store's not like a newspaper, so maybe you don't know."

"We've got our problems too."

"Yeah, you just said it right there. You've got problems. And your problems I don't need."

"What's the trouble, Emil?"

"John, you're a smart guy, I wouldn't kid you. They're working on you."

"Who's they?"

Emil Hartmann spread his hands. "You've got to know the answer to that better than me. So, all right, that's your worry. But when they start in on me on account of you . . . Stern in there, he's a very smart boy. He figures we spend the same amount in the other paper we do with you, we get twice the space, huh? Maybe it hasn't got the prestige of the *Sentinel* but it's got plenty coverage. So we make a choice—"

"And stay out of trouble, Emil?"

"John, you got *controversial.*"

"Is it really hurting your business, Emil?"

"I could show you. I don't mean it really shows up in the books or anything, but I know already we got good customers say until I drop my advertising in the *Sentinel,* Hartmann's can drop dead for their business. A thing like that over a period of time can kill you."

"A few of these people can make an awful lot of noise, Emil. How many have you actually heard from?"

"Enough. I can't risk it, and I'm sorry, John."

"Would you, if you were me, back away from something you believe is right just because it's controversial?"

"You're talking about oranges and lemons. You've got a newspaper to get out, I've got merchandise to sell."

"Emil, I can't believe these people, whoever they are, can hurt you that much."

"What would *you* know, a Gentile, how anybody can hurt you?"

"Oh listen, Emil, race has nothing to do with this."

"To a Jew race has to do with everything. He's poor, he's a nudnik; he's rich, what would you expect? He's meek, he's too spineless to stand up like a man; he's forthright, he's just like all the rest of them. Let him, a young man, admire a *shicksa,* he's certainly got a nerve, but he marries a Jewish girl, it shows they all stick to the same tribe. You want all the arguments, I've got 'em. They don't like what you do in your newspaper, it's that bastard Hagen, but if they don't like what *I* do it's that *Jew* bastard Hartmann. They got a whispering campaign going now about you, they start a good strong one about me, boycott Hartmann's, I could be dead. Takes time, but it could happen. Maybe you've got too much guts for your own good, John. Maybe you'd just like to get a good price for the *Sentinel,* go someplace else, run a newspaper where people like some we've got here should turn blue. I don't know, it's not my problem. But I can't advertise with you any more, I'm sorry, but I'm not going to change my mind."

"I tell you, Emil, they're just not that strong," said John earnestly. "It's a small vocal minority boring in wherever they think there's a pressure point."

"*You* say. I say there's a lot of them and they don't like what you said on this PURIFY. Who uses dynamite? Maybe I'll get stink bombs in the store. Look, John, you think what you want but it's no different. The decision stands."

"If you'd look at it this way—"

"I'm all out of time."

John Hagen arose. "All right, Emil."

"I said it twice, I'll say it three times, I'm sorry."

"Okay." He was at the door when Hartmann spoke again.

"John, when the little girl was killed last January . . ."

"Yes, Emil?"

"It was a nice thing you did."

"It was little enough I could do."

"The ad I ran, closing the store a day. You never billed."

"She was a nice little girl, your daughter."

"Maybe you could—you know—kind of change your mind on this silly political business? A thing like this, it's that important?"

"Good-by, Emil," said John Hagen.

He took another route back to the office. On the way he saw three billboards: Elect/STATE SEN. DAVID O. HAUSNER/Attorney General/*CLEAN UP* CALIFORNIA . . . Assemblyman VICTOR MASSONI/Your Next Attorney General/Dedicated—Able . . . Mark "YES" on Prop. 5/The *PURIFY* Amendment/GET RID OF THE DIRTY BOOKS!!

– *31* –

And another letter. It was on stiff vellum bearing the letterhead of a firm of Los Angeles attorneys. It was in what it omitted rather than in what it said that gave cause for concern . . .

It bore a September date.

Mr. John A. Hagen
President
Sentinel Publishing Company, Inc.
9351 Centinela Avenue
Wellbrook, California

Dear Mr. Hagen:

On behalf of Miss Mary R. Peters, a 20% shareholder in the Sentinel Publishing Co., Inc., and Mr. and Mrs. Henry D. Quentin, shareholders in joint tenancy of a 20% interest in the Sentinel Publishing Co., Inc., and with the concurrence of James A. Malkin, a 20% shareholder in the Sentinel Publishing Co., Inc., I hereby request a special meeting of shareholders of said corporation during the first week of October.

I call your attention to Paragraph 15 of the By-Laws, which requires the convening of a special meeting when requested by a majority of shareholders.

Please let me know at your earliest convenience the day, time, and place that you wish to convene the meeting.

Yours truly,
L. B. Bradbury

cc: Miss Mary R. Peters
     Mr./Mrs. Henry D. Quentin
     Mr. James A. Malkin
     Mr. Allan R. Hagen

"Ready, son?" said his father.

"We may as well find out what they want and get it over with," said John Hagen. He tucked the letter back in his pocket. His father got up from the table rather slowly. In just two months he would be seventy, John remembered.

Emiliano was standing at his habitual post by the cash register, bowing a trio of men out. The door closed behind them.

"Mr. Hagen, I been very pleased to meet your father," said Emiliano. "Mr. Hagen, you got a very fine boy here. You come back and see us any time, sir."

"Thank you," said Allan Hagen gruffly. "Very good food."

"I try to serve the best in Wellbrook. Good-by, gentlemen."

Walking toward the car, Allan Hagen said, "Why is it so many ex-bootleggers run such good restaurants?"

"How did you know he's an ex-bootlegger?"

"Isn't he?"

"So I'm told. I was about four years old when there were such things as bootleggers."

"About the only good thing the Great Brain ever did, getting rid of Prohibition. Of course you know he and Eleanor were just this side of being a couple of lushes."

"Oh Lord, where did you ever hear that canard?"

"It was very well known at the time. When are you going to get rid of this old wreck?"

"About the time you start forgetting some of those stories about Roosevelt," said John, opening the door for his father.

"It's not good for that many years. Now, Hoover, there was the last sound President this country ever had."

John Hagen came around and opened his own door and got in. "Yes, I've read all about the Great Engineer," he said. "The business of this country is business."

"If you're going to make a point with sarcasm, it'd be a good idea to quote the right man. That was Coolidge."

"Oh, yes. Hoover was two cars in every garage and a chicken in every pot, wasn't he?"

"All we have to feah is feah itself," said Allan Hagen. "*My* friends."

"What do you suppose these people want, Dad?" said John.

"Well, I think they're worried about the paper, wouldn't you think?"

"We're still in business."

"Yes, but the gross is way off since you lost Hartmann's."

"We'll get him back sooner or later," said John with a confidence he did not feel. His father grunted and said no more as John drove to the Riviera Lodge, where he had rented a meeting room for a couple of hours. The meeting could easily have been held in his office, but he had not wanted it there. The meeting call was ominous, hinting at hostilities, and if he were facing one or all of the other shareholders in an adversary situation, he did not want to do so in the clublike surroundings of his own working headquarters.

He parked in a palm-lined drive, and father and son walked along the drive until they reached a sidewalk which led under a huge V-shaped porte-cochere to the broad glass double doors of the hotel entrance. It was just one-thirty; they were exactly on time. They walked down a corridor that angled off the spacious lobby. It dead-ended at a room whose door was open. Faces turned toward Allan and John Hagen as they entered. Four persons were seated at a comfortably large conference table. Another, a man, was standing, smoking restlessly. The table had been covered by a maroon spread and had all the usual conference paraphernalia: writing pads and pencils, ashtrays, and ice water and glasses. Behind the table stood a tarpaulin-covered chalkboard and next to it, an easel, both accessory to the room's usual role as a site of sales meetings.

Bradbury, the attorney, the man who was standing, now came forward. "The Hagens, father and son," he said. He was of better than average height, sparely built, and of a somewhat pasty complexion, as though he spent too many hours in the office and not enough on the golf course or gardening. They accepted his handshake in turn.

"Hello, Allan," said one of the two seated men, rising now, as did the other.

"Jim, how are you?" said Allan Hagen to James Malkin, who was one of the four original investors in the corporation. Malkin was a well-preserved, ruddy man with almost theatrical white hair. He could have been a long-retired football coach or Boy Scout executive. The other introductions were made. The other man, now on his feet, was Henry Quentin, co-holder with his seated wife of a 20 per cent share by inheritance. The other, rather mannish-looking woman, who also acknowledged the introduction, was Miss Mary Peters, whose father had bequeathed her his 20 per cent ownership on his death. John Hagen had not met either her or the Quentins until now, because they had been willing to let Bradbury represent their interests at the routine annual meetings of the past several years. Their presence confirmed John's apprehension that something very sticky was in the works. He took his place at the head of the table.

"I'll declare this special meeting of the shareholders of the Sentinel Publishing Company, Incorporated, open," said John Hagen. "It has been called at the request of a majority of the shareholders, namely Miss Peters and Mr. and Mrs. Quentin—as I understand, they requested the meeting—"

"That is right, and Mr. Malkin concurred," said Bradbury.

"All right. We'll keep it informal, as we usually do. It is noted that the officers are present in the person of myself as president, Mr. Allan Hagen as vice-president, and Mr. Malkin as secretary-treasurer. All shareholders are present. Who wants to begin? Mr. Bradbury?"

The attorney steepled his fingers. "I suppose I may as well. Now, as we all know, up until recently the *Sentinel* newspaper has been in a growth situation. It has shown a steady increase in both circulation and advertising, and for the past five years has returned an excellent profit for the investor-shareholders. Last year the net yield was approximately fifteen per cent of gross income. Distribution to shareholders amounted to approximately eight per cent dividend on investment, calculating the present market worth of a twenty per cent share as one hundred and twenty thousand dollars, more or less."

Miss Peters cleared her throat. "We know all that," she said brusquely.

"It is necessary to state it, Miss Peters," said Bradbury with a hint of reproval in his voice. "But let me proceed. Despite this excellent, ah, track record, recent events with respect to the *Sentinel* have aroused certain apprehensions in a majority of shareholders. They have communicated these apprehensions to me and through me, to the end that this meeting has been called."

"Let me straighten the record on that," said James Malkin, pushing his hand back over his snowy hair. "I said if Miss Peters and the Quentins wanted a meeting, I'd go along. If they felt it was necessary to talk this thing out, I was willing. Okay?"

"Your concurrence nonetheless created a majority request, Mr. Malkin," said the attorney smoothly. "I'll continue. Specifically, the reason for this meeting, springing from these apprehensions I spoke of, is to examine the stewardship of Mr. John Hagen as editor-publisher of the Wellbrook *Sentinel*. To decide if the events of the past several months may not have cast considerable doubt on his editorial judgment, his continued ability to publish a financially successful newspaper; in short, to ask ourselves frankly: has Mr. Hagen committed himself to an editorial policy that may well lead to the ultimate failure of this newspaper? That is our purpose here today."

John Hagen was stunned. Never in his ten years had he been so openly challenged. There had been subdued grumbling in times past about his editorial stand on a particularly controversial issue, but never so much as a hint that he was incapable of continuing to steer the ship. For a moment no one spoke. He found his voice.

"I might say I am taken aback, to put it mildly," he said in a dry voice. "Truly—"

"Whose damn fool idea is this?" demanded Allan Hagen. He looked around the table fiercely. "Yours, Jim?"

"I'm here to hear what these people have to say and that's why I agreed to the meeting, Allan," said Malkin frowning. "And I'm not commenting one way or the other until I hear more."

"Well, I want to say—"

"Excuse me," said John Hagen. "We conduct a fairly informal meeting here but in the circumstances I guess we'd better abide by some rule of order. Do I understand you are suggesting I might resign as editor and publisher, Mr. Bradbury?"

The attorney cocked his head behind hands opened like those of a wrestler groping toward the thrust of his opponent's hand. "Wait a minute, we're going too fast. Nothing like that has been said at all. I believe the consensus here is that we want to ask ourselves some questions. Then we can decide which way we go from there."

"Well, I have something to say," said Henry Quentin, nudged by his wife. He was a man who looked to be in his young thirties, with sharp, inquisitorial features.

"I'll interrupt again," said John Hagen.

"Not me you won't," said Quentin.

"As presiding officer I will—"

"Mr. Bradbury, I've got a right to speak," said Quentin angrily.

"Yes, of course he has, Mr. Hagen," said Bradbury sharply.

"I'm going to rule first, Mr. Bradbury, that either you are the spokesman for the Quentins and Miss Peters, holding their power of attorney, or that they will speak for themselves. If they do, you will have relinquished that power of attorney and I'll ask you to leave this meeting."

"That's awfully high-handed," complained Miss Peters, shifting in her chair. "We have a right to our attorney."

"They do indeed, Mr. Hagen," said Bradbury sternly.

"I don't see how a guy can run a meeting fairly when it's him we're discussing," said Quentin sourly, looking across at Miss Peters, who nodded vigorously.

"Since I haven't yet been voted out as president of this corporation, I'll continue to preside," said John Hagen. "I'll give you your say. However, you, Mr. Bradbury, can choose whichever role you want, but not both. If you wish to remain as adviser to the Quentins and Miss Peters, you may, but in that case you will have no voice and no vote in this meeting. I'm no lawyer, but I know that giving you an additional voice would be tantamount to giving you shares in this corporation, which I am in no position to do. Now, who speaks for the Quentins?"

Quentin and his wife looked at each other.

"I'll speak for myself," said Quentin grimly to John Hagen.

"Who speaks for you, Miss Peters?"

"I guess I can handle my end," she said firmly.

"The ruling then is that you may remain as adviser but you have no voice here, Mr. Bradbury," said John Hagen.

"I'll accept that for now," said the attorney abruptly. "Only for now, mind you."

"Now may I talk?" said Quentin determinedly.

"When there is a motion on the floor," said John. "Mr. Hagen, will you assume the chair so that I may offer a motion?"

"I will," said Allan Hagen to his son.

"I move," said John Hagen, "that Mr. John Hagen be discharged as editor and publisher of the Wellbrook *Sentinel* in accordance with a provision of the bylaws permitting his discharge for failure to perform his duties in a satisfactory and competent manner."

There was a shocked silence. Then Henry Quentin grinned. "Second the motion," he said.

"It has been duly moved and seconded that John Hagen be discharged as editor and publisher," said Allan Hagen slowly. He glowered at Quentin. "I relinquish the chair."

"Point of order," said Quentin. "I've never been through anything like this. I'll have to ask my attorney for advice. Mr. Bradbury, would it be legal for Mr. John Hagen to preside as chairman when we're discussing his own job?"

"I see no reason why not, Mr. Quentin," said Bradbury formally. "Providing he takes no part in the discussion."

"I'll go you one better," said John. "Not only will I take no part in the discussion, but I'll declare that the area of discussion is wide open. I'll answer only when I am directly addressed. Does that meet with everyone's approval?"

No one spoke.

"Hearing no objections, the chair will now entertain discussion on the motion," said John.

"Now maybe I can talk," said Quentin sarcastically. "Mr. Bradbury said some of the shareholders—how'd you put it, Mr. Bradbury?—have certain apprehensions about the way Mr. Hagen has been running the *Sentinel* lately. Well, you could say that. You could say, because of this screwball business on state ballot Proposition Five, that Mr. Hagen is running this newspaper straight into the ground. Now, Mrs. Quentin and I aren't any of your original backers, but that doesn't make any difference. We inherited twenty per cent and that gives us as big a voice in management as anybody. I object to this editorial position on two grounds: philosophical and business-wise. I personally signed the PURIFY initiative petition because I think it's a damn fine thing. I don't think any newspaper I've got any connection with should stick its neck out and oppose it. For the life of me, I can't understand why our editor and publisher here should. That's philosophical. The other, more practical reason is, it stands to hit me right in the pocketbook. Well, I don't intend to sit back on my haunches and see a valuable holding go up in smoke, just because of one man's stubborn disposition. I'm going to ask some questions and I'd like some answers." He looked directly at John Hagen, who returned his look impassively.

"Mr. Hagen," said Quentin, planting his right elbow on the table and aiming a forefinger at John, "isn't it true that the Wellbrook *Sentinel* just one month ago lost its single biggest advertiser because the *Sentinel* opposes ballot Proposition Five?"

"Correct," said John.

"Hartmann's Department Store gave you a thirty-day notice that they weren't going to renew, and this month they didn't, isn't that right?"

"Yes. The yearly contract expired and Hartmann failed to renew."

"How much advertising did Hartmann's buy during that twelve-month period?"

"It amounted to some sixty-five thousand dollars."

"Sixty-five thousand dollars," said Quentin slowly. He looked around the table. "The net profit for last year was only a little over ninety thousand dollars. One account, sixty-five thousand dollars." He looked expectantly at John Hagen. John said nothing. "Okay,

Mr. Hagen, let me ask you this: did Hartmann's come right out and tell you they might renew if you changed the *Sentinel's* position on ballot Proposition Five?"

"That, I believe, was implicit."

"Don't give me implicit," said Quentin.

"Don't be impertinent," Allan Hagen growled. "Who do you think you're talking to?"

"I'm a shareholder of this corporation talking to an employee of this corporation," Quentin snapped.

"You're talking to the man who founded and built the newspaper," said Allan Hagen.

"Yes, with some of my father's money."

"A fine man who knew exactly what he was doing when he invested."

"Have you some more questions, Mr. Quentin?" said John Hagen.

"I sure have. What do you mean, implicit?"

"Mr. Emil Hartmann indicated he would renew if I could change my mind on this, quote, silly political business, unquote."

"He laid it right on the line like that?"

"Yes."

"And you didn't grab it? You let a sixty-five-thousand-dollar account go down the drain—just like that." Henry Quentin snapped his fingers.

"I didn't take him up on his offer," said John. "A principle was at stake."

"Yeah, for sixty-five grand, two thirds of a year's profits. I'd like to know if you would tell me and my fellow shareholders just exactly what that lofty principle is that costs so much money?"

"I'm not sure whether the word is lofty or practical, Mr. Quentin," said John Hagen thoughtfully. "I think if the word gets around that your editorial columns are for sale, you're doomed for extinction sooner or later anyway. Mr. Hartmann, I believe, has no philosophical disagreement with the *Sentinel*. He was worried that our position on PURIFY might hurt his own business. I don't think his decision will remain in effect permanently. It is my personal belief and hope that when the heat and tempers cool, Hartmann's will be back in the *Sentinel*. In fact, still practically speaking, I believe he will not derive the benefit from his advertising in the *Progress and Green Sheet* that he has in the *Sentinel*. Meanwhile, he is forced to respect the *Sentinel* for its integrity. He knows that what he buys is advertising space, not our editorial soul."

"Oh boy!" said Quentin disgustedly. "That sounds like a high-school valedictory."

"Is that a question or a comment, Mr. Quentin?"

"Are you through, Mr. Quentin?" Miss Peters said.

"No, but go ahead."

She cleared her throat. "I'd like to ask you, Mr. Hagen, how you can put your own personal beliefs ahead of the best interests of the Wellbrook *Sentinel?*" Her mouth closed firmly.

"I'm not sure that I do," said John Hagen.

"Isn't this position that you have adopted on Proposition Number Five purely a personal one?"

"I didn't take a staff vote, if that's what you mean. We don't run the *Sentinel* by committee."

"Then it *is* solely your own opinion that PURIFY is bad?"

"Not entirely. I got some good legal opinion before making any move at all. You'll notice, by the way, that most other newspapers have since come out against PURIFY too."

"Are they getting the same treatment the *Sentinel* is?"

"Not as far as I can learn. Some crackpot letters, yes."

"Why is it that anyone who disagrees with you is a crackpot, Mr. Hagen?" said Quentin dangerously.

"To me, anyone who writes a vicious, defamatory, threatening letter without the guts to sign his name is a crackpot," said John. "Anyone who equates smut with communism is a crackpot. Anyone who plants filthy rumors about me and my family, makes anonymous, threatening phone calls in the night, drives my wife to the verge of a nervous breakdown—any person who does any one of all these things that have happened to me in the last several months is a grade-A, certifiable nut. Is there any more discussion?" His voice was at the point of breaking with emotion.

Quentin was looking at him curiously. "All this?" he said.

"Yes."

"Can't the police do anything?"

"Apparently not. They've tried. I don't know who these people are. But I'm not caving in. Only if you people fire me."

"I think maybe we ought to vote on it," said Miss Peters.

"Just a minute," said Allan Hagen. "You two people have been doing all the talking. I'm as big a shareholder as either one of you. I think maybe you ought to know that any day my son and I happen to agree on anything in politics, that day the sun will rise in the west. That goes for his opinion on PURIFY, for that matter. I happen to think it would be a good thing myself." He cleared his throat, frowning fiercely. "At the same time, let me remind you people once more that John Hagen is the man that put the Wellbrook *Sentinel* in business as a daily newspaper. He pulled it together out of nothing and he made a success out of it with his brains, his guts, his energy, and ten years of his life. He's going through a bad time right now. The paper's lost some business—a pretty good chunk of it. Some cowardly people are trying to make his life a hell. And because he's got too much stamina and plain damn fool stubbornness, if you please, you characters who came along—yes, you Johnny-come-latelies who inherited a piece of this business and don't know any more about the newspaper business than I do about the moon—you're going to nail his hide to the barn door. You're going to ram your opinions down his throat and he's going to take it or be fired. Well, I'll tell you right now, I am goddamned proud of my son and I'll tell you furthermore that whatever he does with *his* newspaper, he's got my backing all the way."

"It isn't *his* newspaper, Mr. Hagen," said Attorney Bradbury.

"You shut up," said Allan Hagen. "This is a meeting of shareholders."

"I call for a vote," said Quentin tightly.

"Do you move the question?" said John.

"I move the question."

"Is there a second?"

"I'll second," said Miss Peters.

"What is your pleasure?" said John.

"Aye!" said four voices.

"We are voting on the motion to dismiss John Hagen as editor and publisher of the Wellbrook *Sentinel*," said John. "All those in favor of his dismissal respond by saying aye."

"Aye," said Henry Quentin.

"Aye," said Miss Peters.

"Opposed?"

"No," said Allan Hagen, looking at James Malkin.

"The chair casts its vote no," said John. "Mr. Malkin, I don't believe you voted."

"I abstain," said James Malkin. The others stared at him.

"We have two ayes and two noes," said John Hagen. "The motion is—"

"Just a minute," said Malkin, brushing back his snowy hair once more. "I'd like to make my position clear after listening to all you people. I feel pretty much the same way like Allan Hagen here when it comes to this Prop. Five. I think it ought to go through. I don't have his blind loyalty to his son, though. So let me explain my vote —or lack of it. Today, we've got a two-and-two stalemate. Yeah. Here's what I'm going to do. I'm going to wait for the election. Now, if Prop. Five loses, that's the end of it. John Hagen's still in the saddle. *But,* if Prop. Five wins—as I hope it does—John Hagen is going to come out and say in the *Sentinel* that he was wrong— that the people have spoken and that the *Sentinel* accepts their decision. And if you don't, John, no more questions. I'll join the Quentins and Miss Peters in calling for another special meeting and I'll cast my vote to fire you. That's all I've got to say."

"The motion to discharge John Hagen, lacking a majority vote, is lost," said John. "Is there any further business to come before this meeting?" He waited. "Hearing none, I declare this meeting of shareholders adjourned."

The Hagens, father and son, walked back to John's car. Allan Hagen hawked his throat and spat explosively. "Pack of jackals!" he said.

"Thanks for the support, Dad," said John.

Allan Hagen shot him a fierce look. "I don't know how I ever raised such a bullheaded son," he said. "I think if you were a woman you'd let some rapist choke you to death instead of giving in."

"Oh, I don't know," John said. "I guess we never know what we're
going to do until we have to do it."

"What the hell *is* wrong with PURIFY anyway?"

"Read the Wellbrook *Sentinel*," said John. "All the news, all the
time."

His father made a noise in his throat that sounded like "Graw."

— *32* —

John leaned back in his chair and stared at his wall. He was in a
state of bemusement. What was he to do? For the moment he had
chosen his path and he was committed to it, at least until after the
election. But what then? If PURIFY passed, he saw no option. He
could not and would not admit he had been wrong, in which case he
would offer his resignation before his fellow shareholders had the
chance to meet and fire him. But if it failed—what then? Did he
even wish to continue as publisher in a community which had attacked him so viciously? Equally important, would he want his family
exposed any more to fear, ostracism, the back-of-the-hand gossip
and rumors of the past several months? PURIFY would have come
and gone before he knew it, but could its scars be so quickly effaced?
Certainly the *Sentinel* would face issues in the future on which the
community was divided, and be forced to take a stand. And in every
case, no matter which way the newspaper leaned, there would be a
disgruntled faction.

Thinking of his wife reminded John Hagen that his mother-in-law
was due in two more days. Kris had of course mentioned it following
her visit to San Francisco. Late October had then seemed a mercifully
long time away. Well, at that, her mother's presence might prove a
welcome diversion.

He had one more problem to think about—the libel action. With
all the other nastiness, Harry Wells had persuaded his opponent,
Merz, to postpone further deposition taking until after the election.

"He's not happy but there isn't much he can do about it," Harry
reported. "I can't for the life of me understand why he hasn't quietly

dropped the whole thing anyway. You know, that Supreme Court ruling of a few months ago made us look all the better."

"Refresh me," John said.

"It upheld the right of states to help parents assess what is called sex-related material," Harry said. "The whole thing, of course, turns on whether the material Genesee sold your reporter falls under ban as legally objectionable for children. I don't think there is any question of it."

Just the thought of spending more long hours undergoing interrogation by Merz, however, made John Hagen wince. And suppose he were obliged to resign following the election? Until the court action was settled one way or the other, he couldn't even make a clean break with the newspaper. The suit, after all, was against him personally as well as against the *Sentinel*.

While he was mulling over a number of thoughts, most of them unpleasant, his telephone buzzer sounded.

"Yes, Mary?"

"You have a call from Los Angeles, Mr. Hagen," the switchboard receptionist said. "I believe she said it's the Sierra Television Network."

"All right. I don't know what they want, but put the party on."

The phone bell sounded a short ring. He punched the lighted button and picked up the receiver. "John Hagen speaking," he said.

"Mr. Hagen, this is the secretary to Mr. Garry," said a woman's voice. "Just one moment, he wishes to speak to you."

"Who?" he said.

"Mr. *Garry*," said the woman. She managed to convey the thought that John had committed lèse majesté. He shrugged. Probably some network news editor.

"Hello," said a man's voice. It was rather flat and unpleasant. "Hello, is this Mr. John Hagen?"

"Yes, it is."

"Rodge Garry here. You've seen *Time* magazine today, of course. I'd like you on my show. What say?"

"Hold up a minute," said John. "I haven't seen *Time* magazine and I don't even know what show you're talking about."

There was a brief and apparently shocked pause.

"Mr. Hagen," said the man wearily. "This is Rodge Garry. *The* Rodge Garry. *Time* magazine has written you up. I think you've become enough of a newsworthy personality to appear on my show. What about it?"

"What show, Mr. Garry?"

"Well, sir, only about a million people watch 'Sky's the Limit' every week up and down California, but I suppose there *are* some who haven't seen it. You *do* have television in Wellbrook, do you not?"

"It reaches. I apologize, Mr. Garry; I'm not much of a viewer."

"Well, catch it tonight. You'll see what kind of show we've got. Meanwhile, what about you for election eve? I want to go into this question of pornography."

"Why me?"

"Because I told you, you're news today, man!" said Garry. "Go get a *Time* magazine and see for yourself. But I need a commitment from you today—right now."

"Give me a number I can call you back on," said John.

"Well, make it before noon, will you?" said Rodge Garry testily. He gave a Los Angeles telephone number and hung up. John levered the squawk box.

"Yeah, John?" said Gil Dennis.

"Gil, send the copyboy over to Charley's to pick up a *Time* magazine, will you?"

"Right," said his city editor. "Anything for us?"

"I won't know until I see it."

The youngster with the long sideburns ambled in a few minutes later. "Gil Dennis said you wanted this, Mr. Hagen. Charley's *Time* magazines were still bundled."

"Thank you, Roy," said John Hagen. "Get the money out of petty cash."

"I did already."

John thumbed to the table of contents and looked for the Press section. He flipped over to the page. A flashlighted photograph of himself eyeing the hole in the *Sentinel* building jumped up at him. The underline was *John Hagen: ". . . any questions?"* The story was alongside:

BOMBS IN THE NIGHT

John A. Hagen is known as a man who speaks his mind in his medium-small (circ. 41,603) Wellbrook daily *Sentinel,* which serves medium-large (pop. 125,111) Wellbrook, a sprawling, incorporated city about 35 miles from downtown Los Angeles.

By this time Publisher Hagen might well be musing whether forthrightness does not come too high.

Since the *Sentinel* some three months ago informed its readers it "firmly and unalterably" opposed a statewide smut-smiting ballot measure in the upcoming November election, all sorts of unpleasant things have been happening to John Hagen and family.

The proposed constitutional amendment, Proposition 5, is best known under the name chosen by an uptight group of citizens who engineered it: PURIFY (for Public United to Restore Innocence to Fair Youth). Prop. 5 would place sellers of dirty books in the company of armed bank robbers (e.g., up to five years in prison, minimum $5,000 fine for a second offense).

Since setting his face against PURIFY, Hagen has had his plant bombed (none injured), his mailbox drenched with filthy, anonymous letters, his home telephone repeatedly rung by threatening callers.

The Wellbrook rumor mill has had it that John Hagen is a communist and a pornographer. A number of local merchants have canceled their advertising.

Who is behind it all? The beleaguered Hagen professes not to know, knows only that despite the hair-raising harassment he's giving not an inch. Declared normally mild-mannered John Hagen in a recent page 1 editorial:

". . . I have not the slightest intention of budging from Wellbrook or of selling the *Sentinel.* Nor do I intend to withdraw the *Sentinel*'s editorial opposition to Prop. 5. . . . To my enemies of the night: . . . DO YOU HAVE ANY FURTHER QUESTIONS?"

Quincy Broyles came in while John was rereading the piece and he showed it to him. As Broyles looked up, fumbling for a match, John said, "Quin, ever hear of a television program called 'Sky's the Limit'?"

"Oh, yes indeed. A man named Roger Garry, affectionately known as Rodge. I believe he has quite a following."

"What's it like?"

Broyles fired up his burner. "Well, the name Torquemada occurs to me. Maybe that's too extreme. More like a thoughtless little boy pulling the wings off flies. He may or may not know it hurts."

"Are you saying he's irresponsible?"

"Let's say he exists on controversy. He tries to get his guests mad by playing devil's advocate. He makes no pretense of being impartial, I'll give that to him. The yahoos love him because he's strictly belt level." He touched the magazine, which he was still holding, with the stem of his pipe. "Something to do with this?"

"He wants me on what he calls his show."

Quincy Broyles shook his head slowly and emphatically. "Uh-uh, squire. Don't you do it. Mind if I say something?"

"You're going to say it anyway."

"I sure am. If ever I saw a man who's bucking to do time in a rest home, it's you. You need about one more nasty encounter, and believe me, Rodge Garry will provide it."

John looked up at him wearily. "Does it show that much?"

"You're on the thin edge, John. We're all worried about you."

John Hagen smiled. "Thanks, Quin. Things *have* been a little rough but I don't think they can get any worse. I'll relieve your mind: I have absolutely no intention—"

His telephone buzzer sounded. "Excuse me. Yes, Mary?"

"It's somebody named Garry, Mr. Hagen, and he sounds sort of mad."

"He does, does he? Put him on." A light began flashing and he stabbed the button. "John Hagen speaking."

"Rodge Garry. You've had enough time to send to New York for *Time* magazine. What about it, Hagen—can I put you down for the show?"

"No thank you, Mr. Garry. One career is enough for—"

"Now, wait a minute, sir! Do you think I put any schlemiel on 'Sky's the Limit'? A lot of people consider it an honor to be asked. I want *you* because you're a central figure in PURIFY."

"*Against* PURIFY," said John Hagen emphatically. "Why pick on me? If you've been reading the newspapers—"

"I read *ten* newspapers, Mr. Hagen—"

"Then you'll know that just about every other newspaper in California, including the L.A. *Times,* the San Francisco *Chronicle—*"

"Yeah, yeah, yeah, the *newspapers.* I know they're opposed. Big deal. You've been reading the polls too, haven't you, Hagen? They show that Prop. Five looks like it's going to pass. Now, listen to me: I know you run a schlock little newspaper; it wouldn't make one section in the Sunday L.A. *Times.* But you're the guy that spoke up first and you're the guy that's getting all the big heat. Like I told you a while ago, you're *news.* It's not your—whadda you call it?—*Sentinel—*I'm interested in, it's the symbol of John Hagen as opposition. You want a big audience to air your point of view, Hagen, come on my show. Say yes and I'll pencil you in."

"No."

"The little guy who stood up and defied his whole town—"

"I'm not little and I'm not defying my whole town. A lot of people are on my side."

"Yeah, that's why they're setting off dynamite, I suppose."

"That was a bunch of doped-up kids. Only incidentally did it have anything to do with PURIFY. I'm afraid the answer is—"

"Listen to me just one more minute, Hagen. I've got another guest for election eve who's damn happy to appear. His name is Coe—the Reverend Bradshaw Coe." He added, sarcastically: "I do imagine you've heard of him."

"Well?"

"That's all the reaction?"

"What do you want me to say?"

"Do you want him and his point of view to go unchallenged before a million California viewers—and voters? Do you want PURIFY to pass? You wanta prove out the polls?"

"No, of course not, but—"

"Haven't you got the guts, Mr. Hagen?"

"That's a pretty worn-out appeal, Mr. Garry. It doesn't make one iota of difference to me whether you think I've got any guts or not." Quincy Broyles was puffing thoughtfully. He shook his head again.

"Suppose I tell my viewers that I invited the leading spokesman for the opposition to PURIFY and he was too scared to defend his position, because his arguments wouldn't hold water?"

"You'd do that, would you?"

Rodge Garry chuckled nastily. "I'm liable to do most anything on 'Sky's the Limit,' Hagen. Well, it's your affair. If you want to hand the platform over to Reverend Coe, just say no one more time and you've got your wish."

John Hagen clenched and unclenched the fingers of his free hand. "If I don't appear, you won't make an attempt to get anyone to oppose this man?"

"If you tell me you won't do it and hang up, Hagen, the subject is closed. The Reverend Coe gets the whole floor."

"Where and when do I show up?" said John Hagen. Quincy Broyles shook his head once more and walked back into his own office.

— *33* —

". . . And if you elect me your attorney general, I will give you the highest possible type of law enforcement in California—a standard of fairness and justice to all citizens . . . the poor, the middle-level, the moneyed alike," said Victor Massoni. "The least privileged among us will stand just as tall and his voice will be just as loud —to me—as if he were the governor of California. That is my pledge and my promise." For some two seconds his eyes stared into the viewers' before the image of his face cut to:

Elect
VICTOR MASSONI
Attorney General
This November

A voice intoned: "The foregoing political announcement was paid for by the Citizens Committee to Elect Victor Massoni Attorney General." A dog food commercial popped up.

"Why don't you turn it off?" said Kris. "Unless there's something you want to see, Mother?"

"My, no," said Mrs. Wellesley. "One can watch television at home.

He's a very impressive man, isn't he? I thought so when he came to get you that night up in—"

"Are you comfortable, Mother?" she said.

Mrs. Wellesley, hand resting on the crook of her cane, her small, plump body well settled in John's favorite chair, smiled gently. "You'll never hear me complain, darling. John, tell me more about this television program you're going to be on."

"Oh, didn't you tell her this afternoon, Kris?" he said.

"Not in any detail," said Kris. "We had too much else to talk about." She had met her mother at the heliport at two-thirty.

"I'm going to debate the leading spokesman for Proposition Number Five, Mother," he said.

"Yes, that's this awful political thing that's been making all our lives miserable," said Kris.

Mrs. Wellesley looked from one to the other. She pursed her lips. She shook her head. "My, you two children have certainly been having a time of it, haven't you? John, haven't you lost some weight?"

"I don't know."

"Yes, he has," said Kris.

"I haven't weighed myself."

"It shows," she said. The telephone rang—one ring. She stiffened. The automatic answering device cut it off. Her mother raised an inquiring eyebrow. "This is the way we live now, Mother," Kris said. "We don't dare answer our telephone; we take recorded messages and see if we want to call the person back."

"But that's terrible!" said Mrs. Wellesley.

"That's what it's like," she said.

"I think you just ought to get out of this town," said Mrs. Wellesley. "John, why don't you sell the paper and bring your family to live in the Bay Area?"

"And do what?" said John Hagen. "Take a reporter's job on one of your local newspapers? Quit the business and sell used cars?"

"I wouldn't care if you painted signs for a living," said Kris.

"No talent," he said.

"So we stay," she said. "I told you how Gordo got the black eye, Mother."

"Yes, the poor child."

"He was defending his father's honor. Day before yesterday. It's not the first time."

"It's the first time he got a black eye," said John.

"Oh yes, and Pammy," said Kris. "There was this birthday party she so much wanted to be invited to. She was last year. She wasn't this year."

"That's simply awful," said Mrs. Wellesley. "What you've been going through."

"I think I'll find out who's calling us," said John.

"Oh dear," said his mother-in-law, looking at her daughter.

John walked to the alcove, where the telephone sat beside a metal box. He flipped a lever as he picked up the receiver. There was a high-toned *beep* and a metallic voice said, "This is Pete Salzman, Mr. Hagen. I've got some very important information. You can call me back at this number. I'll wait for your call." He gave a number as John used the small gold pencil and wrote on the pad by the phone. He depressed the disconnect, released it, and dialed.

"Hello, Mr. Hagen?" said Pete Salzman almost instantly.

"Right, Pete. What's up?"

"I'm calling from a phone booth out here in county territory," Pete said, his voice higher than normal with agitation. "I've picked up something you've got to see right away."

"What is it, Pete?"

"You'll have to see it, Mr. Hagen."

"Won't it wait until morning?"

"No," said Pete positively.

"Are you on your way back to the office?"

"I'll be there in about a half hour."

"I'll meet you there."

Both faces turned to him expectantly as he walked back into the living room. "It's one of my reporters," he said. "He's onto something hot. I've got to go down."

"Oh, dear," said his mother-in-law.

"At this hour?" said Kris. "It's almost bedtime."

"He said it won't wait. Go to bed. I'll be quiet when I come in."

Kris shrugged helplessly. "Day and night," she said.

"I just don't know," said her mother. "I just don't know."

He parked in the lot and let himself in with his pass key, with an involuntary glance at the fresh concrete patch at the site of the bombing. A police cruiser had rolled quietly up. The man at the wheel saw who it was and waved, and John waved back before closing the door. Chris Smith, who was pulling the night city editor duty, raised his head. "Well, John," he said. Chris had been too many years in the game ever to show startlement.

"Anything stirring, Chris?"

"Pretty dead," said Smith. He stared a moment at his publisher in case an explanation might be forthcoming, but John said only, "It can get awfully dull, can't it, Chris?"

Pete Salzman came in. "Let's go in my office, Pete," John said.

"What's the hot tip?" John said, touching the wall switch. The fluorescents fluttered and beamed on.

"This," said Salzman. "I found it in my car just before I called you." He held out a pink leaflet. John took it. As he began to understand its contents he sank into his seat almost in a trance.

BIRDS OF A FEATHER!

screamed the big black type. The text was crudely printed, as if on some amateur printing buff's basement press:

> Now Wellbrook's got two Big Shots who believe in the filthy kind of Literture the Law won't put down because the "BLEEDING HEARTS" and the U.S. Supreme Court won't let them.
>
> Not to mention their names but they are a well-known Newspaper Publisher and a Politician . . . . . and you get just three guesses. Theyre telling decent Citizens that they should vote down P.U.R.I.F.Y.
>
> Well heres some news for the two Big Shots, who once upon a time used to be room mates in College. THIER FOIBLES AND PECADILLOES IN THOSE LONG-AGO FAR OFF COLLEGE DAYS ARE WELL KNOWN TO SOME PEO-PLE. THEY ARE GOING TO BE REVEALED IN JUST A VERY FEW DAYS.

We're not going to say just exactly what those Foibles and Pecadilloes were right now but its no co-incidence that this notice is printed on PINK paper.

Let's see how the two Big Shots feel when a certain Legal Document, sworn and testified to, comes to light.

"THE FAIRY TELLER"

John Hagen gripped the paper tightly, crumpling it. He felt the sick rage spread through his body like powerful brandy on an empty stomach. "The dirty, filthy monsters!" he breathed. He spread the paper out once more, brushing at its web of wrinkles with his hand. He closed his eyes a moment, fighting for control. He reopened them to become aware that Pete Salzman was watching him apprehensively. He leaned back in his chair. "You found this in your car, Pete?" he said slowly.

"Yeah, out by a coffee shop I was in. I don't know how many of these things are around. I thought you ought to see it right now."

"You did right, Pete. First thing tomorrow morning we're going to see something else. That, I promise."

He spent a restless, dream-filled night and was down at Harry Wells's office at eight o'clock, virtually ordering Harry to meet him there a full hour ahead of his normal schedule.

As always, Harry was trimly dressed as they met outside the locked door of his office suite.

"Well, stranger," he greeted John. "You're giving me a lot of business these days." He fitted a key in the lock. "What have we got now?" He flipped light switches on the way into his office. John had the crumpled pink flyer in his hand and gave it to him almost before Harry had had the chance to seat himself in his massive, padded swivel chair. John had himself well in hand now, his rage cold and controlled. His eyes felt grainy from his troubled night. His stomach was slightly queasy with the only thing on it a hasty cup of instant coffee made with hot tap water. Harry read the document quickly.

"What's my recourse, Harry?" said John.

Harry Wells was shaking his head slowly. "I can't believe it," he said.

"What's my recourse?" repeated John impatiently. "You know what that thing says, of course?"

"I know what it says, but the trouble is, it doesn't say enough," said Harry Wells. He pushed the paper forward as if it had an offensive odor. He kneaded the knuckles of one hand with the other. "Someone is really playing for keeps here, John. I don't know why it is, but the type of fringe element that's been giving you so much trouble always seems preoccupied with homosexuality. It's a nasty weapon, like the imputation of child molesting. I'd say there is only one thing you can do, and that's take this to the district attorney's office." His nearly oriental eyes narrowed on John. "Of course, if this is to be believed, they're going to drop another shoe. I don't understand what this so-called 'certain legal document' is all about. Do you?"

"Harry," said John Hagen bitterly, "I don't know what any of this is about. Some scum is implying that Vic Massoni and I were gay with each other in college. I don't know who the bastard has in mind—not me, of that I'm sure. I'd also take my oath about Vic. Hell, he's about to marry one of my staffers. Besides, Vic and I never roomed together." He clenched his jaw. "Not that facts would ever stand in the way of someone who would stoop to this."

"Have you tried to get hold of Massoni?"

"I'm going to, first thing. I'll have to check his schedule with his campaign headquarters in L.A., see where he is."

"Maybe you'd better have a talk with him before you do anything. It's hard to know who's the principal target in this—you or him. Tell him when you talk to him, however, that the sooner the D.A.'s office can start tracking down the source of this leaflet, the sooner you can take action."

"Isn't this criminally libelous, Harry?" said John, stretching out to pick up the pink flyer.

"Not quite, in my opinion, John. The implication is there, all right. Hard as it might be to believe, there are people naïve enough not to interpret the two most damning elements—the pink paper reference and the 'Fairy Teller' signature. However, if you can find out who's responsible, you can certainly put on enough pressure to stop any further such publication."

"I'd like to see something that spells it right out," said John Hagen angrily. "I'd bust it wide open in the *Sentinel*. You say some people are naïve; I say everyone who reads this will know exactly what it implies."

"Yes, but neither you nor Massoni is named. That's the other thing missing here. I know it sounds far-fetched to assume the writer had in mind some other publisher and politician who attended college at the same time, but it's possible. Massoni's a lawyer. See if he doesn't agree that of itself, this document doesn't provide a handhold for court action. But stopping further publication—that's another story."

"All I can do right now, then, is turn this over to the D.A.'s office for investigation, is that it, Harry?"

"Yes. And wait. I know waiting is tough in a case like this, John, but there's nothing else you can do. Oh, be sure to check with Massoni before you go to the district attorney."

"I'll check with him to let him know what's going on," said John Hagen firmly. "But regardless of what he says, I'm going in anyway. They're trying to destroy me, Harry, crush me completely. If it comes to a hard choice, I'm going to preserve myself and my family, regardless of Vic." He got to his feet.

"Try to take it easy," said Harry Wells.

"I've forgotten how," said John.

— *34* —

Will Naismith came into John's office three mornings later with a worried frown on his normally cheerful face. He had with him a folded section printed on litho stock.

"Morning, Will," said John. "Troubles?"

"I don't know," said his advertising director. "Take a look at this." He spread the tabloid-size section in front of John. Page one was a huge splash of color dominated by the legend:

VOTE "YES" ON
PROP. 5
Help Clean Up California

and was signed at the bottom: *Public United to Restore Innocence to Fair Youth, Inc.*

"So?" said John. He turned the section over to look at the back folio. Sixteen pages.

"Well, the thing is this," said Will Naismith. "They want this insert to run on election eve. Knowing how you feel about this proposition . . ." His voice trailed off.

"They sent you a copy asking whether we'd tuck this in with the *Sentinel* that day?"

"Uh-huh."

John whistled. "Lord, they must really be spending the money! If they can reach this far down on the list with a sixteen-page supplement . . ." He leafed through rapidly. Page after page was devoted to arguments why Proposition Five should pass. He refolded the section. "Full space rates?"

"Full *political* space rates," Will Naismith corrected. "Cash in advance."

"We'll take it," said John. "Cash with copy."

"The letter said they're ready to ship the copies and mail the check on confirmation."

"No problem whatsoever."

Will Naismith grinned crookedly. "I'd have bet you were going to say no, chief. Just shows how wrong I can be."

"I'm just surprised they're willing to spend the money with the *Sentinel*," said John. "This must really be a saturation program." His advertising director turned and started to go. "Oh, Will?"

"Uh-huh?"

"Have you seen Hartmann lately?"

"Not Hartmann. His advertising manager, this fellow Stern." Naismith slapped the folded section against his leg. "I could be wrong again, but I don't think they're doing quite as well with the *Green Sheet* as they did with the *Sentinel*. Stern won't admit it, of course, but I think when the dust settles after the election it won't be long before Hartmann's is back with us."

"Is this just intuition or is it anything he said?"

"Just a hunch, John. Don't can me if I'm wrong."

"Oh, I think you've got a job here, Will." He grinned wryly. "Or at least as long as I have."

Two hours later the bright day was overcast with the arrival of an envelope delivered by messenger. John Hagen hunched over the contents aghast, then picked up the telephone.

"Get me the Massoni headquarters in Los Angeles," he ordered the switchboard operator. "I'll hold."

A few minutes later a woman's cheerful voice said, "Good morning, Massoni for Attorney General headquarters."

"This is John Hagen, publisher of the Wellbrook *Sentinel*. It's urgent that I locate Assemblyman Massoni. Can you tell me where he is today?"

"Uh, just a moment please," said the woman. And a bit later a man said, "Mr. Hagen?"

"Hagen of the Wellbrook *Sentinel*."

"This is Jerry, the assistant publicity director. I understand you wish to locate Vic. He's speaking in Redding today. I can give you the number if you wish and maybe you can have him paged."

"Yes, please."

He hung up and placed the call. It had been several days since he had spoken with Massoni, locating him in Santa Rosa. Vic had heard him out in tense silence, then said, "Don't do anything until I see you."

"I'm paging Mr. Massoni," said the voice now on the telephone.

"Thank you," said John. In a moment there was a click on the line.

"This is Assemblyman Massoni," said Vic.

"This is John Hagen, Vic. I—"

"Hello, Johnny! You seem to track me down wherever—"

"Vic, listen. They fired the other barrel. A notarized, two-page—"

"Hold it!" said Vic sharply. "Not over the phone."

"Well, how then?" said John Hagen.

"Uh—pretty bad?"

"Filthy rotten."

"Are the two parties in question named?"

"They are indeed."

"In alleged detail?"

"About as explicit as you can get."

"I see. Let me think." John drew a deep breath and leaned back, waiting until Vic Massoni said, "Still there?"

"I'm still here."

"I'm going to be back in L.A. Sunday night before election."

"That's the soonest?"

"The very soonest. Can you come to my headquarters?"

"I'll be there. What time?"

"Make it—uh—five o'clock. Is it real dynamite, Johnny?"

"I told you, it's filthy rotten."

"Okay, well sit on it, for the love of God!"

"I'm involved as much as you are, old friend," said John Hagen, and hung up. He lashed the envelope shut with cello tape, then got up and went over to Dwight Henry's office. "Dwight, would you put this in your safe?" he said. "I'll get it tomorrow afternoon."

"Of course," said Dwight Henry mildly. He betrayed not the slightest curiosity. Things were, to Dwight. They would be revealed, if it were meant to be, in due time.

When John returned to his office his telephone intercom was buzzing.

"Yes, Mary?"

"Lieutenant DeGros of the Sheriff's Department would like to speak to you, Mr. Hagen."

"All right. Hello, Lieutenant."

"Hello, Hagen," said DeGros. "How are things?"

"Not good at all."

"I've got some news I think you'll be interested in."

"Oh? What is it?"

DeGros cleared his throat. "I don't want to say it right out. I can't leave the office now, but—"

"I'll come over."

"Good. I'll see you."

The sheriff's substation was a green, one-story building just off

Centinela Avenue in county territory. John parked in a diagonal space marked VISITORS and went in. A young deputy, hatless and jacketless but wearing the suntan shirt and green trousers, looked up from a typewriter. John rested his hand on the dividing counter.

"Mr. Hagen to see Lieutenant DeGros," he said.

"Yes, sir," said the deputy politely. "Straight through, turn right, and all the way back." John nodded his thanks. He walked past a glassed-in enclosure where a girl tended a switchboard and monitored several police radio nets, down a short corridor, and through an open doorway. DeGros, in business suit, watched him enter from his wooden armchair behind a gray steel desk.

"You made good time," he commented, hoisting his body from the chair and putting out his hand. They shook. "Close the door," said DeGros. John complied. He took the wave of a hand as an invitation to be seated. DeGros placed an elbow on the desk and rested his jaw on the palm of his hand, "Things been kind of rough for you lately, Hagen?"

"They reached a new low today," said John.

"What's that?"

"A copy of a purported affidavit spelling out the details of a homosexual incident between me and Victor Massoni. A follow-up to that pink flyer last week."

DeGros took his chin from his hand and leaned back, folding his beefy arms. "Yeah? How'd you get that—in the mail?"

"It was delivered by messenger. Regular messenger service."

"You gonna follow up and see who gave it to him?"

"Yes. From here I'm going to the district attorney's office. They're already investigating the source of the flyer."

Degros grunted. "You want an answer?"

"I don't understand."

DeGros rubbed a hand over his jaw. "Tell me, Hagen; who around Wellbrook might have any reason to harm you?"

"Any number of people, I guess. A newspaper can make itself enemies on a lot of issues."

"We're talkin' about two different things. I mean real, low-down harm. Like this affidavit."

"What do you know that I don't, Lieutenant?"

"I know where that pink flyer, you call it, came from."

John sat up suddenly. "Where?"

"Remember Roberts—got canned along with Hosea?"

"The deputy! Yes!"

"They're your boys."

John frowned, biting his thumb. He dropped his hand and said, "All by themselves?"

"No. Genesee of Art's Arcade is in it with them. That affidavit you got. I saw it two days ago. So did Greives, the deputy D.A. There's only one thing. The name on the affidavit—one William Pilkerson. Know him?"

"I never heard of him before in my life."

"He's real. The D.A. has talked to him. He swears that the act really took place, that he witnessed it, and he's willing to swear to it in court."

"Including the year nineteen fifty-four?"

"Yep. Says he's positive, because that's the spring he graduated from USC."

John said softly, "But Vic Massoni and I were graduated from USC in nineteen fifty-three."

A broad grin spread across Lieutenant DeGros' face. "Well, do tell," he said.

John raised an eyebrow. "Is it possible you and the deputy district attorney really believed this story?"

DeGros said evenly: "I'm a cop, Hagen. If I know anything after twenty years' law enforcement, it's that anything's possible. Don't take it personal."

"Tell me this, if you know," said John Hagen. "You say that Genesee and Roberts and Hosea, your fired deputies, are responsible for printing and circulating the flyer and this affidavit. How do you know, and can you prove it?"

"How I know—just take my word for it, I know. Sooner or later I know everything that's going on in my territory. And I can prove it, all right."

"Then why hasn't the district attorney's office made an arrest?"

"On what?"

"Criminal libel."

"On whose complaint?"

"Well—mine, I guess."

"You have to make one."

"I will," said John Hagen. "And for this fellow Pilkerson too. Where does he live?"

"San Bernardino. Go over to the D.A.'s office, file your complaint, and he'll take it from there."

"There's just one thing I'm puzzled about," said John. "Why did you call instead of the district attorney?"

"Because I asked him if I could."

"Why?"

"Just to show you I can do you a favor once in a while. Remember?"

"You've done it. Any way I can ever repay it—"

"Sure," said Lieutenant DeGros solemnly. "Support your local police." There was the barest hint of amusement on his countenance.

The youthful deputy district attorney, Greives, heard John Hagen out in silence twenty minutes later, twiddling a pencil. Finally he said, "Yes, that's right. DeGros says he'll swear to the source of the flyer and the affidavit."

"Then I want to swear out a criminal complaint. Right now."

The deputy D.A. tapped the pencil tip on his desk blotter. "I can oblige you, but I'd like to ask you a question first." John raised his eyebrows inquiringly. "When arrests are made, this becomes a public matter—you realize that." It was no question, but John Hagen said, "Yes, of course."

"And it will be publicized in the newspapers, including your own *Sentinel*."

"Especially in the *Sentinel*."

"And you do realize the possible effects?"

"Of course I do! This is provably a lie."

"Don't you want to talk to Assemblyman Massoni first?" said the young deputy. He stabbed the pencil point lightly in the desk blotter. Head aslant, he eyed John Hagen.

His mother was on the telephone from La Jolla shortly before two o'clock Sunday afternoon. The election was two days off. His scheduled appearance tomorrow night on "Sky's the Limit" was adding to his tensions.

"Hello, Mother," he said.

"John? Is that you?"

"Yes. How are you?"

"John, I don't want to worry you, but it's your father. They've taken him to the hospital. They think it might be a heart attack. But John—"

He gripped the receiver hard. "Is it bad?" he said tensely.

"John, please listen to me. They're taking tests now. They don't know that it's a heart attack, but could you—"

"I'll be down this evening. I'll be there at eight o'clock."

"He's in the Scripps Memorial Hospital. Come right there, John. I'll meet you."

Both Kris and her mother were quite concerned.

"She said the doctors didn't know whether it's a heart attack or not, but I can tell she's frightened and upset," said John. "She'll be better off just having me there."

"Of course," said Kris. "How do we work this out now, about tomorrow?"

He ran his hand distractedly through his hair. "Well, I'll stay the night in La Jolla, then drive up to North Hollywood for the program if he's all right. If he's not, I'll cancel out—the hell with it. Assuming he is, why don't you drive over and meet me at the studio? Say, about seven-thirty. The program doesn't go on until eight o'clock, but I have to meet this fellow Garry early in the afternoon. Or maybe I could drive back here early—"

"No, don't do that," said Kris.

"I do hope Mr. Hagen isn't too ill," said his mother-in-law.

"Thanks, Mother." He thought for a moment. "Well, I guess I have everything—clean suit, toilet articles—"

"You have everything," said Kris.

"Can you find your way to the Sierra Television studios all right?"

"We'll be fine. I'll see you tomorrow night. You'd better call me first."

"I'll do that. Good-by, hon."

"Good-by, dear." She returned his kiss warmly.

"One of these days things will get back to normal," he said.

"I know they will," said Kris.

Victor Massoni for Attorney General headquarters was a large ground-floor office space in downtown Los Angeles a few blocks from the Civic Center. John put his car in a self-park lot and walked a half-block to the campaign headquarters. The cavernous interior space was all but dark. Only a single light burned somewhere in the back. Vic was waiting on the inside. He unlocked the door.

"Let's go back to my office," he said tersely.

Vic's office, several paces back along a hallway at the partitioned rear of the headquarters, was a rather sparsely furnished room with a desk, chairs, telephone, pad and pencils, and more of the ubiquitous posters. John had his first chance to take a good look at him. He looked bone-weary. There were heavy lines in the light-olive skin below his eyes, and John imagined there was slightly more gray at the temples and a frown line above his nose that hadn't been there the last time they'd seen each other.

"All right, Johnny," he said. "Let's see it." He extended his hand. John took out the envelope. Vic went behind his desk and sat down, ripping open the cello tape with a letter opener. John waited as he scanned the document. He saw the large hands, with the wiry black hairs down to the second knuckle, tighten on the paper. Finally, he said, "God!" When he looked up his face was black with anger.

"I've got some good news for you, Vic," said John. Vic Massoni's eyes narrowed.

"The D.A. and sheriff know who did it."

"Who?" said Vic explosively. "Who is the dirty bastard?"

"Two fired deputy sheriffs and a man who runs a place called

Art's Arcade. A man who's suing me for a series I ran on his place."

"Who in the hell is Pilkerson?"

"Claims he was a student at USC."

"Well, that I can see," said Vic sourly.

"Who claims he saw us together in a shower on a certain March evening of nineteen fifty-four."

"Who claims he saw us naked in that shower playing Frank and Ernest on a certain March evening of nineteen fifty-four. Why, the filthy lying son of a bitch! I was in law school in nineteen fifty-four and you were working for the L.A. *Times*." Vic pinched the bridge of his nose wearily. "This I need like I need a knife in my back." His expression was haggard. "I've seen some dirty pool in this campaign, but this is the absolute worst." He scowled. "Where's this been circulated?"

"I don't know yet. The sheriff's lieutenant and the deputy D.A. have seen copies. It may be all over Wellbrook by now as far as I know. Where else, I couldn't say."

"Do you suppose it's aimed at me or you?"

"Considering who's responsible, I'd say it's aimed at me."

"But I'm the one with the most to lose."

John Hagen stared in amazement. "That's a damned funny thing to say."

Vic waved his hand impatiently. "Sorry, I didn't mean it the way it sounds. I mean—well, hell, right at election time."

"What if it hasn't gone any farther than Wellbrook?"

"It doesn't make any difference. If it gets out, it'll be all over the state of California. True or not—my God!"

"I'm going in Tuesday to swear out a complaint for criminal libel, Vic."

"You're what!" Vic shouted.

"What did you think I was going to do—take this? These men belong in jail and I'm going to put them there."

"Johnny, do you want to kill me?"

"What about me, Vic? You talk about yourself and your political campaign. What about me and my family and my newspaper? My life, Vic!"

Vic Massoni's hands, fingers spread, vibrated with agitation, as if their very urgency could convey the force of his emotion.

"Johnny, listen to me . . . listen to me, please, for *God's sake!* I want you to go to the D.A.! I want you to! I'll go with you when you do and put my name with yours! I want to see these crummy bastards in jail! I'll appear in a courtroom and testify against them, and I hope the judge throws away the key. *But after the election, Johnny, after the election!*"

"So in the meantime I just live with this?" said John sharply.

"Johnny, *after the election!* For Christ's sake, man, that's only two days from now! Go in Wednesday—three days. Don't you see there's only time to get them arrested and publicized on TV with the polls still open? Don't you see what it'll do to me? The Democratic candidate for attorney general of California a fairy—a *queer?* Sure, we'll prove in good time that these guys have published a criminal lie, but I've lost the election. This smear will stick until we get them in court. The people will vote for Hausner. Am I getting through at all?"

John Hagen was breathing heavily with his own mental turmoil. He appreciated his friend's argument, but he had been living with so much strain he was almost beside himself with the overwhelming urge to strike back at last—to lash out immediately against one set of identified enemies. Finally he had a target in his sights and he was being asked to stay his finger on the trigger.

"I don't want you to lose the election, Vic," he said tightly. "But I think the voters might rate you pretty courageous if you came out with this yourself right now."

Vic Massoni groaned. "Oh, sweet Jesus, what you know about politics! You want me to be the bravest man in the cemetery!"

"And you want *me* to be a pariah in my own community. You can be damned sure this filthy paper is being handed around all over town. Do you have any idea how much advertising I've lost already over PURIFY? Wait three days, you tell me. In three days Kris could be driven to a mental hospital."

Vic Massoni was punching his right fist into the palm of his left hand. "No, no, no, no!" he said. "Johnny, I'm pleading with you— for the love of God, don't do it." His eyes narrowed. "This election means a lot to me, Johnny. I've worked myself to exhaustion, put every dime of my own into it, every stinkin' dollar I could beg or steal from friends, supporters, even guys who don't know I hate their guts. I'm on my way up, Johnny, and I'm not going to let anyone stop me—you or anyone else." There was a glint of anger in his eyes. "So help me God, if you go to the district attorney before Wednesday—" His huge fists were clenched. "I think I'd kill you with my bare hands." John stared at him. Almost immediately Vic attempted a grin. It was a disaster. "Oh my God, Johnny, what am I saying? My best friend. I'd never—never . . ." He gulped.

John still stared at him. He said slowly, his own anger a sick knot in his stomach: "Tell me about friendship, Vic."

Vic frowned in puzzlement. "I don't get it," he said.

"Since we're getting down to what people are going to do to each other, let me ask you something that I was never going to mention. Did you and my wife used to go with each other in college?"

Vic's chin came up slowly. "Well," he said.

"Yes, well. Answer my question, old friend."

Now there was genuine pain on Vic's face. "Johnny, there's something I can't tell you."

"You can sure as hell tell me if you went with Kris at any time in college."

"Was Kris my girl friend? No, she wasn't."

"Then what do you mean there's something you can't tell me?"

A guarded expression came over Vic's face. "Anything you want to know you'd better ask your wife."

"By God!" John breathed. "There *was* something between you. Something neither you nor she ever saw fit to tell me. And I encouraged her to go out with you in San Francisco! How many kinds of a fool can I be?"

Vic shook his head vigorously. "Whatever you're thinking, forget it, Johnny. I didn't so much as kiss your wife in San Francisco."

"Do you know something, Vic? I think you are lying. I think Kris has been lying. I think you and she went to bed in San Francisco."

"No, God damn it, no! Johnny, you couldn't be more wrong in your life."

"I guess I walk alone from here on, Vic."

"Johnny, maybe sometimes there are things a man is better off not knowing."

"Whatever that's supposed to mean. Good night, Vic."

"Johnny, what are you going to do about that complaint?"

"I guess we'll just have to see, huh, Vic?"

Vic Massoni half raised his hand as if to detain John's exit and then dropped it slowly. "All right," he said wearily. "See you around, Johnny."

— *36* —

He was tired and apprehensive when he entered the hospital.

"John!" said his mother. To his amazement she was smiling.

"Mother!" he said. She hugged him tightly.

"It's all right!" she said. "He's all right, John! It wasn't a heart attack at all. They took tests and found out there's nothing at all wrong with his heart."

"Are they sure?" he said anxiously.

"Yes, they are. They think now it was only a bad case of indiges tion or gas or something."

He laughed with sudden relief. "Mom, that's wonderful!" He took her arm. "How long are they going to keep him?"

"Just overnight. Oh, John, I was so worried, and you had to drive all the way down here and—"

"Oh, hell, who cares? Can I see him?"

"He'll make it pretty hard on all of us if you don't. Come on, it's this way."

His father's impatience with hospital routine was apparent, even with a thermometer in his mouth. A pretty young nurse smiled at John and his mother as they entered. "We'll just be a moment here, Mrs. Hagen," she said.

"*Mllmph!*" said Allan Hagen. He waved his hand in greeting. The nurse took her fingers from his wrist and removed the thermometer.

"What's it say?" demanded Allan Hagen.

"Oh, it's just fine, Mr. Hagen," she said. "Whoever told you you were sick, anyway?"

"That damned quack who calls himself a doctor and my golfing

partner," said Allan Hagen. "Hello, John. Looks like we got you
down here for nothing. You're going to stay the night, aren't you?"

"Hi, Dad," said John, gripping his father's hand. "Yes, I don't
feel like driving back tonight. Kris figured I would stay. Are you
going to watch me on television tomorrow night?"

His father folded his arms. "Yes. I hope that fella doesn't tear
you to pieces. How's everything going?"

John hesitated. "Not too good. I'll live, I guess. The main thing
is that you're all right." His mother had sat down, smiling, and John
now took a chair himself.

"I'm not quite ready to cash in," said Allan Hagen gruffly. "It
didn't figure to be my heart anyway. Damn thing's always been as
sound as the dollar was before the New Deal. Well, son, do you think
that ballot proposition is going to pass?"

"I hope not, but I don't like the looks of the polls. Of course
they're not infallible either. Look what happened to Dewey in 'forty-
eight."

"Dewey!" said his father. He snorted. "I'll say this—I hope it
doesn't pass now. Not because I wouldn't like to see it, but because
of those pip-squeak Quentins and that dried-up old maid Peters. If
Proposition Five goes through and you don't eat crow, you've had
it. Jim Malkin wasn't kidding, you know. I've talked to him since
the meeting and he says he meant every word he said. He's an old
friend of mine, but he's as bullheaded as you are."

"You can't always tell about old friends," said John.

"Not always," said Allan Hagen. "Well, no use sweating out the
future. The present's bad enough."

"I'll subscribe to that," said John.

"How was dinner tonight, dear?" said his mother.

"All right, I guess," said Allan Hagen. "But I tell you, if Dr.
Quack-old-golfing-buddy doesn't let me out of this mausoleum by
eleven o'clock tomorrow morning, you're going to see some heads
roll. I'll tee off on him with a four wood."

"I don't believe you even had indigestion," said John.

"Well, that's what he said it was when he got over trying to scare
your mother to death with this nonsense about a heart attack," said
Allan Hagen.

John had a good sleep despite, or because of, the pressures of the day. In the middle of an excellent, late breakfast he suddenly remembered to telephone Kris.

"I wondered if you'd call," she said with a trace of reproach in her voice. "How is he?"

"It wasn't anything—not a heart attack. They're letting him out today, I think."

"Oh, that's wonderful!" she exclaimed. "Oh, I'm so happy."

"Original plan in effect," he said. "I'll see you at the network studios at seven-thirty this evening."

"We'll be there," she said. "Oh, I'm so glad to hear the good news about your father. Well, I guess that's about it, then."

"I guess so. Good-by, Kris."

His mother walked him to the door. He put his arm around her and kissed her cheek. "I know everything's going to be all right with Dad," he said.

"I hope everything's going to be all right with you," she said.

"Somehow we'll come up heads, Mom," he said.

"Tell Pammy and Gordo we love them," she said, and smiled.

"Right. Say so-long to Dad, will you?"

During the drive to Los Angeles, thence to North Hollywood, his thoughts were black. His recent troubles paled beside the knowledge newly acquired the night before. The rest was so much blah. He was in torment; the two names drummed in his head like the insidious drip of a leaky faucet in the still hours of the night: *Vic-and-Kris, Vic-and-Kris, Vic-and-Kris.* He made a stop at a service station for gasoline. He vomited in the toilet. He resumed his journey, not wanting to go where he was going, but there was no other place to go, either. There was no place.

There was one way he could serve his *old friend,* yet even as it occurred, he rejected it. What purpose to go to the district attorney before Wednesday, after all? The story was all over Wellbrook— *would* one additional day make that much difference? No, he and Vic henceforth would go their separate paths, but fairness spoke: he's worked hard, give him his chance. Revenge might be sweet, but he knew it would leave a bitter taste on his tongue.

He reached the three-story, block-long green building that housed the studios of the Sierra Television Network.

The Reverend Bradshaw Coe had arrived at the producer's office ahead of him. It was John's first glimpse in months of his foe.

The young man who had escorted him in introduced him to the producer, a Mr. Regal, who in turn said, "I'm sure you know the Reverend Mr. Coe, Mr. Hagen."

"I do," said John. The Reverend nodded at him.

A tall man wearing tight-fitting checkered slacks, moccasins, and a red wool turtleneck sweater ambled through a doorway. "Ah, my Christians are assembled for the circus," he drawled.

"Hello, Rodge!" cried the producer. "Gentlemen, the star of our show, Rodge Garry. Reverend Coe and John Hagen."

The tall, shambling man said, "Well, I'm glad you could come." He shook hands with both in turn. "Stan, I'll just sit here and you can take them through the format." He flopped into the nearest padded armchair and looped one leg over the arm.

"A pleasure, Rodge," said the producer. "Basically the show is simplicity itself." He outlined the simple steps to the opening. "And that's pretty much all there is to it," he concluded.

"Really all there is," murmured Rodge Garry. His fingers were laced over his mop of sandy hair. "Of course," he added in his flat, almost nasal voice, "we deal in adult problems. I ask adult questions. I hope you both came prepared to speak up, because I guarantee my audience their money's worth." He unlaced his hands and waved negligently. "We should all have a lot of fun." He grinned like an urchin who has planted a wad of chewing gum in a classmate's hair. "Fun and games."

The director came in, shook hands all round, uttered a pleasantry, and said, "I'll ask that you both be back here by seven at the very latest." Rodge Garry made his apologies, such as they were, and disappeared.

John Hagen called his office from an outside booth to see if anything was stirring.

"Where are you, John?" said Quincy Broyles. He sounded tense, quite unlike his normally placid self.

"North Hollywood. Any trouble?"

"Bad trouble, John. Someone's circulating the most scurrilous piece of paper I've ever seen. I hate to tell you this, but it's about you and Victor Massoni, and it's disgusting—rotten."

"The affidavit, Quin?"

"Oh, you know about it."

"I do, and I'm going to take legal action on it. Criminal action."

"You'd better. We've had several dozen cancellations of subscriptions today and Will Naismith is over in an emergency powwow with the Brakebills right now. He told me they're talking about pulling all their advertising from the *Sentinel*."

"Does the staff know about it, Quin?"

"Well, you know how these things get around, squire."

"In other words, it's all over Wellbrook."

"I'm afraid so, John."

"All right. You're going to see some action real quick."

"Good. And, squire?"

"Yes, Quin?"

"Good luck in the bull ring tonight."

"Two ears and a hoof," said John.

After that there seemed nothing to kill time for a few hours but to drive in to Hollywood Boulevard and take in a movie. He was back at the studio at seven o'clock.

He was in Makeup, getting a light dusting to cut down the shine, when a courteous young man stuck his head in to announce that Mrs. Hagen and her mother had arrived backstage and had been escorted to the sponsor's booth, per agreement.

"Good," said John laconically.

— 37 —

"If there is anything you know about the candidate Victor Massoni that the voters should know, we'd like to hear about it," said Rodge Garry.

"Such as what?"

"Anything that bears on his qualifications to be California's chief law-enforcement officer," snapped Garry.

"If you know of anything, I'd like to hear what it is," said John Hagen. Now the fine wire of tension stretching between them almost twanged audibly. Garry glanced significantly out at the studio audience and then back at John Hagen.

"Well, let's just get along with our program and see if anything further develops," he said. "Or comes up, as it were." The smirk in his voice said plainly to John, I'm going to nail you yet, my friend. You and Victor Massoni.

Because the Reverend Bradshaw Coe sat near, John was able to see his smug, tolerant smile. He was probably tallying in his mind the vote on Proposition Five and finding a comfortable cushion of Yes votes over No.

Having registered his point, Rodge Garry addressed himself to the Reverend Bradshaw Coe, who returned his interest with the equable air of an ally helping plot the final destruction of the common foe. Garry had modulated his tone now; he spoke almost softly.

"Tell me something about yourself, Reverend Coe. You are a family man, are you not?"

Coe smiled warmly. "Oh, yes indeed, sir. Mrs. Coe and I have been married for twenty years and we have four wonderful kiddies."

"Can you tell us how you first became interested in this crusade against smutty literature?"

"I can and will," said Coe confidently. "It was right after the war—that's World War Two—when I was in the seminary. A certain young man, whose name I needn't mention, published a so-called novel about the war in the Pacific that leaped to nationwide notoriety. It was so crude, so filled with obscenities, that I found it unbelievable anything like it could be put between covers. Now, of course, it is mild by comparison with what we are seeing in the bookstores."

Rodge Garry arched an eyebrow. "Your campaign, then, goes beyond the cheap paperbacks, girlie and nudist magazines, and deviate publications, is that not true?"

The Reverend Bradshaw Coe hesitated, apparently sensing a subtle change of climate. John Hagen noted it despite his own preoccupations. Garry, the immoderate moderator, had seemed to be leading him dangerously close to the precipice by boring in about Vic Massoni and John's personal attitude toward him. Inexplicably he had dropped the subject and changed tack.

"I think," said the Reverend Mr. Coe slowly, "that obscenity should be attacked wherever it may be found. One could say, then, that yes, our campaign goes well beyond the type of matter you describe."

"Would you describe yourself as a well-read man, Reverend?"

Coe made a deprecatory gesture with his hands. "I believe I am as well read as my average contemporary. I am thoroughly acquainted with the one greatest of all books, of course."

"We'd assume that," said Rodge Garry ironically. "But let me get specific. Have you read *Lady Chatterley's Lover?*"

Coe cleared his throat loudly. "Yes. Utterly disgusting!"

"*To Kill a Mockingbird?*"

"No."

"*The Memoirs of a Lady of Pleasure*—better known as *Fanny Hill?*"

"Unfortunately, yes."

"How about *Moby Dick?*"

"I have always intended to—"

"You haven't? What about *The Story of O* and *Diary of a Flea?*"

"Yes. Inexpressibly filthy, both of them."

"*All Quiet on the Western Front* perhaps?"

"I'm afraid that I have not had—"

"*Naked Lunch?*"

The Reverend Mr. Coe rolled his eyes to convey his horror.

"Have you read *Caine Mutiny* or any of Conrad?"

"I confess I have not."

"*Last Exit to Brooklyn?*"

"Yes."

"*Main Street?*"

"No."

Rodge Garry dropped it in quietly. "I have named about a half-dozen classics or near classics which are almost totally devoid of sexual content. Another is also recognized as a classic, but with a highly erotic content. And five books that are heavily sexual in tone. You have read only the one classic that is highly charged with sex and none of the others, but you have read all the specifically sexual books. Why is that, Reverend?"

The Reverend Mr. Coe's expression was that of J. Edgar Hoover placed under arrest by a special agent of the FBI.

"I *beg* your pardon, sir!"

"Do you find my question hard to answer, Reverend?" said Garry. He was now all wide-eyed innocence, the quester after truth who, like Diogenes, carries his lantern into strange alleys. John Hagen for the first time recognized the essential nature of the man. He allied himself with no one. If he seemed to do so temporarily, it was a pact written on water, lulling its victim into delusions of security.

"I don't like the implication but I'll give you a forthright answer," said Coe. John grudgingly admired him for his speed of recovery. He had been fed a wicked low curve and was coiling to slam it out of the park. "It is true that I have read a lot of books of a specific sexual nature, Mr. Garry. Could a doctor diagnose carcinoma if he had never seen cancer cells under a microscope? Could a lawyer draw a legal brief without ever having read a law book? Would you entrust your life to a pilot who had neglected learning how to land an airplane? Yes indeed, I *have* read very many sexual books, Mr. Garry. I have seen much sexual material. I regard doing so a very necessary part of my crusade, and it *is* a crusade, against filth!" His voice had raised to almost platform volume. Challenged, he defended by attacking. There was a cry of approval and handclapping from the studio audience, which John Hagen had almost forgotten was there.

"But I wonder if you secretly enjoy any of this material?" said Rodge Garry. He seemed amused at Coe's vehemence.

"Does the doctor *enjoy* seeing cancer cells?" Coe shot back. More applause.

"You're overworking the parable," said Rodge Garry. "I'll ask you again: do you enjoy reading dirty books?"

"No!" He was getting the audible approval of the studio audience now with every answer.

"Do you think someone who does should be allowed to?"

"Of course not!"

"Why not?"

The Reverend Mr. Coe's face registered incredulity. "Because obscenity erodes and destroys. It rots our moral tissues, it blurs all lines between right and wrong so that we move into a twilight zone in which there is no good and evil and all things become possible. America is sliding into that pit now with a speed that is frightening. Our fibers are deteriorating into uselessness and our enemies rejoice!"

There was an enormous round of applause.

Rodge Garry smiled. "I think we'll take time now for a commercial. But stick around. Things are just beginning to get interesting."

On the screen, gremlins in red jerseys labeled EPC for Edgewater Petroleum Company paraded to mock German band music, formed patterns at a gasoline station island, surrounding a real girl in a real automobile, swarming over the hood, checking tires, polishing glass. The girl smiled in pretty bewilderment.

The Reverend Bradshaw Coe sat staring straight ahead in grim silence. His hands rested on the table, fingers laced. His thumbs were in irritable motion. John Hagen leaned back and looked up at the sponsor's booth. Kris was staring at him fixedly, her expression so typically unreadable. He saw her mother bend toward her, could almost hear her saying, "What's wrong, dear?" Kris's lips moved in brief reply.

"I'll say this," said Rodge Garry, scratching his nose. "You gentlemen are two of the most articulate guests I've had on this show in some time. Keep it up; you're doing great."

Coe turned his head slowly toward his betrayer. "I'd scarcely expected personal insult, Mr. Garry," he said dignifiedly.

Garry grinned. "I thought you handled yourself beautifully, Reverend. You're doing fine too, Mr. Hagen."

"What comes next?" said John. He ignored the intended praise, if that's what it was and not more of Garry's sharp needling.

"Oh, the real fun part of the show," said Rodge Garry. "You people now get to field questions from the studio audience. Doesn't that sound peachy-dandy? Hold it—we're on." He brushed a quick hand over his hair and picked up a piece of paper. The voice from the monitor said, ". . . And now, back to 'Sky's the Limit' and Rodge Garry." The little red light of the stage-right camera flashed on.

"And back to our two guests, Mr. John Hagen, the Wellbrook newspaper publisher, and the Reverend Bradshaw Coe, Wellbrook pastor and leading figure in state ballot Proposition Number Five, the so-called PURIFY amendment," said Garry. "We are discussing the issue of pornography. Mr. Hagen opposes Proposition Five because, he says, it's unconstitutional. Reverend Coe is leading the campaign for it because, he says, it's needed to get the dirty books off the shelves. With that, let's answer some questions from our studio audience." During his speech someone had turned a rheostat. Approximately three hundred spectators were now bathed in light. Almost immediately, a dozen persons were on their feet. "The lady over there," directed Rodge Garry. A young man, one of three roaming the aisles with hand-held microphones, was by her side quickly, holding the microphone to her mouth.

"This question's for Mr. Hogan," she said shrilly.

"Hagen," said Garry. "Yes, ma'am?"

"Well, Mr. Hagen or Hogan or whatever your name is, how come you think our kids oughta read filthy books?" She was quickly applauded, sitting down to the congratulations of her immediate neighbors.

"I don't believe you've been listening," said John Hagen. "I thought I explained very carefully that what I'm against is the wholesale censorship of all reading material that is contained in Proposition Number Five."

"That's his story and he's sticking with it," said Rodge Garry cheerfully. "Yes, the gentleman in the gray suit."

"For Reverend Coe," said a thin, elderly man with gold-rimmed spectacles.

"Question for the Reverend Mr. Coe," said Garry.

"How can a person help put this ballot measure over?"

"Thank you for asking, sir," said Coe. "Tell all your friends and neighbors to vote for it tomorrow and vote for it yourself. Vote Yes on Proposition Five."

"Lady in the flowered dress?" said Rodge Garry.

"For Hagen," she said rudely. "Would you let your kids read pornography?"

"There's a good question for you, Mr. Hagen," said Garry, grinning. "Would you let your own children read pornography?"

"I don't know how many times I have to repeat myself, but I'll try again," said John testily. "I am *not* for dirty books for children. I *am* against blanket censorship of all reading material."

"I'll pursue that, if you don't mind," said Garry. "The lady asked you whether you'd let your own children read pornography."

"I wouldn't thrust it on them, no. But if they ever got hold of some, I don't think it's the worst thing that could ever happen to them." There was a wash of booing from the audience.

"All right, next question," said Rodge Garry . . .

John finally had begun to relax. Twenty-five minutes of the final half-hour had gone by and he was still alive. The questions, by and large, were hostile toward him and nearly all on ground that had already been thoroughly tilled. But in five minutes or so the whole business would be over. Whether he had held his ground ably, he had no way of judging. Certainly the audience and Rodge Garry had carved at him, but his carcass was still generally intact. He wondered whether any minds in the vast unseen audience had been changed over the past fifty-five minutes—and if so, which way? He doubted it. In fact, he doubted whether any amount of logic or persuasion could ever be brought to bear in the area that had given him so much grief. Opinions tended to solidify, hardening with the strength of epoxy that defied bulldozers to pull it loose. John Hagen had reached the rather pessimistic view that whatever people listened with when it came to the political measure known as PURIFY, it wasn't their ears or their center of reasoning. On either side they merely honed their prejudices. Finally, all arguments reached the tonal equivalent of waves against the beach—ultimately unheard.

"One final question," said Rodge Garry. "The gentleman over there in the blue suit."

The one recognized was quite close to the stage. He was a small, dark-haired man whose face was disturbingly familiar. John Hagen exposed it to the file of his mind. This was someone he knew or should know. There was the quick shock of recognition as he spoke. John had never met him, but he had seen him in one slightly under-lighted glossy photograph taken by Mike Brescia with a Minox camera in Art's Arcade. Beyond a doubt, this was Arthur Genesee.

"I'm from Wellbrook," the man said.

"Well, Mr. Hagen's home community," said Rodge Garry.

"Yeah, that's right," said Genesee. "And this question is for Mr. Hagen."

"Well, ask your question," said Garry.

"Sure. I'm kind of curious to know just what there might be between Mr. Hagen and Mr. Massoni that maybe might have some kind of bearing on the whole campaign."

Rodge Garry looked at Genesee, who had sat down, grinning triumphantly, then at John Hagen, who was suddenly frozen with fear. He had told himself it was possible, yet that was an eternal half-hour ago. This man, one of the authors of his misery, now sat showing his teeth like a hyena who knows his prey to be dead.

"I don't understand the question but maybe Mr. Hagen does," said Rodge Garry innocently. The Reverend Bradshaw Coe, John saw through his own mask of apprehension, was smiling comfortably. Rodge Garry saw that, too. His nostrils quivered on the scent. "Mr. Hagen," he went on sharply. "Will you clear up the mystery for me and our audience? The question has been asked, what is between you and Mr. Massoni that might have some bearing on the election? Will you answer that? Our time's almost up."

John Hagen's eyes flicked almost without volition to his wife, who was leaning forward tensely. He faced the questioner.

"You'll have to be more specific, sir. I believe your name is Genesee, is it not?"

"Will you stand up please, Mr. Genesee," Rodge Garry commanded. "I'm tired of this shilly-shallying. What is the meaning of your question?"

"You want me to say it right out here on television?" said Genesee defiantly.

"Whatever you have to say, say it quickly."

"You're darn right I will then!" shouted Genesee. "I got an affidavit right here in my pocket, sworn to before a notary that this here Assemblyman Massoni and our good respectable publisher, Mr. Hagen, was kind of, you know, for each other in college."

There was a collective gasp from the audience. Genesee seated himself proudly, an idiot grin on his face.

"Well, Mr. Hagen?" said Rodge Garry quite softly. For a long moment there was the silence of the tomb.

"Is the gentleman alleging that Victor Massoni and I had a homosexual affair?" John Hagen said clearly and distinctly. The gallery's collective exhalation swept up to the stage like a low moan.

"Is that what you're saying, Mr. Genesee?" said Garry. "Speak up, man! This is a most serious charge!"

"He said it, not me," said Genesee.

"But that is exactly what he means," said John Hagen.

"Well?" said Garry.

"Yes, it's true—" said John.

There was a cry of outrage from the audience.

"Quiet!" commanded Rodge Garry. The crowd stilled. "Mr. Hagen, do you know what you're saying?"

"I know exactly what I'm saying," said John. "It is true that there is such a scurrilous document in circulation. It alleges—quite falsely, Mr. Garry *and* Mr. Genesee—that there was a homosexual relationship between Victor Massoni and me in college. I am sorry that this has been aired in this fashion. Assemblyman Massoni and I had hoped to see it publicized on the day after tomorrow, when he and I are going to file charges of criminal libel against the perpetrators of this outrageous lie. That means, Mr. Garry *and* Mr. Genesee, that we are going to put the people responsible for this disgusting falsehood in the state's penitentiary. That, Mr. Genesee, pertains not only to the man who swore falsely to this filthy paper, but to every person who had anything to do—in any way—with printing it and circulating it. They are all going to go to prison. Does that completely answer your question?"

The grin had faded from Genesee's face. He was staring at John Hagen as if entranced. He licked his lips. Rodge Garry saw that, too.

"Well," he said. "That, I guess, brings us to the end of a *most* interesting session of 'Sky's the Limit.' I'm your host, Rodge Garry, my guests tonight have been the Reverend Bradshaw Coe, a leader in the campaign for Proposition Five on the Tuesday election ballot, the measure best known as PURIFY, and John Hagen, publisher of the Wellbrook *Sentinel* newspaper, who opposes it. Next week, another stimulating and provocative subject—the Pope's encyclical on birth control. Until then—keep fighting."

John Hagen raised his eyes to the sponsor's booth. Kris was openly sobbing. Suddenly his own eyes stung.

— *38* —

From eight-thirty on, with a scattering of precincts reporting from San Francisco, tiny Alpine County, Fresno, and San Diego County, the computers had nearly every important election decided. All that remained was to count most of more than six million votes.

"Damned forecasting by machine," John Hagen grunted. "The infuriating thing is, they're almost always right."

"And in the race for attorney general," said a severe man wearing headphones in front of a wall-sized chart resembling a tote board, "the pattern of early returns shows that State Senator David O. Hausner will defeat Assemblyman Victor Massoni by a very narrow margin. The computer gives Senator Hausner fifty-one point two per cent to Massoni's forty-eight point eight per cent."

"More coffee?" said Kris.

"Please."

"Poor Vic," she said, picking up his coffee cup.

John grunted. "He ran a good race. That business last night could only have hurt him." His easy chair felt especially comfortable tonight. They had seen Mrs. Wellesley off on the helicopter that morning. John had added his insincere urging to Kris's possibly more genuine coaxing to stay a few more days.

"No," she had said. "I don't want to wear out my welcome. My leg feels ever so much better, but I wonder what they put in your water down here. My stomach just hasn't felt quite right since I've been here. Oh well, I don't feel any cold coming on; that's a blessing, and that's why you won't really hear me complain. I'll be home in time to cast my vote."

"For Massoni, Mother?" John asked half playfully. God and Buddha willing, another visitation was a good twelve months' distant.

"Such a fine-looking man, but I just don't know," she said, which meant of course that she did. Hausner—and, John suspected, PURIFY—had her vote.

"In the most hotly contested ballot proposition, Number Five, I'm afraid it's a little early to call the shot," said the severe man. He glowered into the camera as if defying his viewers to challenge his veracity. "A slight lead is reported on the Yes side, but the pattern is confusing. The machine tells us we'd better wait a bit on this one. Now, let's take a look at some of the other races. . . ."

"Kris?" said John.

"Mm-hm?" she said. He waited so long that she turned her gaze from the television screen to look at him.

"I only know one way to ask this," he said painfully. "But now I have to ask it. Did you have an affair in college with Vic Massoni?"

"Dear God," she said. Her hand went to her face; her eyes were closed. "Oh, dear God, no. How long have you thought that?"

"Have you ever had an affair with Vic Massoni? I'm sorry, but I must know."

She opened her eyes, her face anguished. "No, I never did. Oh, John, did you think—oh, my dear, never. But do you want to know the truth? It's very hurtful." She looked at him supplicatingly.

"I've got to know it now. Vic said there was something he couldn't tell me."

"We'll return to our election night coverage after this brief pause for a message from our sponsor," said the stern man on the set.

"I told you about the affair with the professor."

"Yes, and I don't really care, Krissy."

She swallowed hard. "That was, well—pretty shattering. I knew he was married, of course, but it was the same old story. She didn't love or understand him and I did. Etcetera. And when Du Pont offered him three thousand dollars more a year plus fringe benefits, it was the end of our beautiful romance. He vowed to keep me in his heart forever. Etcetera."

He listened, stricken for her. Yet he could not or would not stop her.

"I didn't react too well," she said, smiling wanly. "In fact, before I woke up to what I was doing—was becoming—I'd had two—what would you call them?—quickies with two other men. And then one night I went to this—party." She looked at him swiftly and went on. "The boy I went with seemed nice enough. And in spite of my rapid orientation or whatever you want to call it, I was still pretty basically naïve. Well, there were about twenty or thirty people there; it was in somebody's house out toward Westwood. I—I hadn't much experience with alcohol, if that's any excuse. I guess maybe it is. Are you sure you want to hear this?"

"Does it involve Vic Massoni in any way?"

"Yes, that's exactly why I'm telling you. I guess I sort of half passed out in one of the bedrooms. It's all so dim and hazy, like a nightmare. But one of the girls who was there told me a day or so later."

"What happened, Krissy?" he said tensely.

Her voice was dull, lifeless now. "Five men—used me," she said.

He exhaled deeply. It came out almost a groan.

"And someone was making movies," she said.

He shook his head miserably. "Krissy, I wish I hadn't—"

"There's more," she said.

"Vic?" he said tightly.

"Yes, Vic," she said with a small note of sudden defiance. "And to this day we've never spoken of it. Vic, the girl told me, got to the party late. Some smirking idiot who'd had his—turn—I guess—came up to this big football player and tipped him off to action in the bedroom. Vic barely knew me, but he took one look and went berserk. He picked up a piece of lighting equipment and slammed the man with the camera over the head with it and smashed the camera and found all the exposed film. He pulled another man away from—away from me and knocked him unconscious. Then I guess he went back out into the other room and found the man who had told him, backed him against the wall, and pounded him unconscious too."

She drew a long, shuddery breath. "And then he came back into the bedroom, helped me dress, and took me home. That's why I'll always admire Vic Massoni. It's also the reason he and I could never, never —oh, can't you see!"

"We have more returns now in the statewide election," said the severe man. "In the race for governor . . ."

"My Krissy, my Krissy," said John, holding her tightly. "Oh, my dear, my poor darling Kris." Her body was shaking.

For a long time, until her trembling subsided, he held her in his arms, neither speaking, while the voice from the lighted screen droned on. What a burden for a proud, beautiful woman to have carried all these years, he thought. I have been fighting what I believe to be an evil, repressive law. Yet, how now? Where did one go in his thinking when brought face to face with the other evil side of the coin, that at one time had touched this fine, spirited person who had consented to become his wife? Small wonder that she had acted so agitatedly at his long failure to speak up, that she had wanted only to retreat from threat and snicker and nasty rumor.

"You you've asked me many times why I married you," she whispered. "I wanted so—so desperately to get back. To get back from where I'd been. To start thinking of myself as a whole person again, a normal human being. And there you were, all of a sudden, kind of grave but fun, smart, and so—solid. I needed a rock, and there you were. Strength and security. That's what you gave me."

"Don't say any more, Krissy," he said.

"But I'd never told you, not in all those years," she said, pulling back her head to look at him.

"Don't talk. It's all right, honey, it's all right."

"And for a while I started to forget why I loved you."

"You're going to get spanked if you don't shut up."

"Promise?"

". . . In the attorney general race, Assemblyman Victor Massoni has edged up slightly, but Senator David O. Hausner, the Republican candidate, is still holding about a two-point lead," said the television voice. "The computer *is* wavering a bit on the eventual winner, however, after first predicting victory for Hausner. Maybe this race isn't over yet. It is going to be very, *very* close. And the very hotly disputed Proposition Number Five—so-called PURIFY—is running just about neck-and-neck between Yes and No, and that is all our computer will tell us on that one."

"At this point I don't think I give a damn any more," said John.

She placed a finger against his lips. "Yes you do. You did what you had to do, and you did right."

"I tried."

"John?"

"Talking again, huh?"

"What happens if—if Proposition Five wins?"

He smiled at her. "Then we take a nice long vacation. Permanently."

"What if it loses?"

"We take a nice long vacation."

"That sounds nice."

"Where would you like to go?"

"I'm with you."

"Tahiti? The Virgin Islands? Xanadu?"

"Uh-huh," she said.

He was thinking again of the young Kris and Vic and John those years before at the University of Southern California. His lips tightened for a moment at his recent suspicions. He knew now that he owed Vic an old debt of gratitude. He knew, too, that they could never speak of it, but that he, John, would be forever grateful for what he had learned of Vic, as traumatic as the learning had been. Vic Massoni was simply of that valuable, vanishing species, the gentleman. A pang shot through him. Knock it off, Hagen, he told himself quickly. It's past, it's gone, it never happened. Let the dead past bury the dead. To coin a phrase, as Kris would remind him.

At twelve minutes past twelve midnight, the somewhat haggard-looking man with the earphones said, "As of this hour, the trend that began to show at about eleven o'clock—a No vote on Proposition Number Five—has continued its definite upward surge, for whatever reason or reasons, of course, we'll never know. Our cautious computer has now climbed down off the fence. The prediction is that, while it is going to end up as a comparatively close contest—" He paused to glance away, then nodded at someone off-camera.

"Come on, man!" said John Hagen.

"That was another race. Proposition Number Five seems definitely headed for—defeat—"

"Hallelujah," said John quietly.

"—Possibly by two to three hundred thousand votes," concluded the announcer.

"They don't always show good sense, but once in a while they do," John said.

"Do you think this ends it, honey?"

He shook his head. "No, never; well, hardly ever. They'll be back for another round. Hopefully, next time they'll come up with something I can agree with."

"In the only other tight contest, the final result may well depend on the absentee vote," said Mr. Severe. "I refer, of course, to the attorney general race between Senator David O. Hausner and Assemblyman Victor Massoni. At the moment they are running so close together that we can't get any sort of answer out of our computer. Now, for another rundown on the congressional races."

"Good luck, Vic," said John feelingly.

"Good luck, Vic," said Kris.

"And good night, David," said John Hagen, snapping off the television set. He went arm in arm upstairs with his wife, very much a part of her, quite proud of her.